# A FOOLISH
# CONSISTENCY

# A FOOLISH CONSISTENCY

Andrea Weir

For permission requests, please address
Cedar Forge Press
7300 West Joy Road
Dexter, Michigan 48130

Published 2014 by Cedar Forge Press
Printed in the United States of America
18 17 16 15 14    1 2 3 4 5
ISBN 978-1-936672-73-8
Library of Congress Control Number: 2014939180

This is a work of fiction. Names, characters, places, and incidents are
the products of the author's imagination or are used fictitiously. Any
resemblance to actual events, locales, or persons, living or dead, is
entirely coincidental.

*To my daughters, Rebecca and Catherine,
who wouldn't take no for an answer*

These roses under my window make no reference to former roses or to better ones; they are for what they are; they exist with God today. There is no time to them. There is simply the rose; it is perfect in every moment of its existence. Before a leaf-bud has burst, its whole life acts; in the full-blown flower there is no more; in the leafless root there is no less. Its nature is satisfied and it satisfies nature in all moments alike. But man postpones or remembers; he does not live in the present, but with reverted eye laments the past, or, heedless of the riches that surround him, stands on tiptoe to foresee the future. He cannot be happy and strong until he too lives with nature in the present, above time.

—Ralph Waldo Emerson *Self-Reliance*

# 1

I stepped into the empty waiting room and heaved a sigh of relief. The last place I wanted to spend Christmas Eve was in a hospital emergency room.

A young man perched on a stool behind what appeared to be a pane of bulletproof glass looked up and smiled. "Can I help you?" The glass—or rather its purpose—gave me a slight sense of foreboding. I took another glance around the room.

"I cut my hand and I'm pretty sure I need stitches," I replied, raising the injured appendage. It was wrapped in a dishtowel, but blood had seeped through the cloth, leaving bright red blotches on the pastel fabric. The sight of it made me feel a bit faint.

The clerk pressed a button and a young woman dressed in blue surgical scrubs responded almost immediately.

"Well, what do we have here?" she asked as she stepped through the door that led to the triage area. She spoke in a warm Southern drawl, her voice as smooth and sweet as maple syrup. She began to unwrap the towel, and I explained what happened. It was a simple accident, really. Paying more attention to a conversation I was having with my friend Miranda than to the loaf of French bread I was slicing for dinner, I let the knife slip. The blade skirted across the back of my hand, in the space between my thumb and forefinger.

Very gently the nurse tugged a section of fabric that had stuck to my skin. I felt a sharp pain and gasped lightly. Fresh blood oozed through the cotton material.

"Well, we're just gonna leave that alone for now," she said. "We'll let it be until the doctor's ready to see it." She rewrapped the towel around my hand and patted my arm. "Why don't you come on back to a room?"

Miranda, who had driven me to the hospital, came in just then, and the nurse led both of us down a wide hallway, past several cubicles. In one room, an elderly woman rested quietly on a gurney, the leads of a cardiac monitor affixed to her chest. In another, a young father occupied his toddler son while the child's mother tried to soothe their infant daughter who must have had an ear infection. It had been twenty years since my own children were so small, but I recognized the look of fever on the baby's face and the telltale ear pulling.

We stopped outside a small room at the end of the hall and the nurse directed me toward the empty bed. "Make yourself comfortable, hon."

I felt a little lightheaded, so I stretched out and rested my head on the small pillow.

"Does it hurt much?" the nurse asked, nodding toward my hand. "The doctor will be able to give you somethin' for it after he sees you." Her Southern accent stretched the words like a taffy pull.

"It's not too bad right now," I replied.

"Well, good." She turned to leave. "You just lie back and relax. The doctor will be in shortly, okay?"

I nodded and turned my head in Miranda's direction. She stood against the wall, arms folded across her chest.

"Great way to start a holiday vacation," she chided. "If I'd known you were so incompetent with a bread knife, I would have had you set the table."

"So would I," I answered dryly. I closed my eyes, suddenly very tired. I'd been awake since five a.m., and now all I wanted to do was sleep. I felt surprisingly weak, given the nonserious nature of my injury.

I looked over at Miranda. "I'm sorry about this," I apologized. "I'm sure you're no happier to be here than I am."

She flipped through the collection of magazines on the rack on the wall. "Well, I've had better Friday nights," she replied. "But worse, too." She found a worn issue of *Better Homes & Gardens* and sat down on a stool someone had pushed into the corner of the room.

"Hey, look," she said lightly, "tips for the perfect July 4th barbecue—two years ago."

I listened for a moment to the various noises around me. Things had become fairly quiet. The doctor must have taken care of the baby with the ear infection.

I did hear the murmur of voices down the hall, the squeak of rubber-soled shoes on the linoleum floor as someone passed by the room, and the occasional whoosh of a curtain being opened or closed. From farther away came the rattle of a cart as it was wheeled across the floor.

After what seemed like a long time, a quiet knock sounded at the door and a doctor stepped into the room. I looked over at him, but couldn't see his face. It was hidden behind the chart he continued reading as he introduced himself.

"Hi, I'm Dr. Tremaine," he said, his eyes still directed downward.

My stomach lurched, and I felt as though I'd swallowed a rock. My heart pounded as I sat up. The palm of my good hand became slick with sweat, and I wiped it on my jeans. I could feel Miranda's eyes on me.

The doctor raised his head then and focused his attention in my direction. "And you're—" Almost automatically, he extended his right arm, intending to shake hands. When he saw me, however, it froze in midair and then dropped to his side. His eyes narrowed as he studied my face. He opened his mouth to say something but closed it again. He hesitated, and then spoke.

"Callie?" He glanced at my paperwork as if looking for confirmation. "God, Callie—is it really you?"

"Will," I murmured in response, aware of the tremor in my voice.

"Wow!" Miranda said, looking first at me, then at Will, and back to me. "I never saw this coming."

Will took a few steps toward me. "I can't believe it," he murmured, as though to himself. "And you look just the same."

I blushed slightly in response. "Well, I don't know how that could be. A lot of years have passed ... but thanks."

He gazed at me for a long moment, seemingly unaware of his surroundings. Then, remembering who—and what—he was, he brought himself back to reality and became the doctor in charge again.

"So, what happened?" He pulled on a pair of latex gloves, took my swaddled hand in his, and, as the nurse had done earlier, gently unwrapped the towel.

"This might hurt a bit," he said as he tugged at a stubborn section of cloth that had attached itself to the area around the laceration.

I winced and drew a quick breath as he pulled it off.

I explained about the knife and the bread while he examined my hand and studied the length and depth of the gash.

"You're definitely going to need stitches," he replied, "but it's a pretty simple repair. You're lucky you didn't get a major blood vessel or a tendon— you came pretty close."

"Thank goodness for small favors," I said, and then added, "and for not so small ones, too." He looked directly into my eyes. His face betrayed no emotion, but I think the corners of his mouth turned up just slightly.

When his pager beeped, Will glanced down at it and frowned. "I'll be right back," he said, and stepped out of the room. He left the door open, and though I couldn't see where he had gone, I did notice a young woman, her smooth dark hair swept up in a ponytail, approach the nurse's station. She leaned her forearms on the counter and asked a question. My ears perked up when I heard her say "Dr. Tremaine." She wore surgical scrubs and held what appeared to be a small gift-wrapped package. A Christmas present, perhaps.

The Southern belle who had done triage earlier answered her curtly, saying Dr. Tremaine was with a patient. The woman in scrubs jotted down a note and handed it and the package to the belle and asked her to pass it on to him. The belle smiled and promised to do so. When the ponytail passed through a set of double doors that led to another part of the hospital, however, the belle tore the note in two and dropped it—along with the package—into the trash. I chuckled under my breath.

Will returned to the room after a few minutes, tucking his cell phone back into its holder. The belle was close behind him. She listened in rapt attention, her blue eyes shining, as he told her what he was going to do. It was more than professional attention, I thought, and though I had no real justification, I took an immediate dislike to her. When Will finished speaking, she nodded affirmatively and pulled a suture kit out of the cupboard. She opened it and laid out the contents on a stainless steel tray next to the bed.

"Okay, I'm going to give you a few shots of lidocaine to kill the pain," Will said. "I'm guessing you'll need about six stitches. That's not too bad." He picked up the syringe and pointed it toward the cut. "You might want to breathe," he quipped. "You'll feel better and it will help you stay upright."

"I think I'd prefer three fingers of Jack Daniels," I replied, inhaling deeply.

When my hand was comfortably numb, he went to work with the needle and sutures. I'm generally not very squeamish when it comes to medical procedures, but in this case I preferred to look away. Miranda, who, quite surprisingly, generally is squeamish when it comes to medical procedures, excused herself.

"I think I'll leave you in the good doctor's capable hands and wait for you out there," she said with a smirk, and pointed down the hall.

I focused my attention on Will. He was as handsome as I remembered. And I remembered him well. He'd occupied the last twenty-five years of my life, even though I hadn't seen him once in all that time. If a century had passed, I'd still know that dark hair, those blue eyes, and the warm, full mouth.

"So, what are you doing in Westin?" he asked. "You don't live here now, do you?" His head was bent over his work. I couldn't read his expression.

"No, I'm just visiting for a few days. For Christmas. I live in California—in San Sebastian." If this meant anything to him, he kept it to himself.

From the corner of my eye, I could see the small movements he made as he mended my torn hand. He stopped briefly and looked up at me.

"It's really good to see you again," he said, and then continued his work in silence.

"All right, then. That's that." Will peeled the gloves off his hands and dropped them on the tray beside the array of bandages, syringes, and other detritus of his work. "Keep it covered for the next forty-eight hours, and try not to get it wet. The stitches should be removed in a couple of weeks."

"Well, I guess you're right—that's that." I lifted myself off the bed, using one arm to steady myself. We stood close to each other for a moment, our eyes fixed on one another. I wanted to touch him, but didn't dare. "Thanks for taking care of this," I said instead. "I guess I'll find Miranda and we'll go."

He brushed my arm as I started toward the door.

"Callie, do you think—I mean—I was wondering if—" He took a breath and exhaled sharply. "Just … look after that hand, okay?"

�

Will watched Callie walk down the hall and out to the waiting room to join her friend. He still felt the warmth of her hand in his. He wanted to run after her, to call her back, stop her from leaving. But he couldn't. He had no right.

He slowly became aware of someone speaking to him. A nurse stood at his side, a radiologist's report in hand. The elderly woman in cubicle three had fractured her hip when she lost her balance and fell off the curb. Yes, he told her, she would have to be admitted, and would most likely require surgery. Yes, he'd order something stronger for the pain. And yes, this was a lousy way for her to spend Christmas Eve.

Will glanced down the hallway again, hoping to catch another glimpse of Callie before she left the hospital. He still wanted to go after her. Instead, he signed the admission order the nurse had tucked into the old woman's chart and went on to the next patient.

"You look like you've seen a ghost," Alex Merritt said to him an hour later when they ran into each other in the doctor's lounge. Will had just finished with his last patient and was in a rush to meet Lizzy and Wiley at his in-laws' house. He was late, and they'd be anxious for him to arrive. It wasn't their first Christmas Eve since the accident, but feelings—and fears—still ran high.

"I have, sort of," Will replied. He grabbed his wallet and car keys from his locker.

Alex chuckled as he reached into his own locker and pulled out a small wrapped package. He tucked it into his jacket pocket. "Christmas Past, Present, or Future?" he asked.

"Past," Will responded. "And in more ways than one."

Alex narrowed his eyes and studied his friend's face. "Who, exactly, was this ghost?"

"A patient. Someone I used to know...very well."

"And from the look on your face, I'd guess it wasn't just any someone," Alex noted.

"It was Callie. Callie Sutton—well, Winwood now. She's married."

Alex shut the locker with a slam and twirled the combination lock. "Wasn't she the girlfriend you had when you started medical school, the main one before Joanna? You told me about her, right? Does she live around here now?"

"No," Will replied. "She's visiting a friend for Christmas."

Alex wrapped a scarf around his neck and pulled on a heavy coat. "Well, she must not be very married, then. Otherwise she'd be with her husband."

"Maybe," Will said, shrugging on his own coat. "But whatever the situation, it's Christmas Eve, and I have a couple of kids waiting for me—and I'm late."

He started down the hall toward the exit. He wondered, as he walked, what circumstances had brought Callie to Westin for the holiday. She came to visit a friend, she said, but where was her husband? Will hadn't thought to notice whether she was wearing a wedding ring.

The double doors of the hospital entrance opened automatically as Will approached. But instead of walking out into the cold night air, he stopped just inside, paused for a moment, then turned around and headed back to the emergency department.

"Dr. Tremaine, I thought you'd left already." The nurse with the Southern accent gave him a broad smile. "Just couldn't stay away, even on Christmas Eve, huh?"

"I am on my way out," Will replied. "I just want to check something on one of the charts—the woman who came in with the hand laceration. Can you get it for me?"

"Sure," the young nurse responded warmly. She brushed against him as she walked past. Will took a small step sideways to avoid any further contact. With a slight air of offense, the nurse handed him the file.

"Thanks," he said. He shuffled through the papers until he found the form that contained Callie's cell phone number. He scribbled it on a scrap of paper and shoved it into his pocket. He closed the file and with an unfamiliar sense of anticipation, he left the hospital and walked toward his car.

ℰ

"So that's the infamous Will Tremaine," Miranda declared as she set a mug of tea on the table next to me. I was curled up on the couch in her living room, resting my bandaged hand on a pillow.

She sat down on the opposite end of the couch, cross-legged, and took a sip from her own cup.

"Yup," I replied. "That's the infamous Will Tremaine."

"And did you see the way he looked at you," she asked, more an assessment than a question. "You could have knocked him over with a feather."

"I hardly think so," I replied, slightly embarrassed.

"That was more than just an expression of surprise," Miranda argued. "A lot more."

"Oh, you're imagining things." I watched the whorls of steam as they rose from the tea and vanished into the air. "But you know, I have thought about him almost every day since he drove away." The last time I'd seen Will was on a warm afternoon in late August when he kissed me goodbye and headed east, to Boston and medical school.

"I was thinking about him even on the day Joe and I got married. Certainly not the best frame of mind for taking wedding vows." I shook my head. "God, what was wrong with me?"

"There was nothing wrong with you," Miranda replied with a shrug. "Well, nothing a little courage wouldn't have fixed. I think you knew Joe wasn't the right one because you were still stuck on Will—whether you wanted to be or not. And I think you also knew you had no business marrying Joe, but didn't have the guts to tell him. Besides," she noted, "you were pretty young."

Like any good prosecutor—and she was one of the best—Miranda homed in on the truth and didn't mince words. This particular set had more than just a ring of truth, and their echo reverberated uncomfortably in my head. On our wedding day, just as the processional was about to begin, I had looked down the aisle at Joe—who appeared none too enthusiastic himself—and

7

wanted to take off running in the opposite direction. Still, I went through with it, figuring somehow everything would work out in the end.

"And then you had Ben," she went on. "And as far as you were concerned, you and Joe were stuck with each other. And when Justine came along, well..."

"I don't know if I'd go so far as to say we were *stuck*," I said in defense of myself, and of Joe. "It's not like we were *miserable*."

"Well, maybe not *all* the time." Miranda set her mug on the table, adjusted the cushion behind her back, and looked at me straight on. "We both know you and Joe weren't a great match." She raised her hand to cut short the protest I was about to make. "Not that he isn't a good man—some of the time—but he was never the right one for you. Or you for him—he let you know that loud and clear."

"Well, yeah," I agreed, recalling the evening Joe inadvertently—or, perhaps not—let it be known his affections were directed elsewhere. "I guess he did."

"All I'm trying to say," she continued, "is that if Will still matters to you as much as I think he does, you should be honest with yourself about it. About *all* of it."

I shook my head slowly from side to side. "Listen to you, giving relationship advice. You're the queen of relationship avoidance." I smiled and took a sip of tea.

Miranda crossed her arms. "I'm not opposed to all relationships. It's simply that I, like our forefather Thomas Jefferson, choose to avoid those messy entangling alliances."

She straightened her leg and gave me a gentle nudge with her foot. "But we aren't talking about me."

"Anyway," I argued, "I don't know anything about him anymore, except that he actually did become a doctor."

"And that he's not married," she added.

I looked at her curiously. "How do you know that?"

"He's working on Christmas Eve, when most married men—well, happily married men—would be home with their wives." She leaned back against the arm of the couch and nodded toward my bandaged hand. "When you think about it, that could turn out to be one hell of a holiday present."

She stood up and reached for the mugs. "Well, I'm going to clean up the kitchen and head off to bed. It's Christmas Eve, after all, and if we aren't asleep, we won't have a visit from Santa."

I waved my injured hand. "I'd help, but—"

"Ah, no," she interrupted. "You stay right where you are. I'll take care of it.

The last thing we need is you tripping over the rug by the sink and injuring something else."

While Miranda was in the kitchen, I took the opportunity to check in with Ben and Justine. Each call went directly to voicemail, so I left messages to let them know I was thinking about them and wishing them a very happy Christmas Eve. I dropped my phone onto my lap and stared out the window. The snow was beginning to fall again.

A feeling of melancholy settled over me like a heavy blanket. I thought of Will—somewhere in Westin with the family I was sure he must have, despite Miranda's assertions to the contrary—and of Ben and Justine at a ski lodge celebrating Christmas with their father and his new wife. Will and Ben and Justine were the only people for whom I'd felt a love so pure and unfailing and unconditional that it existed almost on its own. It was without question or purpose. It was—or, in Will's case, had been—its own purpose. I sat there, thinking of Will and Ben and Justine, and I became achingly lonely for all three.

Brushing teeth with only one working hand is doable—awkward, but doable. Washing one's face, however, poses a greater challenge. Being right-handed and not the least bit ambidextrous, I was grateful that my left hand was the one I'd taken out of commission. Every task took more time to accomplish, but at least I could do it. What proved to be the most difficult was pulling my hair—a mass of waves and curls—into a clip so it would be out of the way. I actually needed Miranda's help with that.

My ablutions clumsily completed, I took one of the mild pain pills Will had prescribed to help me get some sleep.

I crawled into bed and held the medicine bottle close to the lamp so I could read his name on the prescription label. "William A. Tremaine, M.D." William Anderson Tremaine. Will. I heaved a sigh, switched off the light, and settled under the covers, the bottle still clasped in my hand. From where my head rested on the pillow, I could look out the window and watch the snow still falling. If it kept up, we'd have a very white Christmas.

Apparently the weather forecast I heard earlier had been correct—a big storm had blown in.

※

The Halloran house, lit up like a proverbial Christmas tree, was almost a welcoming sight as Will followed the curve of the circular driveway. Looks can be deceiving, though, and he was no fool. He sat in the car, leaning on the steering wheel, preparing himself for the evening ahead.

The Hallorans' Christmas Eve tradition consisted of a late supper, after which the family would gather around the huge tree in the living room and each person would be allowed to open one gift. Will knew he had to be there for Lizzy and Wiley—he wanted to be—but he wasn't looking forward to spending time with the rest of the family. It had been difficult even when Joanna was there to run interference. Now that she was gone, he always felt as though he was on the front line with no reinforcements.

Will walked toward the front door. Wiley saw him through the window and opened the door before he knocked.

"Dad!" Wiley grabbed his hand and pulled him into the living room. Eleanor and Edward sat on the sofa; Lizzy and her Aunt Rowan were sharing one of the wingback chairs, and Uncle Chase and his new wife were, appropriately, settled on the love seat.

Eleanor rose and approached Will. Accepting her outstretched hands, he kissed her lightly on the cheek.

"Merry Christmas, Eleanor." He turned to Edward and they shook hands. He glanced around the room then, nodding and acknowledging Rowan first and then Chase and Sarah. Chase moved to greet him as he took off his heavy coat.

"Glad you could make it," Chase ribbed, patting his brother-in-law on the back. "Tough night to be on duty, eh, Doc?"

"Well, someone has to be," Will replied. "And the doctor on the schedule couldn't very well tell his son to wait for a more convenient time to make his entrance into the world." He accepted the glass Chase handed him. "Thanks. Anyway, now I'm finished until after New Year's."

"Da-ad, come on!" Wiley tugged at Will's sleeve. "Gran says we can all open one present. Lizzy and I already picked ours." He pointed to a pair of boxes—one large and rectangular, and the other small and square-shaped—on the far side of the tree.

"Okay, let's go!" Will matched his son's enthusiasm. He sat down on the floor, daughter on one side and son on the other, and pulled the packages out from under the tree.

"Let's see, this one is for Lizzy," he said, reading the tag on the small box. He handed it to her and kissed the top of her head. "Merry Christmas, LZ."

"Thanks, Dad." She held the package in her lap while Will made a show of presenting Wiley with his gift. Wiley tore at the wrapping paper, his face beaming in the glow of the Christmas tree lights.

"Awesome!" he exclaimed as he pulled the paper down one side of the box. "A Spooner Board!" He turned to Eleanor and Edward. "See, Gran? See Grandpa?"

The grandparents smiled. "You're a lucky boy, Wiley," Edward replied.

He ripped open the box and pulled out the curved board that resembled a skateboard minus the wheels.

"And just what is that?" Eleanor asked.

"You can do tricks with it, just like on a skateboard or a snowboard, but you can do it inside," Wiley replied excitedly. "Watch!"

He jumped up and dropped the board onto the floor, curved end up. He planted his feet, and then twirling his upper body and shifting his weight, spun around first in one direction, and then another. "Tanner has one—it's awesome!"

Lizzy unwrapped her package slowly and more carefully. "Oh, wow," she said when she saw the pair of small diamond stud earrings.

Will leaned in close. "Your mom always said a girl's first diamonds should come from her dad."

Lizzy smiled and wrapped her arms around his neck. "Thanks, Dad. I love them." She stood up and moved toward her grandmother and Rowan. "Aren't they pretty?"

Wiley, who had been doing figure eights on the carpet, plopped down next to his father with his board in his lap. "Hey, Dad, aren't you going to open something?"

"Mm, I think I'll wait until tomorrow," Will replied. "I like the anticipation."

After a couple of hours of Christmas carols, games, and as much good cheer as the group could muster, Eleanor corralled Lizzy and Wiley and began to herd them toward the door and up to their respective rooms. "All right, children, it's time to go to bed. You know Santa will pass right by if he thinks you are awake."

Lizzy looked at Rowan and smiled furtively. Wiley glanced at his father, who gave him a knowing wink. Then both children scurried up the stairs with their grandmother and aunt a few steps behind.

Chase moved to the chair previously occupied by Rowan and Lizzy and leaned toward Will as he reached for his wineglass. "She's been saying that every Christmas Eve for as long as I can remember. When I was little, Joanna would tease me and threaten to stay awake all night so Santa wouldn't come. Scared the bejeezus out of me."

Will laughed softly.

"Well," Chase added with a touch of sorrow, "She's not teasing anyone anymore, is she?" He got up, took his wife's hand, and led her out of the room.

Will sat quietly for a moment staring into the fire. Thoughts of Joanna and the last Christmas they'd spent together flooded his mind. She had given him a watch and a portrait of her and the children, which she'd commissioned from a painter who also happened to be a close family friend. It was still hanging in their living room. He had presented her with a pair of mittens into which he had tucked two tickets to the Metropolitan Opera's production of *La Bohème*. They came with a trip to Manhattan, he had told her, and it would be just the two of them—no children. He'd already worked it out with Eleanor. He smiled at the memory. Joanna's eyes had shone bright with excitement on that Christmas morning. It had gratified him to see her so happy.

But the trip never took place. Joanna died a month before they were supposed to go. Will gave the tickets to a colleague who was taking his wife to New York City for their anniversary.

Then Will thought of Callie and the last Christmas he'd spent with her. They were so young. He'd given her a sterling silver bracelet with a heart-shaped charm. It was engraved on one side with her initials, and on the other with his. She'd given him a copy of *Gray's Anatomy* and a scarf to take with him to Boston. He still had the scarf. He wondered if she still had the bracelet.

He reached into his pocket and pulled out the scrap of paper on which he'd written her telephone number. He stared at the digits, studying their shapes. A series of curves and lines, like those on a map. A road, he thought to himself. He traced the numbers with his finger. A road that right now might possibly lead him back to her.

# 2

I awoke on Christmas morning to the smell of coffee and cinnamon. I pushed my arms into the sleeves of my robe and wandered downstairs, yawning. The pain medication had worked like magic, and I'd slept soundly through the night. My hand felt much better, although my wrist and elbow were stiff from having kept them immobile for so long.

"Well, good morning," Miranda said as I trundled into the kitchen. "And a very merry Christmas, too." She gave me a hug. "How's the hand?"

"Better, thanks. Is that coffee I smell?"

"Yes, it is. And fresh cinnamon rolls, too." She handed me a steaming cup.

"Okay, now I'm starting to worry. Between dinner last night and breakfast this morning, there is way too much domesticity going on here. Are you feeling all right?" I touched my hand to her forehead in mock concern.

"Well, I didn't actually make the cinnamon rolls," Miranda admitted, ducking her head. "I just put them in the oven. Not quite the same thing. And anyway, Scrooge, it's Christmas. Put on your happy face, grab your cup, and come into the living room to open up some presents."

I followed her and parked myself in one of the club chairs by the window. "You do have a magnificent tree," I declared, noting the Scotch pine festooned with ornaments, tinsel, bulbs, and angel. "You seem to have become quite a sentimentalist. I wouldn't expect you to have anything more than a few holly branches stuck in a glass jar."

"I know," she said, as she pulled a brightly wrapped box out from under one of the branches and handed it to me. "I surprise myself sometimes. Now, open this one."

I made a feeble one-handed attempt at tearing off the paper. That wasn't much of a problem, but the ribbon posed a greater challenge. I handed the package back to Miranda.

"Here, why don't you do it," I said. "I'll watch and utter the proper oohs and aahs."

"Okay then." She looked down at the tag. "This one says, 'To Callie From Miranda.' Hmmm. I wonder what it could be."

With the gifts unwrapped, Miranda and I sat down to Christmas breakfast.

Just as we finished eating, my cell phone rang. I expected Ben or Justine to call, so I had tucked it into the pocket of my robe. I pulled it out and checked the number. I didn't recognize it, so I assumed Justine was using someone else's phone because she had misplaced hers—yet again.

"Hi, honey," I said cheerfully. "Merry Christmas."

"Uh, Merry Christmas to you, too. Cal?" I looked at Miranda, wide-eyed. The voice on the other end of the phone was Will's.

"Oh, Will, I'm sorry, I was expecting my daughter," I said, trying not to sound flustered. "I mean, I'm not sorry about the Merry Christmas, I just—" I paused and glanced at Miranda. She rolled her eyes and shook her head. "Can we start this conversation over?"

3

Will and I met the next day at a small cafe near the center of Westin. I was running a few minutes late because I'd taken so long getting dressed. The main obstacle had been the tiny buttons on my red cashmere sweater, which were hard to manage with one hand. Making my hair presentable was a challenge for the same reason. The dampness in the air made the curls springier than usual, and after trying to pull it back in a clip, I finally gave up and let it fall in waves over my shoulders.

Will was already at a table when I arrived. He looked more than a little nervous; but then, so was I. I didn't think I'd see him again after I left the hospital.

Right now, I had no idea what to expect, no idea where his life had taken him since we last saw each other. When we lost touch, we had done so completely. And while I often thought about him, I'd never made any attempt to contact him. Too much time had passed, and it wouldn't have been right to intrude in his life.

And, of course, I'd had my life—a marriage and children of my own.

Will rose to his feet as soon as he saw me. He was dressed casually in dark jeans, a button-down shirt, and a teal sweater that contrasted with his dark hair and brought out the deep blue of his eyes. He watched me walk toward him, and I saw the color rise in his cheeks. When I reached the table, he helped me out of my coat and draped it over a chair. He pulled another chair out for me, and took a seat across the table.

"How's the hand?" he asked, eyeing the bandage.

I raised it, examined it briefly as though it were a rare objet d'art, and laid it back on the table. "Oh, it's not bad. It hurt the first night, but nothing one of those very pleasant pain pills couldn't remedy."

"I'm glad to hear it," he replied. Nodding in the direction of my hand, he added, "That had the potential to be a really serious situation."

"Well, I do appreciate your fine craftsmanship. You're quite talented with a needle and thread."

"Yeah, well, I get plenty of practice."

An awkward silence fell over us.

"I hope you don't mind my calling yesterday," he said finally. "I got your number from your chart." He looked slightly abashed. "I'm really not supposed to do that, but I chanced it, thinking you wouldn't mind."

"No, I'm glad you did," I replied, more than a little anxious myself. A waitress with straight black hair and round eyes outlined in dark pencil stopped at the table to take our order. I requested hot tea, and Will asked for coffee.

"This was a great place to meet," I continued when the waitress moved on to the next table. "I took a pretty circuitous route to get here—I borrowed my friend Miranda's car—and it gave me a chance to get reacquainted with this part of town."

"Yeah, a lot has changed. When I came back three years ago, I barely recognized it." As soon as the words were uttered, I wondered what had brought him back to Westin. When he left, he had no intention of ever returning.

The waitress approached the table, balancing a round tray on one hand. She set an empty cup and a carafe of hot water in front of me, along with a basket of assorted tea bags. She gave Will his coffee, asked if we needed anything else, and was gone.

Will and I glanced at each other. The awkwardness had returned. I picked up a tea bag, removed it from the wrapper and dropped it into my cup. Had we been nothing more than friends all those years ago, we probably could have chatted easily. As it was, I wanted to know everything about his life now, but I was hesitant to ask. Our last conversation, which took place more than two decades earlier, had ended with the two of us—at Will's behest, mostly—going our separate ways.

But in the emergency room the other night, it seemed none of that mattered anymore.

"So, you live in San Sebastian and you're visiting here for Christmas," Will said, navigating the conversation. "What else?"

I took a deep breath.

"Well, let's see." I leaned back in my chair. "I teach English literature to high school kids, I have a son and a daughter—Ben and Justine—and I used to have a husband. We divorced two years ago. That's me in a nutshell."

He smiled. "C'mon, there has to be more than that. Tell me about your children. How old are they?"

"Oh, they're practically grown," I replied. "Wait a minute—they are grown. Ben is twenty-three, and Justine is twenty-one. Ben is a landscape designer and lives in Kentfield, about an hour away from San Sebastian. Justine is studying international relations at Middlebrook College, a little bit farther north."

"Are they much like you?" Will asked.

"Well, Ben tends to resemble me physically, but is much more like his father—and his side of the family—in terms of temperament. Justine, I think, has physical aspects of both me and her father, but her personality is a lot more like mine."

"And how do you happen to be living in San Sebastian?"

I gave him a very abridged version of my life from college to present day, but I specifically omitted details about my marriage. No need to reveal everything at once, if at all.

I glanced down at my bandaged hand and then at Will. "Obviously, you made it through your internship and residency—and then some."

I inclined my head toward him, indicating it was his turn. "And what else?"

His expression changed, and I thought I saw a shadow cross his face.

"Well," he said slowly. "I was married. My wife died a couple of years ago. Car accident."

I felt a sudden stabbing pain in my chest, as though an ice pick were boring its way through my breastbone. Sympathy, of course, but I had to admit it had as much to do with his use of the word *wife*. I had no reason to believe he had remained single, but it stung to think he'd planned to live happily ever after with someone other than me.

And yet, I'd done the same thing. The difference, however, was that if his wife hadn't died, Will would still be married to her. Joe lived across town from me, and, by choice, we almost never saw each other.

"I'm so sorry," I said quietly.

He picked up his spoon and began slowly turning it over and over on the table. His eyes were heavy. I sat motionless, waiting for him to continue.

"It all happened so quickly," he said. "She went off the road and into a ravine." He glanced up at me. "It was especially hard on the kids. I have two—Lizzy is thirteen and Wiley is eleven."

I felt a wave of empathy for both children. "I imagine it was hard on all of you," I replied. I wanted to offer him some comfort, but I wasn't sure how to do it.

I leaned forward, rested my hand on his, and gave it a slight squeeze. In response, he attempted a smile and placed his other hand over mine. We sat for a moment, in silence, studying each other's faces, and the chasm that separated us began to narrow.

"Tell me about Lizzy and Wiley," I prompted.

From this point, the conversation got easier. We had revealed the most important pieces of our current selves, and the details could be filled in later.

"Lizzy—Elizabeth—is in eighth grade. She's a great kid, but I tell you, girls are tough."

"Mm. I remember that time very well," I shuddered. "And aside from the perils of technology, it doesn't seem much has changed since my daughter was that age."

Will shook his head from side to side. "Her friends come over and I hear them chattering away about this one and that one and which boys like which girls, and, I tell you, it terrifies me. It was a hell of a lot easier when she was little and I was the only guy in her life."

I added a fresh tea bag and more water to my cup.

"Well, chances are you're still the most important guy in her life. She just doesn't realize it right now," I said reassuringly. "And Wiley?"

Will smiled and chuckled under his breath. "Wiley's just your average kid. He likes sports, video games, skateboarding. But he's also very artistic—like his mother."

I stiffened, but forced myself to relax. Will noticed my reaction. He frowned slightly, as though scolding himself.

"So, how do you like living in San Sebastian?" he asked, running his thumb and forefinger along the handle of his cup.

"Oh, it's great," I replied. "I like that it's close to both the ocean and the mountains. I used to do a lot of hiking and mountain biking, but somehow lately I haven't been able to find the time. Things are always so crazy."

"And do those crazy things involve anyone in particular?" he queried. He rubbed his hand across his face. It was a familiar gesture. "I'm sorry. I shouldn't have asked that. It's none of my business."

I considered the question for a moment, and gave him a mischievous smile.

"If you're asking if there's someone special in my life, I have to say ... most definitely, yes."

Will took a deep breath and let it out slowly.

"Ah," he said simply.

"His name is Bailey," I continued. "We met shortly after Joe and I got divorced. He's handsome and loyal and attentive, and I can't imagine my life without him. I'm really lucky to have found him."

"Ah," Will said again with a slight nod.

"He's strong and amazingly courageous, and he makes me feel safe," I added wistfully. "I have a picture of him, if you'd like to see it. Justine took it the day he moved in."

"Uh, sure," Will said with a disinterested shrug.

I extracted the small photo from my wallet and set it on the table.

"Where is he?" Will asked, squinting as he examined the image. "I only see you."

"He's the one with the stick," I said, pointing to the bottom half of the photo.

Will grinned.

"Ah," he said for a third time. "Handsome, loyal, attentive ... you must be talking about man's—er, woman's—best friend."

"Of course I am. What did you think?"

"I wasn't thinking anything."

"And you?"

"Now it's just me and my kids—and Hank and Piper. Hank is Wiley's hamster and Piper is Lizzy's cat."

We continued to talk easily, then, although we avoided topics that involved my ex-husband, his late wife, or our own shared history.

# 4

It was not a great day for traveling. Another storm had blown in during the night and rain fell in sheets. To make matters worse, I woke with a miserable headache.

"I hope your flight isn't delayed," Miranda said, peering out the guest room window. "Fortunately, Tuesday isn't usually a major travel day."

"They're all major," I replied, rolling a pair of jeans as tightly as I could with only one fully functional hand. I was bound and determined to fit everything in my carry-on bag so I could avoid the hassle of checking luggage. I didn't enjoy airports or flying, and tried to make the experience as uncomplicated as possible. I'd gotten everything in for the flight out to Westin, so I knew it all had to fit for the return trip. I hadn't added that much while I was here.

"Have you taken a plane anywhere lately?" I continued, now stuffing pairs of socks inside my shoes. "It takes forever to get through security, people are packed in like sardines, and take-offs are always delayed so you sit on the tarmac for an hour while some baby screams its head off and the kid behind you kicks the back of your seat."

"Well, you're in rare form this morning. Wake up on the wrong side of the bed, did you?" Miranda looked at me with raised eyebrows.

I sat down on the bench next to the window. "I'm sorry. I guess I just kind of wish I didn't have to leave yet." I picked up a sweater and began folding it.

"Aw, I'm touched," Miranda quipped and then added jokingly, "Or is it Dr. Tremaine who should be touched—er, excuse the pun."

I grabbed a pair of socks I'd rolled into a ball and threw them at her. The ball glanced off her shoulder and skidded under the bed. She laughed, and then got down on her knees to retrieve it.

"Have you heard from him?" she asked, her arm and shoulder completely engulfed by the bed skirt. "Since your coffee date, I mean."

"Yeah, he called me this morning."

"And you didn't tell me?" She dropped the socks in my lap. "Well, what did he say?"

"For crying out loud, Miranda, you sound like you're in junior high!" I spoke more harshly than I had intended. "I'm sorry, I didn't mean to snap at you."

"Don't worry about it," she replied evenly. She picked up my toiletry bag and tucked it in the suitcase.

"The fact is, there's nothing *to* talk about," I continued. "That's probably why I'm so miserable. I saw him and now I'm leaving. And in all likelihood, I'll never see him again."

It did occur to me after Will and I parted two days earlier that we hadn't officially exchanged telephone numbers or e-mail addresses, or even the most casual suggestion regarding future communication. Neither of us had brought it up. He had my cell phone number, obviously, and because he'd called me, his number was stored in my phone. But that seemed more a function of technology than conscious choice. When he walked me to my car and said goodbye, I felt a degree of finality, as though a door were closing.

I was surprised, then, when my cell phone rang as I was getting dressed and his number appeared on the screen.

"I just wanted to say again how great it was to see you the other day," he said. "I wish we'd had a little more time, but I have my schedule at the hospital ... and the kids ... and I know you have to get back."

"Yes," I had replied. "I'd love to be able to stay longer, but I have to get ready for the beginning of school." I paused for a few seconds. "But maybe we'll have another chance to catch up sometime. I'm sure I'll be back in Westin to see Miranda again, and when I am maybe we can get together."

"That would be great," he said. Now it was his turn to pause. "Listen, Callie, I—" he hesitated. "What I really want to say is—" He paused again and then sighed. "Never mind. It's not important."

And, goodbyes aside, that had been the extent of the conversation. I fully expected never to see or hear from him again. The door was not only closed, but the deadbolt had been turned, and I was shut out.

# 5

It was already dark when I pulled into the garage. I heard Bailey's bark coming from the kitchen even before I got out of the car. My welcoming committee, I thought to myself, smiling as I unlocked the door and walked inside. Bailey yipped and whined in excitement, wriggling his body in paroxysms of joy. I took a look around. Home. Funny, though, I felt a little glum.

"C'mon pal," I said to Bailey, who followed me into the living room. The message light on the telephone was blinking, so I hit the button. I had only two new messages.

"Hey, Mom." I smiled at hearing Ben's voice. "Just want to say welcome home. Everything's fine here. No broken bones; not even a sprained ankle. I'll call you tomorrow to talk about the trip. Oh, and Dad said to say Merry Christmas and Happy New Year."

The next message was from Justine, and a very typical one. "Hi, Mama, I can't remember when you're getting home, but call me, okay? I need to talk to you about something."

I sighed, closed my eyes, and shook my head. I picked up the phone and dialed Justine's number. Of course, she didn't answer.

"Hi, Jus," I said to her voicemail. "I just got in a few minutes ago. I'm really tired, though, so I think I'll go to bed early. I'll call you in the morning, okay? G'night, sweetie."

I put down the receiver and looked at Bailey. He was sitting across from me, the tip of his tail swishing softly across the floor.

"C'mon, let's get you something to eat. I'll bet you're hungry."

He padded behind me into the kitchen, where I found a note from Alice McMillan, the woman who owned my cottage, the main house, and the thirty acres on which they stood. Bailey had been staying with her while I was away. She knew I was getting home late, and brought him back earlier in the day so he would be here when I arrived. In her usual concise manner, she let me know that no problems had arisen, and that Bailey had been a perfect gentleman.

"Good boy," I said patting his head.

I scooped some dry food into his bowl and set it down on the mat.

"There you go, handsome. Bon appétit."

Yawning, I shuffled quickly through the mail that Alice left on the counter. Nothing that couldn't wait until tomorrow.

As soon as Bailey finished eating, I sent him outside for a few minutes, then locked the doors, turned off the downstairs lights, and carried my suitcase upstairs.

I unpacked a few things and decided to leave the rest until morning. I was suddenly overwhelmingly tired. I got undressed, washed my face and brushed my teeth, and crawled into bed. Bailey settled in beside me, his big paw across my arm.

"That's right, pal," I said, planting a kiss in the long brown fur at the top of his ear. "Just you and me." I switched off the light and didn't hear a sound until morning.

A sharp knock on the front door roused me from a deep sleep and the middle of what I thought had been a very pleasant dream. Bailey let out a bark and ran down the stairs. I followed after him, pulling on my robe and tying the sash around my waist.

Rubbing my eyes, I peered out the front window and recognized Ben's light brown hair.

"Hey, sweet pea," I said with a yawn as I opened the door. He stepped in and gave me a brief hug.

"Do you have to call me that?" he asked tiredly. He caught sight of my bandaged hand and took hold of my forearm. "What the hell happened?" he cried.

"Yes, I do have to call you that," I replied, moving toward the kitchen. "It's my maternal prerogative. I've called you sweet pea since you were a week old, and I'll be calling you that when we're both old and gray. And my hand's no big deal. I cut it while I was slicing bread at Miranda's house. I needed a few stitches, but it'll be fine."

I reached for the coffeemaker and began filling the carafe with water. I made a clumsy attempt at opening a fresh bag of coffee while Ben stood by looking amused. "Here," he said after a moment of watching me fumble. "Let me do that."

I stepped back so he could take over. "Tell me about the ski trip. Did you enjoy it?"

He finished setting the coffee to brew and then pulled out one of the two stools tucked beneath the counter. "Yeah, I did. It was fun. Dad was more relaxed than I've seen him in years. It was the first time in a long time that he and I were able to just hang out together. You know, talk about whatever. It didn't have to be a serious discussion about school or jobs. He wasn't tense or worked up about anything."

I put a carton of orange juice and a glass in front of him. He filled the glass and picked it up thoughtfully. "I think his new wife is actually good for him," he said.

I turned around to face the sink and leaned against the counter. I wanted Joe to be happy, and I wanted Ben and Justine to be comfortable with the different configurations the family had taken since Joe and I divorced. But Ben's assessment brought home a painful truth. It reminded me that in all the years Joe and I had been together—and there were a lot of them—I'd never really succeeded in bringing out the best in him. Of course, neither had he where I was concerned, but that wasn't the point right now.

"I'm sorry, Mom. I shouldn't have said that." Ben set his glass down on the counter.

"Don't be silly," I replied, popping two pieces of bread in the toaster. "I'm glad your dad is happy. And I'm really happy that you two are getting along."

I'd never said a word to Ben or Justine about their father's infidelities, despite the fact that, as far as I was concerned, it was his extramarital activity that made "till death do us part" pretty impossible. I suspected they had some idea about his second affair—they were certainly old enough to pick up the clues—but I never confirmed it, never even discussed it with them. Ben and Justine would have suffered from the knowledge, and it would have impacted their feelings for Joe and their regard for him. Ben's response to the divorce was proof enough of that.

"Mom!" Ben's voice pulled me out of my daydream.

"What, honey? I'm sorry. My mind was a million miles away."

"I asked if anything exciting happened while you were at Miranda's house. Besides your hand, I mean."

I lifted my coffee cup to my lips. "Not really."

24

# 6

"So what are you going to do?" Alex Merritt tossed his running shoes onto the floor of the backseat and slammed the door.

"What do you mean, do?" Will stood on the sidewalk with his hands on his hips. He glanced toward the house, eyes narrowed, looking for signs of activity. He exhaled heavily, and his breath hung in the air like a wispy cloud.

"Well, you saw this ghost on Christmas Eve, and then met up with her again a couple of days later. And from the look on your face when you talked about it, I'd say you were more than a little spooked." He opened the driver's door and sat down, one foot on the floor and the other on the street. "That means there's more to it than a couple of friends just catching up."

Will folded his arms across his chest and rubbed his sleeves. The air was clear and cold. A powdery layer of white from the snowfall a few days earlier still clung to areas that hadn't been warmed by the sun.

"There *is* more to it," he said, gazing down the street. "But I don't know what."

"Well, I haven't seen you this interested in anyone since—" Alex hesitated. "And, I'm telling you, it's about time. You can't keep living like a hermit."

"I'm not," Will argued. "I mean, I don't want to be. But I do have two kids who are still learning how to survive without their mother. And anyway, I've tried the dating thing." He looked directly at Alex. "Remember Tess?"

Tess Avery was a surgical nurse and the first woman who caught Will's attention after Joanna died. They dated seriously for a while, but Tess was looking for more than Will was able to give. She wanted a husband and a house and a family of her own, and after a few months of getting to know one another he got the distinct impression that the ideal family of her own did not include children from a husband's previous marriage. And while she certainly was attractive—and amenable—their encounters—he couldn't really call it lovemaking—left him dissatisfied, and almost lonely.

The last time he'd talked to her was after Christmas. She said she'd left him a note and a gift before taking off on Christmas Eve to visit her family for the holidays, but he told her he never got it. And when next they spoke, shortly before New Year's Eve, well, he'd met up with Callie by then, and that's where his attention had stayed.

"Tess wasn't long term, but she was a good start," Alex said. "At least she got you out of your house—that's more than anyone else was able to do."

With his arms still folded across his chest, Will tucked his hands under his armpits to keep them warm. "I know, I know." He paused. "The thing is," he continued, "there was something about seeing Callie again. I just—I can't stop thinking about her."

"Well, maybe you need to go with that." Alex pulled his leg into the car, slammed the door, and started the ignition. He pushed the button to roll down the window. "You know, the very least a conscientious doctor would do is check on his patient, particularly one who has stitches to be removed." He gave Will a brief nod and a wink as he started to pull away. "I'll see you at the hospital."

Will smiled and hurried up the driveway and into the house.

7

Fortunately, a few days of vacation remained between the time I got home from visiting Miranda and the first day of classes. I took full advantage of the opportunity to be lazy. My most strenuous activity involved preparing for my winter classes—basic composition, American literature, and, for my honors students, Shakespeare. I decided we'd tackle *A Midsummer Night's Dream* first, and then one of the tragedies—maybe *Romeo and Juliet*.

Despite the rain that seemed to fall incessantly, Bailey and I took walks together every day. Sometimes Alice and Bingo, her terrier mix, would join us. Bingo and Bailey—Alice joked that they sounded like a vaudeville act— enjoyed one another's company tremendously, particularly when they spent their time exploring the orchards and the meadow near Alice's house.

In the few weeks after the holidays, I had hoped to hear from Will again, but as days passed without a call, I became more and more convinced that he was getting on with his life and, I supposed, expecting that I was getting on with mine.

One Sunday evening, however, as I was gathering papers and previous lessons in preparation for school the following day, my cell phone rang and Will's number lit the screen.

"I just wanted to find out how your hand is doing," he said. "I thought I'd be remiss as a physician if I didn't check. Did you get the stitches out?"

"Yes, I did. Last week, as a matter of fact," I replied. "Everything's fine. The doctor was impressed with your handiwork." I glanced down at my hand.

"Well, I'm glad to hear it's okay," he said. Then with mock scolding, he added, "I do, however, strongly recommend that in the future you show proper respect for all your kitchen utensils, and I don't mean just knives. Scissors, graters—and potato peelers. They can be downright treacherous."

I laughed and promised to heed his counsel.

"So, how was your trip back to San Sebastian?" he asked.

"Oh, it was fine. Uneventful. And Bailey gave me a very warm welcome. He was quite happy to see me when I got home."

"I'm sure he was," Will said with a laugh. Then, more seriously, "I was really happy to see you, too."

"So was I—to see you, I mean." Nervous, I picked up the pen that was sitting on my desk and began doodling odd shapes on the back of an old envelope.

We talked for a bit longer, exchanging small, innocuous pieces of information. He asked if I'd done anything special for New Year's Eve, and I told him Bailey and I spent a quiet evening at home.

"Lizzy had a bunch of friends over, and they rang in the New Year with a lot of music and a lot of giggling," he said. "Wiley and I just hung out together watching *Star Wars* movies. Poor guy barely made it to midnight before he was sacked out on the couch."

We chatted a bit longer, and then the conversation wound down.

"Well, I guess I should get going," Will said. "You probably have things to do. Wiley is supposed to give a presentation on photosynthesis tomorrow and I promised to help him with some graphics. Though what I know about plant biology could fit on one quarter of a four-leaf clover."

I set aside my pen and paper.

"Let's see, if I remember correctly from Ben's sixth-grade science class, you—or rather the plants—take carbon dioxide and water, add a little sunlight, mix it all together, and, voilà!—oxygen. Did I get that right?"

"You're more the photosynthesis expert than I am," he joked. "Maybe you should be helping with his charts. All I can say is, thank God for the Internet."

"And all I can say is, 'Been there, done that.' I wish Wiley—and you—all the best."

"It'll be fine. He's a smart kid." Will paused. "And as for you, I really am glad your hand has healed so well. And I'm glad I was able to help."

"Well, thanks for your professional expertise and your concern," I said huskily. "And thanks for calling to check on me. I really do appreciate it. In the words of the famous playwright my students will be studying this semester, 'All's well that ends well.'"

Will was silent for a moment.

"Hm. You just wished me the best, and said all's well that ends well," he remarked cautiously. "Is that what this is then? The end?"

I hadn't considered the various meanings he might draw from either of those phrases, but a cup of coffee and two subsequent telephone conversations being the extent of our renewed acquaintance was certainly not one of them.

"I sure hope not," I replied.

We spoke once or twice a week after that. I left it to Will to call me, not because I thought it was his place to do the pursuing—if that's what it was— but because of the circumstances surrounding our respective marital status. He hadn't sought to end his marriage as I had mine. That decision was made for him when his wife's car careened off the road. Joe and I, on the other hand, parted ways by mutual agreement, and I didn't want to come across as the overly eager divorcée who couldn't wait to get her hooks into the eligible doctor.

So I let him take the lead. At the same time, though, I made clear how glad I was to hear from him.

"Tell me how you got to San Sebastian in the first place," he said during one of our earlier conversations. "You were pretty vague about your life history when we talked in Westin."

Vague didn't even begin to cover it. When we met in Westin, I wasn't sure I'd ever see Will again, and I was not inclined to share any important details of my life.

"Well, let's see," I began. "After you left for Boston, I still had every intention of going to law school. But I decided to take some time off. I was feeling really unsettled."

"Hmm," Will said in a noncommittal tone. I couldn't tell whether it was a response of simple acknowledgment, agreement, or remorse.

I had gotten a temporary job at a private boarding school not far from Westin, and was actually living on campus when I met Joe. He was a young architect just starting out, and very confident and very talented. We made our official acquaintance by running into each other—literally—just outside a grocery store. Coming from opposite directions around a corner of the building, and neither of us paying close attention, we plowed into one another. My bag of groceries tumbled to the ground, with the contents scattering across the sidewalk. While most of the items could be salvaged, a few were completely demolished.

"He asked if he could buy me dinner as partial reparation," I recalled. "One thing led to another, and the next thing I knew, we were engaged. And the next thing after that, we were married."

"Hmm," Will said, in the same noncommittal tone.

When Joe was offered a position as a junior associate at a well-known architectural firm in San Sebastian, we packed up and moved there.

"And what about law school?" Will asked.

"To tell you the truth, I wasn't sure what I wanted to do. Law and law school were sounding less and less appealing."

"And how did you get into teaching?"

"Well, you know what they say about the best-laid plans," I replied. At the boarding school, I tutored advanced readers in the upper grades, and found I really enjoyed it. As my interest in law school waned, I found myself more excited about teaching.

"You know, impacting young minds before they turn criminal," I joked.

When Joe and I got to San Sebastian, I went back to school and finished a master's degree in literature and got a teaching credential at the same time. I hadn't taught even a year, though, when I got pregnant with Ben.

"And then I started doing the mom thing. A couple of years later, Justine came along, and I just kept on doing it. When she started preschool, though, I went back to teaching."

Will was silent. I wondered what he was thinking.

"So I taught, Joe designed houses, and we stayed together until ... well, until we decided not to anymore." I concluded with what I hoped was a suggestion of finality. I didn't want to go any further into the circumstances of our separation.

Will must have picked up on that because he steered the conversation toward my current status.

"And so you've stayed in San Sebastian," he noted.

"There really wasn't any reason to leave," I explained. "I have a great job, I'm in close enough proximity to my kids that I can see them fairly often, and I also have the good fortune of living in a place I really love. It's a small guest cottage on a large piece of property near the ocean. It's very peaceful and very beautiful. Not lavish, but perfect for Bailey and me. And it has an extra bedroom for Ben or Justine when they come to visit."

Landing in the guest cottage was more than fortuitous; it was an example of pure synchronicity. It all came together in the teachers' lounge shortly after Joe and I separated. A colleague, Sally McMillan—a woman I knew fairly well, although we weren't particularly close—was aware of my situation, and had a proposition for me.

She lived with her mother in a large house on what used to be a small avocado ranch. At one time it encompassed more than sixty acres and several hundred trees. When Sally's father died of a heart attack, the business more or less went with him. Sally, the McMillans' only child, preferred teaching to farming, so production and distribution were scaled back to a level that could be managed with an overseer and a handful of part-time workers.

With her father gone, Sally moved back to the old family homestead so she could look after her mother.

Alice McMillan needed very little in the way of attention, though, aside from a bit of company and the occasional ride to the grocery store or pharmacy. She did all her own cooking, and, with the help of a gardener who came once a week, kept thriving flower and vegetable gardens. They even maintained a small orchard of fruit trees that, in the summer, provided copious amounts of fresh peaches, apricots, plums, and nectarines for the pies and cobblers she baked and the jars of homemade jam she put up every year.

When Sally was offered a job as director of a middle school some three hours away from San Sebastian, Alice encouraged her to make the move. She wanted to, but worried about leaving her mother on her own, with only friends and acquaintances to fill in the gaps.

That's where I came in. Sally asked if I was interested in living in the guest cottage—paying reduced rent and utilities—in exchange for checking in with Alice every day and occasionally driving her into town for medical appointments or groceries or other errands.

"As it turned out," I said to Will. "Alice and I have become very good friends, and I feel as though I've gotten the better end of the bargain all around. I live in a beautiful place that I absolutely adore in exchange for spending time with a woman I feel honored to consider my friend."

"It sounds like a really great situation," he replied. "I'm glad you found it—or it found you."

"So what about you?" I asked. "How did you end up back in Westin? When you left, you were pretty adamant that you'd never set foot in that city again."

"Well," he said slowly, "like you said, things don't always end up the way you plan."

"No, I guess they don't."

"I was working in a hospital in Connecticut when Joanna and I got married. We were living there when Lizzy was born and then Wiley a couple of years later. She was from Westin, and toward the end, when things got ... uh ..." He cleared his throat. "When things got ... difficult, we moved back so she could be near her family. And then, after she died, Lizzy and Wiley and I stayed here so they could be close to their grandparents and to Joanna's brother and sister."

I wanted to know more, but didn't feel it my place to ask. I'd wait for him to volunteer, in time, whatever details he thought appropriate. After all, I was doing the same thing—carefully choosing the particulars I was willing to reveal. At one point, Will and I would have felt comfortable sharing the most intimate details of our lives, but right now neither of us knew the other well enough to be completely candid.

"I can imagine how hard that was," I said softly.

"Yeah, it was tough," he agreed. "It still is. Joanna's family—her mother, in particular—doesn't want to accept that Joanna's gone. She's been holding on really tightly to Lizzy and Wiley."

"I guess that's not surprising," I offered. "They are the only physical connection she has to her daughter."

"I just worry sometimes that Joanna's mother—and sister—put too much pressure on Lizzy and Wiley. And particularly Lizzy."

I took a deep breath and exhaled slowly. "Well, I guess all you can do is take things one day at a time. I mean, at any given moment, I suppose we're all just trying to do the best we can."

"Yeah, well." Will paused for a moment. "This discussion has gotten way too serious," he grumbled. I sensed he was less uncomfortable with the gravity of the conversation than he was with the fact that his life was the focus of it.

"Well, it's getting late anyway," I acknowledged, "and Bailey's scratching to go out. He wants to be one with the night prowlers for a little while—at least those he can hear from the safety of the front yard. And then I think he and I will head off to bed. It's been a long day."

8

Will didn't bother knocking before opening Wiley's bedroom door. It was early Saturday morning and Wiley, still sound asleep, wouldn't hear him anyway.

Will stopped for a moment and gazed at his son. His pajamas were askew and he'd kicked the covers down to the foot of the bed. Will chuckled and pulled the quilt up off the floor. Wild night, he thought.

He sat down next to Wiley. "C'mon, pal, time to get up." He patted his son's back. "If you're going to the car show with your Uncle Chase, you have to get moving."

He peered out the window. From the looks of the gray clouds, rain was on the way, and probably a lot of it. More likely than not, the whole event would be canceled.

Glancing around the room, Will noted the clothes strewn across the floor, the piles of Lego pieces, and the assorted video games. He had to get tougher with Wiley about keeping his room neat. Those Lego pieces were a hazard.

Wiley had draped a shirt across the hamster cage next to his bed, and Will leaned forward to pull it off. He peeked in on Hank, expecting to see a tiny pink nose poke out from inside the pile of pine bedding and paper towel strips. Instead, he found the hamster curled up on his side near his food dish. It didn't take any real medical expertise to see that Hank was dead.

Will blew his breath out through his mouth. He covered his face with his hands. *Damn*, he thought. The last thing he wanted to do right now was to tell Wiley that something else he loved was gone. He'd done that once before, and it tore him up inside. A hamster couldn't compare to a mother, of course, but love was love, and Wiley had cherished Hank from the moment he joined the family. The loss would be hard to take.

Will placed the shirt back over the cage to hide Hank's lifeless body. He would tell Wiley about it first, and then, if Wiley wanted to, he could take the shirt away and see for himself.

Will would have preferred waiting to deliver the bad news so Wiley could enjoy the day with his uncle, but Wiley and Hank had a morning routine that Wiley never missed. As soon as he woke up, Wiley would pull a hamster treat from the box in the nightstand drawer and slip it through the bars of the cage. Hank, always bleary eyed and sleepy at this time of the morning, would scramble from his nest to take the treat from Wiley's fingers. He'd stuff it in his pouch and haul it back to bed with him.

Will sighed again.

"Wiley," he called quietly. "Wiley, you need to wake up."

Wiley rolled over, yawned and rubbed his eyes. "What time is it?" he asked.

"It's early," Will replied. "But I have to tell you something."

Wiley looked at Will, wide-eyed and apprehensive. He sat up slowly. The last time his father started a conversation this way, it ended with the knowledge that he would never see his mother again.

Will put a hand on Wiley's knee. God, he hated this. He hadn't wanted the hamster in the first place. It was Joanna who insisted Wiley should have a pet.

That realization hit him like a punch to the solar plexus. Hank and Wiley and Joanna—mother and son had visited four different pet stores before settling on Hank, and together they'd set up his cage and outfitted it with piles of nesting material, an exercise wheel, and an assortment of toys. For Wiley, Hank was more than a pet; he was the last direct link to his mother.

"Wiley, when I came in this morning to wake you up, I looked in on Hank." Will tightened his hold on Wiley's knee. Just say it outright, he told himself. No beating around the bush. No trying to soften the blow. Wiley was too smart for that now. "When I looked at Hank, he wasn't breathing." He paused for a moment, letting Wiley absorb the information. "I think he passed away sometime last night. I'm really sorry."

He waited for Wiley's response.

"What?" Wiley whispered. He turned immediately to the cage and removed the shirt. Will let out a sigh of relief that the hamster's eyes were closed. He looked like he was sleeping—nothing more sinister than that.

Wiley's chin quivered and a tear rolled down his cheek. He opened the cage door and reached in. He touched Hank very lightly.

"He's cold," Wiley noted. He sniffled and wiped away the tear.

"I know. I'm so sorry," Will replied.

"What happened to him?"

"Well, hamsters don't live a very long life, and he'd gotten to be a pretty old guy," Will explained, stroking Wiley's hair. "My guess is his heart gave out and he died in his sleep. I'm really sorry."

"Me, too," Wiley murmured. His eyes filled, and tears overflowed onto both cheeks.

"Come here, pal." Will opened his arms to Wiley, who welcomed his father's strong embrace. He clung to Will's shirt.

Passing Wiley's bedroom on her way downstairs, Lizzy glanced in and saw her father and brother. "What's wrong?" she asked with alarm.

Will sighed. The news wouldn't fall easy on her, either. He motioned for her to come in. She took one step through the doorway and pressed herself against the wall, next to the dresser.

Wiley separated from Will and turned toward Lizzy. His cheeks were damp. "H-Hank d-died," he said and turned back to Will's shoulder amid a fresh round of tears.

Lizzy stood firmly in place, making no move to approach either Wiley or Will. "How?"

Will repeated the explanation he'd given Wiley.

Lizzy nodded in response. She was silent for a moment, and then spoke softly. "Are we going to have a funeral for him?"

"We can," Will replied. "Do you want to do that, Wiley?"

Wiley didn't speak, but nodded into Will's shoulder.

Upon further discussion, which included a telephone call to the grandparents, it was decided that Hank would be laid to rest in the Hallorans' backyard. Eleanor suggested a spot underneath the oak tree, where Joanna's cat and the family's cocker spaniel had been buried many years before.

So a few hours later, beneath a heavy rain, the small group of mourners formed a circle around the freshly dug grave. They stood shoulder to shoulder, huddled under umbrellas that offered little protection from the downpour. Heaven, it seemed, was sharing their grief.

The rain hadn't been falling nearly as hard when Will came out with a shovel an hour or so earlier, and as he watched the heavy drops pummel the soft earth, it occurred to him that at the rate they were going, the hole could easily fill with water, or the ground fall in on itself before the ceremony was finished. The leafy branches of the massive oak formed a canopy that provided some shelter, but after a while, even that wouldn't do any good.

Will glanced down at Wiley. The boy stood next to him, holding in his cupped hands the gray and white ball of fur.

ANDREA WEIR

Well, no matter, he thought. The hole was small; he'd just dig it out again if necessary.

"We have gathered here this afternoon to bid farewell to a great and true friend," Edward began. His deep voice echoed through the rain. He stood solemnly, his arms in front of him, hands clasped. "A friend who was with us in good times and in bad, who supported us, cared about us, and loved us. And we, in turn, loved him."

He shifted his weight from one foot to the other.

"Friends pass through our lives," he continued, "and the best of them leave us with something of themselves. The one we're here to honor today touched our hearts in ways we will never forget."

He turned to Wiley and laid a gentle hand on his shoulder. "Is there anything you'd like to say?"

The boy stood quietly, his attention focused on the small creature that lay still in his hands. He sniffled, and wiped his nose on the shoulder of his coat. Tears trickled down his cheeks.

"Bye, Hank," he said, gently stroking the soft fur around the animal's ear. "Thanks for being my friend." He knelt down and removed the lid of the shoebox that would serve as a coffin. He had stretched one of his old baseball socks across the bottom to make it more comfortable. Very carefully, he laid the hamster on the fabric, fitted the lid on the box, and placed it in the tiny grave. He picked up a handful of wet dirt, intending to drop it on the box, but stopped abruptly. He turned to Will and grasped his sleeve.

"Do you think Mom will remember to feed him?" he asked, eyebrows knitted with worry. "I had to remind her when I went to camp. What if she forgets?"

Will gazed down at his son. Tears filled his eyes. Death and loss had occupied so much of the boy's life during the last two years. He wished he could somehow shield him from the pain of it, to place his own body between that dark abyss and his son's innocence. But all he could do right now, at this moment, was to be with him; to share the burden of grief as best he could, and to help him learn how to shoulder the sorrows he would carry for the rest of his life.

He wrapped his arm around Wiley and pulled him close.

"She'll remember," he said gently.

"I hope she gives him treats, too." Wiley looked up at his father, head cocked to one side. "They have treats in heaven, don't they, Dad?"

Will smiled. "I'm sure your mom will find some," he said.

Lizzy, standing on his other side and flanked by Rowan and Eleanor,

36

quickly wiped away her own tears and wrapped her raincoat tightly around herself. She took a step closer to Will. He placed a hand on the back of her neck and gave it a slight squeeze. He kissed the top of her head very softly. "I'm sorry, Lizzy," he murmured.

Leaning into him, she replied, "It's okay, Dad. I'm okay."

After a moment, he picked up a shovel and began to fill in the hole. Rain continued to fall in sheets, saturating his hair and working its way down the collar of his coat. He tamped down the wet dirt, and then he and Chase, who'd been standing next to his own father, placed two large rocks on top of the grave.

"Goodbye, Hank," Will murmured. "Thanks for everything."

He picked up the shovel again, and with his arm wrapped around Wiley's shoulder, joined the rest of the family as they walked toward the house.

The group filed through the back door and into the mudroom. Will leaned the shovel against the porch wall and stepped inside.

"Be sure to hang up your wet things," Eleanor reminded. Addressing her grandson, she added, "Wiley, I have your favorite chocolate cake, and I'm saving the very first piece for you."

The kitchen was warm and welcoming. The scent of freshly baked cake hung in the air, along with the aroma of strong coffee. The large, round claw-foot table in the middle of the room was already set with plates, napkins, and silverware. Eleanor picked up the silver cake server and began cutting generous wedges and transferring them to plates, which Lizzy distributed among the group.

Cake served, coffee poured, and glasses of milk provided to the children, Eleanor took a seat between Lizzy and Wiley.

"That was a very nice service, Edward," she said to her husband, who sat across the table from her. "Quite dignified."

Edward bowed his head. "Well, Hank deserved it." He looked at Wiley. "And I meant every word."

Seeming not to notice the exchange, Wiley chewed thoughtfully on a mouthful of cake. He swallowed, paused, and addressed Eleanor. "Gran, do you think Mom still loves us even though she went away?" His cheeks, still flushed from the afternoon chill, resembled tiny apples.

Will had been in conversation with his brother-in-law, but overhearing Wiley's question, turned to look at him.

"Well, of course she does. What would make you think otherwise?" Eleanor took Wiley's hands in her own. "Your mother loved you with all her heart, and that doesn't just stop. All the love she ever had for you is still here."

Wiley looked from his grandmother to his father, then rose and walked slowly across the room. He sat down on a chair near the window. Will and Eleanor exchanged glances, and Will moved toward his son. He squatted next to the chair so he could be at eye level with him. "What is it, buddy?" he asked. "Maybe I can help."

Wiley focused his attention on the cuff of his shirt, fidgeting with the button. Aside from his thumb and forefinger, he was completely still. Will stroked the top of his head.

"Wiley, you know you can tell me anything and it'll be okay, right? I promise you it'll be all right." He ran his hand through the boy's silky blond hair. Just like Joanna's, he thought to himself.

Wiley's mouth twitched as though he wanted to speak but was weighing his words carefully. Will waited patiently.

"I heard Mrs. Everett talking on the phone when I was at Tanner's house yesterday," Wiley finally began. He kept his eyes on the button of his cuff. "She said Mom wanted to die." He raised his head and looked directly into his father's eyes. "Does that mean she didn't want to be with us anymore? Did I do something wrong?"

From the moment the paramedics had brought his wife into his own emergency room, Will carried an ache in his chest. Hard and solid as a stone, it exploded now, sending shockwaves of pain throughout his entire body. He lifted Wiley off the chair, sat down himself, and settled the boy on his lap. He held him tightly against his chest.

"It was an accident, Wiley, a terrible accident. Your mom drove too fast around the curve and lost control of the car. She didn't do it on purpose, I promise. She would never choose to go away from you or Lizzy. She loved you too much."

"And she wouldn't want to go away from you either, right, Dad?"

Again Will and Eleanor exchanged glances.

"No," Will murmured reassuringly. "She wouldn't choose to go away from me either." He rested his cheek on the top of his son's head. Neither one moved as they sat together, staring out the window and watching the heavy raindrops bounce off the patio.

"Who is this Mrs. Everett?" Eleanor demanded a short time later, after Wiley joined his grandfather in the living room for a game of checkers. Fury blazed in her dark eyes. "How *dare* she make my family's private affairs a topic of common gossip?"

"She's Tanner's mother," Will replied wearily. "You remember him, don't you? He's Wiley's friend from school. They spend a lot of time together in the afternoons, and it's really been good for him." He rubbed his hand across his face. He was bone tired. It had been a long day, and it wasn't over yet. "I'm really surprised to hear about this, though. I'd expect her to be a lot more sensitive. I'll talk to her about it the next time I see her."

Eleanor leaned slightly to one side, allowing the family's housekeeper to refill her coffee cup. "Thank you, Paulette," she said with a nod.

Using a pair of small silver tongs, she grasped a sugar cube and dropped it into her cup. She stirred slowly and deliberately while considering the situation.

"I have a mind to talk to the woman myself," she snapped. "Joanna is our daughter, and nothing about her is anyone's business but ours."

"And she was my wife and my son's mother," Will replied flatly. "I'll talk to Helen Everett."

The door to the mudroom opened and Lizzy walked into the kitchen. She approached her father and leaned against his chair. He put his arm around her waist and looked up at her.

"How goes it, LZ," he asked. "Are you all right?"

"I'm okay," she shrugged.

"What were you doing in the mudroom, sweetheart?" Her grandmother reached out and gently brushed Lizzy's hair away from her eyes. "It's terribly cold in there."

Lizzy sat down in the chair next to her father. She twisted her mouth and chewed the inside of her lip.

"I just wanted to be by myself for a while."

"But why there?" Eleanor pressed. "You can certainly find more comfortable places in the house."

"I know," Lizzy replied. "But I wanted to look out the window so I could see Hank." She turned to Will. "Do you think Wiley will get another hamster? One to replace Hank?"

Will smiled faintly and touched his hand to Lizzy's face, caressing her cheek with his thumb. "There is no replacement for Hank, LZ He was one of a kind."

It was late when Will finally got the children home. After saying goodnight to Lizzy and seeing Wiley settled, he went into his own room and sat down on the edge of the bed.

He leaned toward the nightstand and switched on the lamp. It produced a dim glow, just enough to form odd shadows on the walls around him. He hated being in here. Too much of Joanna was in this room. Too much of the troubled version of the woman he thought he knew. He looked around. Even after two years, most of her things remained because Lizzy didn't seem ready to let them go. She often came in here, pulled one of Joanna's sweaters out of the drawer, and curled up with it on what used to be Joanna's side of the bed. Or she'd rummage through Joanna's jewelry box, or try on one of the assorted perfumes on Joanna's dresser.

Whatever problems Will and Joanna had, he would not take anything away from his daughter. He trusted that in time her grief would lessen, and she'd be able to relinquish the material things—most of them, anyway, he hoped. But if having them and being in here brought Lizzy comfort, well, that was all that mattered.

His own feelings were a jumbled mix of sadness, remorse, and a fair amount of guilt. Joanna's mood swings—her "quirks," as Eleanor called them—had made life more than difficult, particularly after Lizzy and Wiley came along. Medication smoothed things out considerably, but Joanna deemed it more an option than a necessity.

Will snorted to himself as he remembered uncovering her stash of pills. It was shortly after she had died. He was going through one of her drawers looking for something, and he happened upon a dozen or more prescription bottles—all of them nearly full.

In all his years as a physician, the only time he questioned his own competence was the afternoon he found the bottles. He had believed Joanna when she told him she was following her doctor's orders. He'd wanted more than anything for it to be true—for his wife to be healthy and whole. So he had taken her word for it. Looking back on it, he realized there was so much of Joanna's condition that he had chosen not to acknowledge—so much that he, like Eleanor, more comfortably attributed to her particular sensibilities.

But as he sat on the bed that afternoon—in practically the same spot as he did now—he had stared at the bottles that lay in a pile on his lap, and berated himself for not seeing what had been so clearly in front of him. He was a doctor, for God's sake. If anyone should have known, it should have been him.

If he had, maybe he could have saved her; and maybe he could have protected his children from the loss that was now devastating their lives.

Will blinked hard and shook his head as though to dispel the memory. He grabbed a pillow and blanket from the closet, and walked out of the room, closing the door behind him. As he did most nights, he went downstairs and into the family room, where he stretched out on the couch, tucked the pillow under his head, and pulled the blanket up to his chest. He switched off the light and fell into a fitful sleep.

He dreamed of Joanna. She was lost somewhere in a strange city, and he was trying to find her. But the streets were a maze of circles, and he couldn't make his way from one to the other. Each time he thought he was going in the right direction, he'd hit a dead end. To make matters worse, a heavy fog was rolling in, and visibility was decreasing rapidly. He had to find her before it engulfed them completely and he wouldn't be able to see anything.

Suddenly, he heard the sound of her crying. It came from the center of the maze. On the verge of panic, he jumped out of his car and started walking the circles and half circles, trying desperately to get to her. The sound grew louder, as though she was right next to him. He turned and found himself face-to-face with Callie. Her smile was warm and reassuring, and he wanted to follow her, even as the fog grew thicker and Joanna's crying got louder. She moved easily from one circle to the next, making her way to the center. Will turned in every direction, but could move no more than a few steps. The passageways were closing around him, and he realized he was trapped.

He awoke with a start, his heart pounding. He still heard the sound of crying, and realized it was coming from Wiley's room. He leapt off the couch and took the stairs two at a time. When he opened the door, he found Wiley sitting up in bed, clutching his blanket. His face was red and tear-stained.

In one quick, fluid motion, Will got from the door to the bed and gathered Wiley in close to him. The boy dissolved into wracking sobs. "Wiley, what is it?" Will asked anxiously. "Tell me. Are you sick? Do you hurt somewhere?"

Wiley could barely speak. "I w-w-want H-H-Hank," he cried. "I w-want H-Hank back. And I w-want M-Mommy."

Will held his son, rubbing his back and stroking his head. "I know," he said soothingly. "I know." Just then, Lizzy appeared in the doorway. "Dad?" she asked nervously. "What's wrong with Wiley?" With one arm still around his son, Will extended the other toward his daughter. She ran over to him and crawled under the covers, curling up against his chest. Exhausted after a time, Wiley finally quieted and collapsed on his other side. Will sat with his back pressed uncomfortably against the headboard, holding his children close to him, guarding against whatever demons might approach in the dark. Eventually, they all slept.

# 9

It wasn't the rain that kept us indoors as much as it was the thunder and lightning. Such weather was fit for neither man—or, in this case, woman— nor beast, according to Bailey, and he was happy to curl up on his bed, near the fire, and snooze away the afternoon.

Needless to say, I was in complete agreement. I had a cup of hot tea and a copy of *A Room of One's Own* that I'd started over Christmas vacation but never gotten around to finishing, and nothing short of a lightning bolt striking the cushion next to me would have gotten my attention.

Well, nothing, as it turned out, except a phone call from Will.

"Hey, I hope I'm not interrupting anything," he said.

"No, not at all," I replied. "The weather is atrocious, and I'm just sitting here with Bailey reading a book."

"It's about as bad here. It's cold and snowy, and, to tell you the truth, I can't wait for spring."

His voice sounded heavy.

"I know what you mean." I paused briefly. "Is everything all right?"

He let out a sigh. "It's been a tough weekend. Hank, Wiley's hamster, died sometime Friday night and we had a funeral for him yesterday. Burial, eulogy, the whole nine yards. It was really hard on everyone."

"Oh, Will, I'm so sorry. Is Wiley all right?"

"Yeah, he's okay. But the hamster was kind of a connection to his mother, and losing that was especially hard. He was really upset last night."

He described waking to the sound of crying, and sitting with Lizzy and Wiley from the middle of the night until morning.

"I'm sorry," Will said apologetically, "I don't mean to be so—maybe I should just hang up."

"No, really, it's fine," I assured him. I was, in fact, quite moved by the image of him holding his children—in the dark—using his body and the strength of his presence to protect them and keep them safe.

"I just wish there were some words of wisdom I could offer," I continued. "There's nothing harder than what Lizzy and Wiley are going through, and it sounds like you are doing everything you can to help them manage it. No one can ask for—or expect—anything more."

"Well, thanks. I appreciate hearing that."

"So, what did you all do today?" I asked, trying to lighten the mood a bit.

"I didn't do much of anything," he replied. "Just caught up on some medical journals. But Wiley spent the day at a friend's house, which was good for him. Took his mind off things. And Lizzy went to the mall—again."

I smiled to myself. "Lizzy's what? Twelve? Thirteen? I'm afraid her mall days are just beginning. Your credit card is going to suffer a lot of wear and tear from here on out." I was pleased to hear Will laugh.

"She's thirteen, and I think you're right. I may need to make a whole new category in the family budget for her shopping excursions."

We both chuckled and then were silent for a moment. Will finally spoke. "You know, Cal, I don't think I've told you how really glad I am that we've reconnected." He spoke casually, but his tone was altogether serious. "I mean, really glad."

"Well, I am, too."

# 10

Will walked through the double doors of the hospital entrance on Monday morning and the familiar scent filled his nostrils—the pungent odor of disinfectant mingled with the aroma of brewed coffee and fresh flowers. He took a deep breath and immediately felt himself relax. This was his place. He felt at ease here and in control here. In this place, he had answers. In every other part of his life, he faced a jumble of questions, concerns, and doubts.

Heading toward the trauma center, he turned a corner and ran into Alex Merritt.

"Hey, man, looks like you had one hell of a night," Alex joked as they both continued down a long hallway. "I hope it was worth it."

"Not exactly," Will replied. "Wiley's hamster went to the big exercise wheel in the sky this weekend, and Wiley was pretty broken up." He nodded at a nurse who crossed paths with them.

Alex patted Will on the shoulder. "Oh, jeez. Poor kid, he really loved that little thing."

Will and Alex stepped out of the way to make room for an orderly who was pushing a patient on a gurney.

"I really am sorry," Alex continued. "Listen, why don't you come over for dinner tonight? Julie was just asking about the kids the other day. Said she hasn't seen them in a while. We'll get Chinese or pizza or something." He paused for a moment and studied his friend's face. "You look like you could use a break, too."

Will snorted. "No argument there."

"Here—you hold one with these two fingers, like this, and the other on top, like this." Julie gave Lizzy and Wiley a brief lesson in the use of chopsticks,

44

carefully adjusting the utensils in Wiley's hand. "Then you move them kind of like claws."

To supplement his wife's tutorial, Alex offered a brief demonstration. "See?" He picked up an egg roll, and just as he opened his mouth to take a bite, the chopsticks slipped, and the egg roll—true to its name—bounced onto the table and rolled off the edge.

Alex looked at it lying on the carpet and frowned. "I thought it was meatballs that did that!" Undaunted, he leaned over and picked it up, then held it like a trophy, bowing slightly to the applause of his audience. When the chopsticks slipped again, and the egg roll landed with a splash in his water glass, Lizzy and Wiley exploded in a fit of laughter. Alex directed a good-natured scowl first at the children and then at his wife.

"You know, a man could starve to death trying to eat this way," he said.

Julie smiled at him. "They don't seem to have any trouble with this in Asia."

"Yeah, well. This is the good old U.S. of A., and I do my eating with a fork." He cast a glance at Wiley. "How about you? Are you a fork man, too?"

Wiley, whose luck with chopsticks hadn't been much better, nodded shyly.

"Make that two patriotic Americans," Alex called to Julie, who was already on her way to the kitchen. "And a fresh glass of water wouldn't be bad, either."

Sitting opposite Lizzy and Wiley, Will leaned back in his chair, welcoming the respite the Merritt house provided. He'd known Alex since they were in medical school together. They'd done their internships and residencies at the same hospital in Connecticut. It was Alex, in fact, who put Will in the right place at the right time to meet Joanna.

When he and Joanna moved back to Westin several years later, Alex—who by that time had managed to convince Julie to marry him—decided he was ready for a change himself. At Will's urging, Alex interviewed for—and was offered—a position at Westin Memorial Hospital. His specialty was neurosurgery.

Julie, a social worker, went to work for a nonprofit organization in Westin that advocated for children whose parents were involved in the criminal justice system.

Julie and Alex had been Will's sole support throughout his difficulties with Joanna. While Will looked after her—and Lizzy and Wiley—Julie and Alex looked after him. Had it not been for them he wouldn't have managed the aftermath of Joanna's death.

What's more, they took their role as godparents to Lizzy and Wiley very seriously, and Will had come to count on that. The Hallorans welcomed any opportunity to have Lizzy and Wiley stay with them, and while they offered a safe place, Will's relationship with them was often strained. He worried about the children spending too much time with Eleanor and Rowan. While it was true that they—and Edward and Chase, for that matter—offered a connection to Joanna the children couldn't find anywhere else, they also fostered a certain degree of discord.

After dinner, Alex set Wiley up with his computer and a new video game, and Julie sat down with Lizzy to work on a project they had started. Julie was an expert knitter, and she was teaching the craft to Lizzy. Their first effort together was a yellow-and-purple-striped scarf done in alternating sections of garter, stockinette, and seed stitch.

Wiley sat cross-legged on the floor with the computer in front of him while Julie and Lizzy occupied the couch. Will and Alex, who'd been assigned kitchen duty, hung out in the dining room until they were ready to tackle the dishes.

"So, how are things?" Alex asked.

"You know, I just do what I have to do," Will replied with a shrug. He motioned toward Lizzy and Wiley in the living room. "This is really good for them," he said. "Thanks for inviting us tonight. At home, things are just ... hard. Not much that's really pleasant."

Alex picked up his water glass and took a sip. "I know, man, and I really wish we could do more. It's a tough situation any way you look at it."

Will rubbed his hands across his face. "Yeah, well ..."

"Have you talked to anyone?" Alex asked cautiously.

"What do you mean? Like a counselor?" Will responded.

"Yeah, someone who knows about this sort of thing. Someone who can offer some advice. You're in a tough spot with these kids, and then you add Joanna's family on top of it. No offense, but I've met her mother and sister, and I don't think either one has her head screwed on straight."

Will laughed. "You got that right."

Alex reached across the table and began to stack the plates, separating out the silverware and chopsticks. "Hey, by the way, I meant to ask, what's up with the old girlfriend—the one whose hand you stitched on Christmas Eve."

Will's face brightened and the corner of his mouth curled upward. "Callie," he replied. "I've spoken with her quite a few times, as a matter of fact. I guess you'd say we're getting reacquainted." He picked up the glasses and silverware and followed Alex into the kitchen.

"And that's a good thing, right?" Alex asked in a tone that was more directive than questioning.

Will smiled. "Yeah, I think it is."

Alex rinsed the plates and loaded them in the dishwasher. Will leaned against the counter, watching.

"So what's her story?" Alex asked. "Married? Not married?"

"Not married," Will replied. "Divorced a couple of years ago. She has two grown children—a son and a daughter."

Alex took the glasses as Will handed them to him. "Well, what do you think?"

"What do you mean, what do I think?"

"I mean, I haven't seen such a stupid grin on your face in a long time," Alex responded. "So what do you think you're going to do?"

Will pulled a bottle of water out of the refrigerator, unscrewed the cap and took a long sip. He looked at Alex with one eyebrow raised and a half smile playing at his lips. "Get more acquainted."

# 11

The school day had ended, and the last of my American literature students spilled out of the classroom, laughing and chatting as they went home or off to their respective activities. Two girls, one light haired and the other dark, passed in front of me on their way outside and I caught a snippet of their conversation. It was Friday, and the brunette had a date that night with whoever happened to be the current young man of her dreams. She and her friend were engaged in a heated discussion about the appropriateness of leggings versus jeans, and whether zip-up boots or Uggs made the best "I-want-to-look-fabulous-but-I-don't-want-to-look-like-I-care" fashion statement.

My desk was at the front of the room, and a burst of cold air hit me when they opened the door. Winter, which seemed to have arrived on the wings of the New Year, was making its presence known with a vengeance. December had been relatively mild, but January was cold and rainy, with gusting winds that turned umbrellas inside out and sent hats flying. February was proving to be only slightly more temperate.

I had just begun to gather up my books and papers and prepare myself to brave the outdoors when my cell phone rang. I rummaged through my purse trying to find it before the call went to voicemail. I assumed it was Justine wanting to complain about her chemistry test and how unfair it was that Middlebrook College required her to complete a physical science course when her career aspirations would take her in the exact opposite direction. By the time I managed to grab the phone, however, it had stopped ringing. I waited a minute and then heard the familiar three-note riff that meant someone had left a message.

I opened up my voicemail, although I had absolutely no intention of calling her back right away. At this moment, I would not be the least bit sympathetic. When I saw Will's name and number, however, I pressed the button and listened to the message.

"So, here's the thing," he said. "I know it's only been a couple of months, and I know we've only spoken a handful of times, but I'd really like to see you again. The kids have two days off for President's Day or something, and they're going to spend a long weekend with their aunt and uncle. I took Friday and Monday off because I thought they'd want to hang out with me so the three of us could do something together, but they'd rather go snowboarding with Chase and Sarah. I don't particularly want to join them, so that leaves me with some time on my hands. I thought maybe I'd catch a flight on Thursday evening. Give me a call back and let me know what you think."

I sat back in my chair, took a deep breath, and exhaled. What *did* I think? I certainly wanted to see him again, too, but I wasn't sure about the whole situation. If Will were the only one involved, my response would be unequivocal—he'd find me at the arrivals gate in a heartbeat, waving a "Welcome to San Sebastian" banner. But he had two children to consider. We had to tread lightly. I couldn't step into his life without stepping into theirs, and that was not something I would do precipitously. I knew from my own experience on the other side of the equation what a difficult proposition it would be, and I wasn't sure I wanted to take it on.

I was almost Lizzy's age when my own mother died, and the soul-shattering reverberation had stayed with me—to one degree or another—all my life. When my father broke the news on a cold January morning, it was as though I had been set adrift on a vast ocean, to float rudderless, with no compass, no guide, no anchor, and no land in sight. It was a horrible feeling of being lonely and alone, isolated, and desolate.

I also remembered the anger and resentment I felt when—not long afterward—my father brought Lila into our lives. Not only had he found a replacement wife for himself, he seemed to think he'd found a replacement mother for my brother Lucas and me. He never did understand—and neither did Lila—why we hated her so. Lila had seen us as a ready-made family—two children whom she thought must be in desperate need of a mother. And she was a woman in desperate need of children. She couldn't seem to comprehend, or chose not to accept, that Lucas and I already had a mother. She may not have been physically present, but she had been real, and she had been ours.

I wasn't sure about Wiley, but I was pretty confident Lizzy would resent whatever presence I might have in her father's life. No matter what happened, she would see me as an intrusion. Will and I were only slowly getting to know one another again, but even so, I didn't want to start anything I would be afraid—or unable—to finish. It wouldn't be fair to any of us.

And yet, I had loved him so deeply once. And I couldn't deny that a part of me still did. If he felt the same way about me, would it be fair to either of us to walk away and pretend he didn't exist? The idea of finding him again only to turn my back on whatever future might present itself seemed equally unjust—and, at this moment, unthinkable. Questions, answers, and more questions swirled in my head. I needed more time to figure things out before I saw him again and the whirlwind of joy, excitement, and other emotions overpowered my rational mind.

I picked up my phone and dialed Will's number. Both Ben and Justine had intimated earlier in the week that they might stop by Saturday or Sunday, so I decided to use their visits as a reason to excuse myself from that particular weekend. Will answered on the third ring.

"Hey, it's Callie," I said, a little breathlessly.

"Oh, hi. Hold on for a second, okay?" He spoke hurriedly at first, but more slowly when he got back on the line. "Sorry. I wanted to find a quieter place to talk. I guess you got my message then. Are you free next weekend?"

"You know, Will, I really wish I were," I said. "But I was planning to spend most of Saturday with Ben, and then Justine was talking about coming home for the weekend, and I haven't seen her in weeks." I wasn't telling the complete truth, but neither was I offering up a bald-faced lie.

He must have recognized it.

"Oh," he replied, a touch of surprise and disappointment in his voice. "Okay. I understand. Maybe some other time." He hesitated for a few seconds. "Well, you have my number, so why don't you just call me when you feel like it."

I detected a note of finality in his voice. He'd made a move, I'd rebuffed it, and that was that. It occurred to me that despite what he said, there might not be "some other time," and while I wasn't sure about seeing him so soon, I was absolutely certain about never seeing him again—that simply was not an option.

"Will," I blurted, "I—you—" I stopped to collect my thoughts. "You know what, I'd love for you to come out next weekend. I'll just rearrange things with Ben and Justine."

"Are you sure?" he asked cautiously. "If the timing is bad—"

"No," I interrupted. "It's perfect. I have the long weekend, too."

"You're sure."

"Completely."

When the conversation ended, I dropped my phone onto my desk and sat back in my chair, holding my breath. I felt as though I'd hurled myself off a cliff only to realize partway down that I didn't really want to jump after all. Well, nothing to do about it now but brace myself. I couldn't very well tell him I'd changed my mind—could I?

## 12

"Boy, it is *chilly* out there!" It was Saturday, midday, and I had just come in from running with Bailey. I poured a glass of water from the pitcher on the counter and walked over to Justine. Having made a surprise visit this weekend instead of next, she was sprawled out on the couch perusing a Global Good catalog. I pressed my hand to her cheek and she jerked away from me with a growl.

Bailey, in a fit of uncontrolled exuberance, took a flying leap and landed practically in her lap. Caught off guard, she nearly spilled the mug of cinnamon orange tea she had just poured for herself. "Get off!" she hollered trying to push the eighty-five-pound mass of fur back onto the floor. "Jeez, Mom, would you do something about your dog?"

"C'mon, Bailey," I cajoled. "Justine has no appreciation for such complete and undying devotion." He jumped off the couch and joined me at the foot of the stairs.

"I'm going to jump in the shower," I told her, "I'm taking Alice out to run a few errands this afternoon, and then we're stopping at May's for an early dinner."

I started up the stairs. "You're welcome to join us, if you want. Alice always likes seeing you."

"Maybe I will," Justine replied. "Depends on how much of this stupid paper I get written." She frowned in the direction of her laptop. It sat closed on the table next to her, not even plugged in.

"At the risk of stating the obvious, you'll get more done if you actually turn the thing on," I noted.

"Yeah, yeah," she said dismissively. She sat up and tossed the booklet onto the coffee table. "By the way," she added mildly, "you got a call from some guy named Will Tremaine. Your cell phone rang and I picked it up. I thought it might have been Ben—or maybe Dad. He was surprised when he realized he wasn't talking to you."

"Justine! You can't answer my phone," I sputtered. "It's private!" I wasn't really angry as much as I was flustered. I hadn't told either Justine or Ben about Will, and I had no immediate plans to do so.

"Sorry," Justine apologized with no detectable remorse.

"Well, what did he say?" I asked, a little more calmly.

"He said to tell you he called, he wants you to marry him, and he'll call back tonight for your answer."

"What?" I cried.

"Relax, Mom, I was kidding. He just said to tell you he called and that he'll try back tonight for your answer. I added the marrying part." She picked up her cup. "But that sure got your attention. Are you going to tell me who he is?"

"Well, he's not your new dad, so don't get all excited," I said, starting up the stairs again.

"Are you going to call him?"

"Didn't he say he was going to call me?"

"Oh, playing hard to get, huh?"

I grinned and headed off to the shower.

"So, Alice," Justine said as she held a French fry in front of her mouth. "It would appear that Mom's been holding out on us."

My cheeks flushed and I gave my daughter a harsh look. "Justine," I said firmly, trying to redirect the conversation, "why don't you tell us about the paper you're writing. What class is it for?"

"What do you mean, she's holding out on us?" Alice asked. Her brown eyes were bright and the corners of her mouth twitched on the edge of a smile.

I gave Justine another warning glare. She responded with one of her sweetest smiles.

"I mean, Mom has a gentleman friend that she hasn't told us about. His name's Will." Still smiling, she raised her eyebrows at me, and took a bite of her hamburger.

Alice and I sat next to each other in the booth, and Justine was across from us. Alice turned to me directly, raising her own feathery eyebrows. "Is this true? But why haven't you said anything?"

"Mainly because there's nothing to tell," I said, trying to sound casual. "He's just an old friend. Remember when I hurt my hand over Christmas?"

Alice nodded.

I explained that Will was the doctor on duty when Miranda brought me to the ER, and that he and I had known each a long time ago but hadn't spoken in many years. I told her about meeting for coffee after Christmas, and how we both enjoyed the opportunity to catch up.

"There has to be more to it than that, Mama, or he wouldn't have called you. And you wouldn't be trying so hard to keep from talking about it. So, come on," she demanded. "Spill it."

"Oh, please do," Alice urged. "It can't be anything to be ashamed of."

"Hold on," Justine said, her eyes narrowed and her voice suddenly cold. "Did you know him before you met Dad, or while you were still married?" The irony of her suspicion was not lost on me, given her father's extramarital activities. Still, I had to address it. So much for keeping my private life private.

"All right," I conceded. "I knew him before I met your dad. We went to college together in Westin. We were, uh, very good friends. Then he went to Boston to become a doctor, and I moved to Westbridge. I met your dad a while after that, and I never saw or heard from Will again until now—well, until Christmas Eve."

Justine and Alice cast sidelong glances at one another, their eyes twinkling. "Very good friends, huh," Justine scoffed, her suspicions allayed. "You were a couple, weren't you?"

I took a bite of salad to buy myself a little time. I wasn't sure how much I was willing to share with Justine at this point. I was not prepared to make my renewed acquaintance with Will common knowledge. I glanced up at her and half shrugged.

Justine scowled and chewed her lip contemplatively.

"Wait a minute," she said slowly, her gaze moving in my direction. "Will Tremaine. He's the 'W.T.' on that silver charm, isn't he? You know, the heart-shaped one on the bracelet you keep wrapped in a handkerchief at the bottom of your big jewelry box."

"How do you know about that?" I asked.

"I've seen it dozens of times," she replied. "Remember how you used to let me look through your jewelry and try things on when I was a kid?" She glanced at Alice. "I don't know why I never thought to ask whose initials they were."

She was right about the bracelet. It was wrapped in a handkerchief that Will's mother had given me as a gift on the same Christmas that Will presented me with the bracelet. She had embroidered my initials on one corner, and I'd treasured it as a remembrance of her.

54

I looked at Justine and heaved a sigh. "Yes, he is the 'W.T.' William Tremaine. William Anderson Tremaine."

"And did you love him?" she pressed.

I truly did not want to be having this conversation with her, but she was not to be dissuaded.

"All right. I'll tell you. I'll tell both of you. But it really isn't a very exciting story. We were in love—or, we thought we were, at any rate. We were very young." I fidgeted with my spoon as I spoke. "Then he went his way and I went mine. Each of us married and had families of our own. Had he not been working in the ER on Christmas Eve, we probably never would have seen each other again. And that's it."

Justine and Alice looked at one another and smirked.

"But you did see him again, and now he's calling you," Justine commented. "What about his family? Where's his wife?"

"She died in a car accident a few years ago. Will lives in Westin with his two children."

I raised my hand to get our waitress's attention so I could ask for the check. I was ready to bring this conversation to a close.

"Well, I think it's wonderful," Alice declared. "Not the car accident, of course, but the fact that the two of you have been brought together again. I'm very happy for you." Alice was a true romantic.

I smiled at her. "I think you're making a little too much of one telephone call." I chose not to mention the several that had preceded it.

"How old are his kids?" Justine asked. "Boys? Girls?"

"He has a boy and a girl. Wiley is eleven, I think, and Lizzy is thirteen. Now, can we move on to something else?"

Justine folded her napkin and tucked it under the rim of her plate. She took one final sip of her Diet Coke and set the glass back on the table. "I always wanted a younger sister," she teased.

"Well, don't get your hopes up," I said as I grabbed the check and we slid out of the booth.

# 13

The airport in San Sebastian was small and quaint. It accommodated only three airlines, and passengers boarded the planes via portable stairs that runway crews wheeled right up to the door. Rain or shine. No enclosed Jetways here. They disembarked the same way, walking across the tarmac to the gates.

I arrived at the terminal just as Will's plane landed. I stood among a crowd of people eagerly awaiting their husbands, wives, girlfriends, boyfriends, and other loved ones. My heart raced. I was excited, too—more than I'd been in a long time. I had stood countless times on this exact spot, but never felt such a rush of anticipation. Joe traveled frequently on business, and when I'd come to pick him up, I'd watch passengers approach the gate and see their eyes light up when they caught sight of the people who had come to meet them. They'd run toward each other, arms open wide with the kind of joy that is too powerful to contain. Joe and I never greeted each other that way. We'd say hello, walk to the car, and drive home in relative silence. We were never particularly happy to see each other, and, remembering that, I felt a pang of regret.

My stomach tightened, and I focused my attention on the passengers as they made their way to the terminal. I kept an eye out for Will's dark hair. One by one and two by two, the newly arrived found their friends and families, retrieved their luggage, and headed off for the comfort of home or for whatever adventures awaited them. I felt a warm glow in my chest.

I waited, watching anxiously as the last few passengers approached the gate. Will was not among them. My heart, which had felt so light a moment ago, sank like a stone. He wasn't here. I rummaged through my purse, looking for my phone. Maybe he'd called to tell me he was delayed somewhere or had missed his connection. No messages.

I looked back at the plane and saw two flight attendants chatting as they crossed the tarmac. Each had a small suitcase in tow. One young woman was particularly animated, making wild gestures with her free hand to illustrate her point and to communicate over the din of other planes rolling toward their respective parking places.

There was no sign of Will.

I walked inside the terminal to check the monitor and confirm the flight number and arrival time. No mistake—I had the correct information and the right gate. Will, it seemed, simply hadn't been on that plane.

He must have changed his mind about coming, I thought to myself. Maybe he decided it wasn't a good idea after all. Or, maybe one of the children was sick and he couldn't leave. My mind raced through a list of possibilities. But whatever it was, surely he would have called. Outside, in the brisk evening air, excitement gave way to disappointment, and angry tears stung my eyes. I adjusted my coat and started toward my car.

All of a sudden, from somewhere behind me, I heard my name.

"Callie!"

I turned to see Will slipping sideways through the doorway just as the agent was about to close it.

"Callie!" he called again. He rushed toward me, dropped his duffel bag onto the ground, and gathered me into his arms. The tweed of his jacket was rough against my cheek. I closed my eyes and breathed in the scent of him.

Realizing himself, he let go of me and took a step backward. He cleared his throat and brushed a knuckle across his upper lip. "I'm sorry," he said awkwardly. He paused for a moment before continuing.

"Right after we landed, the co-pilot started having chest pains, and while we were taxiing toward the gate, one of the flight attendants asked if there was a doctor on board. I was checking the guy out while everyone got off the plane. I'm pretty sure it wasn't his heart, though. More likely the airport enchiladas he had for dinner."

I tried to smile, but my feelings must have shown on my face. He looked down at me, and his expression softened. "You didn't think I'd decided not to come, did you?" He seemed to have read my mind.

"Well, that possibility had occurred to me," I replied coolly. I hoped my feigned indifference would mask my very real fear that he'd decided not to show up.

He grinned in response. "Not a chance."

"Are you hungry?" I asked as I merged the car onto the freeway. "We can stop somewhere or go back to my place and I can throw something together. I have to warn you, though, I'm not much of a cook anymore."

"I haven't eaten since this morning and I am starving," he replied. As if on cue, his stomach let out a long rumble. "But I don't want you to go to any trouble."

It was after eight o'clock and May's Diner was practically empty. The dinner crowd had long since dispersed. As directed by the sign just inside the entrance, Will and I sat down and waited for someone to bring over a couple of menus.

I was about to say something when a familiar voice rang out.

"Well, look who's here!" I turned toward the sound and saw May's big smile as she approached the table. "I was wonderin' when you'd stop by for a visit." She set down two glasses of water and handed us the menus she had tucked under her arm. She glanced at Will and then gave me a wink as though we shared some big secret. "And you, missy," she admonished, "Where's my hug?"

I stood up and wrapped my arms around her as best I could. She did the same to me and rocked from side to side, holding me tightly against her ample chest. Taking a step backward and placing her hands on her hips, she looked me up and down. "Baby girl, you need to eat."

"I was here just last week," I argued, "with Justine and Alice. You must have missed us. And we all ate very well, by the way."

May looked at me with one eyebrow cocked and her lips pursed. "Mm-hmmm." She turned to Will then, and in her most matronly tone inquired, "And just whose acquaintance do I have the pleasure of makin' now?"

"May," I replied, gesturing to Will. "This is Will Tremaine. Dr. Will Tremaine." With my hand on May's arm, I turned to Will. "And, Will, this is Maybelle Haines, the owner of this fine establishment. Not only is she one of my best friends, but her grandson is in my honors English class."

"Smart boy, that one," May said, beaming. To Will, she added, "Well now, I am pleased to make your acquaintance."

Will rose from his seat and extended his right hand. "Uh, thanks. I'm happy to meet you, too."

"I've known May for a long time," I explained after we'd both sat down again. "We met when I was ..." I hesitated for an instant. "... When I was going through kind of a hard time."

58

May patted my arm and turned her attention to Will. "So, you're the doctor she told me about—the one who fixed up her hand." Leaning closer, she lowered her voice and added, "The one that put that smile on her face."

The face in question turned as red as a tomato, and I raised my hand to my forehead, hiding my eyes. I peered through my fingers to see if Will was looking at me. He was. And his face was split in an ear-to-ear grin.

"So, what do you have planned for us this weekend?" Will asked as he brought a forkful of eggs to his mouth. It was well into the evening, but we'd both decided to order breakfast.

I hadn't given much attention to how he and I would occupy our time while he was here. Now that I thought about it, I realized I had no idea what he might want to do. And that in turn reminded me of how little I knew about him now.

"Well, you're the guest," I replied. "It's your choice. We have the mountains, we have the ocean, we have museums ..." I sounded like a chamber of commerce brochure.

"To tell you the truth, I don't really have any preferences," he responded, "but I kind of like the idea of the mountains. Or the ocean. You know, commune with Mother Nature. I don't get to do much of that at home."

"Well, here it's pretty easy to have both," I replied. "Bailey and I go out every morning and walk—or run, depending on how ambitious we are—along the bluffs beyond the edge of the McMillan property. They overlook the ocean, and it's very quiet, very peaceful, and very beautiful."

"That sounds like a great place to start," Will said. "I heard something about rain tomorrow, though."

"Doesn't matter. Bailey and I are tough. We brave the weather, whatever it is."

"Well, if you can, so can I."

"Then I guess that is the place to start. Depending on how the day turns out, maybe we can go for a hike on Saturday. There's a particularly beautiful trail up in the backcountry." One of the servers came around with a pot of coffee and refilled our cups. I smiled at him. "We've had a lot of rain in the last month and a half, so Rock Creek is practically full and all the streams are running." I added cream to my cup, paused, and leaned slightly to one side, making a point of examining Will's legs. Half smiling, I continued, "But if you're agile enough, you shouldn't have any problem."

"Oh, I'm agile enough," he replied.

We sat quietly for a moment, and then I changed the subject.

"How did your kids feel about your leaving for the weekend?"

"They didn't mind," he replied. "I told them I was visiting a friend from college." His eyes caught mine and held them for a moment. Not a lie, but not exactly the truth, either.

"And anyway," he continued more casually, "they'll take any opportunity to spend time with their grandparents. Lizzy and Wiley are the only kids, and they're spoiled rotten." He spread strawberry jam on a piece of toast, folded it in half, and took a bite. I smiled to myself. He still ate toast the way he had so many years ago. Okay, so not *everything* about him was new.

"All they have to do is think about something they might possibly want, and someone is at the ready with cash or a credit card," he continued. He licked a bit of jam off his thumb and looked at me. "That makes them sound like little mercenaries, doesn't it? The truth is, the kids like being with them. It gives them a connection to their mom that they really seem to need right now."

I put down my fork and refolded the napkin on my lap. I chewed the inside of my lip nervously. The mere mention of Will's wife made me uncomfortable. It generated an unease deep in my core. I couldn't help thinking that, given the choice, she was the woman he'd want sitting across from him right now, not me. It didn't matter that coming to visit had been his idea or that he was the one who'd made the effort.

"Well, I know how important that is," I agreed quietly. "And it's good that all of you make it available to them."

Will sat back in his chair. "It never really goes away, does it?" he asked more rhetorically than in expectation of an answer. "I mean, I'm an adult— and a not so young one at that—and I miss my parents. It's so hard for kids."

I shrugged. "No, it doesn't go away, but you learn how to live with it. And if you're a kid, you just learn a lot earlier than most." I picked up my coffee cup and took a sip. "I'm sorry to hear about your parents. I always liked them. They were very kind to me." In truth, I hadn't spent a lot of time with Will's family. He and I visited them for Thanksgiving a couple of times, and then for a few days during the summer before he left for Boston. But his mother was very warm and maternal, and being with Will and his parents gave me a taste of the family life I'd always craved. In fact, when Will and I went our separate ways, I grieved almost as much for the loss of his parents as I did for him.

"Well, they each did it the right way," he said, wiping his napkin across his mouth. "I mean, my dad was, for the most part, okay until his heart gave out, and when my mom got sick, well, she went really fast." I saw the shadow pass across his face.

"But, that's the way to do it, I think," he continued. "Feel great until you don't, and then just go. No drawn-out treatment protocols, no lingering, and no discomfort to manage. Live well until you're done."

"I really am sorry, Will." I wasn't sure what else to say.

He pushed his plate away, crossed his forearms and rested them on the table. "And what about your family? How is your dad? And your brother? And you had a stepmother, didn't you?"

There wasn't a lot to say about any of them. I explained that my father was in fairly good health, although I didn't see him or my stepmother very often. They had moved to a retirement community in Greenfield, and Lucas, who a year or so ago took a job in a town about forty-five minutes away, checked in with them once or twice a week, and that was enough for everyone. We weren't a close family growing up, and not much had changed.

I considered it a stroke of luck when Lucas and his wife settled a short distance away. Lucas's tolerance level for my father was much higher than mine—most likely because his degree of animosity was much lower.

"My dad also has a few minor health problems, but everything seems to be going okay. He doesn't drive anymore, and that's probably a good thing. The community where they live is pretty self-contained, so they don't have to go out and about much, anyway. I guess my dad's happy," I said as an afterthought. "It's always been hard to tell."

It occurred to me as I looked at Will that we were now roughly the age our parents were when we first met. It was hard to believe so much time had passed.

Apparently Will was thinking the same thing. "I remember when my father was my age and I thought he was so old," he said. "But here I am, and I don't really feel much different than I did twenty-five years ago. Maybe I'm just fooling myself. Lizzy seems to think I'm ancient and completely out of touch with the modern world."

I gazed at him. He looked so much the same as I remembered, but also different. I saw a glimmer here and there of the college boy I'd known so well—the slightly crooked bottom tooth and the deep blue eyes that crinkled at the corners when he smiled. But overall, he was a more seasoned, more comfortable version of his younger self. I wanted to reach out and touch him to know he was real. "No," I replied, "you're not fooling yourself."

After dinner, Will and I decided to stop at the waterfront and take a walk along the pier. It was nearly ten o'clock, but because of the holiday weekend the area was crowded with couples strolling hand in hand, and even a few children running back and forth across the oiled boards. Off to the side, a few old men were trying their hand at night fishing. They had tucked their poles between the slats of a bench and wedged the non-business ends between two planks. They sat on either side of the poles, toasting one another with bottles of beer, laughing, and slapping each other on the back.

Will smiled as we walked past them. "My grandfather used to do that," he said with a nod in their direction. "Sometimes he'd take me with him."

"Really? What did you catch?"

"Cold, mostly," he joked. "Even during the summer. My grandfather wasn't much with a rod and reel. To tell you the truth, it wasn't the fishing he enjoyed so much as the opportunity to get away from my grandmother and spend his own version of happy hour with his buddies and a six-pack of Miller. My grandmother didn't cotton much to any kind of drinking. A one-woman temperance movement, she was."

We continued walking. "From what I can tell, this really is a pretty place," Will said as we strolled beneath the three-quarter moon that hung in a nearly black sky. The night air was cold, and a light breeze blew in from the ocean, carrying the tangy scent of salt water and seaweed. Rain was in the forecast for the next day, but from the looks of the sky, any storm heading our way was a long way off.

The pier extended more than four hundred yards beyond the surf, and we stopped occasionally to look over the railing and watch the moonlight rippling on the water. The ocean was calm, but the current caused tiny wavelets to break against the pylons beneath us. Their gentle *whoosh* was a comforting sound in the dark. When we reached the end of the pier, we sat down on a bench. Will took hold of my hand.

"You know, Cal, I can't tell you what I thought when I saw you in the ER on Christmas Eve," he said. "It was the last thing I expected, but it was also the thing I most wanted. It caught me so off guard I didn't realize it then, but I do now."

I looked up at the stars that shone like pinpricks of light in the velvety night sky. To the south, I could make out Orion's Belt, and to the north, the Big Dipper. "I felt the same way. I just wasn't sure what to do about it. I'm still not."

"What do you mean?"

I regretted the statement as soon as the words left my mouth. I was in no way prepared for a conversation about where we were or what we were doing or what our reconnecting might mean. I adjusted my position on the bench and waved my hand in a gesture of dismissal. "Oh, I don't know what I mean. Never mind."

In a blatant attempt to redirect the conversation, I got more personal. "So, how is it that an eligible bachelor such as yourself has managed to stay unattached?" I asked. "Assuming you are, that is."

Will looked at me with bland amusement, aware of my diversion but willing to follow. "I am," he said in reply. "And I could ask the same of you."

"You must have had plenty of opportunities in the last couple of years." I gave him a wry smile. "Not the least of which might be that young nurse who did triage on my hand in the emergency room. You know—the Georgia peach. She seemed pretty sweet on you," I joked. "Not that it's any of my business, of course."

"Ah," he said, nodding his head. "You mean Natalie. Well yeah, I guess she is a little sweet on me. But the fact of the matter is there's no way I'd get involved with anyone who works in the ER. That would just be asking for trouble. And even if I did, it wouldn't be with her."

"Okay, so that takes care of Natalie," I said dryly. "But I just can't believe you've been all alone for the last two years."

"And what about you?"

"We're not talking about me."

"We could be."

"But we aren't."

"Okay," Will sighed. He bit his lower lip while he pondered. "I have dated a bit, but suffice it to say I've not been particularly successful."

"And the woman in surgical scrubs who asked for you?" I continued my inquiry. "The Southern belle—er, Natalie—got rid of her in very short order—along with the Christmas present."

"Ah, so that explains it," he said. "Now I understand what she was talking about after Christmas." He added, "You don't miss much, do you?" And then, more seriously, he explained his connection to the woman with the dark ponytail.

"She's a surgical nurse, and she and I did spend a few evenings—uh ..." I couldn't tell in the dark, but I'd have bet my shoes that he was blushing.

"Studying anatomy together?" I finished his sentence for him. "Will, you don't have to be uncomfortable about it. It really isn't my business and certainly not my place to pass any judgments."

"Actually," he said, "it didn't take long for me to realize there wasn't a whole lot there." He must have felt some need to explain. "I don't mean her nursing abilities—she is really smart, and she has a great way of making patients feel at ease."

He looked down at me. "But she's young, and we don't have a lot in common. And there are Lizzy and Wiley to think about." He raised one shoulder and let it drop. "To tell you the truth, I just don't like the whole dating thing—particularly with women who were barely out of kindergarten when I was graduating from medical school."

"Not looking for the trophy wife, huh?"

"Not that kind," he said. "And as for it not being your business, I don't mean to be presumptive, but after the conversations we've had—and granted, they were over the phone—I'd sort of hoped that by now you would consider it your business. Or would from here on, anyway."

I got up and walked to the railing. If not for the moonlight flitting here and there across the surface, the water would have been black. "You know, Will," I said, turning to look at him, "a lot of years have passed since we were… whatever we were. We were a lot younger then. We were a lot different then. But now—" I paused, searching for words. "We barely know each other anymore. We can't just pick up where we left off."

He approached the railing and stood next to me, his body so close that I could almost feel the heat radiating from him. "That's true, and I understand it. But something happened when I saw you at the hospital. Something from a long time ago. It scared me at first, maybe because it was so powerful. But, Cal, I really do want us to know each other again."

I turned to face him. The breeze picked up and a layer of clouds I hadn't noticed before began to drift in toward the beach. I shivered and pulled my jacket around me. He raised his hand and caressed my cheek with his thumb and fingertips. His touch was feather light, and my heart pounded like a kettledrum. He leaned forward and brushed his lips against mine. They were soft, and warm. His male scent, which I recognized even now, was familiar and inviting.

"I mean it. I really do want us to know each other again," he murmured.

I closed my eyes and leaned my head into his hand. It was like heaven to stand so close to him.

Heaven. I opened my eyes, and took an abrupt step backward. The immense joy I felt at being with Will again suddenly turned into immense fear.

"We should head back," I said, turning toward the waterfront. "It's going to get cold."

"Is it always like this?" Will asked, peering out the car window. "It's a little spooky."

I guided the car along the familiar curves of the long driveway, past

Alice's house and on toward the cottage. With no light save that from the moon and stars—and given that they were shrouded in wisps of clouds—the area between the main house and the cottage was dark. The headlights shone like beacons, but otherwise blackness surrounded us.

"Yup, it is," I replied. "But you get used to it. The worst is when I have to let Bailey out in the middle of the night. I turn on the porch lights, but he can always meet up with raccoons or skunks or possums. I've even seen the occasional coyote around dusk. Ben put up a picket fence in the front yard and an enclosed area out back so I don't have to worry about him—Bailey, I mean—taking off, but he can still try to make friends with the wild beasts that wander into the yard."

Will shivered involuntarily. "And you like this?"

"It's really not that isolated," I replied, "and not at all rustic. I do have a telephone, after all, and electricity, and running water. And it's only a quarter mile to the main road. It only seems like it's far away. But that's what I like about it. It feels remote, but it isn't. I can be at the center of town in ten minutes."

We came around a bend and the lights from the cottage welcomed us. I always kept a few lamps on timers so they'd turn on automatically at dusk. Bailey got anxious if he was alone after sunset, when the house grew dark. I learned that the hard way the first time I'd left him at home in the afternoon and didn't come back until well into the evening. Greeting me when I opened the door was kitchen trash strewn all over the floor, the arm of my favorite chair shredded down to the wooden frame, and poor Bailey huddled in a corner of the laundry room.

I parked in the small garage, and led the way into the house. I was a little nervous, not sure how Will might have interpreted my suggestion that he stay with me. I hadn't meant anything in particular—the nearest hotel was several miles away, and if Will was going to be here only for a few days, I hated for him to spend a lot of that time by himself. That's what I told myself, anyway.

Bailey, who had been sleeping on the sofa while I was gone, immediately launched into his welcome dance when Will and I walked into the living room. After a minute or two, he finally settled down enough for me to make formal introductions. "Bailey, this is Will. He's going to be visiting for a while so you need to behave." Bailey regarded him suspiciously, and even let out a low growl.

"I'm sorry," I said. "He's a little protective of me." I turned to Bailey. "Relax, buddy. Everything's fine."

Undaunted, Will extended his hand and Bailey took a good long sniff. "It's okay. I come in peace." Apparently satisfied, Bailey wagged his tail and gave Will's knuckle a lick.

"All right, mister," I said. "Go lie down." Both Will and Bailey looked at me quizzically. I patted Will's arm. "I meant the dog," I said.

"What a great place," Will noted, glancing around the living room and kitchen. "Really cozy."

"Well, that's a nice way of putting it. Very diplomatic," I replied. "It's small, but just right for me and Bailey. How about I give you the quick tour. It ought to take a good minute and a half."

"Okay. Lead the way."

"Well, as you can see, this is the living room, dining area, and kitchen," I said, casually extending my arms.

As I looked around, I realized Will was right. It was cozy—from the hardwood floor, to the bead-board wainscoting, to the plaster ceiling. In the living room, a couch and two overstuffed chairs, positioned around a heavy wooden coffee table, faced the fireplace, and a rolltop desk with a matching chair was pressed against a wall near the stairs. A huge picture window next to the front door faced eastward, with two long shelves underneath it. Other floor-to-ceiling built-in shelves and cupboards provided ample space for my books—of which there were many—and other artifacts of my life.

The small dining area was outfitted with a round table and four chairs, an antique sideboard that came from the Winwood house, and my grand-mother's curio cabinet. More built-in cupboards with glass doors provided additional space for the china, glass, crystal, and sterling silver that I rarely used, but felt the need to keep. Some pieces had been passed through my family—from my grandmother to my mother and then to me—and I held them in safekeeping for my own children. Others were remnants of my marriage to Joe, and while I wasn't particularly attached to any of them, I couldn't bring myself to dispose of them.

"There's the small laundry room between the kitchen and the garage, as you saw when we came in," I told Will, "but otherwise, this is it for the first floor."

I walked to the stairs with him behind me. As we climbed them, my heart began to beat faster. I wanted to turn around and fling myself at him, and I was sure he wouldn't have minded if I'd followed that inclination.

"This is the guest room," I said, opening the first door off the hallway. He peeked inside. It contained a full-size bed with nightstands on each side, a dresser with attached mirror, and the old rocking chair in which I'd nursed both of my children and sung lullabies to them in the wee hours of the morning. That also came from the Winwood house. "Looks comfortable," Will said.

"Ben and Justine like it," I replied. I pointed to the next door, near the end of the short hall. "The bathroom is right there, and the master bedroom is across from it. I don't know why I call it the master bedroom," I said, speaking more quickly than was necessary. "It's really not much bigger than the guest room. But the window has a better view, and it's where I sleep, so I sort of think of it as the primary bedroom and—"

"Are you nervous, Cal?" Will interrupted. He looked slightly amused.

"Uh, um, a little, I suppose. I've not had anyone stay with me except Ben and Justine—and Miranda a few times. And you're, well—" I interrupted myself. "Are you nervous?"

"Not at all," he replied.

Back downstairs, Bailey scratched at the front door. He needed to go out once more before he could settle in for the night. I grabbed a flashlight from the top drawer of the desk.

"Want to join us?" I asked Will. "You'd better bring your jacket if you do. It's pretty chilly out right now." I pulled a wool shawl off one of the pegs next to the door and wrapped it around myself. With the flashlight illuminating the path beyond, we stepped out into the yard.

"Wow! Look at that sky," Will exclaimed, gazing upward. It was clear and dark, the stars standing out like glitter against a backdrop of black satin. In the distance, I could see the clouds moving toward us. They were on their way, but it would be a few hours yet before they arrived.

I closed my eyes and took a deep breath. I loved the pungent smell and the feel of the cold night air, particularly when rain was coming. All around me, nature gave off strong fragrances—the cold, dank earth, the wet grass, and the eucalyptus trees. The scents converged and filled my nostrils. The wind picked up slightly and blew strands of hair across my face. I reached up and pulled them away.

Standing beside me, Will touched his hand to my back, between my shoulder blades. I felt its warmth even through the heavy wool. I leaned against him just slightly, enjoying his closeness.

It was late, and after calling Bailey inside, I began to close up the house for the night—locking the windows and the deadbolts on the front and back doors, turning off the lamps. Will picked up his duffel bag and moved toward the stairs. "Well, I guess I'll take this up to the guest room." He looked at me for confirmation.

As much as I wanted to direct him to my own room, I simply couldn't. Some odd sense of propriety got in the way. Or maybe my feelings were simply too overwhelming. I'd spent years dreaming about being with Will again, and having him near—close enough to touch. How often I had awakened in the middle of the night, my nightgown damp with sweat, basking in a warm satisfaction that had nothing to do with the man lying beside me.

Now Will was here. The dream pressed against reality. And I was afraid of trading one for the other, and losing both.

"Yeah, I think so," I replied.

By the next morning, dark clouds had rolled in, and although the rain had not yet begun to fall, the air was heavy and damp. I was still wearing my thin cotton nightgown when I heard a soft knock on the bedroom door.

"Cal? Are you awake?"

"Uh, yeah, come on in," I responded, pulling on my robe. Will opened the door and glanced around the room. He was already dressed, in worn jeans, a T-shirt, and the same teal sweater he'd been wearing the day we met for coffee. I saw him take note of the unmade bed, the clothes strewn across the chair, and my own state of dress. He looked as though he wanted to say something.

Realizing he had decided to keep whatever it was to himself, I spoke instead.

"I was about to throw on some clothes so Bailey and I could take our morning constitutional. Want to join us?"

"Sure. I'll just grab my jacket."

He closed the door behind him, and I pulled on a pair of jeans and a long-sleeved shirt. Reaching into the dresser drawer for a pair of socks, I took a quick look at my reflection in the mirror. "What's wrong with you?" I scolded. "Get a freaking grip! This is what you've wanted. Don't screw it up by being scared."

The clouds threatened rain any minute, and the air was thick. We walked along the path that led to the bluffs above the ocean. It was cold and wet, but also incredibly beautiful. Will and I were the only people in sight. The grasses were tall and cloaked in vibrant shades of green, and even though spring was more than a month away, the pink and purple larkspur and the yellow clover were beginning to show their faces.

The dirt path crunched beneath our feet as we walked. "This is truly spectacular," Will declared, taking in the view that swept from the mountains to the ocean. "I can see why you love it here."

We strolled along the cliffs, stopping every so often to gaze at the ocean. It was gray and forbidding and dotted with whitecaps.

"I'd love for my kids to experience this," Will said, looking across the expansive meadow.

"Tell me more about them," I urged.

"Let's see," he began. "They're both very lively and very funny. They each have a great sense of humor. Lizzy is quite dramatic, although that might be her age, and Wiley can be really funny, but also very serious—a lot like his mother."

I took a quick breath, and Will saw it. "I'm sorry. I shouldn't have said that."

"No, don't be silly." I tried to sound casual. "She is half of who they are. You can't ignore it. You shouldn't ignore it." I paused briefly. "Go on. What else?"

Over the next hour or so I learned, among other things, that Lizzy and Wiley were named for their grandmothers—Lizzy for Will's mother, and Wiley for Joanna's. "'Wiley' is actually a nickname," Will explained. "His formal name is William. William Anderson Tremaine II." He glanced over at me. "I think it sounds a little pretentious, but Joanna liked it. And calling him Wiley was a good way to recognize his other grandmother. That was her maiden name."

Will added that Lizzy was named not just in honor of his mother, but for Elizabeth Bennet, the heroine of Jane Austen's *Pride and Prejudice*. "It was one of Joanna's favorite books."

"She's a lot with you, isn't she? Joanna, I mean," I said quietly. We had stopped at a small grassy area that jutted out over the beach.

Will took a deep breath and exhaled heavily.

"Right now, I guess so." He hesitated. "But it's not what you think, Callie." He turned his gaze to the ocean, and suddenly seemed very remote. "It's hard to explain."

I brushed his forearm with my fingertips. "It's okay. You don't have to explain anything." I turned, called to Bailey, and continued walking.

By the time we got back to the cottage, the rain had begun to fall in large drops. We hadn't bothered to bring umbrellas, so our coats were not quite sopping wet, but close. After stopping on the front porch to give himself a good shake, Bailey trotted inside and curled up on his bed near the fireplace. Will and I went upstairs to our respective rooms to change into dry clothes.

We met at the top of the stairs.

"What do you say we go into town for a while?" I suggested. "We can have some lunch, and then I'll show you around a little bit."

Will took a deep breath and let it out. Again, he looked as though he wanted to say something, but decided against it. "Sure," he replied. "That sounds good."

# 14

San Sebastian was not a bustling metropolis, but it was generally pretty easy to find something to do. With no particular plan in mind, we left the car in a parking structure and walked through the center of town. By the time the afternoon had passed, we'd roamed through the art museum, a small independent gallery, and a couple of used-book stores. My favorite, which was owned by my friend Alistair Lowell, was closed, however. I'd hoped to say hello to him, and even introduce Will, but Mr. Lowell was visiting his niece in Chicago.

"Hey, Cal, isn't this the same edition of *Sonnets from the Portuguese* I got for you before I left for Boston?" He stood beside me in one of the other bookstores and skimmed the pages. "I always wondered why they're 'from the Portuguese,' though. Elizabeth Barrett was English, wasn't she?"

I peered over his arm at one of the poems.

"She was English," I replied. "But Robert Browning referred to her as his 'little Portuguese.'" I closed the book partway so I could see the cover. "Yes, that's the edition. I have no idea what happened to it, though."

"Hmm," he said.

I turned my attention to the shelf in front of me and perused the titles. "So, what sorts of things do you like to read?"

"Right now, aside from the newspaper and medical journals, most of my reading is confined to what Wiley likes," he answered. "We do a lot of reading together—*The Last of the Mohicans*, *Treasure Island*, *Huckleberry Finn*, that sort of thing. We've been going through some of the classics my dad used to read with me."

"That's a great thing to do. I used to read like that with Ben and Justine. It was easier with Justine, though. Ben was always far more interested in comic books, which I never really considered great literature. Although," I added absently, "there are those who would disagree with me."

I moved into a different aisle and lost sight of Will. I found myself in the old books section, where volumes dating as far back as 1809 lined the shelves. I picked up a collection of works by John Milton and was reacquainting myself with the first few lines of *Paradise Lost* when Will came up behind me and touched his hand to my waist. Startled, I jumped and let out a muffled cry.

"Don't *do* that," I said, exhaling loudly.

"Relax," he chuckled. "I was only going to suggest we get something to eat."

The rain had let up and the late afternoon sky was beginning to peek through the scattering clouds. It looked as though the storm—such as it was—had moved on. We ducked into a small bistro a few doors down from the bookstore and took a table near the window.

I pulled off my raincoat and draped it over the chair next to me. Will handed his coat to me so I could place it with mine. It seemed a little heavy, and I thought I heard the clunk of something solid hitting the wooden chair when I tossed it over the back.

"I've really had a good time today," Will said when we'd settled into our chairs. "Even with the rain."

I smiled. "Me, too."

We talked and laughed over bowls of minestrone soup and thick slices of warm French bread. The conversation was light and we became more and more familiar with each other. Sharing a generous slice of chocolate cake, we talked about favorite books and movies, places we'd like to visit, and things we still hoped to accomplish.

"So, what's something you'd really like to do?" Will asked.

I was pensive for a moment. "Well, I've always wanted to dance the role of the Sugar Plum Fairy in *The Nutcracker*," I said, "but seeing as I don't own a pair of toe shoes and haven't taken a ballet lesson since I was nine, I'm starting to doubt the likelihood of seeing that dream come true." I considered the question for another moment. For so long, my focus had been on the dreams and desires of the other people in my life—my children, Joe—that I never really paid much attention to my own. In many ways, the life I led now was the thing I'd always wanted.

"How about you? What would you like to do?"

"Me? Let's see ..." Now he was pensive. "I've always wanted to climb Mount Everest. And take a cross-country road trip on a motorcycle."

"Really? I never knew that."

"I never knew you liked ballet."

We both stared out the window and watched people walking hurriedly past the restaurant. Raindrops clung to the glass and shimmered in the glow of the streetlamps.

I felt Will's eyes on me, and stole a quick glance at him. He was watching me casually.

"What?" I asked.

"Last night—you wondered how it is that I'm still unattached," he said.

I answered with a nod. "And?"

"Well, I've been wondering the same thing about you."

"Ah," I replied.

"Well?"

As much as Will and I had already revealed to each other, I still wasn't willing to share details about my marriage or my life with Joe. The truth of it was that I had remained unattached simply because I preferred it that way. I had dated occasionally, but no one had come along for whom I would surrender my newfound independence.

"My friend Miranda—the one who was with me in the ER—describes it as avoiding entangling alliances," I said with a chuckle. "It's not that I'm averse to relationships, it's just that I spent almost my entire adult life in a marriage that—" I stopped myself.

Will eyed me curiously.

"Let's just say that Bailey represents the only entangling alliance I've been interested in."

Will nodded and then looked away.

"Well," I continued, "until now, that is."

He glanced back at me and our eyes met. The corner of his mouth turned up.

I glanced at my watch and was surprised to see that it was almost eight o'clock.

"Remember when you said this morning that I didn't have to explain anything?" Will asked, suddenly serious.

"I remember."

"Well, I do. I want you to understand." He looked down at the empty plate on the table and then at me. I sat with my hands in my lap, completely unsure of what he was going to say.

"Since Joanna died, my life has been focused on work and on Lizzy and Wiley. They've needed so much from me. And it has been really, really hard," he began. "When I saw you in the ER, it was as though a light turned on and I realized just how dark everything had become." He paused. "I don't know how to say what I want to say without sounding like a complete jerk."

"Just say it," I said quietly.

"I really want to be here—with you—and the fact that ..." He stopped and sighed heavily. He wadded up his napkin and tossed it onto the plate. "I'm sorry. I shouldn't have said anything. It's just way too complicated."

"Okay." I wasn't sure how else to respond.

He reached out and took my hand. "But, Cal, I'm telling you the absolute truth when I say that if I could be anywhere right now—*anywhere*—I'd want to be here—with you."

We got back to the cottage a half hour later. We came in through the garage, and I switched on the light in the kitchen. Bailey twisted and twirled in exuberance for a minute or so and then ran to the front door. I opened it and he scooted out into the yard. I went into the kitchen to fill his food dish, and then back outside to call him in for dinner. I found Will standing on the driveway looking up at the sky. The clouds had broken temporarily, to reveal a partial moon and a sprinkling of stars.

I stood beside him. "It's really beautiful, isn't it?"

He didn't say anything, but nodded almost imperceptibly. I thought I caught the glimmer of tears in his eyes.

I called to Bailey who, by this time, had completed his patrol. He trotted inside and made a beeline for the kitchen. I followed, and Will walked in behind me. He pushed the door shut, tossed his jacket onto the chair, and grasped my arm. I turned, and he pulled me toward him. Pressing me to his chest, he wrapped his arms around me and buried his face in my hair, whispering my name.

I held him close, my hands on his back, feeling his muscles taut through the warmth of his sweater.

He pulled away from me slightly, cupped my face in his hands, and kissed me urgently. Like a silly schoolgirl, I felt my knees go weak.

"Do you do this on all your dates?" I asked when he stopped for breath.

"Not as a general rule," he replied and kissed me again, his tongue exploring my mouth.

I switched off the lights and led him, in the dark, up the stairs. So much for my rational mind, I thought to myself.

"Are you sure?" he asked as we stood outside the bedroom. "Once we start, I don't think I'll be able to stop."

I kissed him lightly. "I'm sure." As far as Will was concerned, right now I had no concept of anything beyond this moment; but the truth was, I didn't care. All parts of me—mind, body, and spirit—were being called to him, and I had no choice but to answer.

He sat down on the end of the bed and held out his hands to me. I hadn't turned on a lamp, but the moonlight shining in through the window bathed the room in a silvery glow.

I took Will's hands, and he pulled me toward him so I stood between his knees. With his arms encircling my hips, he rested his cheek against my stomach. I held him there, my fingers wrapped in the soft dark curls at the back of his neck.

He looked up, finally, and without taking his eyes from mine, he pulled off his sweater and then unbuttoned his shirt. Slipping it off his shoulders, he let it fall onto the bed. I wanted him, in a way I hadn't wanted anyone for a very long time, and the sight of his bare chest made my body ache. I rested my hands on the broad curves of his shoulders and then drew one hand slowly down his chest, letting my fingertip just brush his nipple. He closed his eyes and let out a deep sigh. Then he stood, and very carefully and very deliberately began to remove my clothing.

I became more than a little self-conscious—I had managed to take pretty good care of myself over the years, but I was not the same young woman he'd made love to all those years ago. Two children, two decades, and gravity had taken their toll.

If he noticed the changes, though, he didn't let it show.

When the last article of clothing landed on the floor, he took a step back and gazed at me for a long moment. I pulled the clip out of my hair and let the rest of my long chestnut curls fall across my shoulders.

"You are so beautiful," he whispered. He pulled me to him again, kissing me deeply. I unbuckled his belt and fumbled with the buttons on his jeans. They were uncooperative, but with one experienced tug, he had all four undone at once. He slid his pants down over his hips and stepped out of them. I could see immediately that he was as ready as I. He raised one eyebrow and shrugged lightly. I moved toward him and wrapped my arms around his neck. I felt the hard swell of him between us.

With his hands on my waist, he guided me toward the bed. I reached behind me with one hand and pulled back the quilt. I slipped between the cool sheets, and then slid back against the pillow. I lifted the covers, inviting him to join me.

He pulled the quilt up over his hips as he rolled onto his side, raising himself on one elbow. His eyes locked on mine and a smile played at the corners of his lips. He shook his head from side to side, almost imperceptibly. Raising his hand, he caressed my cheek with the side of his forefinger.

"I can't believe I found you," he said softly. "I didn't think I'd ever see you again, let alone touch you. Not like this."

"I didn't either," I replied, my eyes on his. "Not in my wildest dreams." I smoothed away a lock of dark hair that had fallen across his forehead.

His hand slid downward, his finger gliding along my neck, into the space between my breasts, and finally resting lightly on my stomach. "Your skin is like silk," he murmured.

He leaned toward me, his face just inches from mine. His hand ran along the curve of my waist and hip. I felt the warmth of his breath as he exhaled slowly through his nose. His lips brushed mine, barely a touch. Very lightly, he stroked my bottom lip with the tip of his tongue. A spark ran through my body, and I shivered. I could feel my heart racing. With my hand on the back of his neck and my fingers entwined in his hair, I pulled him toward me. His mouth found mine, and our lips parted. Sliding his hand upward, he cupped my breast before enveloping it in the warmth of his mouth. The nipple was hard and he tickled it with his tongue. I moaned softly and arched my back slightly in response to his touch. With one hand on his shoulder I held him close to me, and with the other I took hold of him and felt his own body reply. He pressed himself into my hand as I stroked him.

"I want you, Callie," he whispered, his breath coming fast and warm against my neck. "I can't wait." I could feel the urgency in his body even as he kept it under control. The muscles in his arms and legs trembled.

"You don't have to," I replied, pulling him on top of me. My legs opened to him, and I inhaled quickly. He held his weight on his forearms, lifting his upper body slightly.

He studied my face for a moment and then gave me a smile so sweet I thought my heart would melt.

"Is this really happening?" he asked, and before I could answer, his mouth closed onto mine. I raised my hips just slightly, inviting, and he found his way home.

"Oh, God," he murmured, dropping his forehead onto my shoulder. "You feel so good." He moved just slightly within me, and my muscles contracted in spasms that drew him deeper. He answered suddenly by plunging hard and fast, and my body welcomed him. He reached his hands beneath me and held my hips tight against his. The feel of him between my legs brought me to the brink over and over.

"Don't stop," I gasped.

He kissed me, hard, his tongue intent on mine. I wrapped my legs around his so I could bring him farther into me.

After a moment, he lifted himself on his hands, closed his eyes, and cried out in a hoarse whisper. My release met his, and together we rode a wave that crashed against a rocky shore and then receded back into the sea.

"Don't go," I said a few minutes later, as he moved to separate his body from mine. My hands grasped the muscles around his hips, trying to hold him in place. I wanted to keep him there forever with nothing between us, and each a part of the other.

We were damp with sweat, our bodies glued together. He chuckled, lifted himself gently away from me, and fell back onto the pillow. Heaving a sigh, he laid his hand on my thigh.

"Don't worry," he said, eyes closed and the corners of his mouth upturned. "I'm not going anywhere."

I turned onto my side and rested my hand on his chest. "Promise?"

He looked over at me. "Do you?"

I don't know how long we lay there, fitted together like two spoons, his body molding itself to mine, one hand resting on my breast, cupping it gently. He was completely still, and I thought he might have fallen asleep. I gazed out the window, watching as the moonlight faded in the dark night sky. The window was open partway, and a cool breeze ruffled the gauze curtains.

I felt an utter contentment I hadn't known in years—if ever—and accompanying that, an odd sense of wonder. For the first time, I somehow felt right inside. An unfamiliar calmness radiated throughout my body. Whenever Joe and I had made love, I was always left with a knot in my stomach and a sense of longing that emanated from somewhere deep within my soul. I knew it wasn't his fault, but still I could never make sense of it. It was an odd feeling of homesickness, but I could never tell what, exactly, I was homesick for.

As I lay there listening to Will breathe quietly and evenly, it suddenly became clear. The object of my longing had been him. I had been homesick for Will, and that longing had been my soul crying out for him. Like the physical body hungers for vitamins, minerals, and other nutrients, my soul also hungered for the nourishment that came from my deeply rooted connection to him. Despite the intervening years and distance, my very being had remained as fixed on him as when we first fell in love some twenty-odd years ago. I just hadn't realized it.

I covered his hand with mine and squeezed lightly. His voice rose quietly from the darkness. He wasn't asleep after all.

"A penny for your thoughts," he murmured. He moved onto his back, and I rolled toward him, laying my head in the hollow of his shoulder and my arm across his chest. As the sheets rustled, I caught the musky scent of sex and satisfaction. He caressed my waist and hips with the tips of his fingers, and I closed my eyes for a moment, savoring the feelings that lingered in my body.

"I'm just really happy you're here," I replied finally.

"So am I," he said, holding me tighter. "You have no idea how much."

My eyes filled with tears then, and one escaped and trickled down my cheek onto Will's chest. I brushed away another and sniffled. Will cocked his head and looked down at me, an expression of alarm crossing his face.

"Are you crying?" he asked.

I dabbed my eyes with a corner of the sheet. "No, not really," I answered. "Just a spontaneous overflow of powerful feelings, I guess."

I glanced up at Will. "Wordsworth's description, not mine—but it fits."

"I'm not overly familiar with his work," he commented, "but I think he hit the nail on the head with that phrase."

"He was actually describing poetry."

Will grinned and rolled over so he was practically on top of me. He kissed me deeply, taking my breath with his own. "Well then, I'd say the guy was right. Because that's what this is—pure poetry."

# 15

The sun shining in through the window blanketed the foot of the bed. The clouds and gray sky of the day before had practically vanished overnight. I sat up, yawned, and stretched. "So, what do you want to do this morning? It looks like it's going to be an absolutely beautiful day."

From his own bed, Bailey lifted his head, looked over at me, and wagged his tail.

"I wasn't talking to you, pal." I reached down to give him a scratch behind the ears. "I know what you want to do."

I turned back to Will. He had raised himself, tucked the pillow behind him, and was leaning back with his arms folded across his chest. His hair was tousled, and he looked sleepy and sweet. All at once, I had the slightly disconcerting sensation of being in one of my own dreams.

"You mean besides this?" he asked in response to my question. He reached an arm out to pull me closer to him.

Obliging, I tilted my head up and kissed him lightly.

"Besides this," I replied, lifting the covers and scrambling out of bed. I slipped on my thin cotton robe and tied the sash around my waist. "C'mon, Bailey. You have some business to take care of." The dog followed me downstairs and into the kitchen. Holding open the back door, I waited while he took a few sniffs of the cold morning air and then ran outside.

I put on a pot of coffee and pulled two mugs down from the cupboard. I set them on the counter and smiled. I could hear water running in the bathroom, and I felt an uncommon—and strangely uneasy—joy in knowing that Will was in the house with me.

He appeared in the kitchen a few minutes later, barefoot, but clad in a pair of flannel pajama bottoms and a gray T-shirt. I stood at the counter, my back to him, pouring coffee into the mugs. He came up behind me, wrapped his arms around mine, and rested his chin on my shoulder.

I slid the carafe back into the coffeemaker and turned to face him. I put my arms around his waist and held him close. I gazed up at him.

"I meant what I said last night," he murmured, "that I can't believe I've really found you again." He kissed me then, his lips warm and full. He tasted of mint toothpaste, and his shirt smelled of laundry soap and fabric softener.

"Last night was unbelievable," he said. "I mean really unbelievable. I've never felt that way before. God, I've never wanted anything the way I wanted you—the way I still want you."

I laid my head against his chest, my arms wrapped even tighter around his waist. "Me, too," I murmured into the folds of his shirt.

We stood that way for a few minutes, completely enclosed in one another. I felt Will's chest rise and fall beneath my cheek and the light touch of his hands running up and down the length of my spine. Bailey scratched on the door and let out a whine, but I didn't move.

"You know," Will said abruptly when we'd finished breakfast, "in all our conversations, you've never said anything about why your marriage ended." He lifted his mug, took a sip of coffee and glanced at me. "I mean, it's not really my business, but ..."

"And not to be presumptive, but ... after last night, maybe it should be?" I asked the question for him. "Am I keeping some deep, dark, dangerous secret about my past? Or about myself?" I picked up my plate and carried it to the sink. I rinsed it and set it in the bottom rack of the dishwasher.

"Well, I wasn't thinking that, but I guess I'm wondering what would have made him let you go after all those years," Will replied.

I turned to face him. "Someone else," I said matter-of-factly. Will stared at me wide-eyed. "You mean he left you for another woman?"

"Well, yes," I said with slight hesitation. "But I suppose it's more accurate to say we left each other. He just happened to find a replacement before we made it official."

I sat down again, resting my hands on the table. I picked up a paper napkin and began folding and refolding it. "I can't really hold it against him, though," I said. "I'm not sure I wouldn't have done the same thing if I'd had the opportunity."

Will reached out and covered my hand with his. His eyes searched my face. I dropped the napkin and pulled back, suddenly uncomfortable. I detected a note of pity in his action, and that was one thing I did not want from him—now or ever.

As if he knew what I was thinking, he lifted my hand and pressed my fingers to his lips. "I'm sorry," he said, holding them in place. Then, letting go, he added, "But I can't say I'm not grateful. Otherwise, I might not be here with you."

We sat quietly for a moment and then I got up and began to clear away the rest of the breakfast dishes. I stacked them in the sink and then stood by the counter, staring out the window. The small lawn needed mowing, I noticed, and the pink and white carpet roses spilling over the picket fence were beginning to look overgrown. So were the hydrangeas. And the willow tree. The long slender branches hung so low they nearly touched the privet hedge along the side of the yard. And that small tree Ben had planted to replace the one that died last summer was also far from thriving. I wondered for a moment whether the problem was the soil itself. Could anything grow there?

"Actually, it was after Joe's second affair that I finally filed papers," I said quietly, almost to myself. I was aware of Will's eyes on me, watching, waiting. "The first one was harder, though. It happened when Ben and Justine were very young—Justine wasn't much more than a year and a half."

I still remembered him telling me about it. In truth, I remembered as if it were yesterday.

*It was late. The house was quiet, Ben and Justine long since tucked in their beds. I was curled up on the couch in the living room reading a book.*

*Joe had just returned from some errand. He seemed agitated as he stood next to the fireplace with his elbow resting on the mantel. "I have something to tell you and it's not pleasant," he said.*

*"What?" I asked, looking up at him. I had no idea what to expect.*

*"I've been seeing someone."*

*"What?" I asked again, but confused this time, not sure I understood what he'd said.*

*"I've been seeing someone and I'm in love with her." His voice was calm and even.*

*I shook my head, like a fighter who's taken a surprise blow. I was trying to absorb the words and their meaning. "Wait a minute. I don't understand. You've been sleeping with someone?" I felt as though the world had suddenly gone sideways and I was having trouble staying upright.*

*"Yes," he replied. "We love each other and we want to get married."*

*I stared at him for a long time. I swallowed hard, working the tense muscles in my throat. "How long?" I demanded. "How long has it been going on? And who is she?"*

*"About a year, and it's someone from work," he replied.*

*"And you're just now telling me about it?" I exclaimed.*

*The clock in the living room chimed softly. It was midnight. The witching hour.*

*"Her husband found out and said he'd tell you himself if I didn't. I thought you should hear it from me."*

*"Ah, I see. Backed into a corner, were you?" I paused for a moment. Then, glaring at him, I snarled, "You son of a bitch."*

*The weight of all his words suddenly felt like lead in my lap. I rose quickly, refusing to hold them any longer.*

*I don't remember leaving the house, but somehow I found myself at an all-night diner several blocks away. I slid into a booth, crossed my forearms on the table and let my head drop. I was exhausted. It was nearly one in the morning.*

*The waitress, a heavy-set woman with shimmery eye shadow and red lipstick, filled my coffee cup without saying a word. When she returned with a fresh pot several minutes later, she set it down on the table and shook her head from side to side.*

*"Mm-mm-mm," she said in time with the movement. "I recognize that look. Man trouble, huh?"*

*I gave her a half smile and shrugged slightly. "How can you tell?" I sniffled, rubbed a wadded-up napkin across my eyes, and then blew my nose.*

*"Hard to miss. You, in here after midnight, alone, and wiping tears from your face? It's no mystery. If it were something else, you'd be somewhere else." She patted my hand and then started to turn away. She stopped abruptly and turned toward me again with a look of concern on her face. Her eyes narrowed. "He didn't hurt you, did he?" she asked carefully. She didn't have to elaborate; I knew what she meant.*

*"No," I replied softly. "He didn't hurt me."*

*"Well, you'll be okay," she said reassuringly. "Honey, you aren't the first woman to have man trouble—whatever it is—and you won't be the last. And no matter how you feel right now, it isn't gonna kill you."*

*Her skin was smooth and soft, and almost as dark as the coffee. She was big-breasted, with a chest like an overstuffed down pillow. I longed for her to take me in her arms so I could lay my head there and cry like a baby while she rocked me and stroked my hair.*

*I desperately wanted my mother.*

*She refilled my cup and walked back to the counter. Returning a few minutes later, she set a dish of apple pie on the table.*

*"On the house," she said with a wink.*

*A fresh round of tears flooded my eyes. I felt so alone that even this small act of kindness seemed overwhelming.*

*"Will you share it with me?" I asked. My voice was barely more than a squeak.*

*She glanced around the room. The place was empty, save the two of us and the cook, who sat at the counter reading a newspaper.*

*"I don't see why not," she answered. "Wouldn't mind taking a load off for a few minutes, anyway." She sat down across from me. "Name's Maybelle. Maybelle Haines. But people just call me May."*

*"Callie," I replied. "Pleased to meet you."*

*It was around three a.m. when I left the diner and headed back home. I had to be there when Ben and Justine woke up, and I had to pull myself together. May strongly encouraged me to take a taxi, but I told her I wanted to walk. It probably wasn't a good idea, but I did it anyway.*

*When I got home, I found Joe asleep on the pullout couch in the living room. The image of him lying there so peacefully struck me like a blow. He had dropped a bomb that over the course of thirty seconds obliterated the world as I knew it; then he watched me run out of the house in anger and despair; and although it was the middle of the night and he had no idea where I was, he was still able to go to sleep.*

*"I didn't think you'd want to share the bed with me," he'd stated calmly in his own defense. The knowledge that he could have so little concern for my welfare would eventually become a chasm that neither one of us could bridge.*

Focusing on the lawn, the clouds, or something farther away, I wasn't aware of Will's presence behind me until I felt his hands on my shoulders. I swung to the side, away from him, and began to rinse the rest of the dishes. I suddenly felt very exposed, as though I were standing before him uncomfortably naked and vulnerable, unable to hide the parts of myself I didn't want him—or anyone—to see. I hadn't intended to tell Will about Joe's infidelities. I felt they were in some way my failings, too, and I wasn't ready to lay them all out before him.

Will took a step back, putting a few feet of distance between us, and leaned against the counter. His arms were folded across his chest. "So that's how you met May," he said. I nodded in reply.

"And what did you do about Joe and the other woman?" he asked.

"I had a talk with her," I replied with a half shrug.

"You what?" he asked, his eyes wide with disbelief. "Holy shit!"

*A few days after the details of the affair had been revealed, I told Joe I wanted to meet the woman who had stolen his heart—or to whom he had given it. I had a few choice words for her, although at that moment I wasn't sure exactly what they were.*

*Very reluctantly, Joe gave me her work number, and a day or so later I picked up the telephone and called her.*

*She answered on the fourth ring, and didn't seem particularly surprised to hear from me. I thought she must be expecting my call, and I wondered for a moment if Joe had warned her.*

*"I'd like to meet with you," I said quietly. "I think we have some things to discuss." My body was trembling and the hand that grasped the telephone was damp with nervous sweat, but my voice was steady. I'd be damned if I'd give her the upper hand by revealing the fear and anguish that for the last two days had permeated every fiber of my being.*

*She suggested a coffee shop near her office building, and I arrived five minutes past the appointed time—as was my intention. I wanted to make her wait for me, rather than the other way around. Let her sit there and wonder exactly what was to come, I thought to myself.*

*As I parked my car in front of a window, I saw her sitting at a table. I'd met her in passing a few times, most recently when she stopped by the house to show off her son's Halloween costume. I remember thinking it odd that she would come so far out of her way for something that had very little to do with us, but dismissed the thought and went about my own business. It was after Joe let the tomcat out of the bag that I realized she was sharing the event with the little boy's would-be stepfather.*

*I took a deep breath, squared my shoulders, and began walking toward the door. I wanted to appear tough and fearsome, despite the fact that underneath the steely exterior I displayed, I was as solid as melted ice cream. I was just as nervous as she, but there was no way I'd let her see it.*

*I sat down across from her. She was clutching a worn tissue, which she used to dab her eyes.*

*"Thank you for meeting me. Given the circumstances, I think we have some things to discuss." I spoke quietly, my voice cold and even. My forearms were crossed and resting on the table. Keeping my face expressionless, I leaned forward and focused my eyes directly on hers. She looked away, but I didn't. Weak, I thought, wondering what it was about her that had attracted Joe. I'd have expected him to be drawn to someone who could hold*

her own. But, then, what did I know? Stupidly, I had expected him not to be drawn to anyone at all.

"So, what did you want to say to me?" she asked.

That was all the invitation I needed.

"First of all," I said, my eyes boring into her like lasers, "I want to say how truly abominable I think your behavior is. And I mean both of you. You have caused immeasurable damage to two families, and risked the well-being of three young children—including your own. As a mother, I am thoroughly disgusted by your selfishness."

I could see her cringe as my words struck her like one tiny arrow after another. Tears welled in her eyes while mine remained clear and cold. She twisted the tissue in her hand.

"And furthermore," I continued. "I'm not stupid enough to think there is any way I can keep him from leaving me for you if that's his choice, but I'll tell you this much: I sure as hell won't make it easy—or pleasant—for him. Or you, for that matter. I will do whatever it takes to protect my children."

I paused for a moment, allowing my words to settle into her brain. With her head bent forward, she simply stared at her hands.

"Although," I added, with as much disdain as I could muster, "I can't understand for the life of me why you'd be interested in a man who's willing to cheat on his wife and abandon his family. I don't know what makes you think you'd have any better luck."

She looked up at me then, her expression softening. She appeared almost wistful.

"But he's so ... so ... wonderful," she said.

I snorted, and shook my head in disbelief. "Well, my guess is you've seen only his best behavior so far," I replied.

She raised her hand to swipe at a tear that rolled down one cheek. I simply stared at her, dry eyed, still leaning forward. I meant to create as much discomfort as possible. I knew that I had little or no say about what Joe ultimately chose to do at this point—and I had no idea what I wanted to do—but I wanted this woman to know that if she was to have any role whatsoever in my children's lives, she should be prepared to deal with me.

More tears welled in her eyes. Weak, I thought to myself again.

She lowered her gaze to her lap once more and sniffled. Taking a deep breath, she raised her head and looked directly at me. It was the most courage she'd demonstrated yet.

"What are you going to do?" she asked. "Are you going to leave him?"

"I don't know," I replied.

*"So if you believe what we've done is so terrible," she challenged, "how can you think about staying with him?"*

*I leaned in closer, and she responded by pressing herself further into the back of her seat.*

*"That," I said through clenched teeth, "is between me and my husband, and none of your business."*

*I rose, turned on my heel, and walked away.*

*From the parking lot, I could see her watching me as I moved toward my car. I got in, started the engine, and backed out of the space. I steered the car around the corner, pulled into another space, turned off the ignition, and promptly went to pieces.*

"As it turned out," I said, glancing at Will, "she had the final word—with Joe, anyway. Shortly after our meeting, she told him that she and her husband had decided to try to work things out. I like to think my conversation with her had something to do with it. It gives me some perverse sense of satisfaction."

Will stepped behind me and put his arms around me as he'd done earlier in the morning. This time I didn't move away.

"Well, I am impressed," he said, speaking into the crown of my hair. "That took a lot of guts."

I shrugged.

"Not really," I replied, my gaze directed out the window and away from him. "If I'd had real courage, I would have told him to leave."

"Why didn't you?"

"I don't know," I said with a sigh. "I was young and scared. It didn't occur to me that I could—or should—stand up for myself. And, too, I guess I thought it was partly my fault." I stepped away from Will, folded the dish-towel in thirds and hung it from the handle on the oven door.

"And I worried about Ben and Justine," I continued. "I wanted them to have one home, not split themselves between Dad's house and Mom's. I thought we owed it to them. And when all was said and done, it's not as though Joe and I had terrible fights or even major disagreements. I guess I thought we could work things out."

I refilled my coffee cup and sat down at the table again. Will joined me.

"We never really did, though. That's not something you can work out. But it took me a long time to realize it. Eventually, though, I stopped being angry and I saw the affair for what it was. And I saw Joe for what he was." I paused for a moment, examining the intricate floral pattern on my cup. "But I think it was a mistake to try to hold things together for so long. It kept both of us—him and me—from really being happy."

Will leaned forward and cupped his hand over the side of my face. Neither of us said anything. Then he drew me toward him and kissed me very gently.

When he pulled away, I shook my head and ran my hand through my hair. "What do you say we get dressed and head to the mountains?"

# 16

We drove to the trailhead with Bailey, who knew every landmark along the way, becoming increasingly animated the closer we got. By the time I'd parked the car and opened the door for him, he could hardly contain himself. Hurling himself past me, he hit the ground unceremoniously. He got up, wagged his tail sheepishly, and parked himself on my foot.

It was a beautiful winter day—the air was crisp and the sky was a clear, crystalline blue. Not a hint of clouds, except those far off in the distance. They may have been heading in our direction, but it would be well after dark before they'd bring any precipitation.

"Which way?" Will asked, looking up at the live oak and pine trees that towered above us. Dressed in worn jeans, a T-shirt, and an unbuttoned plaid flannel overshirt, he reminded me of a lumberjack heading off to work. By contrast, I wore a pair of black leggings, a long-sleeved cotton shirt, and an old pair of running shoes. It was chilly, but not particularly cold. I wrapped a fleece pullover around my waist on the off chance the temperature dropped during the afternoon.

"Well," I said, "we can start at the creek—the trail is relatively flat and very pretty—or we can hike up the mountain. It's also very pretty, but a little more strenuous. What do you think you can handle?" I raised my eyebrows.

"Whatever you can," he assured me.

As it turned out, we decided to follow the creek because that seemed to be Bailey's preference, and it was as good a trail as any. Given the recent rain, the creek itself was near full. Bailey scampered up and down the banks with ease, chasing leaves, sticks, and anything else that caught his attention.

Will held my hand as we walked, letting go only when the trail narrowed so one of us had to step in front of the other, or when we reached a stream crossing and had to balance as we hopped from rock to rock. We were silent for the first several minutes, listening to the sounds of the sparrows, finches, and warblers, the rustling leaves, and the water as it bubbled over the rocks.

After a while, we reached a wide spot in the trail. Several large boulders that must have come loose and rolled down the mountainside following a storm had landed in an orderly but off-kilter configuration that struck me as a cross between a miniature Stonehenge and the Flintstones' living room. Will stopped and took a deep breath. I sat down on the flat top of the rock closest to me. The branches of a tall pine tree hid the sun, and the shade was cool on my face.

"It is really beautiful here," Will said, looking up at the treetops. "I'm so used to being in the city that I've almost forgotten what it's like just to hear birds sing. I don't even pay attention to it at home."

I took in the landscape around me. "This is one of my favorite places. Sometimes I come here and just sit on a rock next to the creek. It's a great place to think."

Will was close enough that if he angled his leg just right, his knee touched mine.

"What do you think about?" He picked up my hand and began playing with my fingers.

"Oh, I don't know," I replied. "Everything. Nothing."

I pulled my hand away and awkwardly tightened the pullover around my waist. He leaned forward slightly, resting his forearms on his thighs, and turned his shoulders toward me.

"Can I ask you something?"

He spoke with such gravity that I almost laughed, thinking he was about to make a joke. But his serious expression made it immediately clear that humor was the last thing on his mind. My heart fluttered briefly, and I wiped my suddenly damp palms on my jeans.

"Um, okay," I replied. "I guess so."

"What are you afraid of?" he asked, as matter-of-factly as if he'd asked my name.

I looked at him quizzically.

"Afraid of? What do you mean?"

"I mean, you seem kind of reserved. Distant. You have been on and off since we first saw each other in Westin. Even on the phone. So I wonder if you're afraid of something."

I glanced over at Bailey who was busily trying to dig up a tree root. He attacked it first from one direction and then another, scratching and pawing at the dirt. I chuckled at the futility of the task, but at the same time, I marveled at his perseverance.

I turned back to Will.

"I don't think I was so reserved last night," I said, a little more defensively than was necessary.

He laughed softly.

"No, you weren't reserved—or distant—last night." He bowed his head slightly, one corner of his mouth curving into a smile. "And I have to say, I thank you for that." He paused, focusing his attention on the pink and purple lupine that grew in bunches alongside the trail. When he spoke again, he kept his eyes on the ground.

"Last night was—well—it was incredible. But afterward—and even this morning—you seemed to pull back, as though you were avoiding something. Or were afraid of something. Or … maybe wanted one of us to be somewhere else." He took my hand and placed it on his thigh and covered it with his own. The muscle beneath my palm was strong and tight.

"Cal, if something's going on, let me know. Please. Don't shut me out. Not now." His voice seemed to catch in his throat.

Now I took a deep breath. The last thing I wanted to do was shut him out. If anything, I wanted to wrap my arms around him and hold him so tightly he couldn't get away. I wanted to breathe him in so he could live next to my heart. But he was right. From the moment I had seen him at the hospital, I'd been open and amiable one minute and restrained the next. But how could I explain to him what I didn't completely understand myself?

"You know, you're the only one who has ever called me Cal," I said, changing the subject. "Everyone else uses Callie—except my dad, who used to call me Calamity, and sometimes still does. I always wondered whether there was something passively aggressive in that." I rambled on, nervous, trying to redirect the conversation. "And then most of my teachers called me Calista. I hate Calista."

"I know," Will replied simply. "I also know you're avoiding my question."

I looked down at his hand covering mine. Even after all the time and distance, he could still read me.

"The truth is, I'm afraid of you," I said softly. "I mean, of my feelings for you. I'm not sure what they are, but it's the power of them, I think, that scares me. I'm afraid to—to—" I grasped at words. "I don't know; I'm afraid I'll begin to care for you again. Like I did before."

He looked at me, eyebrows drawn together. "And that would be bad because …" He stopped, waiting for me to explain.

I stood up and took a few steps toward the tree where Bailey had been digging. He had abandoned his excavation project, and turned his attention to simply digging a hole. He glanced up at me, wagged his tail, and returned to his work. It was cool in the shade, and I shivered slightly. I pulled the fleece on over my head and turned around to face Will, holding my arms tight around my middle.

"Because our lives are in such different places," I said. "And I don't mean that we live in different cities or even different parts of the country. Our lives are different. You're still raising children and mine are, for the most part, grown. You have a medical practice in Westin and I have a job and a place I love here."

Will rose and walked toward me. "Is that what it is?" he asked. "The fact that my kids are younger than yours?"

The breeze rustled the silvery leaves on the tree branches, etching lacy patterns against the blue sky. I glanced up just in time to see a gray squirrel scurry up one of the tree trunks as though he were ascending a spiral staircase. He stopped, peered down at us, and continued his climb.

I turned to Will. He stood with his hands on his hips, eyes intent on mine.

"Maybe that's part of it," I conceded, "and maybe those are just excuses. With my voice just above a whisper, I continued. "The truth is, I don't seem to be good at loving people—or being loved in return."

"What did you say?"

"I said I'm lousy at relationships, and I'm afraid of starting one with you because it probably wouldn't work."

"What do you mean?"

"I mean, I couldn't make things work with you all those years ago, I couldn't make my marriage work, and I can't seem to let anyone except Bailey get really close to me—and he's a dog."

I walked toward the edge of the creek, moving from shade into sunlight. The leaves, dry despite the earlier precipitation, crunched beneath my feet with each step. I knelt down and dipped my hands in the cool water, and touched them to my cheeks and forehead. I felt as much as heard Will come up behind me. His body cast a shadow that enveloped me like a cloak.

He stood for a moment, and then dropped down next to me. He sat with his legs bent and knees drawn close to his chest.

"*We* couldn't make things work before. It wasn't just you," he said. "I was young and stupid and wanted my own way. I thought I knew what was right for both of us, but I didn't. I was completely wrong."

I wanted so much to lean against him, bury my head in his chest, and forget all the years that had passed. I wanted to pretend we could pick up where we left off, as though our separate lives hadn't happened. But I couldn't. For good or ill, we had left each other behind. He had created a life that didn't include me, and I had done the same without him.

And even if it were possible to wipe away the years as though they were marks on a blackboard, that would mean erasing Ben and Justine, and I couldn't imagine my world without them. The same way Will couldn't envision life without Lizzy and Wiley.

Lizzy and Wiley. A knot formed in my stomach when I thought of them. I was, in fact, as much afraid of them as I was of my feelings for Will. My children were an integral part of my life, but they had lives of their own that didn't always include me. With Justine away at college, weeks and even months went by when our only communication would be by telephone or e-mail. Ben was closer in proximity, and while he checked in with me on a fairly regular basis, he, too, was otherwise occupied with his own friends— including a charming young woman of whom he was particularly fond.

But Lizzy was barely a teenager, and Wiley just approaching adolescence. Will was still in the process of raising them, and they required his immediate attention every day. He was their only parent, and they relied on him entirely. Perhaps more important, though, because Ben and Justine were older, I'd had more years with them to establish relationships that wouldn't be impacted by the addition—or subtraction—of other people. Will hadn't reached that point yet with Lizzy and Wiley, and their circumstances made the road particularly bumpy. For Ben and Justine, who had both of their parents, there would be no competition for affection, no anxiety about misplaced loyalties, and no worries about losing the memory of someone very, very special.

Still, as arduous an undertaking as all this would be, I knew I could at least attempt it if I simply trusted myself and had faith in Will. And there, I realized, was the rub. I wasn't at all sure I was capable anymore of either faith or trust.

Will put his hand on the back of my neck and squeezed gently. "What?" he asked with a quiet insistence. "Tell me."

I took a deep breath and exhaled heavily through my nose.

"Okay, I'll tell you." I brought my fingers up to my lips while I thought for a moment, trying to choose the right words. "I am afraid," I began. "Over the course of my life I have been wrong so many times that I don't trust myself anymore. And aside from my children, it's so hard for me to be close to anyone. I don't really trust other people. I thought Joe and I loved each other—or loved each other enough, anyway—but I was wrong. I thought you and I loved each other, but I was wrong about that, too." I looked at him squarely. "I have thought a lot of people loved me at various times in my life, and too often I discovered I was wrong." God, I sounded pathetic. I wanted to jump into the hole Bailey had dug and cover myself with dirt.

Will took hold of my wrist and turned me around so I faced him. "They probably did love you, in whatever way they could—including me. Weren't you the one who said that at any given moment everyone is just trying to do the best they can?" He gazed up at the tree branches that towered over us, and then back at me.

"You weren't wrong about us," he went on. "We did love each other. We were just too young to know what it meant. I didn't want to leave you all those years ago. But I didn't think it was fair not to. And I figured you'd find someone else anyway, whether we were together or not. And you did. Maybe I was trying to protect myself and it backfired for both of us."

"Maybe," I replied, looking down at the fingers closed tightly around my wrist. I paused for a moment and then focused my eyes directly on his. "Will, your coming into my life again over these last couple of months has brought such joy that I can hardly believe it's real. Sometimes it feels as though life has been breathed into parts of me that have lain wasted for years."

I hesitated before continuing. I didn't want to sound even more pitiful. So many people had come and gone from my life, and those I cared about and trusted the most made their exits long before I was ready for them to leave. Consequently, I tended to keep people at a safe emotional distance, never allowing anyone close enough to do any real damage—except Ben and Justine, of course. And that was simply because a mother's love for her child—as I realized the moment Ben was placed in my arms—trumped all other fear and feeling.

Will touched my cheek. "I get it," he said. "I do. But doesn't it also seem like maybe we're getting a second chance here? To get right what we got so wrong before? Are you really willing to waste that?"

I stood, brushed away the dirt and leaves that clung to my leggings, and walked toward Bailey. He'd given up on hole digging and was snoozing in the cool dirt at the foot of a huge oak tree. I bent over to scratch his head before turning back to Will.

"Maybe that's the case," I agreed. "But what if we still get it wrong? We aren't the same people we were then. And what's even more significant is that it isn't just us anymore. There are Lizzy and Wiley to consider."

Will came close and pulled me toward him. I pressed my forehead against his chest.

"You're right," he said calmly. "Lizzy and Wiley are an important part of it. But they aren't the only part." With his thumb and forefinger under my chin, he tilted my face up so my eyes were inches from his. "Cal, I walked away from you once, but I sure as hell don't intend to do it again."

I closed my eyes and held on to him. With our bodies pressed together, the beating of his heart—or my heart—or our two hearts beating in the same rhythm—pounded in my chest. He pushed a lock of hair away from my eyes. With his arms still around me, he studied my face for a moment. Sunlight slicing through the trees lit the back of his head as though he were wearing a halo. "There are going to be complications," he said, "and things won't be easy. But we don't have to figure it all out this afternoon. Let's just be happy together right now. Later will come, and it will take care of itself."

Farther along the trail, the water picked up speed as it made its way down the mountains. It was by no means a rushing current, but it moved swiftly enough that when Bailey dashed across a wide section in pursuit of a ground squirrel, I subconsciously made a sharp attempt to stop him.

He had already zigzagged across a row of rocks and headed into some brush on the other side when I started to cross behind him. I had no trouble maneuvering the first two rocks, but only a narrow edge of the third stuck out of the water, and at an angle, to boot. I stopped on the second rock, trying to keep an eye on Bailey—who by now was out of sight—while at the same time assessing my position and figuring out how to get from the center of the creek to the far bank. I'd have to use knife-edged rock number three as a springboard to get from where I stood on rock number two to rock number four, which was more than a step away. If I timed it right and extended my leg far enough, I could make it, and use the momentum to propel myself to the opposite side. Not a problem—except the knife-edged rock was very slippery, and the tread on the part of my shoe that made contact with it was rather worn. Instead of pushing off on the edge, my foot slipped, and I lost my balance. I tried to catch myself, but before I knew it, I was on my backside, gasping, with water swirling around my hips. Fortunately, my fleece, which I had removed a few minutes earlier and wrapped around my waist again, provided a fair amount of padding. I fell slightly to the left as I landed, however, and the front of my shirt on that side dipped into the water before I caught myself. It took me a few seconds to realize what happened; and when I did, I stood up in the middle of the creek, soaked to the skin. Errant leaves, twigs, and other natural debris stuck to my shirt and pants. The water, little more than knee deep, was crystal clear, and, given the time of year, extremely cold.

After a quick visual assessment determined no medical attention was required, Will stood on the bank and doubled over with laughter. Bailey, who had crossed from the far side of the creek back to where he started, sat next to him. His fur was sopping, and a puddle had collected around him. He eyed me with an expression of bemused confusion. He wasn't sure why I was standing in a foot and a half of water, but if I wanted him to join me again, he was all for it.

I glared at him with one hand on my hip and the other pointing a finger at him in reproach. "Don't you even think about it, mister!"

With as much dignity as I could muster, I took one step and then another, and attempted to climb up to dry ground. My shoes were slippery, though, and I couldn't get a good foothold. With nothing to grab onto, I was forced to accept Will's outstretched hand.

"Thank you," I said politely, when I stood beside him on dry ground.

He looked down at me, biting the inside of his cheek to keep from smiling. The sight of me—waterlogged, with dirt clinging to my face—got the better of him, though, and he exploded in another fit of laughter.

Feigning offense, I unwrapped the fleece from around my waist and wrung it out so the water splashed on Will's shoes.

"I'm going home," I announced. I picked up Bailey's leash and walked to the car. He followed close behind. My own shoes made a squishing sound with each step, and left tiny pools of water in their wake. It wasn't the dramatic exit I'd intended.

Bailey hopped onto the backseat, and I grabbed an old towel from the trunk. I tied it sarong-style around my lower half, slipped off my shoes and socks and tossed them in the trunk, and slid into the driver's seat. I glanced in the rearview mirror and saw Will approaching the car. He was still snickering, but was trying to hide it behind his thumb, which he held to his closed lips. I smiled briefly to myself, turned the key, and revved the engine as though I was going to leave without him. I backed up slowly, and when he was close to the passenger door, I came to a stop and pressed the button to roll down the window.

He leaned against the car and peered inside. "Willing to give me a ride back to your place?" he asked. "Or, failing that, maybe to the bus station?"

"Well, since you don't know the way to either, I suppose I have to," I replied. "I shouldn't think I could just leave you to the kindness of strangers."

"I would appreciate that," he replied.

I twisted my body around and addressed Bailey, who was perched on the backseat. "What do you say? Should we take him with us?" Bailey let out a woof, and I turned back to Will. "Lucky for you, he's on your side. It's a long walk in any direction."

Will opened the door and dropped onto the seat next to me.

"I'm sorry," he said, still biting his lip. "I really am. I didn't mean to laugh, but—okay, maybe I did. But the sight of you chasing after the dog and then waving your arms as you tried to catch your balance—"

"Yeah, yeah, and even funnier when I landed on my backside in the water, I'm sure," I responded. "Well, I'm glad I could provide the afternoon's entertainment." I bowed slightly.

He touched my cheek and, raising one eyebrow, gave me a half smile. "You also look more than just a little enticing with your shirt clinging to your chest like that." His eyes followed the direction of the conversation. He leaned forward, pulled aside the collar of my shirt, and placed a kiss in the hollow of my neck, just above my collarbone.

"If you're trying to change the subject," I said, sighing contentedly, "it's working." I shifted the car into drive, and turned toward the road.

"You can do whatever you want to." I tossed a wet towel onto the washing machine in the laundry room. "I'm going upstairs to take a shower."

I'd just finished bathing Bailey, who was now curled up on the living room floor gnawing contentedly on the piece of rawhide he had sandwiched between his front paws.

I turned to face Will. "And, I don't want to hear so much as another snicker from you." I narrowed my eyes and pointed a finger at him in a vain attempt at looking fierce. "Not a twitter, not even a snort."

He stepped around me toward the couch. With his hands in front of him, palms facing forward, he was the picture of innocence.

"Not a sound," he said settling himself among the cushions, "I promise." His mouth curved into a grin, and his eyes twinkled. "But you have to admit—"

"*I* don't have to admit anything," I replied, gingerly reaching into my sleeve with my thumb and forefinger and pulling out a damp leaf. I regarded it with disdain and dropped it into the wastebasket next to the desk. "As I said, you can make yourself at home. I'm cold and tired, and I just want to get cleaned up and into something warm and dry."

Upstairs, I flipped on the shower and went into the bedroom to undress. I wanted nothing more than to peel off my wet clothes and let the warm water pour over me. Indoor plumbing, I thought to myself as I adjusted the water temperature, is not the least bit overrated.

I glanced in the mirror and saw a line of mud smeared across my jaw. Another extended down my right temple, from hairline to cheekbone.

"Stupid dog," I muttered. I had to admit, the episode was pretty funny, and I began to laugh in spite of myself. I should have known that Bailey, agile and sure-footed, would have traversed the wet rocks with no difficulty. I, on the other hand, with a higher center of gravity and the instability of two legs rather than four, was far less steady on my feet. Well, it wasn't the first time I'd sacrificed my dignity for a dog, and if history were any indication, it probably wouldn't be the last.

I stepped into the tub and under the showerhead. My whole body warmed as the hot water washed over me. It saturated my hair, and I pulled my fingers through the tangles to remove bits of leaves and other debris. With eyes closed, I reached for the bottle of shampoo.

"Here, let me do that," said a low voice.

I wiped my face with my fingertips and turned around. There stood Will, bottle in hand, wearing nothing but a silly grin. He had moved stealthily—I hadn't heard the shower curtain rustle, nor felt the air change, when he stepped in behind me.

"You said I could do whatever I want," he shrugged. "This is what I want."

He put the bottle back on the shelf and moved toward me. The water fell over both of us. Resting his hands gently on my shoulder blades and drawing me close, he bent his head and kissed me very softly. I leaned in and opened my mouth to him.

"Well," I said, aligning my body with his, "I did tell you to make yourself at home."

He picked up the bottle again and poured a dollop of shampoo into the palm of his hand.

"Mmmm, this is heaven," I purred, as he massaged it into my hair.

I tilted my head back under the shower and he rinsed out the shampoo. When he finished, he picked up the bar of shea butter and rose oil soap, turned it over in his hands a few times to work up a lather, and began washing my body. His hands glided along the skin on my shoulders and chest, and down my abdomen and thighs. He didn't say a word, but concentrated on his work.

When he was satisfied, I stepped back under the spray and let the water carry away whatever remained of my foray into the creek.

I had been facing him at first, but he put his hands on my hips and turned me around so my back was toward him. He pressed his body against mine, and I felt the hardness of him. His hands cupping my breasts, he kissed my neck and slid his tongue along the curve, out to my shoulder. I let my head fall back against his chest. The water continued to break over us.

I reached back and took hold of his buttocks, marveling at the tightness of his muscles. I squeezed, and he abruptly turned me around so that I faced him again. Then his mouth was on mine, and his hands had hold of my hips. I slid my own hand between his legs, gently stroking him. He closed his eyes and uttered a quiet moan.

He moved suddenly then, lifting me slightly so I stood on my tiptoes. He pressed my body against the wall. I pulled him toward me. He bent his legs, and with one quick thrust we were joined. Just the feel of him inside me was almost enough to bring me to climax.

I wrapped my legs around his hips.

"Come to me," he whispered, his breath hot on my cheek. After no more than half a dozen strokes, I did exactly that.

# 17

"Do you ever cook?" Will asked as we perused my extensive collection of takeout menus that evening.

"Mm, not much," I replied, leaning against the counter. I turned over the one-page flier from a new natural foods restaurant.

Once, when Ben was three years old and I was pregnant with Justine, Joe came home after work and asked if there were any plans for dinner. I was about eight months along, and after chasing Ben all day, by evening time I was too tired to boil water let alone prepare a meal. And Joe was astute enough not to expect one. So when he asked about dinner, Ben grabbed the packet of takeout menus, picked up the telephone, and ceremoniously dropped both on my lap. Joe and I looked at each other and burst into laughter.

I thought of that while Will and I decided what form of dinner would come from the telephone tonight. After our hike earlier in the day—not to mention my impromptu dip in the river—I was in no mood for any kind of meal preparation.

"How about this? Healthy enough for you?" I handed him the menu from the natural food place.

"Too healthy," Will answered, studying the offerings. "Tofu? Really? And what the hell is spelt?" He grimaced and picked up another menu. "How about Italian?"

We settled on pizza, and after a bit of a set-to, during which I had to remind him that I was a big girl and often ventured out by myself after dark, I went to pick it up while Will stayed home with Bailey. By the time I returned, he had not only gotten a blaze going in the fireplace but had rummaged around the kitchen and found a couple of placemats and arranged these—along with plates and napkins—on the heavy wooden coffee table in the living room. He'd also opened a bottle of wine and set that out, along with a pair of glasses.

"It's really turning cold outside," I said as I pulled off my jacket and hung it in the closet. "The wind is picking up and it looks like we might get some more rain tonight. I don't think we'll be doing much outside tomorrow." Will had taken the box from me and set it on the table.

"Well, I can think of worse things." He winked as he walked past me.

I glanced around the room, from the fireplace to the table to the man who put it all together. "Oh, Will, this is really wonderful." I held my icy hands out to the fire to warm them.

I gave Bailey his dinner and tossed a piece of rawhide in his direction. I hoped it would keep him occupied for a good long while. Then Will and I sat down on the couch. Flames danced around the oak log, which every so often let out a soft crackle or hiss.

As we ate slices of pizza and drank wine, we talked about our respective children, and some of the perils of parenting. We joked and laughed about funny firsts and the embarrassments we suffered at the hands of innocent children who had no idea what their words or actions meant.

"I can't imagine trying to do it alone," I said quietly. "I mean, Joe and I didn't have a lot between us, but we were united in our support for Ben and Justine. There were a lot of really difficult times that would have been impossible if he and I hadn't been able to count on each another."

Will started to sit back against the cushions, and with his hands on my shoulders drew me back with him. I was still holding my glass, but I leaned my head against him. I felt the vibration in his chest when he spoke.

"I'll be the first to admit it's tough," he said. "And I have a lot more questions than I do answers." He brushed his lips absently against the side of my head. "I sure never anticipated doing this job solo."

"Speaking of questions—and of doing the job solo," I said tentatively, running my finger along the rim of my glass, "can I ask what happened—with Joanna, I mean?" I quickly added that I'd understand if he didn't want to talk about it.

Will kept his arm around my shoulder, but the expression on his face changed. It wasn't serious as much as pensive, but he suddenly seemed very far away.

"No, I don't mind," he answered quietly. "And I guess you have a right to know."

I sat up straight so I could look at him. The firelight cast the room in a warm glow, with dark shadows hovering around us like benevolent ghosts. The reflection of the flame glimmered in Will's eyes as he stared into the fire.

He took a deep breath and began.

He and Joanna met at an art exhibit. He'd been talked into going by his friend Alex, who was at that time working up the courage to ask the gallery owner out on a date.

"She turned him down, by the way," Will said with a chuckle. Then, more soberly, "I really didn't want to go—I'd been on duty for five nights straight. But Alex kept after me. So I finally gave in and agreed that we'd go to the gallery, he'd see how far he could get, and then we'd stop on the way home so he could buy me a beer to compensate me for my trouble. Pretty simple."

Alex struck out, but Will didn't. Joanna Halloran had approached him as he studied a painting of yellow, orange, and magenta squares on a green and blue background. They looked to him as though they might represent a landscape, but he wasn't sure. She stood beside him, a glass of white wine cradled gracefully in her hand.

"I don't get it," she whispered, leaning toward him. "I mean—it's just a bunch of squares, isn't it?"

Will smiled down at her. "I don't get it either," he replied. "But then, I am no authority on art. All I know is I'm not a fan of this abstract stuff. I like to look at a fruit bowl and know it's a fruit bowl."

"Ah," Joanna replied, brushing her long blond bangs away from her eyes. "A realist. What do you do for a living?"

"I'm a doctor. Is that significant?" he asked.

"Could be," she said with a grin. "What's your specialty?"

"Emergency medicine, why?" She had piqued his curiosity.

"Well, then, you don't really work in the abstract, do you?" she said, more as a statement than a question. "A bone is broken or it isn't. Someone is bleeding or he isn't. Someone needs surgery or he doesn't. There isn't a lot of abstract thought there. You get a person through the immediate crisis and then leave him—or her—in the care of someone else who handles the abstract stuff."

Will looked at her, amused. "I'd like to think there's a little more to it than that, but I guess in a way, you're right."

"Joanna Halloran," she said, extending her right hand. "Pleased to meet you."

"Will Tremaine," he replied. "Likewise."

In the end, Alex went home by himself, and it was Will and Joanna who stopped off for a beer.

"I had no idea, then," Will said, glancing over at me. "She was so lively and bright."

They dated for nearly six months before Joanna introduced him to her family. They welcomed Will with open arms.

After a two-year courtship, Will and Joanna got married and settled into a regular life. Joanna had been an artist—a photographer—and when Will spent days—and, often, nights—at the hospital, she spent most of her time working in her studio.

"She had her first episode—at least the first that I'd seen—a year or so after we got married," Will explained. "It was pretty bad. The mania came first, and she went nearly two weeks without sleep. She did some really wild things like drive two hundred miles in the middle of the night because she'd gotten it in her head that she needed to watch the sun rise from a particular place. Or go shopping and come home with bags and bags of things neither of us needed—or could afford. Or rearrange all the furniture at three in the morning. Sometimes she'd lock herself in her studio and turn the music up really loud and spend hours taking pictures of random things she found in there."

After the mania came the precipitous drop.

"I'd seen depression before, but nothing like this," he recalled. His eyes were dull, and his lips were a straight line. "For weeks she just wouldn't get out of bed. She barely ate anything, and she barely spoke—only one- or two-word answers to simple questions. Sometimes she'd just turn away from me and cry in complete and total silence."

"Did she not tell you about her illness before you got married?" I asked. It was astonishing to me that she would not reveal something of that magnitude.

"No," he answered, shaking his head slowly from side to side. "I honestly had no idea." He glanced at me again and snorted to himself. "Can you believe it? Me, a doctor. I don't know how I missed it, but I did. Maybe I just didn't want to see it."

He removed his arm from my shoulder and rubbed his face with his hands. He hadn't shaved that morning, and I could hear the rasp of the stubble against his smooth palms. Still leaning forward, he twisted his body so he could look at me. "I found out later that she'd been taking medication but she hid it from me, and made her family swear not to say anything about it. She was afraid that if I knew, I'd think she was damaged and wouldn't want her." He shook his head at the notion.

"And her parents, of course, went along with it," he continued. "Her father thought they'd hit the jackpot when I came along—that by marrying her off to a doctor she'd always have someone to take care of her." He paused for a moment, still looking at me, and shrugged slightly. "And he was right."

He fell back against the sofa cushion and picked up the throw pillow next to him. He began playing absently with the tassel that hung from one of the corners. "Edward, Joanna's father, finally filled me in when she had to be hospitalized. I thought it was a new medical issue, but he told me they'd been dealing with it since she was sixteen." He glanced over at me. "Sixteen."

Dealing with it for Edward and Eleanor Halloran meant throwing money at whatever destruction, devastation, or simple inconvenience Joanna left in her wake. They reimbursed people whose property she damaged during manic periods, and they gave generous "gifts" to people who'd been adversely affected by her behavior. There was her college roommate, for example, a young chemistry student struggling to make ends meet, who planned her days around the bus schedule and suddenly found a brand-new Volkswagen Jetta in the driveway as a "thank-you" for dealing with the inconvenience Joanna caused when she forgot to turn off the stove after heating some soup and started a small kitchen fire in their apartment. Joanna left school, and her roommate was forced to move out so the apartment could be cleaned and repaired. The Hallorans paid for that, too.

"What a way to find out," I said, trying to keep my tone even. "You must have been furious—to have been deceived like that, I mean."

"I didn't really have a chance to be," Will said, focusing on the fire. "One of the things we found out while Joanna was in the hospital was that she was pregnant with Lizzy."

"So, she had stopped taking her medication," I ventured. "And that's why she had the episode. Is that right?"

"Well, the whole thing might have happened anyway, but, yeah. She had talked about having a baby—she really wanted a child—but it didn't seem like the right time. I was working really long, crazy hours and our life just didn't seem settled enough."

Will leaned forward and pulled a poker from the stand next to the fireplace. The flame was beginning to die down, and he moved a fresh log onto the charred remains of the previous one. The fire responded with blazing embers and sparks that danced up the chimney. The log popped and crackled. Will returned the tool to the stand and eased himself back against the cushions. I had taken the opportunity to adjust my position and move just slightly away from him.

He picked up where he left off. "You're right. She did stop taking her medication. She thought the drugs wouldn't be good for the baby. But as it turned out, not having them was even worse for her. Of course, she never took them with any regularity anyway."

"She was trying to protect her child, then," I said. "That's quite admirable. You have to give her a lot of credit."

Joanna had been discharged from the hospital within a few days, and although she still refused medication, she began to manage quite well. The doctors—Will included—were mystified by the sudden change. They wondered if the hormonal fluctuations that accompanied pregnancy were affecting her brain chemistry and keeping the symptoms at bay even without the help of drugs.

"Maybe it was all strength of will, but it was amazing," Will recalled. "She was really happy—so excited about the baby. And I mean a normal happy. Not mania. And after Lizzy was born Joanna became this really involved, attentive mother. Edward and Eleanor wanted to hire a nanny, but Joanna refused it. She wanted to do it all herself."

After a time, their life fell into a regular rhythm. Will moved up the ranks and became the number two in charge of emergency medicine, and Joanna even began working on her photography again. Not surprisingly, she had taken hundreds of pictures of Lizzy, and she used them as the foundation for a series of collages.

"Her career was picking up," Will noted. "She was showing her work and it was really in demand. She had a great eye. She'd take different images and scan them into the computer and then combine them with other photos she'd taken—landscapes and still life—and then tint all of it by hand. Sometimes she'd incorporate excerpts from poetry or prose that meant something to her. It really was beautiful."

I sat silently at the end of the couch, my back pressed into the padded arm and my knees drawn up below my chin. I wanted to hear whatever Will wanted to tell me, but it seemed necessary to keep some physical distance between us, even if it was no more than half a foot. I was not a part of this story, and even just touching his hand at this point seemed unfitting.

"So life continued, but after a while it got to be like a roller coaster again. Some days she was great, and other days she had to force herself to function and take care of Lizzy," Will continued. "She did finally agree to have someone come in and help with things at home, and that made everything a lot easier."

Strangely enough, it was around that time that Joanna started talking about having a second child. They'd never discussed the idea specifically, or made any mutual decisions, but Will had assumed that Lizzy would be their only offspring. The demands she placed on Joanna seemed about as much as Joanna could manage. But she was adamant. Lizzy must have a brother or sister.

"I didn't think it was a good idea, but she argued that if we had two children they could grow up together and share a family history. She said that with two children, neither one would be completely alone when she and I were gone," Will explained. "Being an only child myself, I couldn't really fault her logic. But I still didn't think it was a good idea in this case."

"And yet a little while later, Wiley came along," I added quietly.

"Yes," he replied, biting his bottom lip. "I should have known better—should have been more careful—but then a little while later, Wiley came along."

He turned to me and began to speak very quickly. "Don't get the wrong idea—it's not that I don't love Wiley or that I'm not glad to have him, I just mean..."

I touched his arm lightly. "I understand."

"It wasn't an accident," Will announced after a few minutes of silence. His eyes were fixed on mine. "I can't prove it—and I'm not sure I'd want to even if I could—but I know she drove off that cliff on purpose. And somewhere down deep, so does her mother. Eleanor Halloran is a very perceptive woman, and nothing about her children gets past her."

He turned his gaze to the fire once again. "Of course," he added, "she'll do anything to let herself believe it was otherwise."

According to the police report, Joanna had been driving on a mountain pass early on a rainy afternoon. The road twisted and curved, with the craggy mountain on one side and a sheer drop on the other. Traveling at a high rate of speed—but not fast enough to indicate she had *intended* to go off the road—she lost control of the car as she rounded a particularly sharp curve. The car flew off the pavement and hit the rocky ground below. It rolled several times before coming to rest in a ravine. Joanna was rushed to the hospital, but she died shortly after arriving.

Will, who had been on duty in the emergency room, met the paramedics when they pulled up to the door. He had no idea the woman on the stretcher was his wife.

"It was awful. It was worse than awful. I'd never faced anything like that before, and I hope to God I never will again." The color drained from his face. He closed his eyes and held the pillow to his chest. "The paramedics had intubated her, and one of them was squeezing the bag to keep her ventilated. It was obvious, though, that she was gone—or close to it. There was nothing anyone could do—her chest injuries alone were too massive. Her heart stopped, and they couldn't restart it."

The head nurse on duty that morning recognized Joanna immediately. In a quiet, soothing voice, she spoke comfortingly to Will as she gently tugged at his arm and pulled him out of the cubicle where doctors and nurses—his colleagues—were tending to his wife in the frenzied but orderly way they responded to all emergencies.

Will stood in the doorway, watching them, hearing the doctors bark out orders. He recognized the words—he'd used them countless times in other situations, with other patients. They were eerily familiar, but at this moment, also very surreal. The world was shifting right before his eyes. What had been true that morning, when he kissed his wife and children goodbye and drove off to work, was not true anymore and never would be again. The face of reality wore an entirely new expression.

I reached up and ran the back of my hand along the side of Will's face, from temple to jaw. His two-day beard was rough against my skin. He turned his head and took my hand in his, and silently, as tears rolled down his cheeks, pressed his lips against my fingers.

"Will, I'm so sorry," I murmured.

He blinked away the tears, cleared his throat, and spoke strongly then. "The hardest part was telling Lizzy and Wiley. How do you tell two children they'll never see their mother again?"

"There's no easy way," I replied, thinking of my father, who had been tasked with the same horrible job. "Whatever words you choose, they're going to feel like knives have been plunged into their hearts. If not right then, they will later. The best you can do is what you have done—to be present for them, to let them know they aren't alone."

If telling Lizzy and Wiley was the hardest, informing Eleanor and Edward was a close second. Will called them from the ER to tell them their daughter had been in an accident. He waited until they arrived at the hospital to deliver the news that she was gone. That sort of report was best given in person.

"Edward responded with his usual stoicism," Will recalled. "But it was strange. I remember noticing something about his reaction that made me think he'd been expecting the call. He seemed—I don't know—prepared in some way."

Eleanor summoned every ounce of self-control she had in order to maintain her composure. When it looked as though she might faint, Will helped her to a couch and sat with her, holding her hand and telling her to take slow, deep breaths.

He continued to hold my own hand, but lowered it to his lap.

"She looked up at me with tears in her eyes." He spoke softly, remembering, as though I weren't there. "All she said was, 'How could she?'"

I waited for a moment before responding. "And that's how you knew," I said.

He looked over at me then, and seemed almost surprised to find me sitting there. He closed his eyes and sighed. "Yes," he replied. "Eleanor's never spoken of it since. As far as she's concerned, it was a terrible accident. But somewhere, in some part of her mind, she knows that Joanna killed herself."

Eleanor's grief, according to Will, cut so deep that, for several weeks, she refused to acknowledge her daughter's death. "She didn't even go to the funeral," he recalled. "She told Edward she didn't want to know anything about it. Wouldn't even admit it was taking place."

The service was held a few days after Joanna died, and Will readily allowed Rowan and Edward to make all the arrangements. He required only that the casket remain closed. He was adamant that the children's memories of their mother not include images of her lifeless body. They were having a hard enough time already, he said.

When Joanna was buried in the old cemetery at the edge of Westin's city limits, she was surrounded by her husband and children, father, brother and sister, and dozens of friends. "I'm sure people wondered why Eleanor wasn't there," Will commented, "but no one said anything or asked about it." He cast a glance in my direction. "I didn't really care who was there. I was only paying attention to Lizzy and Wiley. They seemed so fragile."

"I'm sure they were—they are," I replied. "It's about the worst thing a child can face." I turned my attention to the fire, remembering my own experience. The flame still burned strong and hot.

"So when did Eleanor finally accept the truth?"

"Well, she could deny it for only so long," Will said with a shrug. "She realized how much Lizzy and Wiley needed her—and she needed them. But it's strange—even now she acts like Joanna's away on a trip or something. And she refuses to contemplate the possibility that Joanna chose to ... to ... do what she did."

I didn't want to pry, didn't want to travel into a part of Will's past where I simply didn't belong, but I had to know. "Why did she do it?"

Will frowned, cutting two parallel lines between his eyebrows. "She thought ..." He stopped and breathed another deep sigh. "She tried so hard to be a good mother, to be a good wife—whatever she perceived that to be—and no matter how much I told her otherwise, she thought she was failing me and the kids." He stopped for a moment to massage his forehead and temple.

"She thought I wasn't happy with her—with us." When he looked at me, his face bore an expression I had never seen before. It was a cross between realization and guilt. "And, you know, the truth is, I don't think I ever loved her the way she wanted me to. Not even in the very beginning."

I was startled by his admission. "And yet you married her," I said.

Will reached for the glass on the coffee table. He took a sip and set it down again. I saw a flicker of sadness in his eyes.

"I did love her, but not in the way I thought I should—the way I thought a man should love his wife. And I never really understood why. To tell you the truth, I never really bothered trying to understand why. I just accepted it for what it was," he went on. "And after a while I started to think that maybe what I thought I was supposed to feel wasn't real to begin with."

He watched the firelight's reflection glisten on one of the wineglasses. "I was completely committed to Joanna and to Lizzy and Wiley. I was faithful to her, and I took care of her and the kids—we were always a family—but as I look back on it, I realize that something had been missing from the very beginning."

"Like what?" I asked.

His eyes met mine. He opened his mouth to speak, hesitated, and started again. "For all these years—I think ... I never stopped wanting you, Cal—or, at least, what we had, or what I felt for you. And I think Joanna knew it. Or something like it."

Slightly stunned, I sat back against the sofa cushion. "If that's true," I said, "it's an awful thing to live with—believing the person you're married to would rather be with someone else. I know that from experience."

"She didn't know it was you," Will replied. "Christ, *I* didn't know it was you until I saw you in the hospital." He was quiet for a long minute. "That's what I meant the other night when I said things are complicated."

He leaned back and closed his eyes. He looked tired, and I could see deep lines etched around his mouth and between his eyebrows. I could tell the recollection was a painful one. "The day she died—that morning—we'd had another discussion about the state of our marriage."

I wasn't sure I wanted to hear what would follow, but I took a deep breath and listened for Will's sake.

"They were always the same. She worried that I wanted to leave, I told her I didn't. But I was in a hurry, and probably more abrupt than I should have been. I told her we could talk about it when I got home that evening. We could drop the kids with Eleanor and Edward and go out to dinner, just the two of us. As I was about to head off to the hospital, she took my hand and said she was sorry for everything. I told her she didn't have anything to be sorry for, kissed the top of her head, and left. But I didn't tell her I loved her. And I think she needed to hear that. I think it would have made a difference."

I leaned forward, put my hand on Will's forearm, and squeezed gently. "You can't believe you're responsible for her death," I said.

He raised one shoulder and let it drop. "Everyone else does."

"That can't possibly be true," I argued.

"I was supposed to protect her," he responded flatly. "I was supposed to protect her and take care of her, and I didn't do it. And they all know it."

"Oh, Will," I whispered. I didn't know what else to say.

We sat in silence. I felt the immense weight of everything Will had just told me. I was suddenly overcome by a wave of guilt, as though I were betraying someone—either Joe or Joanna, or both—by sitting here with him. Guilt that my happiness with Will came at the expense of two marriages and a mother whose children desperately needed her. It didn't matter that Joe and I had divorced long before Will and I found each other again, or that Joanna had died two years earlier. Each of us had made a vow to someone else and then, in some way, not followed through. I contemplated what I perceived at that moment to be my own failure, and from the expression on Will's face, he seemed to be doing the same. Finally, he reached over and took my hand. He curled his fingers around mine.

"But you and me, together," he said firmly, "it's not wrong."

"No?" I asked. "Does it not seem in some strange way that they—I don't know—sacrificed something so we could be here? Joe would have stayed married to me if I had been willing."

"But what about his affairs?"

"It took a while after the first one, but I think he truly regretted it," I replied. "He was really sorry about it on a lot of different levels. And I think there was a period in the middle when he really wanted to make me happy. I don't know that I reciprocated very well. By the time the second one happened, the marriage was already over. We just hadn't filed the paperwork."

"And Joanna and I would still be married if she hadn't died. But even so, isn't it also the case that we sacrificed for them? We did it willingly, but still we did it. Neither one of us was really happy, but we stayed anyway and honored the commitments we'd made. I don't mean to sound cold and uncaring, but should you and I be sorry or feel guilty about our feelings for each other or that we have the chance to start over?"

"No," I replied, looking down at the hand covering mine. "I suppose not."

"I wouldn't have abandoned my family for this," he continued, releasing my hand and gesturing with his own to encompass all that existed between the two of us. "But I'll be damned if I'll let it go now. I'll be damned if I'll let you go."

We looked at each other for a long time. I picked up the wine bottle and refilled the glasses.

"I've never told any of this to anyone," Will said, staring into the fire again. "Not even Joanna's family. They know about her illness, of course, and that she wasn't doing well—obviously—but I don't think they knew how scared and insecure she was. I didn't say anything—she was adamant about that—and I doubt she did either. Joanna didn't like to share much with her mother. Eleanor tends to have strong ideas about how things should be and what people should do, and she doesn't handle it well when anyone questions or challenges her."

"And this is the woman with whom Lizzy and Wiley spend so much time?" My voice contained a hint of sarcasm.

"They have to," Will replied. He drained his glass and set it back on the table. "Joanna's family is their only family and their only link to her. I won't take that away from them. Besides, like you said, raising kids alone is hard. I need all the help I can get." He lifted one hand and massaged the back of his neck.

"I do have to be careful, though. Eleanor would like nothing more than for me to hand Joanna's children over to her permanently. Forget the fact that they're my children, too. But Joanna would turn over in her grave if I did anything like that. She, too, was very perceptive. She knew her mother—and sister—better than anyone else in that family did—or does. She would never let them get their hands on Lizzy and Wiley."

"And yet she left them." I had tremendous sympathy for Joanna's condition, but as a child whose mother fought desperately to live—and failed—it was hard for me to empathize with a woman who would do what I considered tantamount to abandoning her children.

Will stared at me. His face was expressionless, but his eyes had turned to steel.

"I'm sorry," I said, placing my hand over his. "That was very cold and unfeeling and unkind. I didn't know her, I didn't know the situation, and I have no right to say anything."

His demeanor softened. "She wasn't a monster. She loved her children." His voice was low and even. "But I think she honestly thought that by leaving she was doing what was best for them. And who knows? Maybe it's better to grow up without a mother than with one who—" He paused, staring at the fire before turning his eyes back to me. "And anyway, she didn't leave them with her family," he added curtly. "She left them with me."

By the time the conversation ended, a bit of a chasm had grown between Will and me. For the first time since we became reacquainted in Westin, we felt awkward with each other. It was almost as though Joanna was in the house with us.

I picked up the plates and glasses, brought them into the kitchen, and stacked them in the sink. Will followed with the pizza box and the empty wine bottle. He set both down on the counter.

I gave the plates and wineglasses a quick rinse, and loaded them in the dishwasher. I closed it up, pressed the "on" button, and called for Bailey to come outside with me. I was tired and wanted to go to bed, but he had to take one final pass around the yard.

Will stood in the doorway. "Are you okay?" he asked.

"Uh, sure," I replied, trying to sound cheerful. "Why wouldn't I be?"

"Maybe because things got a little heated in there," he answered.

"No, everything's fine." It wasn't fine, and we both knew it, but I didn't know what else to say. I couldn't explain what I was feeling, mainly because I didn't understand it myself. Bailey walked back inside, padded over to his water bowl, and slurped noisily. "C'mon, pal," I said to him when he'd had his fill. "Time for bed." As Bailey and I started up the stairs, I turned to Will. "Would you do me a favor and get the lights?"

I didn't specifically ask him to join me, but neither did I indicate that he was unwelcome. I left it to him to decide what he wanted to do. Clearly, his emotions were still raw where Joanna was concerned. He hid them well, but they existed at some core, like an abrasion that had scabbed over. Left alone, it wasn't bothersome, but chafe it a little, or scrape off even a tiny bit of the protective layer, and the pain flared almost as though the injury were brand new.

Contrary to what Will might want to believe—if that was even the case—I was not the balm that would soothe the pain and heal this particular wound. I couldn't be a replacement for Joanna, nor could I be a diversion from whatever grief or anguish he still carried with him. Whatever might grow between Will and me had to be cultivated independently of his relationship with her—or mine with Joe. I remembered one of Alice's gardening principles. It made for an apt analogy. "When you're putting in a new crop, you have to take out everything that's left of the old one, and then work the soil so the young plants have a place to thrive," she said. Maybe Will still had some tending to do.

I washed my face and brushed my teeth, and when I finished I heard Will downstairs. It sounded as though he was making sure the fire was out before he came up to bed himself. I wiped my hands on a towel and hurried into my bedroom.

I wasn't sure where Will wanted to be—wasn't sure where I wanted him to be—so I left the door open about halfway. Then I slipped into bed and picked up a book. My eyes skimmed over the words on the page, but none of them registered in my brain. My mind was focused elsewhere.

I heard Will trudge up the stairs a few minutes later, and then the sound of water running in the bathroom. He walked quietly down the hall, stopping just outside the bedroom. He paused briefly, and then went into the guest room and closed the door.

Well, I thought to myself, I guess that was that. No matter what he'd said yesterday morning or over dinner last night—or even just now—clearly she was still with him. He wasn't kidding when he said it was complicated.

I laid my book on the nightstand and turned off the light. Darkness filled the room. Will had switched off the lamp in the hall, and nary a single particle of light escaped from the guest room. The entire house was steeped in black.

I had trouble getting to sleep. First I was too hot, then I was too cold. Bailey snored too loudly, then the silence was deafening. At some point I must have dozed off, though, because I became aware of a quiet knock on the door. It still wasn't closed all the way, but apparently Will wasn't sure he should walk right in.

"Cal?" he called softly.

"I'm awake," I replied, pulling myself into a sitting position. "Come in."

He took a few steps toward the bed. My eyes had grown accustomed enough to the dark that I could see his shape a foot or two away.

"Cal," he murmured again. His voice, barely audible, held a note of despair that almost frightened me. "I wasn't sure ... I thought maybe you wouldn't ..."

"I'm here, Will. I'm right here." I lifted the covers, inviting him to join me. He hesitated for a second or two, and then accepted. Rolling onto his side, he settled in close, pressing his face against my shoulder. I put my arm around him and held him as I might have done with Ben or Justine. His head rested on my chest, pressed against the thin fabric of my nightgown.

"Callie," he whispered. With his arm across my abdomen, he held me tightly. He sniffled, and I felt dampness between his cheek and my chest. I stroked his hair.

"It's okay, Will. It's okay," I whispered.

"God, it's been hell," he said. "I've had to hold everything together for Lizzy and Wiley, and for the Hallorans. Christ, I've had to protect Lizzy and Wiley from the Hallorans. It has been so damn hard." He closed his eyes and sighed. He was motionless for a few minutes, then tilted his head and looked up at me.

"I really never have told anyone the things I told you tonight. I couldn't. I've had a hard enough time admitting them to myself."

I didn't say anything. I simply continued stroking his hair and waited for him to speak.

"What I felt when I saw you at the hospital—it's nothing I've ever felt for anyone, not even Joanna," he continued. "Not even what I felt for you when we were younger. And at first it scared me. But then I started to feel this incredible guilt, too."

"About what?" I asked.

"Ever since Joanna died I've wondered whether things would have gone differently if she had married someone else. Would someone else have been able to give her what she needed, and would that have changed the outcome? Would she still be alive?"

"You'll never know," I answered softly. "And it doesn't matter anyway. Because someone else isn't who she wanted." I touched his cheek. "She wanted you. And that was her choice."

# 18

It did rain again. Not in sheets, but a steady shower.

Between the rain, the soft bed, and the close proximity of Will's body, I had no intention of getting up, even when the first streaks of light crossed the sky. Neither did Will. When the alarm on his watch beeped unexpectedly, he silenced the offending object, and, with a growl, tossed it onto the chair on the other side of the room.

He took a gulp of water from the glass on the nightstand, and then rolled over to face me. He raised one eyebrow, and I smiled. Question asked and answered. He lowered his head and kissed me, softly at first, and then more intensely. His hand roamed across the front of my body, cupping my cheek and then resting on my chest, abdomen, and beyond.

This was only our third encounter, but I was quickly becoming familiar with the feel of him—the smooth skin across his back, the muscles rounding his shoulders, and the flat plane of his abdomen.

As we touched, it was almost as though I had some kind of cellular memory of him that awakened with every sensation. There was an exciting newness to our lovemaking, but also a comfortable familiarity.

I told him as much later in the kitchen as he leaned against the counter and watched me put a pot of coffee on to brew. I had just shoved a pan of Miranda's cinnamon rolls into the oven to bake.

He reached into the cupboard right above me and pulled out a couple of mugs. "Yeah, and it sounds really corny, but I feel sort of like I'm home or something. Like I've been away for a long time and now I'm home."

I ducked under his arm and set the sugar bowl and a small pitcher of cream on the table. "I know what you mean," I replied. "Hard to know how much of that is real, though, and how much is memory." I turned to him, wrapped my arms around his neck, and kissed him lightly. "But, you know, maybe it doesn't matter."

He opened his mouth to reply, but was cut off by Bailey, who sat up and issued a loud "Woof!" With his tail held high, he pranced to the front door in response to a sharp knock.

Will and I looked at each other.

"You expecting anyone?" he asked.

"Hardly," I replied. "And whenever Alice comes over, she uses the back door. Besides, the weather is too ugly for her to be out walking."

I tightened the sash on my robe and followed Bailey to the door. Will waited in the kitchen.

I glanced out the window as I passed, and my shoulders dropped. Standing on the porch were my son and daughter, who, apparently, had decided to make an impromptu visit. I opened the door to greet them.

"What are you two doing here?" I asked. "And why together? Justine, shouldn't you be at school?" I took a step backward as they came through the doorway.

"Well," Justine replied with a smile as she pulled off her raincoat and hung it on a peg next to my wool shawl, "it's a long weekend—no class on Friday or Monday—so I decided it would be a great opportunity to visit my brother, who I haven't seen in at least a month."

"Yeah," Ben agreed. "And then we thought, what the heck, Mom doesn't have school either, so why not come by and say hello. We figured you'd be glad to see us."

I narrowed my eyes and addressed Justine. "You're behind this, aren't you?" I said, giving her arm a little pinch as she turned toward the dining area. "You knew Will would be here, and you just wanted to get a look at him."

She responded with mock disbelief. "How could you think that? Ben told you, we just wanted to say hello."

I glanced from Justine to Ben and then back to Justine. "And you traveled a hundred and fifty miles to do it." Half smiling myself, I looked at each of them and shook my head. "Right."

Meanwhile, Will, whose view of the front door had been obscured by the stairs, came into the living room. He stood near the couch, his arms folded across his chest, and watched the exchange playing out before him. He coughed lightly, and we all turned toward him.

"Whoa," Justine uttered under her breath.

Ben looked at me—in my robe—and then at Will—clad in worn sweatpants and a faded T-shirt—and back to me. I felt my cheeks burn, as though I'd been caught misbehaving.

Will hung back, not sure how I wanted to handle the situation. I noticed that he didn't seem nearly as uncomfortable as I was. I moved toward him and took his arm. "Will, remember when I said I thought I might be seeing my children this weekend, but that I'd rearranged my plans with them?" I glowered at Ben and Justine. "It seems they didn't quite get the message."

Will nodded, a slight smirk catching the corners of his mouth. "Ah."

"That being the case," I continued, "May I present my son, Ben, and my daughter, Justine." I turned to my children. "Ben, Justine, this is Will Tremaine."

Will shook hands first with Ben and then Justine. "Pleased to meet you," he said warmly.

"Apparently, my oh-so-thoughtful offspring decided today was the perfect day to pay their mother a call."

Justine responded first. "So, are we in time for breakfast? And are those cinnamon rolls I smell?"

I stared at her for a moment, and sighed. "Yes, they are. Come into the kitchen and I'll see what else I can find."

While Will went upstairs to change, Ben and Justine perched on the wooden stools next to the kitchen counter and I rummaged through the refrigerator. "Let's see, I can scramble some eggs if you're really hungry." I closed the refrigerator door to see my daughter grinning at me.

"What?" I demanded.

"Just a friend?" Justine prodded. "C'mon, Mom. You can lie a lot better than that."

Ben was more pensive. His initial enthusiasm had faded.

"I don't have to, you know," I said, pulling the frying pan out of the cupboard next to the stove. "I'm an adult."

Ben poured a glass of orange juice from the pitcher. He emptied the contents in one long gulp and set the glass down with a sharp rap.

"Anyway," I continued, "we weren't expecting company — particularly the two of you."

"Obviously," they said in unison. Justine laughed, but I detected a note of derision in Ben's tone.

I looked over at him, but didn't say anything for a moment. When I did speak, I changed the subject to landscaping and some of the work I needed him to do in the front yard. I pointed out the jasmine bushes that were a bit overgrown, the camellias that had lost their shape, and the little tree we needed to replace yet again.

"There must be something about that spot." I stirred the eggs in the frying pan. "Maybe it's haunted by the ghost of some native plant that once stood there and now refuses to relinquish its small piece of earth."

Ben gave me a sideways glance. "Yeah, sure," he said. "Maybe you should have a priest come and sprinkle it with holy water or perform an exorcism."

"Maybe I should at that," I answered.

In perfect saved-by-the-bell fashion, the oven timer rang just then to let me know the cinnamon rolls were done. I set the hot baking dish on a cast-iron trivet on the counter so it could cool.

A moment later, Will came down the stairs. He was dressed in jeans and a long- sleeved T-shirt. He approached me from behind and rested his hands on the curves of my shoulders. I watched Ben's eyes follow the movement. His demeanor was neither rude nor particularly friendly. Clearly he was sizing up the man he thought was taking his father's place.

"Okay, then," I broke in. "Why don't we sit down. Ben, would you bring over the coffee? And Justine, grab a couple of plates and some silverware, would you?"

I set a bowl of scrambled eggs on the table and then reached for the cinnamon rolls. I picked up the square baking dish bare-handed, thinking it had cooled enough. I was wrong. Uttering an expletive or two, I let go immediately and the dish landed with a thud on the counter. I turned on the cold water and thrust my fingertips into the stream. Will was beside me in an instant.

"Here, let me look at that," he said, pulling my hand away from the water and examining it closely. The pads of two fingertips were red and sore. It was a very mild burn, but stung nonetheless. "An ice cube would be better." He grabbed one from the freezer and put it directly onto my hand. I tried to pull back, but he held on tightly.

"What's this thing you have with your hands?" he asked jokingly. "You only have two of them, you know, and they can take only so much abuse."

"Funny, funny," I retorted. We looked at each other for a moment, eyes shining. Remembering suddenly that we weren't alone, I turned my head and saw Ben and Justine watching us. Justine was clearly entertained, but Ben's face was entirely unreadable. He might have been amused, but then again he might have been upset. He'd always been good at hiding his feelings.

"Ahem." Will cleared his throat and, looking slightly admonished, sat back down at the table. I dropped the ice cube in the sink, grabbed an oven mitt, and picked up the baking dish.

"So," I said, taking a seat near Justine. "What do you two have planned for the day?"

Justine offered Will a cinnamon roll and then took one herself. Ben extended his plate and she served one to him. "Mm, I don't know. Maybe just hang around here for a while." With a smirk, she glanced at Ben, who was scooping spoonfuls of fluffy scrambled eggs onto his plate.

"Or not," I replied.

Purposely ignoring me, she turned to Will. "So, Mom says you're a doctor."

As it turned out, Ben and Justine did hang around for a while, and we all spent a lazy afternoon watching old movies. A second wave of last night's storm brought more rain and a fair amount of gusting wind, so any outdoor activities we might have considered were nixed. I commented on Will's and my good fortune the previous day when a brief dry spell gave us the opportunity to do some hiking.

That, of course, put him in mind of Bailey's and my adventure—or misadventure, depending on how one wanted to look at it—and he regaled Ben and Justine with a blow-by-blow report of my dash across the rocks to rescue a dog that, in reality, had no need of my assistance, and of my subsequent dip into Rock Creek. As I listened to Will's account, I found myself contributing details and laughing as hard and long as everyone else.

Toward late afternoon the rain began to let up and the wind died down enough that Ben decided it was a good time to make the drive back to Kentfield.

"He has a date tonight, and he needs time to primp," Justine teased. "Wait until she gets to know him better. If she's still around, he'll be showing up in dirty jeans and a grubby T-shirt."

I put my arm around Ben's waist and hugged him. "Don't make fun of your brother, Justine. If his jeans are dirty and his shirts are grubby it's because he's making the world a more beautiful place, one flower at a time." I looked up at him and smiled. "Aren't you, sweetie?"

Ben rolled his eyes. "C'mon, Jus, let's go. I want to get home before it starts raining again." He turned to Will and each extended a hand to the other. "Glad to meet you," Ben said.

"And you," Will replied. "It really was a pleasure."

"Bye, Mama," Justine said as she gave me a hug. She let go of me and then opened her arms to Will and embraced him lightly. "I'm so glad we got to meet, and I hope we see you again soon."

"So do I," Will answered.

Ben shifted his weight impatiently. "Come on, Justine. Let's *go*."

I opened the door for them, and Ben kissed my cheek on his way out. "Bye, Mom."

"Drive carefully," I instructed. "The roads are slick."

"Yes, Mom, I know," Ben answered back.

I watched them walk toward his car. "Call or text to let me know when you get home," I called after them. "And, Ben, have a good time tonight."

"Pretty great kids, you have," Will commented as I watched them drive away. "And pretty obvious how much they care about you."

"Most of the time," I replied, referring to their unannounced visit. I tucked the DVD cases back on the shelf and picked up the few glasses and plates that had been left on the coffee table. "I certainly didn't expect you to meet them so soon, though," I said as I walked into the kitchen.

Will followed me with the platter on which he and Ben had piled the sandwiches we consumed while watching the movies. He plucked an apple slice off the plate in my hand and popped it into his mouth.

"Not so soon, huh?" He set the platter on the counter and pulled me to him. "That would imply then that you did, in fact, expect me to meet them."

"Well, I assumed you would—sometime," I agreed. "We are friends, after all."

"A little more than that, I'd say. Anyway," he added, "they just wanted to make sure you're all right. You do have a stranger in your house—at least as far as they're concerned. I think it says a lot about them that they'd come all this way just to check on you."

I laughed. "I suppose it does." I put my arms around his neck and played with the curls that touched his collar. The feel of his hair around my fingers brought on an almost visceral sense of familiarity.

He held me closer, pressing my body to his, and gestured with his chin toward the dishes and glasses on the counter and in the sink. "What do you say we let this wait," he suggested. "I can think of a much better way to spend some time."

"Oh, really?" I replied teasingly. "Well, I'm all ears."

He bent his head and kissed me. He tasted faintly of Sprite and apple. "Actually, I was thinking about an altogether different part of your anatomy."

The patter of drops hitting the window woke me before dawn. I sat up and looked out the window. The sky was dark, and even without glancing at the clock, I could tell morning was still a long way off.

I pulled the covers back over me and snuggled up to Will. He turned toward me with a sigh and wrapped his arm around me. His breathing was steady and even.

"I wish you didn't have to go," I whispered.

"Mmm," he murmured in response.

I fell asleep again with my head against his shoulder.

"You know, Cal, I meant what I said about not walking away from you."

We were sharing a quick breakfast before I drove him to the airport.

"Well, you aren't walking, are you?" I replied and broke a blueberry muffin in half. "You're flying."

"You know what I mean." He spoke sharply. It was clear that he wanted to communicate something, but was having trouble finding the words. He hesitated for a moment. "I know you have some reservations—maybe a lot of reservations—but—" He stopped abruptly and rubbed his hand over his face.

I took advantage of the pause. "Will, I have no idea where we'll go from here, and you're right that I do have reservations." I rested my hand on his. "We just … well, we have to be careful. We can't rush into anything. Lizzy and Wiley, remember?"

He nodded.

"A week ago I had no idea we'd be sitting here together like this," I continued. "Hell, a week ago I had no idea we'd be doing a lot of the things we've done together this weekend." I cocked an eyebrow at him and smiled.

"Yeah, well, I had my hopes," he joked.

"I don't want to walk away from you either," I went on, serious again. "Especially not after the last few days. But I think we need to give ourselves some time. It's important for everyone's sake."

I pulled my hand away and sat back in my chair. "Will, I remember what it was like to be a kid and to have people step into my life. And I remember how hard it was when they stepped back out. The only way I could do that with Lizzy and Wiley—in any capacity—is if I planned to stay."

"Does that mean you don't?" he asked.

"It means I don't know," I replied. "And neither do you, really."

Will looked down at his empty plate. He took a deep breath and exhaled through his nose. "You're right. I don't know. This is all too new."

I laid my hand on his arm. "What I do know, though, is that I am really, really glad to be with you again. And I am not ready to let go."

Will went upstairs to pack his things while I put the dishes away and straight-ened up the kitchen. I was feeling a twinge of melancholy at the thought of him leaving. I wasn't sure when I'd see him again.

Fortunately, I had papers to grade and lessons to plan, and Alice had invited me to be her guest at an opening reception at the art museum. The day—and evening—would be filled, and after saying goodbye to Will I'd return to the rhythm of my own life.

I wiped down the counter, rinsed the sponge, and climbed up the stairs. I walked into the bedroom just in time to catch Will zipping up his duffel bag and pulling it onto the floor. He turned toward me and my breath caught in my throat. All the feelings I'd had for him, all the dreams and desires I'd harbored throughout my marriage to Joe, suddenly coalesced into one unde-niable force. At that moment, I wanted him with every fiber of my being. Not just physically, but emotionally, spiritually, and any other way two people can be joined. Miranda was right—I'd never fully committed to Joe because I'd never stopped wishing for Will. And on some level, Joe must have known that. It was no wonder he sought satisfaction elsewhere.

As I stood in the doorway, I caught Will's eye and glanced over at the unmade bed. I raised my eyebrows.

He shrugged, smiled, and started to unbutton his shirt. Fortunately, I knew a shortcut to the airport.

# 19

"Hey, Dad, here's another one." Wiley spoke into the paperback book he held close to his face. "What's a question you can never answer 'no' to?"

Lost in thought, Will didn't immediately respond. After his long weekend in San Sebastian—and a lot of careful consideration in the weeks following—he had decided to tell Eleanor and Edward about Callie. Things were serious enough, at least as far as he was concerned, that he felt they should know about it. He believed he owed them that much. When Wiley spoke, Will was contemplating the Hallorans' reaction to the news. He didn't expect them to take it well.

"Dad!" Wiley repeated sharply.

"What?" Will glanced in the rearview mirror and saw his son's reflection staring back at him, eyes twinkling from beneath the bill of a Detroit Tigers baseball cap. "Oh. Is that the book Chase got you when you went snowboarding a couple of weeks ago?"

"Yeah, it is," Wiley replied impatiently. "C'mon, Dad, guess. What's a question you can never say 'no' to?"

"I don't know. What?"

"C'mon, Dad, you have to guess!"

Will snorted softly. "Okay, let's see ... well, if it's a question for you, I'd say it has something to do with ice cream. You'll never say 'no' to that."

"No-o-o," Wiley scoffed. "Guess again. I'll give you a hint—it's not about a thing."

Will glanced out the side window, pondering. "I don't know. I give up. What?"

"*Are you awake?*" Wiley answered with a laugh. "Hah! That's the question—*Are you awake?* If you're asleep, you can't say 'no.'" He turned the page and perused the list of riddles. "Okay, Lizzy, now it's your turn. Here's one. What can fill a room but takes up no space?"

Lizzy, sitting in the front seat next to her father, stared straight ahead. "I don't really care," she grumbled.

"Come on, Liz," Will admonished. "He's just trying to have a little fun with you."

Lizzy rolled her eyes and let out an audible sigh. "Fine," she muttered. She twisted her body to face her brother. "Air. That's my answer."

"Enhnhnh—you're wrong," Wiley responded gleefully. "It's light. Light fills up a room but doesn't take up any space."

"Well, yeah," Lizzy argued, suddenly becoming more interested in the question. "But air does the same thing." She looked to her father. "Right, Dad?"

Will glanced in the rearview mirror again at Wiley, who now wore an expression of serious deliberation. "She's got a point," Will said.

After several minutes, during which Wiley regaled his father and sister with a slew of tongue twisters, knock-knock jokes, and even a few limericks—one of which Will forbade him to repeat in the presence of his grandparents—Will navigated the car up the Hallorans' long driveway. He came to a stop next to the front walkway.

"Okay, everyone out. Don't forget to grab your stuff." He walked around to the back of the Range Rover and lifted the hatch. "Let's get inside," he ordered, as he handed overnight bags to the kids. "I'm sure your grandmother's wondering what happened to you. I told her we'd be here a half hour ago."

Paulette opened the door before anyone had a chance to ring the bell.

"Come in, come in," she welcomed.

Eleanor joined them in the foyer. "I'm so glad to see you," she exclaimed, wrapping an arm around each child. "We expected you sooner, though."

Will and Lizzy exchanged glances, their eyes twinkling with mutual understanding.

"Well, no matter." She turned to her grandchildren. "Why don't you two run upstairs and put your overnight bags in your rooms. Then go into the kitchen. Paulette has something special for you."

Lizzy and Wiley picked up their satchels and raced each other up the stairs.

"Hey, you two, be careful," Will called as they pushed themselves alternately against the wall and the banister. "This is a house, not a playground."

He turned his attention to Eleanor. "I'd like to speak with you and Edward about something, if you have a moment. Is he here?"

Eleanor hesitated for a split second. "Of course. He's in the living room with Rowan. Shall we join them?"

Will took a deep breath and exhaled heavily. Better get it over with, he thought to himself. It wouldn't be easy. No matter how he presented it, they would perceive his relationship with Callie as an act of treason, punishable by God knows what.

Will followed Eleanor into the living room and greeted his father- and sister-in-law.

"Will, my boy, good to see you!" Edward stood and shook his hand. "Take a seat. Can I get you a drink? I've got a very tasty stout in the refrigerator."

"No, no thanks," Will replied. "I really can't stay long. I'm on my way back to the hospital to take care of some paperwork that's piled up this week. It's probably best if I have a clear head."

"Quite right," Edward said, returning to his place on the sofa. "I'm sure the board would appreciate that."

Eleanor took a seat beside her husband. "So, you said you wanted to discuss something with us?"

The silk damask sofa and two matching wingback chairs formed a large triangle around the cherrywood coffee table. Eleanor and Edward occupied the sofa, and Rowan had one of the chairs. Will sat down in the other. He adjusted his position so he could address all of them.

He coughed lightly before beginning. He'd been dreading the conversation he was about to start. Until Callie, he'd never felt the need to say anything to them about any woman he had dated since Joanna.

He wasn't seeking their permission, as far as Callie was concerned—or their blessing—but he felt he owed them a degree of honesty. After all, he had been married to their daughter, and was still connected to them through Lizzy and Wiley.

"So, what is it?" Eleanor asked warmly. "Has it something to do with the children?"

Will cleared his throat and took a breath. "In a way, yes. I want to let you know that I am seeing someone. I don't know how serious it is or will be, and I haven't told Lizzy or Wiley about it yet because it's too early." He did, indeed know how serious it was, but he thought it better to let them take in the situation by degrees. "I'm mentioning it to you now only because I don't want it to look like I'm hiding anything." He sat back against the cushion, bracing himself for the onslaught.

He expected the worst to come from Rowan, but to his surprise, she simply rose and, without even glancing in his direction, left the room.

Eleanor sat quietly, her hands clasped in her lap. Edward placed one large hand over hers, patting it lightly. "Well," he said, "this is a bit of news we hadn't expected."

"No, indeed. We hadn't expected this at all," Eleanor concurred. She looked at Edward and then back to Will. "What about Joanna?"

The question took Will by surprise, and he blinked a few times as he tried to make sense of it. "What about her?" he asked.

"We thought you still considered yourself married. She's only—well, we've seen it that way, at least." Eleanor paused for a moment. "And what about the children?"

Will leaned forward in the chair. "Eleanor, I'm not married anymore," he answered calmly. "I was—before—but now I'm not. I loved Joanna, and always will, but she's gone."

Eleanor raised her chin and spoke sharply. "You can say that, but as far as I am concerned, Joanna is still your wife. And again I ask, what about the children—her children?"

"My children, too," Will replied firmly. "I don't want them to know about this yet. It's too soon. But when the time is right, I'll tell them myself. And they'll be fine. I'll make sure of it. I always have."

Eleanor looked down at her hands. The delicate muscles in her neck contracted as she swallowed. "I don't know what to say."

Edward, who never beat around the bush in matters either business or personal, tackled the issue head on. "What can you tell us about the woman? Is she someone we might know?"

"I doubt it," Will replied. "I knew her long before I met Joanna. Before I'd begun my internship and residency, in fact. We ... er ... lost touch when I went to Boston. I hadn't seen her in twenty-five years, but she came into the emergency room after a minor accident."

"Ah," Edward responded. "Does she live here in Westin? Perhaps we are acquainted with her family."

"No, she was here visiting a friend when she came into the ER. She lives in San Sebastian."

"I believe that's on the California coast, is it not?"

"Yes."

Eleanor spoke up then. "And does she know you're married?"

"She knows I was," Will replied.

"Well, then." Eleanor rose and walked to the piano on the opposite side of the room. The dark wood, recently polished, gleamed in the sun that filtered in through the silk sheers. She picked up a silver picture frame and gazed at the image beneath the glass. Joanna's face, caught in a moment of unguarded joy, stared back at her. Very lightly, Eleanor's finger traced the shape of the image—high cheekbones, full mouth curved into a broad smile, round eyes looking straight into the camera.

Putting the frame back, she turned to Will and stiffened. "I guess that's all there is to it then, as far as you're concerned." She turned back to the photo.

Will sighed and looked down at his hands. He didn't move for a moment. Finally, he stood up and took a few steps toward Eleanor. Standing behind her, he rested his hand gently on her shoulder. "Eleanor, I loved Joanna. I still do. And I cherish the part of her that is still alive in Lizzy and Wiley. But she isn't here anymore. And we can't arrange our lives as if she were. It's not fair to anyone—especially not to Lizzy and Wiley."

Eleanor whirled around and glared at Will. Her eyes were dark and fierce, and her tone quiet and controlled. "You may be willing to let her go, but I am not. You may think she is replaceable, but I do not. And I'm sure her children are not so inclined, either."

Edward positioned himself beside his wife, gently taking her arm. It was a protective response. "I assume we will have an opportunity to meet this woman," he said almost questioningly.

Will looked from one to the other. "Of course, Edward. I'm telling you this specifically because I don't want to keep anything from you, and I want to be sure nothing impacts the relationship you have with Lizzy and Wiley."

Eleanor sat down again, and smoothed her skirt. "Well, I should hope you'd feel the same about their relationship with their mother."

Will closed his eyes. The exchange was proving no more difficult than he'd anticipated, but it was wearing just the same.

"Eleanor, I will always do everything I can to keep Joanna's memory alive for them—photographs, stories, hell, I've kept all of her things almost exactly the way she left them just because that's how Lizzy wants it. I will never take her away from them, but we can't keep living our lives as though she's in the next room. She's gone, and the kids need to learn how to live with that."

"You may believe that," Eleanor replied coldly, "but obviously Lizzy does not. The fact that she still needs her mother's things clearly shows that she's not ready to—as you so callously put it—'learn to live with it.' Forcing Lizzy to accept some other woman is not simply detrimental to her well-being, it's downright cruel."

Edward poured his wife a glass of sherry, which she accepted gratefully. "Will," he said calmly, "I'm sure you can see things from our perspective—"

"You may choose to have other women," Eleanor interrupted, squaring her shoulders and facing Will directly. "But Lizzy and Wiley cannot have another mother." Her voice was cold as ice. "If you cannot be sensitive to that, perhaps you are not the father we believed you to be."

Will was about to reply when he heard a sound and turned to see Lizzy and Wiley standing in the doorway. He had no idea how long they'd been there, or how much of the conversation they'd heard. He glanced at Eleanor.

She composed herself quickly, smiled broadly, and welcomed them into the room. "My sweet darlings," she exclaimed. "Come sit by me. Your father was just leaving, and I want to hear all about your snowboarding adventure with Uncle Chase and Aunt Sarah."

Both children stopped to give their father a hug. Will exhaled heavily. Whatever they'd heard, it didn't seem to have upset them. "Bye, Dad," Lizzy said cheerfully. "See you tomorrow."

"Yeah, bye, Dad," Wiley echoed. "See you tomorrow."

Will put a hand on each child's head. "Have fun, but don't give your grandparents any trouble, okay? I'll pick you up tomorrow afternoon."

# 20

In the Halloran family, birthdays were a big event—particularly for the children. When Wiley's came along in late March, it was no exception, and his weekend celebration included two parties. On the Saturday before the actual day, he and a group of eight boys—plus Will and Chase—played laser tag and rode bumper cars in an indoor park, and gorged on as much pizza and birthday cake as their stomachs could hold. The second party took place at the Hallorans' on the Saturday after his actual birthday, with the whole family—plus Alex and Julie Merritt—in attendance.

Lizzy and Wiley were spending the night with Eleanor and Edward, and Wiley, who in the last few weeks had become overanxious about being away from his father, cajoled Will into staying the night too.

"So, Wiley, what's your favorite present so far?" Alex asked after dinner. The family had gathered in the living room waiting for Paulette to bring in Wiley's "official" birthday cake. As Wiley blew out the candles, the celebrants would honor him with rounds of "Happy Birthday To You" and "For He's a Jolly Good Fellow." The latter was a Halloran tradition.

"My dad gave me a new bike," Wiley replied brightly. "It's for riding off road and it has twenty-one gears."

"My goodness," Eleanor broke in. "Twenty-one—how will you ever use all of them?"

Wiley was about to reply when Will's cell phone rang. He jumped up to answer it, excusing himself and slipping into the foyer where he could speak privately. He thought it might be Callie.

Instead, it was one of the two ER doctors on duty that evening. A problem had arisen that required Will's immediate attention.

"I'm sorry, pal," Will told Wiley as he adjusted the collar on his coat. They stood by the front door, Wiley looking distraught. "I'll only be a little while.

I just have to take care of one thing and I'll be right back." As Alex walked by, Will caught his attention and gave a slight nod in Wiley's direction. Alex read the situation immediately.

"Hey, Wiley, there you are." He put a hand on the birthday boy's shoulder. "Why don't you come try out that new video game with me until your dad gets back."

"Okay." Wiley sounded less than enthusiastic, but took a few steps with Alex back to the living room. Alex stopped and turned to Will. "But, hey, don't you dawdle," he ordered. "We're waiting on you for cake, but we're not waiting forever. Right?" He nudged Wiley's shoulder as though they were allies.

Wiley smiled and pointed a finger at his father. "Right. We aren't waiting forever."

When Will came back to the house not quite an hour later, Wiley ran outside to greet him as he got out of the car.

"Dad, Dad, come on, come see," he cried. "Gran and Grandpa gave me my birthday present. Hurry!" He pulled at Will's sleeve.

"Okay, okay, I'm coming," Will said, laughing.

Alex met them just inside the front door. He leaned his head close to Will's. "You ain't gonna believe this," he said in a voice just above a whisper.

Will looked at him quizzically.

"Da-ad, come on!" Wiley dragged Will into the living room. Turning toward Lizzy, Will saw that she was holding something light colored and furry. She glanced up at him with a shy smile.

"Come look, Dad."

Will didn't have to get any closer to see the object of her attention was a puppy. No more than ten or twelve weeks old, Will guessed.

"His name's Winslow," Wiley said triumphantly. "Grandpa found him. Uncle Chase and Aunt Sarah picked him up today."

Will closed his eyes for a few seconds, calculating his response. Surprising Wiley was one thing, but ambushing Will was quite another. The last thing he wanted in the house was something else that required care and feeding. Lizzy's cat was the most he could handle right now.

Edward approached him. "I hope you don't mind, Will, but we thought a puppy would be a great friend for Wiley."

"Right," Will replied. He could argue that a dog—and more specifically, a puppy—was not a responsibility any of them could take on at this point, but he knew he'd be speaking into the wind. A puppy required almost constant attention, and between work, school, and extracurricular activities, he and the children would be hard-pressed to provide it; but that didn't seem to matter. Anyway, one look at Wiley's beaming face—the happiest he'd seemed in a long time—told Will they'd just have to figure out how to make it work.

He took a seat on the chair opposite Lizzy and Rowan. Lizzy walked over and handed the puppy to him. "See, Dad? He's really sweet."

Will smiled. "Yeah, he's sweet." He scratched Winslow's ears, and the puppy twisted his head so he could grab onto Will's hand with his sharp baby teeth. "Hey!" Will cried playfully, pulling his hand away. "Be careful with that." The puppy cocked his head and looked into Will's face. He lunged forward, and slid a soft pink tongue across his cheek.

"Winslow, huh?" He gave the dog another pat. "And where is Winslow going to sleep?"

"With me," Wiley piped. "In my bed. Grandpa said so."

"I don't know about that," Will replied. "You and I are sharing a room tonight, remember? That means if Winslow sleeps with you, he also sleeps with me."

"It'll be like a slumber party," Wiley said joyfully as he took the puppy in his arms.

"Right," Will said and let out another sigh.

## 21

"**W**ell, you're absolutely right that they should have asked you about it first," I acknowledged when Will told me about the Hallorans' birthday gift to Wiley. "A puppy *is* a huge undertaking. On the other hand," I added, "Winslow could also be just the companion Wiley needs right now."

"Yeah, well," Will grumbled.

"Bailey made all the difference for me after Joe and I split," I continued. "He kept me from being alone, but more than that, he loved me—loves me—unconditionally. Every day. No matter what. He doesn't care what I look like or what kind of mood I'm in. He just loves me. And that's huge."

"I know," Will said wearily. "But, to tell you the truth, I'm already stretched to the limit—beyond the limit. And this is going to be like having another kid."

"I wish I could help," I said, hoping to soften his mood.

"Well, Edward offered to send Winslow to some puppy academy, and I think I'll take him up on the offer."

"Good idea," I agreed.

"Anyway, speaking of birthdays, yours is coming up, isn't it? What are you hoping for?" he asked.

I laughed. "Not a puppy, I can tell you that."

## 22

My birthday happened to fall right in the middle of spring break this year, and while I was more inclined to let the occasion pass with little fanfare, Justine maintained that some kind of acknowledgment was absolutely essential. She wanted to drive down from Middlebrook—maybe picking up Ben along the way—and spend the day with me.

Alice had a better idea. She proposed that we take Bailey and Bingo on a nice long walk and then have breakfast at the little patisserie we discovered downtown. Then I could have the rest of the day to myself—maybe to spend with Justine and Ben, and maybe not.

As it turned out, however, Will had the best idea of all.

"Let's go away somewhere," he suggested during one of our regular telephone calls. "Just you and me. Chase and Sarah are taking the kids—and Winslow—camping, so we can have a few days to ourselves."

"Well, that certainly has celebration potential. But what about Wiley? Won't he have trouble being away from you?"

"Not as long as he has Winslow with him." In the five weeks since Winslow joined the Tremaine household, he and Wiley had become practically insepmarable. The only time they weren't together was during school hours. Wiley could manage without his father, Will said, as long as Winslow was on duty.

"So where are you thinking?" I asked.

"I don't know, but someplace new to both of us. Not San Sebastian or Westin." He was silent for a moment or two. "How about Bell Island? You've talked about wanting to go there."

Bell Island was situated along the coast in the northern part of the state, and The Inn on Bell Island was actually the original Bell mansion, which dated back to the 1860s. It was very formal and very elegant.

"I think that sounds perfect," I said.

"All right, then," Will answered. "I'll make the arrangements. All you have to do is show up."

"I think I can manage that."

A few days later, I received a cryptic e-mail from Will that contained nothing more than a date and a reservation number.

"Don't I get any details?" I asked when I spoke with him that evening. "How am I going to know what to pack?"

"The only thing you need to know is when to be there," he replied, "and don't worry about packing. For what I have in mind, you won't need much more than a toothbrush."

# 23

I was in the process of rounding up said toothbrush—and a few other necessities—the following week when I got a telephone call from Joe. Hearing from him always took me by surprise. We'd managed to put aside the rancor that marked the end of our marriage, but, still, our conversations were few and far between.

"So, Justine tells me you're taking a trip," he said lightly. "Running from the law, are you?"

I tossed the pair of sandals I was holding onto the floor. "Well, I am going away for a few days, but the law has nothing to do with it," I responded with equal levity. "Why? Do you know something I don't?"

"Well, I'm not sure," he replied. "Some guy came nosing around my office this morning, asking a bunch of questions about you."

I sat down on the bed. "What kind of questions? Who was he?"

"A private investigator. Wyatt, I think he said his name was. Wouldn't tell me who sent him, though. He wanted to know how long we'd been married, why we split up, whether you'd ever done anything I considered ... uh ... 'questionable' was how he put it."

I felt a burning sensation in the pit of my stomach. Why would someone be asking questions about me? My voice shook when I spoke. "What did you say to him?"

Joe snorted. "I didn't tell him anything, except to get lost. He didn't argue, just closed his notepad, and left." Joe paused briefly. "So, who is he?"

"I have no idea." A vague feeling of dread trickled up from somewhere deep in my core.

"Well," Joe said, "I wouldn't worry too much. There's probably been a mix-up somewhere, and this guy Wyatt is investigating the wrong person. It's been known to happen."

I couldn't imagine why anyone would take this kind of interest in me. The only marks on my record—public or private—were my dissolution of marriage, a few parking citations, and one speeding ticket.

"You're probably right," I replied.

I had managed to put my conversation with Joe out of my mind when the school principal stopped by my classroom the next day. He hemmed and hawed a bit before getting to the point: Wyatt had paid him a visit as well, posing questions similar to those he asked Joe, but regarding my professional life.

"Anything you need to tell me?" the principal asked with a note of concern.

By late evening, after Sally McMillan called to ask—with only a touch of sarcasm—if I was a secret sociopath, my mild anxiety had turned into full-blown panic. I had absolutely no idea what—or who—was behind this Wyatt person's inquiries.

I was desperate to talk to Will, but he was away at a medical conference and wouldn't be home until the next day. I spent a long night tossing and turning until he answered the message I left on his phone. Unfortunately, his response did little to assuage my fears. According to Will, Wyatt was a private investigator the Hallorans' law firm kept on retainer. They called on him when they needed to dig up dirt on a client's behalf. And right now, I was the dirt.

"So, I take it you told them about me," I said flatly.

"Yeah, I did," Will replied. "But I sure as hell didn't expect anything like this."

Will and I had agreed that Lizzy and Wiley shouldn't know anything about our relationship—at least not until we had something certain to tell them—but I knew he felt very strongly that he should say something to the Hallorans. I was thoroughly opposed to the idea, arguing that the philosophy we applied to the children should extend to Joanna's parents and the rest of her immediate family. From what Will had told me about them, I was certain anything else would just be asking for trouble.

And, apparently, I was right.

He, however, had disagreed. "I think in the long run, not telling them would be asking for more," Will argued. "There's nothing wrong or immoral about my feelings for you, and Joanna's family just has to accept it. Whatever goes on between the two of us is not going to change how Lizzy and Wiley feel about them."

I made the case that while I agreed wholeheartedly, I also understood Joanna's family and their likely response to this new development. I had walked in shoes very similar to theirs, and I understood the overwhelming need to keep alive the memory of someone important, no matter what the cost.

But Will was unwavering. Lizzy was very astute, he argued, and he was concerned that no matter how careful he might be, something would slip. "If Eleanor or Rowan were to somehow hear about it from one of the kids, it would be a lot more difficult for everyone than if I'm just up front with them," he said.

I remained unconvinced, but ceded to his judgment.

Now, however, the knowledge that some private investigator was sifting through my life—and at the Hallorans' behest—turned my initial fear into rage.

"Don't worry," Will responded with a calm I found both comforting and disconcerting. "I'll handle it."

The door to the living room was closed as Will approached. He heard voices, two of which he recognized as those of Edward and Eleanor. The third was not familiar, but right now he didn't care who was with them. He pushed the door open and strode into the room.

"Will," Eleanor exclaimed, "what's the matter? Is it one of the children?"

Edward rose and, with the same expression of concern, faced his son-in-law.

Will looked from one to the other, not so much as acknowledging the individual in the corner. "What the hell do you mean by hiring someone to investigate Callie Winwood?" he demanded.

Edward motioned toward one of the chairs, inviting Will to sit down. "Let's see if we can't talk about this calmly, shall we?"

Will remained standing. "Answer me, Edward."

It was Eleanor who responded. "We are only looking out for our grand-children," she said calmly. "If this woman is to be involved with them in any capacity, it is our responsibility to know everything we can about her."

"And it didn't occur to you to just ask? I told you I'm not hiding anything." Will fought to control his anger. "And even if I were, what I do with my life is my business."

"Not when it involves Joanna's children," Eleanor replied sharply. "We have an obligation to them—and to her—to protect them from—"

"Lizzy and Wiley are *my* children," Will broke in. "Do you understand that? Mine. I am their father, and *I* will look after them. So call off the god-damn dogs."

With the slam of the front door signaling Will's departure, the stranger, who had kept himself in the corner, out of sight, stepped forward. "I guess this means my services are no longer required."

Eleanor glanced toward the foyer. "Perhaps not at the moment, Mr. Wyatt. But you have been very helpful, and we will call on you again, should the need arise."

# 24

Given the Wyatt situation, I was inclined to abandon the Bell Island trip altogether, but Will argued that we should not allow the Hallorans' actions to dictate our own.

So, despite my skepticism, I found myself at the Bell mansion a week later, waiting for Will in the room he had reserved for us.

Situated at the end of a long expansive hallway whose width equaled that of my bedroom, the room was light and spacious. A set of French doors opened to the balcony, and big windows looked out on the back gardens and to the water beyond. The first piece of furniture to catch my eye when the porter unlocked the door was the four-poster bed, with its fluffy white down comforter. *Happy birthday to me*, I said under my breath. A gas fireplace was set in the opposite wall, and with the flip of a switch a roaring fire added to the romantic ambiance. I peeked in the bathroom and spied a claw-foot tub that would easily accommodate two.

I unpacked my things and then walked out to the balcony.

The sun reflecting off the water sparkled like a thousand tiny diamonds. I leaned against the railing, my elbows resting on the upper crossbeam, and watched a group of brown pelicans dive into the water. The concierge had told me that dolphins often played in the surf around this time of day, and I kept my eyes trained for dorsal fins. It was mid afternoon, and a warm breeze rustled my skirt and passed gently across my face and arms. I took a deep breath and the ocean scent filled my nostrils.

Will was due any minute, and as I stood on the balcony watching the waves, I was glad I arrived before he did. I welcomed the little bit of time to myself. This was Will's and my first excursion together, and I was excited to see him, but also a little nervous. This trip—brief though it would be—seemed to represent some kind of milestone. The last time we spent a long weekend together was in San Sebastian, on my turf. Then, I felt safer. Now, however, the landscape was new to both of us. We were beginning to operate without a compass, so to speak, and the idea made me more than a little anxious as I continued to fret over Lizzy and Wiley—and the Hallorans. The more time Will and I spent together, and the closer we became, the more involved I'd have to be with his children—and, by extension, the rest of Joanna's family. And they, obviously, were not inclined to welcome me with open arms.

I was beginning to understand how my stepmother Lila might have felt.

I turned my attention to the activity on the beach and a group of what appeared to be college students who had lined up on opposite sides of a worn and sagging volleyball net. They laughed and called to one another as they passed the ball back and forth, and the sound carried all the way to my perch on the second floor. One of them had brought along a dog—a big chocolate Lab—that was running crazily among them, weaving in and out of the rows of players. Every so often he let out an excited bark, and someone would reach down and pat his head or scratch his ears or throw a smaller ball for him to chase. The dog reminded me of Bailey, and the students made me think of Ben and Justine. I smiled, remembering my conversation with Ben a few days earlier.

I knew from the beginning that Justine would have no issues with whatever relationship developed between Will and me. She had always been close to her father, and I encouraged that, even after Joe and I separated. I also suggested—rather adamantly—that she try to be friends with his new wife. Justine and I were also very close, and I had no fears about how a stepmother might impact our relationship—particularly that one.

Ben, however, was a different story. He didn't take the divorce well, and for more than a year, he laid the blame squarely at Joe's feet, no matter how much I tried to explain that his father and I just didn't belong together anymore. Somehow, Ben had learned the truth about Joe's infidelity, and he believed his father had betrayed not just me but the entire family. From the initial separation on, he refused to have any contact with him. Phone calls went unanswered, e-mails ignored, every overture rebuffed. Finally, out of desperation, Joe asked me to intercede on his behalf. I wasn't feeling particularly magnanimous, but for Ben's sake, I obliged. No matter what else, I didn't want my son to be estranged from his father.

I arranged to meet Joe for coffee one afternoon last summer, and convinced Ben to come along. After an hour of accusations, allegations, and arguments, they finally began listening to one another, and a fragile truce was achieved. Ben was willing at last to accept that things turned out the way they had to, and his parents could sit at a table and drink coffee together precisely because they had made the choice not to be married anymore.

Still, Ben became quite protective of me, and I wasn't sure how he would react to another man coming into my life. To my surprise—and relief—after the initial meeting, he was quite comfortable with it. In fact, when I told Ben I'd been considering spending my birthday on Bell Island with Will, he told me I should stop considering it and just do it.

I had just opened a bottle of water when I heard a knock on the door. I felt a rush of adrenaline, and my heart quickened. I hesitated before walking toward the door. This was the first time I'd seen Will since February, and although we'd spoken on the phone nearly every day, I wasn't sure what to expect. My fingers tingled, and I fumbled with the deadbolt before finally unlocking it. I opened the door, and saw him standing on the other side, holding a bouquet of flowers. His eyes sparkled and his mouth broke into a grin. I opened the door wide enough for him to step inside. He picked up his suitcase, and, once in the room, promptly let it drop to the floor along with the flowers. He gathered me to him as he pushed the door closed with his foot.

"God, I missed you," he murmured. His breath was warm on my neck. "I thought I'd never get here." He cupped my face and kissed me softly.

"So did I," I said, wrapping my arms around his neck and pressing my body against his. It felt so good to touch him again.

"Have you been here long?" he asked after a minute or so. "I can't believe how long that stupid flight was delayed. I was hoping to get here before you."

I pulled away slightly, looked up at him, and smiled. "Oh, I've been here for a little while," I replied, adding playfully, "but I've managed to wait patiently."

"Patiently!" he exclaimed, with mock indignation. "I don't know whether to be appreciative or disappointed. I sort of hoped you'd be breathless with anticipation."

"Well," I said, leaning in for another kiss, "you got the breathless part right."

When Will finally let go of me, he picked up the flowers and held them out to me. "Happy birthday," he said.

I fingered one of the creamy white roses and held the bouquet to my nose so I could breathe in its sweet fragrance. "They're beautiful. Thank you." I looked around the room and caught sight of a glass pitcher. I filled it with water, carefully arranged the flowers—a combination of roses, freesia, and purple and white calla lilies—and set them on the desk.

"They really are lovely," I said, turning to Will. He was stretched out on the bed, ankles crossed, and arms folded behind his head as he watched me tend the flowers. He extended a hand in my direction and I took a few steps toward him. He pulled me down so I was practically on top of him, the length of my body across his. I resisted playfully, pushing against his chest and raising my head so I could look at him.

"We have all night, you know." I squirmed slightly under the tight hold of his embrace.

"That and more," he replied. "And I plan to put every minute to good use." He kissed me then, deeply and soundly. I stopped squirming.

We rolled over so I was on my back and he lay on his side next to me, propping himself on his elbow. He undid one button of my blouse, and then another, and another. He pushed the fabric aside and lowered his face to my chest, kissing me lightly. The feel of his breath on my skin gave me goose bumps.

"Mmmm," I murmured, and stretched my arms above my head. He ran his hand along my thigh and up under my skirt. I was hypersensitive to his touch, almost as though electricity passed between us. I took a quick breath.

"We do have all night," he whispered, giving my neck a tiny bite, "but I'm thinking we should practice a little now to make sure we get it right later."

"You mean a dress rehearsal?" I asked, attending to the buttons on his shirt.

"Something like that," he replied, "but without the dress."

# 25

Will clicked on the light by the bed. We had fallen asleep, and when we awoke, the sun was just starting to set. Through the open window, I could hear the waves lapping at the shore.

He picked up his watch and checked the time. "Are you hungry?" he asked. "It's almost seven o'clock. Maybe we should think about getting ready for dinner. I believe our reservation is for eight."

"Mmm," I murmured, adjusting myself closer to him. "How about room service?"

"Can't get that here," he reminded me. "It's the dining room, or nothing until breakfast."

I tilted my head up and kissed him lightly. "Are you hungry?"

"Starving," he replied, returning the favor a little more fervently. "But I think I want dinner, too."

His stomach let out a growl just then and I laughed. "I guess you do."

He held me tightly to him. "What do you say we go to the dining room for dinner, but come back here for dessert?"

I started to scramble out of bed to take a shower, but Will caught my hand in his. He pulled me back under the covers for a few minutes. His body was warm and musky. I loved the smell of him—I always had.

He held me close, and I felt him take a long, slow breath.

I reached up and caressed his cheek with my thumb. He took my hand in his and pressed it to his lips. "I love you, Cal."

I smiled up at him. "Funny, I was just thinking the same thing about you."

He leaned over me and brought his face within inches of mine. "I love you," he whispered again, and kissed me fully and completely.

I jumped in the shower finally, and Will followed while I finished getting ready. I had brought a new dress—iridescent dark blue silk, cut in a low V-neck in both the back and front. With a single long strand of pearls around my neck and a gold bracelet on my wrist, the presentation was elegant but sexy.

Will let out a low whistle through his teeth when he saw me.

"Wow," he said. "Maybe we don't need dinner after all."

I picked up my small clutch and took a step toward the door. "No dinner, no dessert," I said smiling over my shoulder at him.

The dining room was small, with only a dozen or so tables, each formally set with crisp white linen, china, crystal, and silver. Most were already occupied, and the low hum of conversation floated around us like bees as we followed the maître d' to a table by the window. In the distance, moonlight floated on the water, creating a rippling effect that looked like ribbons of black-and-white satin.

Will held my chair for me and I sat down. He seated himself, and then reached for my hand. He brought it to his lips and very softly kissed my fingers.

"Happy birthday, Cal."

I smiled. "Thanks. But you do know it's not until tomorrow."

"I do," he replied.

I gazed across the table at him and thought how stunningly handsome he was. He wore a dark suit with a white shirt and a burgundy tie whose subtle geometric pattern, I saw upon closer inspection, resembled the work of M.C. Escher.

A candle flickered in the center of the table. It was set in a small hurricane lamp, surrounded by a ring of fresh flowers. The flame cast a soft glow across Will's face, making his eyes shine particularly brightly, especially when he smiled.

On Bell Island, dinner spanned several courses and lasted for hours. Each table had only one or two seatings, so everyone moved at a leisurely pace. The menu was limited, but the food was spectacular.

"I can't remember the last time I ate this well," I said, taking a bite of poached salmon. "This is absolutely delicious. A far cry from the micro-waved whatever I usually have for dinner."

Will chuckled. "No kidding."

"How do you deal with that at home?" I asked. "Dinner, I mean. Do you don a frilly apron and cook for everyone?"

Will cocked an eyebrow and leaned toward me. "Listen, if anyone dons a frilly apron, it'll be you," he said dryly, "but it won't be in the kitchen—well, not to cook, anyway." This time I chuckled—and looked down at my plate, slightly red-faced. Apparently I was wrong when I told Justine I was too old to be embarrassed by anything.

Will swallowed a bite of prime rib and shook his head. "As to the cooking," he continued, "I don't do it, but someone else does. Alex's wife, Julie, set it up. It's one of our two luxuries," he said. "I have someone who prepares meals—dinners, mainly. All I have to do is heat it up. Isabel—that's her name—comes to the house on Monday and brings all the ingredients for a week's worth of dinners. She cooks it all there and leaves it in the freezer."

"What a great idea."

"Well, between our school and work schedules—and that's not counting sports and other after-school stuff, and the puppy—there's no way I could add cooking into the mix, even if I wanted to, which I don't. And we can't be eating out all the time. Although there's the pizza place Wiley likes, and we go there almost every Friday. It's become sort of a tradition."

"So what's the other luxury?" I asked curiously.

"Someone who cleans the house every week," he replied. "Lizzy and Wiley have things they're supposed to do—and are constantly trying to argue their way out of doing—but I don't want them to get too wrapped up in stuff at home. It's hard enough for them. I don't want to dump too many responsibilities on them so soon."

I blotted my mouth with my napkin, thinking of all the years I spent cooking, cleaning, and doing laundry for my father. "I'm really impressed," I said. "And I don't mean that facetiously. It would be very easy to let—or even encourage—Lizzy to take on too much, given the circumstances. Wiley, too. You're really doing them a great service by allowing them to be kids, and only kids.

After the dinner plates had been removed from the table, I excused myself to visit the ladies' room. When I returned, a trio of musicians—two men and a woman—were just taking their places at a setup near a small wooden dance floor. The ensemble consisted of a vocalist—the woman—accompanied by a piano and a bass.

Will held out my chair again and I sat down.

"Looks like entertainment," he said with a nod toward the musicians.

"Wonderful," I replied.

The music began softly—a slow rendition of *Our Love Is Here to Stay*. The singer had a beautiful voice, sultry but clear. A few couples stepped onto the dance floor. I glanced at Will, whose odd half smile reminded me of a cat that had just feasted on a juicy canary.

I eyed him suspiciously, but he merely shrugged.

The song ended, and the few couples on the floor returned to their tables. The musicians whispered among themselves, and then the singer, a gorgeous blonde who looked as though she'd stepped out of a 1940s film noir, turned to the audience. She wore a long, sequined off-the-shoulder dress that fitted her form like a well-tailored glove. A silver bangle bracelet glittered in the narrow spotlight that illuminated the group.

Her gaze traveled over the audience as the music rose slowly. I recognized the tune after just a few notes. It was a favorite of mine, and Will knew it. I had told him so just last week when we were talking about music and what we considered the top songs of all time. He said it had to be something by Led Zeppelin; I argued in favor of Etta James's rendition of *At Last*.

Will stood and extended his hand to me. I rose, and he led me to the dance floor. He wrapped his arms around my waist, and I rested mine across his shoulders, my wrists crossed at the back of his neck. We swayed to the music, our eyes locked on one another's. The singer stepped toward the small microphone, took a deep breath, and began.

"At last, my love has come along ... my lonely days are over ... and life is like a song ..." Will rested his cheek against the side of my head. One arm stayed around my waist, and with the other he reached back for my hand and then held it between us. "Oh, yeah, yeah, at last ... the skies above are blue," the singer's smoky voice floated around us. "My heart was wrapped up in clover ... the night I looked at you..." Will twined one of my loose curls around his forefinger. I closed my eyes and melted into the music and him. "I found a dream that I could speak to ... a dream that I can call my own ... I found a thrill to press my cheek to ... a thrill that I have never known ..." Our bodies pressed together, we took small steps as we moved to the music. "Oh, yeah, yeah, you smiled, you smiled, and then the spell was cast ... and here we are in heaven ... for you are mine ... at last."

The music faded. I looked at Will. His eyes were the color of sapphires. "So," I murmured, smiling softly and raising one eyebrow, "are you ready for dessert?"

I awoke before dawn. The room was quiet and still. Out the window, the sun was just rising, and streaks of orange, pink, and lavender colored the sky. I moved closer to Will and rested my head on his chest, my hand lightly stroking his abdomen. I wished that I could freeze the moment—the feel of his warm skin, the quiet rhythm of his heartbeat, the slow rise and fall of his chest. I wanted to preserve this feeling of pure happiness, so I could wrap myself in it when he was in his place and I was in mine.

I felt him stir as he raised his hand to brush my hair away from his face. I angled my head upward. "Here we are in heaven," I whispered.

He opened his eyes and one corner of his mouth curved upward. "Happy birthday," he said, and rolled toward me.

Lying with Will afterward, basking in the warm peacefulness that spread through my body, I sighed contentedly.

The sun had risen, and the sound of birds chirping mingled with the voices of people walking along the path toward the beach and wafted in through the open window we'd never gotten around to closing the night before.

It didn't take long, however—even with my head on Will's chest, his fingers caressing my side, and our legs intertwined—for the familiar sense of dread to begin churning in the pit of my stomach. It was the warning not to get too comfortable. The reminder that one way or another—one day or another—Will would be gone.

I learned three important lessons early in life: nothing lasts, no one stays, and counting on anyone but myself invariably ends badly. I've often heard that for most children who lose a parent, abandonment—or, more specifically, the fear of it—becomes a lifelong adversary. It's always there, skulking in the background, waiting to move in when we aren't looking. That first separation—the one that cuts straight to the soul—never truly heals. And though we stitch it up or hold it together with Band-Aids and adhesive tape, every parting that comes after tears it open again.

In the interest of self-preservation, we avoid those partings simply by not allowing ourselves to become truly attached to anyone in the first place.

In the end, of course, all we manage to preserve is our own isolation. But it really doesn't matter.

With my children, I loved wholeheartedly, without reservation, and without fear. I had, for some reason, a strange intuition that they would always be safe—no major illness or accident would strike. Perhaps it was simply that I couldn't contemplate either possibility, but I preferred to believe they were the beneficiaries of some kind of cosmic protection. And so far, I'd been right.

With Will, though, it was different. I loved him completely—and, perhaps, recklessly. With Will, I felt a sense of wholeness, and of safety I'd never known with anyone else. When he headed off to Boston and shortly thereafter told me there was no room in his life for me—for us—I was like a turtle whose shell had been ripped from its body.

That protective covering grew back over time, but I kept myself at a safe emotional distance from everyone around me—even from Joe. Maybe that was part of the reason he formed attachments elsewhere. Maybe I had chosen Joe in the first place because I knew on some level that I'd never love him the way I'd loved Will, and that he preferred to maintain an emotional distance of his own anyway.

"Will you promise me something?" I asked Will, my voice barely audible. He bent his head toward mine and kissed me lightly on the forehead.

"Anything," he replied.

I didn't look at him, and my hand on his belly was still, except for my thumb, which continued to caress him softly, just beneath his breastbone. I hesitated for a few seconds and then spoke.

"Promise me that if there comes a time when you think you've stopped loving me, you'll be honest and tell me."

He snorted and chuckled. His arm was curled around me, his fingertips moving gently up and down my back from shoulder to hip. He brought his other arm around and settled me closer. "That will never happen," he murmured. "I will love you for the rest of my life."

"Maybe," I said. "But you don't know for sure. There aren't any guarantees. And I think I'd rather be alone than with someone who wishes he were somewhere else. I've done that once, and I just can't do it again." I paused for a moment before continuing. "Nor could I—" I stopped.

"Could you what?"

"...Could I live the way you did with Joanna."

Will inhaled sharply at that, and tightened his grip on my arm. I glanced up and saw that he'd closed his eyes, and a slightly pained expression marked his face. I'd hit a nerve, I knew, but I felt that—for both our sakes—I had to be honest. I'd spent more than twenty-five years in a marriage that, for the most part, I simply tolerated, even though it was to a man I respected and, in many ways, admired. I would not—could not—live under those circumstances again, even for a day.

"Will, please don't think I'm passing judgment. Truly, I'm not. What you and Joanna had was, well, between the two of you. It was whatever it needed to be, and I am in no position to say otherwise. It's just that—" I paused, carefully choosing my words. "After so many years of just okay, and not even that a lot of the time, I know what I want—and what I don't want—and I'm not willing to settle anymore."

I studied Will's face. His expression was unreadable. I couldn't tell whether he was hurt or angry or just pensive. I raised my hand to touch his cheek. "You're an honorable man, Will Tremaine. It's one of the things I love best about you. But I want you always to be honest—with me and with yourself."

I started to pull away from him slowly, but he raised himself abruptly, turning onto his side and propping his upper body on his elbow. His eyes sought mine and held them, as if by force. In his face, I could see anguish, concern, frustration, and love all battling each other. I could also see that he understood what I was telling him, what I was asking of him. He understood that what I wanted to avoid, at all costs, was a repeat of what he had with Joanna, and what I had with Joe.

He brushed a curl off my cheek. "I know that I will love you, always," he said quietly. "And I promise that I will tell you the truth—always. Even if it hurts."

# 26

The cobblestone streets and European-style architecture made the small town on Bell Island more akin to an old English village than to a twenty-first century municipality.

Will and I wandered up and down the quiet streets, pausing every so often to look in shop windows, or visit one of the numerous art galleries. It was early April, and while the spring equinox had marked the official end of winter a few weeks earlier, the weather was still a bit cool.

Turning a corner, we happened upon a tiny cottage, complete with thatched roof and glazed windows. A small sign affixed to the Dutch door identified it as a restaurant. Will suggested we stop in for lunch.

"I wonder which of the seven dwarfs we'll run into," he quipped as he opened the door for me.

I smiled. "If you're lucky, maybe Snow White will be our waitress."

Seated at a small wooden table, I commented on the decor, pointing out the exposed beam ceiling, the plaster walls, and general fairy-tale motif of the restaurant's interior. It was surprisingly authentic—based on what I remembered from the Grimms' fables I read to Justine when she was little.

"She loved them," I mused. "But she always listened with a very critical ear. I remember her asking why it was that biological mothers were generally absent, and stepmothers were always cruel."

"What did you tell her?" Will asked.

"Not to believe everything she read in fairy tales. Although," I admitted as an afterthought, "the more she saw my strained relationship with my step-mother, the more she thought there was some truth to them."

After lunch, we meandered down to the beach and strolled along the surf.

"This really is a wonderful way to spend a birthday," I said, taking Will's hand. "I'm glad you suggested it."

We were barefoot, having left our shoes on the grass, and the cold waves licked at our toes.

"So am I," Will said, and wrapped an arm around my waist. I moved closer to him and pressed my cheek to his chest as we walked, feeling the softness of his sweater and the strength of the muscles underneath.

After a while, Will checked his watch and suggested we turn back. It was late afternoon, and I was looking forward to a long bath before dinner. Passing through the gardens again on our way to the inn's main entrance, we came upon a secluded bench beneath one of the jacaranda trees. Will took my hand.

"Let's sit down for a minute, okay?"

I eyed him a bit suspiciously. "Okay."

He reached into his jacket pocket, withdrew a small box, and held it out to me. "This is for you," he said.

I glanced up at him and reached out tentatively to accept it. It was more rectangular than square, as though it might hold a necklace or a bracelet. Opening the box slowly, I did, indeed, find a necklace, and I gasped when I saw it—a single oval ruby, nearly an inch wide, set in a border of scalloped gold. It looked to be an antique.

"Oh, Will, it's beautiful," I exclaimed as I took the necklace from the box and held it by its gold chain. "It's absolutely beautiful!"

Will flushed slightly. "It belonged to my mother. It's been in the family for a long time. She got it from my grandmother, who, I think, got it from my great-grandmother."

I gazed at the pendant, slightly stunned. I actually recognized it. Even after all these years. "I don't know what to say. It's just … it's so beautiful."

Will took the necklace from me. "Here—let me put it on you."

I turned and pulled my hair up off my neck so he could clasp the chain. I swiveled back to face him and let my hair fall. I fingered the pendant where it rested against my chest, just below the hollow of my neck. "Well, what do you think?"

"You're right," Will replied. "It is beautiful. And so are you." He leaned forward and kissed me. "Happy birthday."

Although the claw-foot tub in the bathroom was, indeed, big enough for two, right now I had it all to myself and I was enjoying every inch of it.

Completely stretched out, I luxuriated in the hot water and the lavender and rose-scented bubbles. My hair was pulled up in a clip, with only a few tendrils falling across my shoulders. Closing my eyes, I rested my head against the terry cloth bath pillow and swirled my hands in the water, sending soft ripples across my body.

Will was in the bedroom, on the phone first with Lizzy and then with Wiley. The quiet murmur of his voice floated around me. I couldn't tell what he was saying, but his words were punctuated occasionally by laughter. Lizzy and Wiley must have been enjoying themselves. I heaved a sigh of relief for Will's sake. He didn't mention it, but I knew he was worried about them—particularly Wiley. He would be more relaxed knowing his children were happy and having a good time.

He walked in a few minutes later and perched on the edge of the tub. I opened my eyes and smiled at him. "Why don't you come in? The water's fine."

No further invitation required, he undressed and joined me.

"Is this not a little bit of heaven?" I asked as I stroked his chest and shoulders. He sat with his back pressed against me, and my knees on either side of him.

He closed his eyes and exhaled, resting his head against my chest. "More than a little. I could stay like this forever." He caressed my lower legs.

"So the kids are okay?"

"Yeah, they're fine. Having a great time."

"I'm glad."

We both sat quietly for a few minutes. I had taken off the ruby necklace before getting in the bath and set it in a crystal bowl on the counter. I glanced over at it.

"Will, can I ask you something about the necklace?" I spoke cautiously.

"Sure," he replied. "What?"

I hesitated before continuing. I didn't want to bring up what might be a sore subject. "Had you ... I mean ... after your mother ... did you ..."

A smile hinted at the corners of his mouth. He knew what I wanted to ask. "Had I given it to Joanna before giving it to you? Is that what you want to know?"

"It would make sense if you had."

He brought his hands up to my knees. "It might, but, no, I didn't."

As much as I hated to admit it, I was relieved. Stunning as the necklace was, I couldn't have worn it knowing it had once adorned the décolletage of his first wife.

"There were a few things Joanna wanted—or wanted to save for Lizzy—but I held on to this one," Will said. "I'm not sure why."

I sat quietly, not moving, pondering the red stone in the crystal dish. "I remember her wearing it once," I said. "Your mom, I mean." Will twisted around and glanced at me, surprised. "It was on Thanksgiving—the last one you and I spent together." He faced forward again, but I could tell he was listening carefully. "I commented on it when she and I were in the kitchen, and she told me how she'd always preferred rubies to diamonds. She said diamonds represent love and purity, but rubies are the stone of love and passion. I've never forgotten that."

Will sat up and turned his body so he almost faced me. I moved across him and straddled his hips. He leaned against the back of the tub and pulled me closer. With his hands resting lightly on my waist, he kissed me long and deep. "Love and passion, huh?" he asked when we stopped for breath. "I guess she was right. Smart woman, my mother."

All too quickly, the three days at Bell Island came to an end and Will and I found ourselves at the small airport waiting to board separate planes.

"I think this has been the best birthday I've ever had," I said as I stood at the gate waiting for the boarding call. My flight took off a little less than an hour before his. "If they're all like this, I may not mind marking the occasion on a regular basis—even if it does mean acknowledging I'm a year older."

"You may be older," Will said with a twinkle in his eye, "but you're also most definitely better—if you know what I mean."

I felt myself blush. "Well," I said, looking up at him and smiling sweetly, "you're not bad yourself, old man."

# 27

While the academic powers that be had lists of required reading for all the English classes, I sought to expand the literary experience of my students—not to mention their critical thinking skills—by studying a quote or passage from what I—and sometimes they—considered an important work. After discussing it briefly in class, the students would write a paragraph about how it might apply to themselves or their lives.

The whole purpose of the assignment was to encourage them to stretch their minds, and to develop a healthy respect for their own ideas.

This week's selection—*A foolish consistency is the hobgoblin of little minds*—came from Emerson's essay on self-reliance. It was one of my favorite quotes. I heard it first when I was my students' age, in a classroom discussion about freedom of thought and the inherent danger of clinging to a particular way of thinking or being. As I read Emerson's words again tonight, I thought of Eleanor Halloran and the meaning she might derive from them.

I had just crawled into bed with a stack of papers and was about to begin reading when the telephone rang. Startled, I glanced at the clock, which was partially hidden by my teacup. Ten thirty. All at once, my maternal alarm sounded.

I exhaled with relief when I saw Will's name on the caller ID.

"Is this a bad time?" he asked. "Am I interrupting anything?"

"No, no, not at all," I said. "I'm just sitting in bed getting ready to read over some essays. When the phone rang I thought it might be Justine. But I'm glad it's you." I smiled as I spoke.

"Well, I just sent Lizzy to bed, and I wanted to talk to you before I hit the sack myself. The ER was really busy today and I'm beat."

"Anything particularly interesting?"

"Not really. Just a lot of it. How are you?"

I settled back against the pillows. Bailey wiggled his way up the bed until he had stretched out against my legs. He licked at the air a few times, twitched his ear once or twice, and dozed off.

"I wish you were here. I miss you."

He chuckled softly. "I miss you, too. After the last few days I've had, I'd give anything to be able to crawl into bed with you and shut out the entire world."

"So I guess absence really does make the heart grow fonder," I teased. I reached down and scratched Bailey behind his ear. He let out a quiet groan and adjusted himself into a more comfortable position.

"That it does," Will said. "I've been thinking about you all day." He paused for a few seconds. "I want you something fierce," he said evenly, and then, almost as an afterthought, "There is way too much geographic distance between us."

"I know." Now it was my turn to pause. "So, tell me, what *would* you do if you were here?" As I contemplated the possibilities, my whole body began to feel warmer, as though the temperature in the room had risen by several degrees.

"I would touch you all over," he murmured. "I'd kiss your neck just below your ears and then the space where your collarbones meet. And as long as I'm in the vicinity, I'd move to that smooth place between your breasts, and I'd keep moving downward until I was, well…"

As if drawn by his words, my fingers immediately went first to my chest and then to my abdomen in a light, feathery touch.

"Is that all?" I asked a little coyly. "I mean, as pleasant as that would be, it hardly seems worth making the trip."

"Oh, it'd be worth it," Will assured me. "It would definitely be worth it."

I did wish he were here. I longed for the touch of his fingers caressing the curve of my waist and hips. I wanted to taste his lips, feel the tautness of his muscles, and see the look in his eyes as his body hovered over mine. And I wanted to hear his quiet sigh of pleasure as he came into me.

Forcing myself back to reality, I took a deep breath, shook my head slightly, and changed the subject.

"So," I asked, "How are Lizzy and Wiley? And what's been going on the last few days?"

"Aarghh," Will grumbled good-naturedly. "I was just in the middle of a great fantasy. They're fine. Well, Wiley's fine. Lizzy's more—" He paused briefly. "Uh…more challenging."

"Lizzy's a girl. And a teenager. Challenging is in her job description."

"It's not just that. She's—" He spoke carefully. "She is aware of you—of us—and she's let me know in no uncertain terms what she thinks about it."

"Ah," I replied, my body temperature cooling significantly. So that's why the only communication I'd had from him since Sunday afternoon were a few brief text messages. "And what terms were those?"

"Well, they involved a lot of tears and a lot of anger."

Although Will had made it clear to the Hallorans that he would be the one to tell Lizzy and Wiley about us—and would do so when he decided the time was right—Rowan seemed to believe she was the better judge of what Lizzy should know and when she should know it, particularly as it related to her father's "involvement" with another woman.

The children had spent the weekend with the Hallorans, Will said, and Rowan took Lizzy shopping on Sunday. Over lunch, Rowan just happened to mention that she'd heard about Will's "new girlfriend." She asked Lizzy's opinion, knowing full well Lizzy had no idea what she was talking about. When it all came out, Lizzy not only perceived a threat to her family but felt betrayed by her father because he hadn't told her himself.

"Needless to say," Will noted, "she didn't take it well."

When he arrived to pick her up late Sunday afternoon, all hell had broken loose. He found Lizzy huddled on the couch in the living room, sobbing into a pillow. Eleanor sat beside her, rubbing her back and stroking her hair. "Lizzy, sweetheart, you have to calm down. You'll make yourself sick."

Rowan, Will commented, was in her usual spot, wineglass in hand, looking very smug and self-satisfied.

Alarmed, Will rushed to his daughter and squatted down so he could be at eye level. "Lizzy, what's wrong? Tell me what's the matter so I can help you."

Lizzy raised her head. "You can't help me!" she screamed. "I hate you!" She buried her face in the pillow and dissolved into sobs again.

Will touched Lizzy's shoulder, but she jerked away from him and pressed herself against Eleanor. He looked helplessly from Lizzy to Eleanor to Rowan and back to Eleanor. "Someone please tell me what's going on!"

Rowan spoke first. "Apparently your daughter doesn't welcome the idea of having a new mother."

"What the hell are you talking about?" he demanded.

"Will, please." Eleanor addressed him calmly. "Please don't use that language here, particularly in front of Lizzy."

"She'll hear a lot worse than that if someone doesn't tell me what's going on!"

Lizzy faced him, her eyes blazing. "Aunt Rowan told me about your girl-friend," she snarled. "She thought I knew about it, but I didn't because you didn't tell me! You lied to me! You've been lying to me!"

Will turned to Rowan, who raised her eyebrows and shrugged lightly.

"Can't argue with the truth," she said.

Teeth clenched and jaw tightened, Will rose and faced his sister-in-law. He opened his mouth to speak, but stopped himself.

Rowan leaned forward, looking up at him. "Someone has to look after Lizzy and Wiley. And, obviously, that's not you. Not when you're busy sleep-ing with—"

"Don't," Will cut in. He glanced at Lizzy and back to Rowan. "Don't."

Rowan sat back against the cushion, rested her elbow on the arm of the chair and brought two fingers to her mouth as though holding her lips closed. Silent, she directed her attention to the picture window on the far side of the room.

Will turned back to Lizzy and touched her arm. She wrenched herself away from him again.

"Lizzy, we have to talk," he said softly. "But just you and me. C'mon, let's go home."

"I don't want to go home with you," she cried. "I don't want to go any-where with you—ever!"

Will took a deep breath, working to maintain his composure. "Lizzy, we're leaving. Go get your things."

"I told you, I don't want to go anywhere with you. I don't want to go home," she shot back. "Gran was right—you are a bad father!"

Will blanched as Lizzy's words sliced through him.

"Really, Will," Eleanor broke in, "as upset as she is, why not just let her stay here and calm down a bit? Chase can bring her home a little later."

Will responded with an angry stare. The last thing he intended to do was leave his daughter to the further manipulations of her grandmother and aunt. If Lizzy didn't come home now—with him—it would be much more difficult to get her there later.

He turned to his daughter. "I'm afraid you don't have a choice. You are coming home with me. Now go upstairs and get your things."

Lizzy glared at him, and he stared back just as fiercely.

"Lizzy, you're coming with me—now—whether you have your things or not," he said firmly. "Your choice."

She heaved an angry sigh, got up, and stomped out of the room.

Will turned to Rowan. "Satisfied?"

"Don't blame me," Rowan replied. "You're the one who started all of this by bringing another woman into Joanna's bed."

Will eyed her, stone-faced. "I'm not having this discussion with you, Rowan. What I do with my life is none of your business."

She stood abruptly and took a step toward Will. Her face was inches from his. "That may be," she hissed, "but what you do with Joanna's children *is* my business."

Eleanor remained silent, but nodded in agreement.

Will glanced from one to the other. "If you think you can control me—or Lizzy and Wiley—you are mistaken. They are my children. Do you understand that? Mine. And I'll decide what's best for them."

"I tell you, I have never been so furious with anyone before," Will said to me. "Rowan used Lizzy as a pawn to get to me, without any consideration for how it would impact her. And then she had the balls—and I do mean balls—to say it's my fault because I am the one who brought you into their lives. I swear, if I'd had a baseball bat I would have used it on her, Hippocratic oath or not."

When Lizzy came back downstairs, Will said, he planted his hand on her shoulder and directed her toward the door.

"She was totally silent in the car. She refused to look at me, and as soon as we got home, she ran up to her room and slammed the door. I tried to talk to her, but she didn't want to have anything to do with me."

As the main antagonist at the center of this drama, I wasn't sure what to say. It was all sounding so ugly that my first inclination was to suggest that Will and I just call it quits and save everyone the grief. But it wouldn't help. Not at this moment.

"I'm so sorry, Will." I couldn't think of anything else to say.

"What's really hard," he went on, "is that Lizzy and I have always been able to talk about things, especially since Joanna died. She's always come to me with problems or issues because she wants me—her father—to help her work them out. But in this case, I'm the problem."

"No, I'm the problem. And it seems Rowan is hell-bent on taking advantage of it."

Eventually, he said, Lizzy had come out of her room, eyes red and swollen from crying. Still, she refused to speak to Will, and maintained her silence for a full two days. It wasn't until this evening that she was willing to sit in the same room with him.

"She told me she couldn't trust me anymore because I'd kept this secret from her," Will explained. "And worse than that, she said, is that I'm not being loyal to her mother. I'm acting like she never existed. I swear, even though they weren't there, I could hear Rowan—and Eleanor—coaching every word she said."

The war has commenced, I thought to myself. But this was just the first skirmish. What would it look like when they brought out the big guns?

"How did you respond?" I asked, my finger absently tracing one of the embroidered flowers on the quilt.

"I told her the truth," he replied. "Like I always do."

"What did you tell her?"

"That I've met someone who has become very important to me. That we knew each other a long time ago, that we ran into each other unexpectedly, and that it happened long after their mother died. But I also told her how much I love her and Wiley—and their mom—and that nothing would change that, no matter what. And I reminded her that Joanna would always be their mother, and no one would ever take her place."

"I think you handled it really well," I said quietly. I tried to ignore the tiny stab of jealousy that rose in my chest when Will used the words "love" and "Joanna" in the same reference. Of course he loved her, I scolded myself. He had married her. And he'd be married to her still if she hadn't separated herself from him. What's more, she was the mother of his children, and he would—should—always love her if for no other reason than that. He owed it to them.

"What did she say to that?"

He drew a breath, cleared his throat, and exhaled loudly. "Well, I think she appreciated it, particularly what I said about her and Wiley and Joanna. She's definitely not happy about you and me, and I'm willing to accept that for now, but I'm not willing to let her—or anyone else—direct my life."

"But they will direct your life, Will. They already have—or have begun to, anyway. This thing with Lizzy is just a sample of what they—well, Rowan, at least—are willing to do. It's going to be really hard."

"They tried with Lizzy, but they didn't succeed," he argued. "And besides, Lizzy and Wiley are *my* kids. If Eleanor and Rowan want to cause trouble, I'll just keep Lizzy and Wiley away from them. I'm their father. I can do that."

"Like I said, it's going to be hard. Everything is so complicated."

Will was silent for a moment and then said calmly, "Actually, it isn't." He seemed to have experienced an epiphany of some kind. "I love my kids, and I love you. I love you. It's that simple."

I'd have given anything to believe the situation really was so simple. But nothing is, particularly where families and love and loss are concerned. Rowan and her mother were clinging to whatever they could in a vain attempt at keeping Joanna alive. Will moving on—and taking his children with him—was, to them, the first step in erasing her memory, and they would take whatever action they deemed necessary to prevent it. Anyone hurt along the way was simply collateral damage.

On the other hand, I thought, maybe Will had it right. Maybe the love that existed *was* all that mattered—our love for each other, his love for his children and theirs for him, and even the love, or at least affection, that would, I hoped, grow between his children and me. Any obstacles Rowan and Eleanor threw in our way were, in reality, nothing more than a hindrance. They would affect us only to the extent we allowed them to. So maybe at the most basic level, it really was simple. All that mattered was that we loved each other.

My throat tightened and I coughed lightly. "So what are you thinking?"

"I'm thinking you should come to Westin and meet my kids," he said. "I'm thinking it's time to make this official."

# 28

Walking out of the air-conditioned terminal into the Westin heat was like hitting a wall. Even in early summer the air was thick, and I stopped for a moment to acclimate myself. Living so close to the ocean, I was accustomed to cooler, more temperate weather. The high temperatures would take some getting used to.

I sat down on a bench to await the arrival of the shuttle bus that would take me to the car rental counter. Miranda wanted to meet me at the airport, but I told her I'd rather pick up a car and drive to her place myself. I wanted access to a motor vehicle for the short time I'd be with her so I wouldn't have to rely on her for transportation or inconvenience her by using her car. More important, I wanted to have the means for making a quick getaway should the weekend with Will and his children go less than swimmingly.

I decided to arrive early and give myself some time with Miranda. I was more than a little nervous about meeting Will's kids, and she'd bring a dose of equanimity to an otherwise charged situation. Besides, it would give her and Will a chance finally to meet officially.

After a couple of days with Miranda, I'd move to a hotel more centrally located in Will's area for the weekend proper. That would give the four of us—Lizzy, Wiley, Will, and me—only one full day in one another's company. And really, how much conflict and discord could develop in so short a period of time?

Miranda came out to greet me when she saw me turn into her driveway. "You can take the same room you had the last time you were here," Miranda said as we walked arm in arm up the pathway to the front door.

Standing in the foyer with my small suitcase in tow, I caught a glimpse out the big windows in the living room and gasped. The hillside was swathed in pinks and violets and reds and oranges. It was a far cry from the solid white snowbanks that covered the ground when I was here at Christmas.

"Beautiful, isn't it?" Miranda noted. "It's a pretty incredible sight to wake up to every morning." She turned toward the kitchen. "Are you hungry?"

"Not really," I replied. "I think I'll go upstairs and unpack a couple of things."

"Well, *mi casa es su casa*, as they say, so make yourself at home." She disappeared into the other room.

I pulled a pair of slacks, a couple of skirts, and a cotton blouse out of my suitcase and hung them in the closet. I was excited about being in Westin. Excited about seeing Will, though my feelings were most definitely tempered by a sense of trepidation. His children would hate me. I knew it as well as I knew my own name. And I wasn't looking forward to it. I was entirely sympathetic to their feelings—I knew from whence they came—and I was entirely certain that nothing I said or did would alter them. My only strategy could be to give them time—to give all of us time. Time for me to show that I didn't want to take their mother from them; time for Will to demonstrate that Joanna was as important to them—and him—as she ever was; and time for them to get used to someone new in their father's life.

I didn't expect Lizzy or Wiley to approach the situation with any more enthusiasm than Lucas and I did when my father brought Lila home. But I was bound and determined not to make the same mistakes she did.

"So, what time are we meeting your Prince Charming?" Miranda asked when I joined her in the kitchen. "And where?"

"Um, seven o'clock, I think. He's going to call me when he's finished at the hospital," I replied. "As to the where, I don't think that's been figured out."

I hesitated, and Miranda glanced over at me. "Why the frown?"

"Well, I'm just thinking that maybe we shouldn't meet Will tonight. Maybe it should be just you and me. I hate to breeze in here, take advantage of your hospitality, and then—I don't know—it just seems rude to create a threesome."

Miranda looked at me reprovingly. "Are you kidding? We'll have plenty of girl time." She filled two glasses with cold sparkling water and handed one to me. "And I want to get to know this guy. I've heard a lot about him over the last fifteen years, and my curiosity is killing me. I want to decide for myself how much of your description of him is true and how much is exaggeration." She winked. "Given the fact that you are head over heels—and don't try to tell me otherwise—I'm not sure I can trust your judgment."

It was closer to seven thirty when we finally met Will. The restaurant, some new place Miranda suggested, wasn't far from her house. I offered to drive, but she insisted on taking her car so that, should the need arise, she could see herself home. She was counting on Will and me finding a way to have some time alone. I assured her that was unlikely—he did have children at home, after all. But she was adamant, and I just gave in. Debates with Miranda were futile. She was especially gifted in the art of rhetoric, and arguing with her was a no-win proposition. Little wonder she had the highest conviction rate of anyone in the Westin district attorney's office.

We hadn't made reservations, and by the time we arrived at the restaurant a line had already formed. Miranda went inside to put her name on the list while I waited on the sidewalk. Looking toward the parking lot, I kept my eyes peeled for Will's dark hair. My attention was so focused that I didn't hear his footsteps when he walked up behind me. Feeling hands on my waist, I let out an involuntary cry and spun around.

"Hey, it's me," Will said, touching my cheek. "It's me." He smiled, pulled me into an embrace, and held me tightly.

"God, I've missed you," he said when he finally let go.

I took his hand. "Me, too."

Looking over Will's shoulder, I saw Miranda approaching. I nodded in her direction. "Here comes Miranda."

Will turned around.

"So, Prince Charming, we meet again." She held out her hand to him.

Will looked at me quizzically. "What?"

"Prince Charming," I explained, giving my friend a cold stare. "It's Miranda's attempt at humor."

The two shook hands. "I'm glad to meet you—officially," Will said. "I'm not sure the time in the ER really counts."

"No, I don't think it does," Miranda said with a warm smile.

We followed the hostess to a table outside. Will held the chair for me and I sat down. He started to do the same for Miranda, but she had already settled herself across from me. Will took a seat between us.

"So," he said, resting his forearms on the table, "Callie says you work in the DA's office. That must be interesting."

"Most of the time," she responded. "But let's talk about you."

As it turned out, Miranda was right about bringing her own car. Will and

I did split off after dinner, although it wasn't of our own volition. Miranda had gotten a phone call from one of her own gentleman friends inviting her to a spur-of-the-moment gathering of some mutual acquaintances. A friend from law school was passing through town, and they were all meeting for drinks.

"Well, this works out perfectly," she said as we walked to the parking lot. "You two go on and do whatever it is you're going to do." She gave me a conspiratorial wink. "You have a key, right?"

I checked my purse. "Yup. Right here."

"So, Prince Charming," she said, giving Will a brief hug, "I look forward to seeing you again soon." Will returned the gesture. "Have fun, you two," she said as she turned toward her car.

"Where to?" Will asked. We were sitting in his car, wondering what to do next.

"I don't know. What do you have in mind?"

"You know what I have in mind."

I chuckled softly.

"No, not that—well, yeah, that, but mostly I just want to be alone with you." He dropped his gaze to his lap. "The kids are with their grandparents tonight, so we could go to—"

"No," I said emphatically.

"What?"

"Not your house. I don't belong there, and I don't want to be there."

"But—"

"No."

He paused. "I suppose you're right." He scanned the view from one side of the windshield to the other, his knuckle set against his upper lip. "This is ridiculous," he muttered. "We're like teenagers with no place to go."

I understood his frustration. I felt it, too. Absence had made my heart— and a lot more—grow quite a bit fonder.

I looked out the passenger side window and studied the scenery. The parking lot was emptying—it wasn't particularly late, but people who'd been out to dinner were beginning to move on. "There," I said, nodding toward a hotel on the corner. It was a Marriott, or Hilton, or Holiday Inn, or some other large chain.

I turned back to him and raised an eyebrow, questioning. His mouth curved into a smile and he started the engine.

It was a nondescript room, but when the door closed behind us, it was ours.

Will held me close, his arms completely enfolding me. I felt the heat of his body through the lightweight fabric of his shirt.

"I'm not accustomed to renting a room for just a few hours," I murmured as I ran my hands across his chest. "Seems a little bit sinful."

He lowered his face, barely brushing my lips with his own.

"Shh," he whispered, and set his soft, warm mouth on mine.

It was pure bliss to lie with Will in the quiet of the hotel room. We hadn't seen each other since April, and I relished the simple act of reaching over and touching him. I think that's what I hated most about the long-distance aspect of our relationship—not feeling his physical presence every day.

I had my own life to keep me occupied, but at night, after dark, lying in bed with only Bailey for company, I longed for the feel and the taste and the smell of him.

"The telephone just can't compare, can it?" I was lying next to him, my head on his chest and my hand stroking his abdomen.

He ran his hand up and down my arm. "Do you think we'll ever get tired of this?"

I adjusted the sheets and then tilted my head up and kissed the hollow space just above his collarbone. "I can't imagine so—we're making up for a lot of time." I was silent for a few minutes before continuing. "Can I tell you something?"

His hand stopped moving on my arm. "Well, that sounds kind of ominous. Is it something I'll want to hear?"

"It's about Joe and me."

"You want to talk about that now? Here?" Will exclaimed, his free hand gesturing toward the sheets and blankets.

Ignoring his question, I sat up and pushed my hair away from my face. "Actually, it's more about me."

He spoke tentatively. "All right." He was lying on his back with one arm bent and his hand behind his head. The fingertips of his other hand very lightly caressed my bare thigh. It felt like a feather brushing across my skin. His eyes, though, were serious.

"After my mom died," I began hesitantly, "and maybe even before, while she was sick, I always felt like I was invisible. Everyone was so wrapped up in their own grief it was like they forgot Lucas and I even existed."

I ran my thumbnail along the edge of the sheet. "And after a while, it began to feel like we were invisible. It seemed that only some people saw us, and even then, it was only sometimes, and usually only for a little while."

I took his hand and interlaced my fingers with his.

"But when you and I were together—in college, I mean—I didn't feel invisible. I felt real. And safe. And happy."

I dropped my eyes to our hands, linked together in my lap.

"And when we split up, well, it was like I became invisible again."

Will squeezed my hand. "Callie, I am so sorry for all of that. Like I said before, I was young and stupid. I had no idea what I was doing."

I rested my other hand on his. "No, that's not what I'm getting at. What I want to say is that I continued to feel invisible until Joe came along. He saw me. And I felt real again. And I was so afraid of going back to being invisible, that when he asked me to marry him, I said yes. Except, I didn't really love him. I don't think I was capable of loving anyone. Maybe not even you."

I pressed my fingertips against my temples, beginning to question the wisdom of having embarked on this conversation. What I was saying made no sense to him, and not even that much to me right now. But I went on.

"In a way, I think I did Joe a disservice through practically our entire marriage. It wasn't fair for me to promise something I knew I couldn't deliver."

Will pulled his hand away. "Well, he found ways to take care of himself. I don't think you have anything to feel guilty about." He folded his arms across his chest.

"I'm not talking about that, either," I replied, dropping my hands to my lap. "The fact is, when I married Joe, I didn't know how to love anyone."

My eyes locked on Will's. "What I'm trying to say is, I love you. I really love you. I mean, I finally know how. It took a lot of years, but I finally learned that I am not invisible—no matter what. And I never was."

I stretched out next to Will again and nestled into the crook of his shoulder. He wrapped both arms around me and pressed my body to his. He was warm and strong. "I guess what I'm really trying to say," I concluded with a sigh, "is that I don't think I'll ever get tired of this."

He kissed my forehead, just on the side. "Well, you're real to me, and thank God for it. And," he added, rolling toward me, "I'm pretty damn sure I won't get tired of this, either."

# 29

Miranda had told her secretary she wouldn't be in until the afternoon, so we enjoyed a lazy breakfast around midmorning. In a display of culinary skill that rivaled her Christmas performances, she greeted me with pancakes, sausage, and good strong coffee.

"Mmmm, this is the best!" I said, savoring the steaming brew. "You and Ben make the best coffee. It must be an innate ability, because I sure can't do it."

"Well, enjoy," Miranda said. She set plates of pancakes and sausage on the table and sat down across from me.

"So, how was your evening?" she asked as she drenched her plate with warm maple syrup. "Though I'm sure I can guess." She sucked a drop off her finger. "You got in when? Two?"

"Closer to five," I corrected her. "And we had a wonderful time, thank you." I took a bite of sausage.

"Take you back to his place, did he?"

"He wanted to, but I refused."

She looked at me quizzically. "What do you mean you refused? Why? Were his kids home?"

"No, his kids weren't home." I poured some syrup onto my plate. "But I just don't think it's right for me to be there. It's his home. Their home. And I'm including his first wife in that."

"Ah. I see."

I cut off a bite-size piece of pancake and dipped it in the syrup. "It just doesn't feel right. And to tell you the truth, I don't want to be in the place where he lived with her. And I sure as hell don't want to be in their bed."

"So what did you do?"

"Went to a hotel. One on the corner, near the restaurant."

"Have you thought about where you'll live when you get married?" Miranda pierced a sausage link with her fork.

"Don't you think you're putting the cart before the horse? We haven't even talked about marriage."

She looked up from her plate. "Oh, you're altar-bound all right. It's just a matter of time."

I took a bite and chewed contemplatively.

"To tell you the truth, if Will and I were to get married, staying here would probably be easier for the kids, but I don't relish the idea of living in the city where he and Joanna spent their life together—even if you're here."

Miranda helped herself to another sausage. "Well, I get your point, and I certainly can't say I blame you."

When we finished, I stood up and carried my plate to the sink. "By the way, I hope you aren't counting on me for dinner tonight. Will made tentative plans for us to meet up with Alex Merritt and his wife. I think I told you about him—he and Will have worked together for years."

Miranda walked toward me and I took her plate. "Oh, thanks," she said. "Actually, it's fine. I have some things to take care of, and since I'm not going into the office until this afternoon, it will give me time later." She snapped the cap on the maple syrup bottle and put it in the refrigerator. "But don't stay out too late this time—I'll want a full report."

# 30

Alex's wife, Julie, answered the door when Will rang the bell. In one hand he held a bottle of wine; the other rested lightly on my lower back. I felt the pressure of his fingertips through the thin cotton of my blouse. I was nervous, although I couldn't say exactly why.

"Come in, come in," Julie said, opening the door all the way.

Will handed the bottle to her as he stepped inside, and at the same time they kissed one another's cheeks. She patted him on the back. "Alex is on the patio, manning the barbecue." She turned her gaze to me. "And you must be Callie. Will has told us all about you, and we've been so excited about finally meeting you."

"Thanks," I replied huskily. "So have I." Not the least bit shy in most situations, I found myself, for some reason, completely tongue-tied.

Casually dressed in faded jeans, a violet tank top, and a sheer floral tunic that complimented her long frame, Julie had an air of dignified informality. Her shoulder-length black hair, slightly wavy, was cut in layers that curled around her face, and long bangs swept to the side revealed deep-set brown eyes. She smiled easily, and I had an immediate sense of warmth and easy friendliness.

She closed the front door just in time to keep a couple of small dogs from dashing out to the yard. I recognized them as a pair of Welsh corgis, a breed I knew from my adolescent days as a pet sitter. A neighbor had one—Mr. Peeps—and she hired me to look after him when she traveled.

"Aren't they adorable," I said, bending down to pat the dogs as they danced around my feet. "What are their names?"

"That one's Melly—short for Melanie," she replied, pointing to a tan and white female that couldn't have been more than twelve inches tall. "And that one over there is Ashley Wilkes." With his oversized pricked

168

ears and similar coloring, the male very closely resembled his female counterpart.

I smiled at her and she rolled her eyes.

"They already had names when we got them," she explained. "I recently inherited them from an elderly aunt who was, as you can guess, an avid fan of *Gone With the Wind*."

"I'm surprised she didn't call them Scarlett and Rhett," I quipped, patting Ashley Wilkes behind the ear and then standing up straight.

"Her lovebirds had that honor," Julie noted as she turned toward the kitchen, "and fortunately for us, they went to someone else." She handed Will a basket of tortilla chips and a bowl of salsa. "Do me a favor and take these out back, would you? And make sure Alex isn't setting the backyard on fire or smoking out the neighbors."

Julie offered me a glass of wine, and I followed her out to the patio, where Alex was, indeed, tending the barbecue. Will stood beside him, a bottle of Guinness in hand. He brightened when he saw me, and gestured for me to join them. I sidled up to him and he wrapped his arm around my waist.

"Alex Merritt," he said almost triumphantly, "this is Callie Winwood." Pointing with his bottle, he added, "Callie, this is Alex—friend, colleague, and grill master."

"My pleasure," Alex said, reaching out to shake my hand. "I've heard a lot about you." He nodded toward Will. "I've been looking forward to meeting the woman who has occupied this man's every non-work-related thought."

I glanced at Will, raised an eyebrow, and smiled. He bowed his head self-consciously.

"Well, thanks," I said, taking Alex's hand. "I'm glad to meet you, too."

He was tall—as tall as Will—clean-shaven, with close-cropped black hair. He was muscular, but in a way that suggested general strength as opposed to bodybuilding. He wore khaki pants and a light-blue polo shirt that brought out the warm brown of his skin tone. He had a calm manner, and, like his wife, smiled easily.

I peeked over at the barbecue. "So, what's on the menu, grill master?"

It was a warm evening. The sky was clear and dark, and the branches of the trees swayed in a wisp of a breeze. We sat on the patio after dinner, drinking wine and eating strawberries. Will, who'd known Alex and Julie for years, interacted easily with them. I, however, felt like an outsider, a status highlighted by the inside jokes and references to people, places, and circumstances that were entirely unfamiliar to me. I found myself sitting back in my chair and listening attentively, but having no idea who or what they were talking about.

"I'm sorry," Will said following one such exchange when he realized I had been excluded from the conversation. "That was rude." His arm rested across the back of my chair, and he brushed my shoulder with his thumb.

"No, it's fine, really." I leaned forward and away from him, crossing my forearms on the table. "You all have a long history together. I understand. Honestly."

Julie put her hand on mine. "You're right—the three of us do have a long history," she said, tilting her head in the direction of Will and Alex, "but the four of us have an even longer future." She squeezed my hand. I heaved a sigh of relief, only then realizing why I'd been so anxious.

Alex and Julie were Will's friends. Will and Joanna's. They had been a part of his life with her. I had a subconscious fear that, despite their innate kindness, they wouldn't accept me. Or, worse, they would consider me a sorry replacement for Joanna—the woman who should be here.

"Callie, I'll tell you something." Alex leaned forward. "I've known this guy for a long time." He looked over at Will, who cast a wary eye in return. "And I know what he's been through. He probably told you, I was the one who—well, I didn't actually introduce him to Joanna, but it was because of me that they were in the right situation to meet. So he and I go way back."

I nodded cautiously.

"All I want to say is, I've never known him to be as happy and content and comfortable as he's been in the last six months." He smiled. "And I, for one, am really glad to see it."

We didn't stay late—I promised Miranda I'd get back to her place early enough to chat.

"They're really good people," I said to Will as we turned onto the express-way leading away from Alex and Julie's house. "I'm glad you've had them in your life."

"I don't think I could have managed without them," he acknowledged. "The Hallorans are a huge help, but it's just easy with Alex and Julie. There are never any issues. And Lizzy and Wiley really love them."

I was a little chilly and pulled my thin wrap closer around my shoulders. "And it's clear how they feel about Lizzy and Wiley," I said. "I could see it in some photos Julie showed me. But I'm kind of surprised they don't have any kids of their own."

Will reached out to turn up the heat. "I think it just never happened. I don't think they ever made a conscious decision about it." He rested his hand on my thigh. "But they're the best godparents my kids could have."

When we arrived at Miranda's, Will walked me to the door.

"I feel like I'm on a date," I laughed. "And any minute my dad is going to flick the porch light on and off to let me know it's time to go in."

"So I guess this is where I hope to score a goodnight kiss," he joked.

I wrapped my arms around his waist. "Play your cards right," I murmured, tilting my face up to his, "and you'll score a lot more than that."

I didn't see Will at all the next day. He wanted to spend it with Lizzy and Wiley, preparing them, I supposed, for our meet-and-greet the following day. Although, I wasn't sure anything he said would soften the blow of coming face-to-face with a potential stepmother. It wasn't going to be easy for any of us.

Miranda took the afternoon off, but we didn't do much of anything except appreciate having the chance just to relax with each other.

After dinner, I packed my things to move to the hotel.

"Thanks again for letting me stay," I said as I dropped my suitcase in the trunk. "You do understand why I'm going over to the hotel, right?"

"Don't worry about it," Miranda replied. "I think it's a good idea. It'll give you more flexibility."

I opened the car door.

"Besides," Miranda continued, "I'll see you before you go back to San Sebastian, right?"

I gave her a brief hug. "Absolutely."

# 31

I met Will the next morning in the hotel lobby. It was after breakfast, which, for me, consisted only of toast and coffee. I was far too anxious to eat anything more.

The plan was to start with a few hours at the zoo. According to Will, that was one of the kids' favorite outings. Even Lizzy, at thirteen, still enjoyed the animals, the carousel, and the zoo train.

Will smiled when he saw me. He took my hands and kissed my cheek, careful to maintain a level of discretion lest either of the children was watching from the car.

"Are you ready?" he asked nervously.

"As I'll ever be."

We moved toward the door, but Will made a sudden turn that took us behind a wide post and out of view. He gathered me to him and kissed me fully. He tasted faintly of coffee mixed with maple syrup and cinnamon.

"Okay," he said, taking a deep breath, "let's do this."

The sun was bright, and I squinted when we walked outside. Lizzy was leaning against the car, arms folded across her chest, and Wiley was squatting down to examine what I later saw was a caterpillar making its way into a flower bed. Lizzy had been watching us, but turned her back as we approached.

Will took Wiley's arm and pulled him to his feet. At the same time, he put a hand on Lizzy's shoulder and spun her around so she faced us.

"Lizzy, Wiley, I'd like you to meet Callie Winwood," he said, gesturing toward me. "She is the very good friend I told you about. Callie, these are my children, Lizzy and Wiley."

"I'm very happy to meet you," I said, extending my hand first to one and then the other. At Will's urging, each shook hands very tentatively. "Your dad has told me a lot about you."

"I bet," Lizzy said. I recognized the bitterness in her voice.

"Hi," Wiley said quietly.

Will and I exchanged glances. "Well, then, shall we go?" he asked, trying to sound cheerful. I was more inclined to hightail it back to my hotel room and then to San Sebastian, where Bailey was waiting for me; but when Will opened the front passenger door and invited me to take a seat, I accepted. Lizzy and Wiley took their places in the back and buckled their seat belts.

"Okay, then," Will said as he started the ignition and navigated the car out of the parking lot and onto the main road.

We drove most of the way in silence. I could feel Lizzy's eyes on me, sharp as daggers. I was not optimistic about the weekend. At this moment, I was not optimistic about the future in general. It was clear from the get-go that Lizzy had no intention of allowing her happy trio—father, daughter, and son—to grow into a foursome. Or worse, a sextet, when I included Ben and Justine. I wasn't surprised. I hadn't felt any different when I was her age and in the same situation.

Will occasionally glanced in my direction or in the rearview mirror at Lizzy or Wiley. He did his best to make conversation that included them, but they sat stone-faced. I did my best to keep it going, but after a while the quiet just seemed easier.

Finally, Wiley spoke up.

"Do you like my dad?" he asked. Will coughed and sputtered in response to his son's question. I turned around to look at Wiley. His face was round and smooth-skinned with big blue eyes and pink cheeks that made him appear almost angelic. He wore a dark green T-shirt, khaki shorts, and a Boston Red Sox baseball cap. From what I could tell, he must have more closely resembled Joanna than Will, although his nose and chin definitely mirrored his father's. Will was tall, and it appeared Wiley would be also. But there the similarities ended. While Will was dark haired, Wiley was ash blond. And where Will's hair was wavy and curled around his collar, Wiley's hair was silky straight.

If Wiley took after his mother, though, Lizzy was most definitely her father's daughter. She, too, had dark hair, although hers was long and straight. It was parted on the side, and on this particular day she wore it pulled back and secured with a claw clip. Her eyes were the same vibrant blue as Will's, and fringed with thick, dark lashes. Like Wiley's, her nose and chin resembled her father's, but she also had Will's broad forehead, and their smiles were almost identical.

"My dad says he likes you," Wiley spoke again.

"I'm glad," I said. "Because I care about him very much."

"Do you have children?" he asked.

"Yes, I have two—a son and a daughter. Ben and Justine."

Lizzy shot her brother an icy glare. "Why don't you just shut up?"

"That's enough, Liz," Will said. She caught his eyes in the mirror, crossed her arms against her chest, and stared out the window.

Wiley continued his line of questioning. I was grateful that at least one of them was speaking to me.

"Did you know my mom?"

I felt a tightening in my chest. "No," I said, shaking my head. "I never met her. But your dad has told me a lot about her. It sounds like she was very special."

Wiley looked down at his lap. "She died," he murmured.

Will and I exchanged glances again.

"I know," I replied, turning my focus back to Wiley. "And I'm very sorry about that."

"She had a car accident. My friend's mom said she died on purpose, but my dad says that's not true. He said Mom wouldn't leave us if she could help it."

Lizzy faced him again, her eyes blazing. "Wiley, I swear, if you don't shut up ..." She jutted her chin in my general direction and added: "This is none of her business. She's not even supposed to be here."

*Game on*, I thought.

Fortunately, we arrived at the zoo before Lizzy was able to ratchet the tension up any higher. Will pulled the car into a parking space and turned off the engine. He opened the door to get out, and directed Lizzy to join him. She obliged, grudgingly, and they walked several feet away and stopped. I watched them through the windshield. They stood facing each other. He rested his hands on her shoulders as he spoke to her, but she refused to look at him. Instead, she stared at the ground and kicked at a rock that was embedded in the dirt.

*What am I doing here*, I wondered to myself. *This is crazy. How can we possibly think we can make any of this work?*

My heart went out to Lizzy. She was angry and hurt and frightened, and, despite the presence of a loving father, very much alone in her grief. I knew exactly how she was feeling. But there was nothing I could do, nothing I could say that would make anything better. At this moment, I was part of the problem.

The worst thing that could happen to Lizzy had, indeed, happened, and at this point, nothing could fill that empty place in her heart. The passage of time would bring some relief, and her family—aunt, uncle, and grandparents included—could provide comfort, but the healing—such as it is—comes from within; it's a solitary process, and it moves at its own pace.

I couldn't hear what Will was saying to Lizzy, and I wasn't much at lip-reading. From their body language, however, it was obvious they weren't reaching any kind of agreement. Lizzy held her arms tightly across her chest, still refusing to look at him. Occasionally she brought a hand up to her face to wipe away her tears. It looked to me as though Will had asked her a question, and her response was a slight shrug. He pulled her into a hug, said something else, and kissed the top of her head.

Watching Lizzy and Wiley during the drive—and, more particularly, over the last five minutes—I realized just how young they were, and how much growing they had left to do. Once a parent always a parent, I knew, but eventually children take charge of their own lives, and the parent can fade into the background. Will had a long way to go before he wouldn't have to be front and center, and I had to consider whether or not I wanted to be standing there with him.

I had raised my children. I had done the soccer thing—as well as baseball and gymnastics and ballet and a thousand other activities. I had seen them through chicken pox, strep throat, colds and flu, broken bones, and even their first hangovers. I endured the unrelenting torment of their adolescent and teen years, when they broke practically every rule, and were, by turns, rude, insolent, and just plain smart-asses. And I had done this with the children that I bore—children I chose to bring into my life, and who, at the very core of their beings really did love and respect me. Children with whom I now enjoyed very close relationships. Did I really want to reenlist and take up arms—metaphorically speaking—with someone else's children, particularly when one of them would just as soon push me off a cliff as look at me?

But balancing all of that, of course, was Will. I loved him. I had for more than twenty-five years, and we finally had the opportunity to build the life together that had eluded us two decades earlier. Would I throw that away?

As I sat there thinking, I became aware of Wiley's eyes on me. I turned around to face him. His expression displayed a mixture of innocence and confusion. "This is all very strange, isn't it?" I commented. He nodded. "You miss your mom, don't you?" He nodded again, and I saw the shimmer in his eyes. I wanted to pull him onto my lap, hold him close and tell him that things really would be okay. Instead, I simply reached my hand back and touched his cheek, smiling faintly.

# 32

The Westin Zoological Garden encompassed thirty-five acres and boasted a resident population of nearly five hundred animals, including the assorted insects and reptiles in the aptly named "Can You Say, Eww?" exhibit.

Wiley, as I soon learned, was a budding entomologist—no surprise that he'd been studying the caterpillar in the parking lot earlier in the day—and at his behest, we all entered the long curved structure that was home to a host of creepy crawlies that included a Madagascar hissing cockroach, a giant millipede, a pair of very hairy tarantulas, a Puerto Rican crested toad, three tiger salamanders, and a gecko. After no more than five minutes in their presence, I found I was not only capable of saying "Eww!" but also wholly inclined to do so.

Separated into individual sections, the structure was, by turns, dank and shadowy or hot and dry, depending on the preferences of each resident creature.

Behind me, someone mentioned something about bats hanging from the ceiling, and I shuddered. Hoping the young man was speaking for dramatic effect, I didn't look. I was not a fan of bats, and I wasn't entirely sure I could maintain my composure if I saw one or two or, heaven forbid, several, dangling above me.

Now that I thought about it, I wasn't a fan of large spiders either, and I had absolutely no affection for snakes. Once, when Ben was in junior high school, he found a tiny garden variety in the backyard, and in true practical joke fashion, buried it in my lingerie drawer.

The blood-curdling scream that came out of my mouth when I reached into the drawer for a pair of stockings was loud enough that the neighbor behind us thought I was the victim of foul play and actually called the police.

Foul play, indeed. The two officers, taking seriously their oath to protect and serve—while doing their best not to smile—kindly removed the offending reptile. One of them spoke to Ben afterward and suggested that playing such a joke—particularly on his mother—was probably not in his best interest.

When I told Joe about it that evening, he laughed so hard he could barely breathe. Still, he gave Ben a stern lecture, and, for good measure, I added a week's worth of extra kitchen duty as punishment.

In the Westin Zoological Garden exhibit, Wiley approached the hissing cockroach with great enthusiasm. "Listen to this, Dad." He pressed a button and the cockroach's song emanated from a speaker set into the glass. "Isn't it cool?"

"Well, I don't think I'd want one as a pet," Will said, squinting his eyes as he examined the insect, "but as far as cockroaches go, I suppose it's a pretty interesting specimen."

Walking slightly ahead of Will and his kids, I turned a corner just in time to see a large boa constrictor, its body in a coil and its head extended and moving from side to side, almost in slow motion. Startled, I gasped and took a step backward. A white mouse scurried from one side of the habitat to the other, and I saw the snake eyeing it. Apparently, it was lunchtime.

"Look at that!" Wiley exclaimed when he caught sight of both the snake and the object of its attention.

Will stood behind Wiley, who leaned in to watch the interspecies interaction. "Does the mouse know what's gonna happen to it?" he asked with great concern.

"I don't know," Will answered.

"Is it scared, do you think?"

"I don't know," Will said again.

Wiley watched as the boa slithered across the bottom of the cage, moving slowly toward its prey, which, quite abruptly, had settled back on its haunches and begun washing its face, oblivious to its surroundings or impending doom. As the snake was about to strike, Wiley cried out and covered his face with his hands. He turned away from the enclosure, and although Will was still behind him, I happened to be in closer proximity. He pressed himself against me and buried his face in the crook of my arm. His own arms were pulled up against his chest.

"I don't wanna see," he whimpered. "I don't wanna see. I wanna go out."

"Okay," I said soothingly. "It's okay. We'll go. Come on." With one arm around his shoulder, I guided him toward the exit. Will followed, with Lizzy's hand tight in his.

Back in the daylight, Wiley sniffled and wiped away a couple of tears. Lizzy parked herself on a bench a few feet away, looking either bored or put out. "Are you okay, pal?" Will asked, resting a hand on Wiley's shoulder.

Wiley pressed the heels of his hands against his eyes, stopping the tears. He didn't say anything for a moment, then glanced up at his father. "The mouse didn't know what was going to happen to him, did he?"

Will stroked Wiley's head. "No, I don't think he did."

Will and I glanced at one another. "What do you say we head over to the giraffes?" he suggested to Wiley. "We can stop and see the elephants and the lions along the way." He turned to Lizzy. "How does that sound to you, LZ? Maybe the cubs will be out playing."

Lizzy shrugged as she scraped her thumbnail across the wood grain of the bench. Expressionless, she rose and walked ahead of her father and brother. Wiley adjusted his hat and quickened his pace so he could catch up with his sister. Will and I followed behind, keeping both children in sight.

Over the next couple of hours, we visited the giraffes, gibbons, and the entire lion family, as well as a father-daughter pair of leopards—which were particularly meaningful to Will and Lizzy—a giant anteater, a lowland gorilla and her mate, and ten different species of rare Asiatic birds.

We stopped at the enclosure across from the lemurs to watch the flamingos. There were a few youngsters among the flock, as we could tell from their downy gray plumage. Will laughed as Lizzy imitated one of the adult birds, trying to keep her balance while standing on one leg. Every so often she'd lean to one side or the other and Will would catch her and hold her upright.

From the flamingo habitat, the next stop was the train station. With Wiley at his side, Will stood in line at the ticket booth while Lizzy and I waited near the great birds of prey.

"This is a really nice place," I said, trying to make conversation. "Just the right size. I can see why you like it."

Lizzy didn't respond except to roll her eyes. With pursed lips and arms folded across her chest, her body language spoke volumes. And I knew exactly what she meant it to say.

"Do you come here often?" I asked. She shrugged.

To my relief, it wasn't long before Will and Wiley returned with four tickets.

"You and Wiley and I can ride together, just like always. Right, Dad?" Lizzy asked. The glance she shot in my direction was clearly intended to put me in my place.

"We do that so no one has to sit alone," Will answered. "This time we can ride two and two."

"But, Dad—" Lizzy started to argue.

"But nothing, LZ This is how we're going to do it. Who do you want to ride with?"

A stone wall no more than three feet high outlined the waiting area near the ticket booth. Lizzy approached the wall and sat down heavily, lips pursed—as usual—and arms folded—as usual—across her chest. It seemed to be her go-to stance. She had defiance down to an art.

"I'm not riding with her," she said flatly, glancing again in my direction. "Or with Wiley."

Her plan, executed with great precision, was to keep Will and me separated as much as possible. I recognized the strategy. I had employed it myself a long time ago.

"Don't be rude, Liz," Will warned. He turned to Wiley. "How about you, pal? Who do you want to ride with?"

Wiley also shrugged, but in his case it indicated nothing more than uncertainty or, perhaps, ambivalence.

I'd score no points if I came between Lizzy and Will this afternoon—and coming between them wasn't something I wanted to do anyway—so I suggested that father and daughter take the first seat in the train car and Wiley and I share the second. "Do you mind if we sit together?" I asked Wiley. "I'd understand if you'd rather ride with your dad and sister, though. I can just wait over by the bald eagle. We've actually become quite chummy, he and I."

Wiley's mouth twitched in a smile and he shook his head back and forth. "It's okay, I don't mind," he replied.

The fact of the matter was that, wanted or not, I was the guest here. Interloper, some might say. The zoo was their place—Will and Lizzy and Wiley's. On this first afternoon with them I had to occupy as unobtrusively as possible whatever space Lizzy and Wiley granted me.

The Westin Zoo Train was typical of every other train at every other zoo. The open-air cars were small, and the bench seats with wooden backs easily accommodated two passengers, but could fit three if circumstances warranted. The sides of each car were decorated with heavy wooden facades cut in the shape of zoo animals and painted in cartoon style.

Wiley monitored the track, watching for the train to make its way around the bend, through the tunnel, and then come to a stop at the gate.

Will touched my cheek as we waited. "Are you okay?"

I smiled, but kept my own hands to myself. "I'm fine," I assured him.

"I'm sorry about Lizzy. I know she's not making you feel very welcome," he said quietly so she wouldn't hear.

I glanced over at her. She was intent on something several yards away. I followed her line of sight and saw a woman and a young girl about Lizzy's age laughing together. From their general resemblance, I guessed they were mother and daughter. They stood with their arms linked, sharing some private joke.

Returning my gaze to Lizzy, I saw the expression of longing on her face. I immediately recognized the feeling behind it, and my first inclination was to approach her and say whatever I thought might help fill the void. At the same time, however, I knew nothing I could say would make a difference, and she wouldn't want to hear it from me anyway.

I sighed and turned to Will.

"It'll just take time," I said.

Sitting with Wiley for the fifteen-minute train ride gave me an opportunity to study his manner and demeanor. He didn't make an obvious point of positioning himself as far away from me as possible, but he did lean toward his side of the car. He kept his hands in his lap, as the conductor directed, but tilted his head outward so he could watch the tracks ahead of us. His silky hair moved lightly in the cool breeze generated by the train's movement.

In terms of emotion, Lizzy was an open book; Wiley, however, was more of a mystery. I knew he missed his mother, but I couldn't get a read on how he perceived my presence. On his own, he didn't seem to resent me the way Lizzy did. But there was a reticence in his interaction with me, particularly when Lizzy was nearby. Perhaps he felt the need to align himself with her as much as possible—heaven knows Lucas and I did our best to present a united front against Lila.

More likely, Wiley was simply doing his best to navigate the situation the best way he knew how—just like the rest of us.

# 33

We followed our zoo excursion with a late lunch at a diner that had been fashioned from an old railroad car, and topped that off with a stop at the duck pond in Westin Park.

To call it a duck pond was truly a misnomer. It seemed more the size of a small lake, with a tiny island in the center. Lizzy pulled a bag of stale bread from the back of the car, and she and Wiley followed the walkway from the parking lot, across the grass to the dirt path that circled the perimeter of the pond. They hurried down to the water's edge, where the ducks congregated.

Will and I strolled along behind, careful not to get too close either to them or to each another.

"It's beautiful out here," I said, nodding toward the trees, the tall grass, and the blue-green water. "Very peaceful."

"Yeah, the kids like it," Will said. "We've been coming here since they were little. We used to—" He was interrupted by the sound of a splash, which was immediately followed by a chorus of mad quacking, the flutter of wings, and then Lizzy's voice shouting to him from behind a screen of scrub brush and bushes.

We were no more than twenty feet from the spot where she and Wiley had turned down toward the water, and Will took off after hearing Lizzy call out. I followed behind. With his long stride, and because he knew exactly where he was going, he reached them well before I did. When I came around the bushes I saw him in the lake, the water up around his knees, fishing out Wiley, who was drenched practically from head to toe.

I covered my mouth with my hand, reminded of my own watery mishap in Rock Creek the first time Will had visited San Sebastian.

"Home. Now," Will commanded when they'd stepped onto the bank. "You have to get out of those clothes and into the shower." Wiley stood grimacing at the mud, algae, and other pond scum that covered his arms and legs.

"Eww, Wiley, you stink!" Lizzy held her nose and took two giant steps away from her brother.

Fortunately for all of us, Will found an old blanket in the back of the car, which he used to swaddle Wiley and thereby contain most of the smell. The boy was completely enveloped, with little more than his face showing.

"So, anyone want to tell me what happened?" Will asked as he drove home.

According to Lizzy, she had been holding the bread bag, and distributed a few slices to Wiley. When he had exhausted his immediate supply, the ducks and geese, in what can only be described as a show of extreme ingratitude, pursued him with great fervor in hopes of extracting a few additional morsels. They weren't vicious, Lizzy said, but they were pushy. Literally. A particularly feisty white goose actually poked Wiley in the backside, and he lost his balance at the edge of the bank and fell into the water.

The corners of Will's mouth twitched, as did mine, and he simply shook his head.

No one said anything more as we drove back to the house.

Winding through the neighborhood streets, I suddenly realized where we were headed—the Tremaine family home. The one place in this entire city where I specifically did not want to be. I took a deep breath.

"Is she coming, too?" Lizzy asked coldly.

Will shot her a warning look, but didn't say anything.

I watched the scenery and read the street signs, imagining Will driving this same route with Joanna next to him and their children in the back. My stomach turned over on itself a few times. I knew Will hadn't orchestrated this turn of events, but I was feeling trapped, and angry. Everyone was already uncomfortable, and for me to be in their home, when the children and I had only just met, was asking too much of us.

I weighed my options as we drove. I could just wait in the car while Will and Wiley got themselves cleaned up, but that would be awkward; I could have Will drop me off somewhere and pick me up later, but that would be awkward, too; or I could have him drop me off and I'd call Miranda to give me a ride to my hotel. From there I'd be free to go wherever I wanted—including my own home. Not nearly so awkward, but probably not a good idea, either.

Will knew what I was thinking.

"I'm sorry about this," he said when he pulled into the driveway and turned off the ignition. Taking his father's orders and warnings seriously, Wiley went straight to the shower; Lizzy, who couldn't get away from me fast enough, bolted out of the car and into the house.

I stared out the windshield at the house. It was a rambling ranch style, with a huge maple tree in the front, and big picture windows framed by wide blue shutters. I glimpsed a figure watching us from one of the windows. Startled, I actually thought at first it was Joanna herself. In reality, though, it could only have been Lizzy.

Will put his hand on mine. "I really am sorry," he said again. "I know how much you didn't want to be here."

"No," I replied coldly. "I don't think you do." I turned away from him. "But there's not a lot to be done about it now, is there."

He took a breath, exhaled heavily, and gazed out the driver's side window. "Well, I have to go check on Wiley and make sure he's getting off all that pond crap, and then I have to change. Will you come in?"

I looked out the passenger window for a moment, studying what I could see of the neighborhood. Partway down the street, someone was pushing a baby stroller, and a little farther away a couple of boys did tricks on their skateboards. Just a regular neighborhood, I thought to myself, but definitely not mine. "All right," I said with complete resignation.

I went no farther than the living room, and I didn't sit down. I stood, with my arms across my chest, trying to occupy as little space as possible. Lizzy was, I supposed, in her bedroom; Wiley and Will were in theirs, respectively, each putting on clean clothes and shoes.

I glanced around the living room, noting the photographic images on the walls. I assumed they were Joanna's. Will was right—they were quite beautiful. What grabbed my attention, however, was the painting that hung over the fireplace. It was a portrait of Joanna, seated on a park bench, with Lizzy on one side, and Wiley on the other. They were obviously mother and children—the family resemblance was undeniable. I wondered if it struck Will every time he saw them. Joanna had one arm wrapped around each child, holding them close. Lizzy leaned against her mother, and Joanna's cheek rested on the top of her daughter's head. It was a precious scene that I imagined elicited both comfort and sorrow.

I bit my lip as I stared at the portrait. The words "intruder," and "usurper," circled through my mind. To Lizzy and Wiley, I was both. Just as Lila had been to Lucas and me when she came into our house.

Tears smarted in my eyes, and I shivered as though a cool wind passed through me. This all was going to be a lot more difficult than I anticipated—for me, for the children, for everyone.

It was early evening when Will finally drove me back to my hotel. We had deposited Wiley at his friend Tanner's house, and Lizzy had been chauffeured to a movie theater, where she met up with a group of girls from school. Both had overnight plans and wouldn't come home until Will picked them up in the morning.

"Do you want to come up?" I asked when he pulled the key out of the ignition. It was a rhetorical question—I was pretty sure what the answer would be. He leaned over, and with his fingers entwined in my hair, kissed me long and deep.

"What do you think?" he replied with a chuckle. "I've been waiting for this all day."

The hotel room was cozy, decorated in an English country motif with lots of flowers in shades of pink and lavender.

"I guess I know why they call this the Rose Inn," Will said, taking in the wallpaper borders that almost identically matched the floral pattern on the quilt and throw pillows.

In addition to the queen-size bed, the room was furnished with a club chair, a small writing table, and a dark wood armoire. The air was a little stale when we walked in, so Will opened the window.

We both felt slightly awkward, as though we were sneaking around behind someone's back—which, I guess in a way, we were. Lizzy might have assumed that Will and I would spend the night together, but if she did, she gave no indication—no snide comments, anyway. Then again, she may have expected us to go our separate ways and not meet up again until breakfast. In any case, here we were, finally alone together and feeling almost shy.

Will took the throw pillow from the chair, tossed it onto the table, and sat down. I took a seat opposite him on the edge of the bed.

He cleared his throat nervously. "Well," he began, "I suppose things went about as well as we might have expected. What do you think?"

I massaged my forehead and temples with my fingertips. I was suddenly extremely tired. I hadn't realized how tense I'd been all day, and I felt physically as well as emotionally exhausted. Meeting Will's children and spending the day with them added a new dimension to my sense of him and of us, and I wasn't sure I liked it. Until today, Lizzy and Wiley—and even Joanna—had been abstract concepts. I knew they were real, of course, but somehow they'd always seemed separate from us. On the few occasions that Will and I had seen each other, we'd been in San Sebastian or some other place where the children weren't. It had been as though they existed on an entirely different plane. They hadn't really been a factor in our relationship up to now.

But now there was nothing abstract about Lizzy's contempt for me. And, at this point, nothing to make me think there was anything temporary about it, either.

"As well as we expected? Oh, you're probably right," I looked over at him, and added humorlessly, "But then, we didn't really have high expectations, did we?" Will moved from the chair to the bed and took my hands in his.

"I know it was hard. But it won't always be like this. It's all so new for everyone."

"Well, at least Wiley doesn't seem to think I'm evil incarnate." I pulled my hands away, picked up one of the bed pillows, and hugged it to my chest. "So what was it you said to Lizzy outside the car this morning?"

"Well, first I told her she couldn't be rude. It's not acceptable for her to behave that way toward you or Wiley or anyone else," Will replied. "I told her she could speak up and say what's on her mind, but not like that. Then I asked her just to give all of this a chance. I asked her to trust me."

"Will, I understand what Lizzy's going through. I really do," I said, still holding on to the pillow. "I've been there. When my father first introduced Lila to Lucas and me, I could barely acknowledge her. And when he married her and she became my stepmother, I hated her. I treated her like dirt. I was so angry that she was alive and living in our house, but my own mother wasn't. And there was nothing I could do about it. Lizzy is that kind of angry, and, to be honest, I just don't know if I can take it on. It's a lot more than hard." I stood up and walked to the window. It overlooked the empty back section of the parking lot and beyond that, a small park.

After a few minutes Will came up behind me and put his hands on my shoulders. I leaned back against him and closed my eyes.

"It's just going to take a little time," he murmured, his mouth close to my ear. "You said it yourself—we're all trying to figure this out as we go along. But it is worth the effort, isn't it?" We stood together for a long while, gazing out the window and feeling the closeness of each other. I reached up and laid my hand on his.

He turned me so I faced him. "It is worth the effort. I love you, Cal, and I know we can do this." He kissed me gently. "We *can* do this."

"I wish I had your confidence," I said. "I look at them and remember how hard it was on that side and how much I hated the changes my father brought into our lives. How much I hated him."

I turned away from Will and looked out the window again.

"We're different, Cal," he said quietly. "Our situation is different. How much easier would it have been if your stepmother had any idea how it felt to be where you were, the way you do with Lizzy?"

I felt his eyes on me, but I kept my focus on the landscape in the distance.

"You get it," he continued. "You can relate to her in a way that no one else can."

I turned around and leaned against the windowsill, my hands on either side of me, pressing against the wood. "So you're saying I should happily take all this on simply because I understand it."

He reached out and smoothed the hair away from my eyes. "No. I'm just saying it will be different with us." He tucked a curl behind my ear. "But the truth is, even that doesn't matter. I'm not looking for someone to help me raise my kids. If I were, I'd hire a nanny. I'm looking for you. Just you."

He smiled and my own expression softened. Holding my hands between us, he leaned forward and kissed me again. "I love you, Cal. I can't make it any plainer than that."

The night air that floated in through the open window was fresh, but also chilly. Beneath the cool sheets, we wrapped ourselves around each other for warmth.

Will sighed, running his hand as far as he could reach along the entire expanse of my body. His touch made me shiver. He rolled on top of me and my legs separated for him. I arched my back slightly as he entered me. Pushing a few errant curls away from my face, he smiled at me, dipped his head down, and kissed me. We moved slowly together, asking and answering, our bodies speaking the language they knew fluently.

"This is where I want to spend my life," he whispered, his face just a few inches away from mine. "Here, inside you. Loving you."

He moved again, and my muscles contracted to hold him.

"Will." I breathed his name as he kissed me again. He ran his tongue along my bottom lip and then into my mouth. We continued to move in rhythm. With my hands on his hips, I pulled him farther into me. He let out a low moan and pushed deeper and deeper with each stroke.

My body responded, opening to him, and he began to move faster and with more force.

"Please," I begged him, although I wasn't sure what I was asking for. His own body seemed to know, and he pressed harder into me. The release began in some deep recess of my soul and grew like a tidal wave until it couldn't be contained. At last, a feeling of pure ecstasy washed over and around and through me, carrying me into and out of myself. I held Will tight against me, urging him, until his own release came, slowly at first, but then so overpowering that he raised himself on his hands and cried out breathlessly.

When he finished, he collapsed his body on mine and lay there for a few moments before lifting himself away from me and rolling onto his back.

I snuggled in close to him, laying my head on his chest. He was slightly damp from the physical exertion, and his breathing was deep and regular. I felt the steady, reassuring beat of his heart. The covers had gotten kicked away, and he pulled them up over us. His arm was wrapped around me, holding me to him.

"God, I love you, Callie."

"And I love you." I stroked his chest with my fingertips.

I did love him. That was the plain and simple truth. I felt right with Will, in a way I never had with Joe—or anyone else. And as I lay there breathing in the scent of him and feeling the light touch of his fingertips on my skin, I realized somewhere deep in my heart that he and I were bound to one another. No matter what the circumstances, nothing could tear me away from him.

Neither of us said anything for a while, then Will picked up my hand and interlaced his fingers with mine. His thumb caressed the faint scar between my thumb and forefinger; it was all that remained of the Christmas Eve accident that brought us together. "Cal, I haven't felt so … safe, I guess, in a long, long time." He spoke haltingly, and so softly I could barely hear him. "The last couple of years have been so hard—hell, the last fifteen years—but now—when you're with me—everything just feels like it's all going to be okay. No matter what happens, no matter what we have to deal with, and no matter how anything turns out, if you're with me, it'll be okay."

I kissed him lightly on the neck, just below the jaw. "I do love you, Will," I murmured. "I always have."

He smiled and stroked my arm. "That's how I know it's all going to be okay."

He kissed me again, and for the first time in as long as I could remember, although I was uncertain about the future, I wasn't afraid.

# 34

Will left my hotel room around eight o'clock the following morning. He had arranged for Lizzy and Wiley to spend the day with Alex and Julie, and he went home to shower and change his clothes so appearances would suggest to Lizzy that he'd spent the night in his own bed. He retrieved the children from the homes of their respective friends, took them to their favorite pancake place for breakfast, and then left them with their godparents.

I, meanwhile, took a long bath and contemplated the afternoon ahead of me. Will had arranged for the two of us to have lunch with Joanna's family, and frankly, I was terrified.

It was clear the Hallorans would not welcome me, but I hoped they'd accept me—not for my own sake, but for Lizzy and Wiley's. The children's lives would be infinitely better if the adults around them all got along. Joanna had been the middle of the three children—Rowan was the oldest and Chase was the baby. I knew, of course, that the three of us would never become friends, but I hoped Chase and Rowan would realize I had no desire to come between them and their niece and nephew. In fact, quite the opposite was true. Lizzy and Wiley were all that remained of their sister, certainly; but more important, Chase and Rowan and their parents were the children's only physical connection to the mother they had lost. I would never interfere with that.

Lizzy and Wiley had Will, of course, but it was Chase and Rowan who could share the family history. Chase and Rowan who could tell the stories of Joanna as a child, of Joanna as a teenager, of the Joanna that Will never knew.

"Wow," I said flatly as we pulled around the circular driveway and came to a stop near the front walkway.

Will shut off the ignition and leaned against the steering wheel, peering out through the windshield. He glanced at me. "Yeah, the place is big," he replied.

I gazed out the window in blank astonishment. "Wow," I said again. "I had no idea."

Though large and impressive, the house was not ostentatious. Rather, it possessed a sort of dignified splendor. It was three stories, with dormer windows at what I thought was the attic, but which Will later clarified had been the servants' quarters when the house was originally built in the early 1920s. The attic, he explained, was even farther up.

The expansive lawns were manicured, and the gardens awash in pink, purple, and white. Meticulously trimmed wisteria and morning glory vines climbed the tall columns that supported the portico. A wide porch wrapped around the house, from one side to the other, and I imagined the family—Will and Joanna included—gathering on warm summer evenings. I could almost hear the laughter.

Will had done his best to prepare me for the experience of meeting Joanna's family, but nothing he said could have come close to matching the grandness that greeted me when we walked through the extra-wide front door.

The housekeeper answered when Will rang the bell, and we stepped into the foyer. The polished marble floor glistened, and the crystal chandelier, which hung from the center of a Florentine-patterned ceiling medallion high overhead, sent slender shafts of rainbow light in all directions. Directly beneath the chandelier stood a heavy, round claw-foot table. Obviously an antique or family heirloom, it was made from some kind of dark wood—mahogany, perhaps—and was accented by a huge bouquet of flowers set in a tall crystal vase. Together, vase and table were large enough to occupy practically my entire living room.

"Dr. Tremaine, it's always so good to see you," the housekeeper said, smiling warmly.

"And you, Paulette," Will replied. "I'd like to introduce you to my, uh, my—" He looked at me questioningly. I shrugged in response. I didn't know what he should call me. Girlfriend? Lover? First wife's replacement?

"I'd like you to meet Callie," he said finally. "Callie, this is Paulette. She's been the Hallorans' housekeeper for … well … for a long time." Paulette extended her hand to me. She was tall and thin, and her bluntly cut short hair was dark, but gray-streaked. She was dressed simply, in a white blouse, gray skirt, and black flats. She invited us into the living room where Eleanor and Rowan had gathered. Edward Halloran, along with Chase and Chase's wife, Sarah, would be joining us presently, she said, as we entered the room.

Sitting next to her mother on the damask sofa, Rowan regarded me with an immediate and obvious loathing. She posed elegantly, her legs crossed, one hand holding a glass, and the other draped over the arm of the sofa. She wore a short black skirt and a turquoise silk blouse that accentuated her ash blond hair, which, in contrast to my own tresses, was smoothed back into a chignon with not one strand out of place. Her eyes were large and round, like Wiley's, and she'd accented them with brown shadow and liner. Her full lips were dark burgundy, with an odd sheen that gave her the appearance of having recently sucked the blood out of some living creature.

Eleanor rose and approached Will. Rather formally, she took his hands and he kissed her cheek.

"It's so nice to see you," she said.

"Hello, Eleanor."

She turned to me and smiled. She wasn't particularly warm, but neither did she seem hostile or antagonistic. So far, so good, I thought to myself.

The resemblance between mother and daughter was noticeable, but not particularly strong. In this case, hair color—which I was pretty sure Eleanor touched up regularly—and a well-defined chin seemed to be the only characteristics they had in common.

As I calculated it, Eleanor must have been in her midseventies, although she looked much younger. Her short hair was carefully arranged, and only a few deep lines marked her otherwise smooth complexion. Her lips were a color similar to Rowan's but lacked the disconcerting sheen.

Sparks of light shot out from the diamonds in her heavy wedding rings as she gestured toward two chairs on the other side of the coffee table.

"Please, sit down and make yourselves comfortable. Will, can I have Paulette bring you something to drink?"

"Uh, no, no, thank you. I'm fine," he replied. I detected a note of caution in his voice.

Eleanor looked over at me, but made no similar offer. I felt very subtly put in my place.

The room was elegantly furnished in a combination of stripes and floral patterns. White wainscoting and crown molding accented the soft celadon walls, and a large family portrait hung over the fireplace. It looked to have been painted when Chase was no more than two. He was sitting on his mother's lap, with his sisters on either side, his father in the back, and the family's cocker spaniel lying at Eleanor's feet.

"So," Eleanor said, "you must be—" She glanced back at Will. "Will, dear, what did you say her name was?"

Will's face was entirely devoid of expression. Before he could answer, though, Rowan turned slightly and addressed Eleanor.

"We know who she is, Mother." Her voice was colder than ice. She spoke to me directly then, and I felt as though I'd been slapped across the face by an Arctic wind. "You're the slut who's sleeping with my sister's husband."

"Rowan!" Eleanor exclaimed. She seemed as shocked by her daughter's comment as Will and I were. "How can you be so vulgar?"

"I'm sorry, Mother," Rowan replied. Sarcasm dripped from her voice like honey from a beehive. "Did I say something wrong?"

Well, so much for getting along. I cleared my throat and licked my lips. I hadn't expected a warm welcome, but neither had I anticipated this kind of attack. I took a quick look at Will, unsure how to respond to Rowan's accusation. Aside from patches of red on either cheek, he'd gone pale, and his eyes were dark with fury.

"Um, excuse me?" I said to Rowan.

Will rose abruptly, reached for my hand and pulled me to my feet. "Come on, Cal, we're leaving." His eyes narrowed as he addressed Eleanor. "We didn't come for this," he said. "And I won't stay here and listen to it. We aren't going to spend the afternoon dodging insults." He took a step toward the door, still holding my hand. I followed behind.

Eleanor rose and came after us. "Will, please. I must apologize for Rowan." She glanced at her daughter, whose icy gaze was now directed toward whatever activity was taking place outside the tall windows across the room. "This is a difficult situation for all of us. I'm sure you can appreciate that. Rowan and Joanna were so close, and it's hard for her to see you with ..." She glanced at me. "Well, it's hard for all of us."

I could understand Eleanor's perspective. Perhaps she wasn't the heartless vulture circling her prey after all.

I exhaled, and my shoulders relaxed slightly, although I wasn't any happier to be there.

"Please," Eleanor continued, gesturing toward the chairs we had occupied previously. "Come back and sit down."

Will glanced at me with raised eyebrows, clearly giving me the option of going—or staying and facing the inquisition. I raised one shoulder slightly and let it drop, then turned toward the room. Any future Will and I had would include his children and, of necessity, their family. That they happened to be the lunatic relatives of his deceased wife was something I'd have to accept.

I could feel Rowan's eyes follow me as Will and I returned to our seats. They bore through me like lasers. I refused to be daunted, however, and gave her a warm smile.

It didn't help. She glared at Will, narrowing her eyes as she spoke. "I can't believe you had the nerve to bring her here," she said, the note of contempt ringing clearly. "Did you actually think we'd welcome her with open arms?"

Will took a deep breath. I could see the muscles tighten along the side of his face as his jaw clenched. He was obviously working hard to keep his temper in check. When he spoke, his voice was quiet and even.

"I brought her because I—we—thought you all should be acquainted with one another. Callie is going to be involved with Lizzy and Wiley, and it's important for their sakes that we all get along as best we can."

Rowan snorted. "Didn't take you long to find a replacement, huh, Will?" She leaned forward, the fingers of one hand toying with the cuff bracelet she wore on the opposite wrist. The bracelet was a single length of gray metal—brushed silver, perhaps—that wrapped around three times. Accented with small pointed tips that extended outward at roughly one-inch intervals, it looked more like a section of barbed wire formed into a wide coil.

"Or were you working on this—" she made a gesture of disdain—"*before* Joanna died?" Rowan was runway-model thin, and her high cheekbones gave her face an angular and sharp appearance that seemed to match her personality.

Will gave her a cold stare. "No, Rowan, I was not. But think whatever you want." Any goodwill that may have existed between brother- and sister-in-law had been destroyed when Rowan took matters into her own hands and told Lizzy about us.

Eleanor laid a firm hand on her daughter's arm. "Rowan, please." She turned to me. "Calista, isn't it?" I nodded, and she continued. "Calista is a guest, and I insist you treat her as you would any other visitor to our home."

Next to me, Will rolled his eyes and looked up toward the ceiling.

"So, Calista," Eleanor asked sweetly, "do you have children of your own?"

"I do," I replied hesitantly. "A son and a daughter. But they're grown now."

"And their father?" Rowan looked at me with raised eyebrows.

I paused before answering politely. "Not really any of your concern, I shouldn't think." From the corner of my eye I saw Will's mouth twitch as he tried to keep from smiling.

The door opened then, and Edward and Chase walked into the room with Chase's wife, Sarah, close behind. Introductions were made and Chase and Sarah sat down on the love seat near the fireplace. Edward settled himself in one of the matching wingback chairs.

"Calista. A lovely name," he said. "It's Greek, I believe."

"Yes, thank you," I replied. "It was my grandmother's name."

"And where is your family, Calista? Do they live near you?" Eleanor inquired. I felt rather like a suspect being interrogated by a police detective already convinced of my guilt.

"My father lives a couple of hours away from me, and I have a brother who lives not far from him. My mother died when I was very young."

"I am sorry," Eleanor said sympathetically. "But I imagine you had other family." I wasn't sure where she was going with her line of inquiry, but I was definitely on guard. If she meant her warmth to be disarming, it was having the opposite effect. It only made me more cautious and suspicious.

"My family is not particularly close," I conceded.

Rowan leaned forward from her place on the sofa. "Well, ours is," she snarled. "And it's not available for the taking."

From where I sat, I could see the muscles and tendons in Will's jaw tighten. He stood up again. It was clear that this time we *were* leaving. "Eleanor, Edward," he said, looking at each one in turn. He reached his hand out to me, glanced over at Rowan, and nodded. "Rowan, as always." He guided me out from behind the coffee table.

"Chase, Sarah," he acknowledged his brother- and sister-in-law.

When we reached the living room door, Will stopped and turned toward the others in the room. "It would be wise for you to remember that Lizzy and Wiley are my children," he said, a touch of ice in his voice. "I want to keep them as close to you—and to Joanna—as I possibly can. And having Callie in their lives isn't going to change that. But if you can't accept it, if you're going to make things unnecessarily difficult—" He didn't look directly at Rowan, but I knew his last sentence was intended for her. "If you make things harder than they need to be, I will do what I think is best for them, even if it means you don't see them anymore."

With that, he turned and we made our way to the foyer and then out the front door into the fresh air and sunshine.

"Well, that went well," I grumbled when we got in the car. "I can't wait for

Christmas when we get to do it all over again, but with even more people who despise my very existence."

Will laid his hand on my knee. "I'm sorry, Cal. I really am. I had no idea it would go that way."

"Have they always been like that, or is it new since Joanna's been gone?"

"They've always been difficult, but it has gotten worse since, well ..." Will put the key in the ignition and started the engine. "She just knew how to handle them."

"Wow," I said again, shaking my head. "I thought Lucas and I were tough. But compared to this, we were a walk in the park."

# 35

Rowan stood at the window and watched as Will held the car door for Callie and then took his own place on the driver's side. She waited until they were out of sight before turning to her mother. "He's going to marry her," she said bitterly. "He's going to marry her and it will be as if Joanna never existed."

"Isn't that a little dramatic?" Chase scoffed. "Will spent almost fifteen years with Joanna. He's not going to pretend they never happened."

Rowan glared at him in response. "So, tell me something, brother dear. If Sarah weren't here anymore," here eyes went briefly to her sister-in-law, "how quickly would you find a replacement?"

Chase rested his hand on the small of Sarah's back. "I love my wife," he replied. "And she loves me. But I know that if something happened to her, she wouldn't want my own life to grind to a halt. And I wouldn't want that for her if I were gone."

"Nice sentiment," Rowan snorted. She addressed Sarah. "Isn't it comforting to know you mean so much to him that he'd welcome someone else into your bed before the sheets were even cold?"

"All right, Rowan, you can stop now." Edward scowled at his daughter. "You've caused enough discord for one day."

Eleanor moved to Rowan's side and touched her arm. "Edward, you know she's right. If Will marries that woman, we will lose our grandchildren—Joanna's children—forever. Do you really think she's going to allow him to maintain contact with his wife's family?"

"If he marries her, she'll be his wife," Chase reminded Eleanor.

Eleanor gave her son a cold stare. "Joanna will always be his wife."

Chase shook his head. "You make it sound like he'd be a bigamist, Mother. Or an adulterer." He walked over to the cabinet against the far wall, picked

195

up a cut-glass decanter, and poured himself a drink. He closed his eyes, took a long sip, and turned to face the group. "For all it pains me to say it," he continued, "and you damn well know it does because I loved her as much as anyone here, Joanna is gone." He addressed Eleanor. "And you know better than anyone, Mother, how good Will was to her. And it wasn't always easy. He deserves whatever happiness he finds."

Sarah rose and walked toward her husband. "I think Chase is right," she said timidly. "Will doesn't seem like a monster. And he made it clear that he wants the children to stay close to all of us."

Eleanor took her daughter-in-law's hand, smiling warmly. "I know you mean well, dear," she replied, "but you are new to the family. Perhaps it would be best if you just kept to yourself."

Sarah took a step back. Though delivered gently, Eleanor's rebuke was equivalent to a backhand across the face. On the other side of the room, Rowan watched with smug satisfaction.

"All right, Mother," Chase said through clenched teeth. He set his glass firmly on the chest.

Eleanor gazed at her son. "I certainly didn't mean to offend anyone, sweetheart. But don't you agree that Sarah ought to wait until she has a better understanding of the situation before expressing an opinion?"

"She has a brain, and some sensitivity, and it seems to me, that should be enough," Chase replied, looking from his mother to his sister. "Which is more than I can say for either of you." He poured himself another drink.

Eleanor nodded toward his glass. "Don't you think it's a bit early in the day for that?"

Chase frowned and then placed the glass gently on the silver tray that held the decanter.

A soft tap on the open door interrupted the sparring, and Paulette peeked in to announce that lunch was ready to be served. She glanced around the room, looking for Will and Callie. She sighed when she realized they were gone.

"Will it be just the family, then?" she asked.

"Edward, you must do something." Eleanor's declaration was more a directive than a suggestion. The couple sat alone in the living room, following a mostly silent lunch. Chase and Sarah had gone home, and Rowan, who feigned a headache, had gone to her room.

"And just what would you suggest?" he asked. "Will is his own man, and makes up his own mind. I can't very well forbid him from marrying this woman if he so chooses."

"But surely you're concerned for the well-being of your grandchildren," Eleanor argued. "It's not enough that they've lost their mother; now he wants to wrench them away from the only family they've known and the only people who can in any way keep her alive for them." She set her cup down and paused. "Edward, this woman will not want to be involved with our family. Nor will she want that for Will. If he marries her, she will force him to make a choice. It may not seem like it now, but she will. And when she does, Joanna's children will be lost to us. And she will be lost to them. Don't you see?"

Edward stroked his wife's hand. "Please, Elly. I wish you wouldn't upset yourself like this. You don't know anything about her. It's as likely as not your fears are completely unfounded. And Will has clearly shown again and again that he understands the importance of family. Remember, he never really wanted to come back to Westin in the first place, let alone continue living here after Joanna—well ... but he's doing it for the children."

Eleanor rested her forehead on her hand. "Oh, Edward, sometimes I think I just can't bear it anymore." Her eyes filled. "I see photographs of her and she seems so happy and full of life. It is all so unfair. Mothers are not supposed to outlive their children, nor are young children supposed to live without their mothers." She dabbed at the corners of her eyes with a white linen handkerchief. "I long for Joanna every day. I long to see her beautiful face, her bright smile. And, oh, Edward, how she loved her children." Eleanor clung to her husband's hand.

"I know, Elly," he said, holding his wife's just as strongly. "I know. So do I."

# 36

Will drove the long way back to the hotel. Each of us occupied with our own thoughts, we didn't say much.

Finally, the silence got to be too much for me.

"I know it's gauche to ask, but how did Edward Halloran amass so much wealth? It looks like he has more money than God."

Will laughed quietly. "I don't know that I'd say more, but I wouldn't be surprised if they were neck and neck. Part of it is inherited—both Edward and Eleanor come from fairly well-to-do families—but a lot of it is what Edward made through investments. He's a pretty savvy businessman."

"Hmmm," I replied.

"What does that mean?"

"Oh, not really anything. The Hallorans just seem to be an example of money not buying happiness. I don't know that I've ever seen a wealthier— and more miserable—group of people.

"Of course," I added, "I don't have a lot of experience with the upper crust."

We continued on in silence, but my mind replayed the afternoon discourse, analyzing the details.

"What's the story with Rowan?" I asked. "I can't say I've met anyone like her. What does she do—for work, I mean? I don't expect a regular nine-to-five is part of her lifestyle."

"She designs jewelry," Will said. "Like that bracelet she had on today."

"The barbed wire, you mean?" I snorted. "Well, it fits, I suppose. She takes sharp and mean-spirited to a whole new level."

Will chuckled under his breath as he glanced over at me. "She wasn't always that way," he said, returning his attention to the road. "There was a time when she was, well, I wouldn't call it warm and friendly, but she wasn't angry and bitter either. That was before the wedding debacle."

"Wedding debacle? What, did someone stand her up at the altar?"

"Not quite," Will replied. "It didn't get that far. A month or two before the wedding—I don't remember exactly when, but it was after the invitations had been sent out—Rowan's intended decided he had different intentions and called the whole thing off. Packed up and moved away to an entirely different state. Montana, I think."

"Jeez," I said, shaking my head. I was taken aback, but it certainly put her behavior in a perspective that made at least a bit of sense. It must have been a humiliating experience for her, and she'd probably been living on anger since the day he left. I wondered how anyone would dare do that to Eleanor Halloran's daughter. It was wise of him to settle in another part of the country. I hoped he was smart enough not to have left a forwarding address.

"Why did he do it?" I was more than a little curious.

"I don't know. Maybe he got a taste of what he was in for if he married into the Halloran clan and took off before they could slap the ball and chains around his ankles." The sarcasm in Will's voice was hard to miss.

"Too bad you didn't see that," I said, watching the scenery pass by. "Could have saved yourself a lot of heartache."

Will took his eyes off the road just long enough to send a cold stare in my direction. "Joanna was not Rowan," he said flatly.

I closed my eyes and pressed my fingers to my forehead. I realized I had misspoken. "I'm sorry," I said, looking back at Will. "I just can't seem to say anything right here, can I? And I don't mean that to be flippant. I really don't know what to say. I mean, all I know of the family is what you've told me, and what I've just experienced myself, and I hate to think of you trapped in all that miserable dysfunction for so many years."

"Like I said, Joanna wasn't Rowan. Or Eleanor." The edge in his voice was still there, and his hands tightened on the steering wheel.

"I don't know how things would have been if Lizzy or Wiley hadn't been born, or if Joanna hadn't been sick," he continued. "What I do know is that I sure as hell wouldn't walk out on them."

I considered his words for a moment, and then his implication struck me like a lit match hitting a drop of gasoline. A spark of fury ignited in my chest. I glared back at him. "And is that what you think I did? Walk out on my family?"

"Well, didn't you?"

"Wait a minute," I said, raising my hands in front of me as though pushing his words back toward him. "This isn't about me. And anyway, my situation was completely different. My children were grown when I left. And I'd spent more than twenty-five years in a marriage I hadn't wanted in the first place. And, for God's sake, my *husband* was sleeping with another woman!" The spark had fanned into a full flame, but I kept my voice low and controlled. "Are you suggesting that doing what was best for me was selfish? Because if that's the case, you really don't know anything about me. You've seen Ben and Justine. Do they seem damaged to you?"

Will jerked the wheel and steered the car off the road and into a strip mall parking lot. He pulled the wrong way into a space several rows away from the other cars and stopped short. I pressed myself back into my seat to keep from falling forward.

He was angry—and his wrath was clearly directed at me—but I honestly didn't understand why. More important, though, I wasn't going to accept it. He turned off the ignition, and I immediately reached for the door handle. I wanted to get away from him and find my way back to the hotel and then home to San Sebastian. After the dressing down I'd received from the Hallorans, and now the suggestion from Will that I'd deserted my own family, I was beginning to think this whole thing was one big mistake and I had been better off when Will was just a fond memory. I had been crazy to think we could meld our disparate lives and histories.

"Thanks for pulling over," I said. "I think I should just get out and take a cab back to the hotel."

"Wait!" He gripped my forearm, his fingers pressing into the bone and flesh.

I looked down at his hand. "You're hurting me."

He let go at once and I pulled my arm away. "God, I'm sorry. I didn't mean to. You know I'd never ..." He turned and focused his attention on a young woman carrying a grocery bag in one arm and a toddler in the other. She stepped lightly across the uneven pavement, careful not to trip as she approached her car.

"Callie, what's happening?" Will asked quietly.

"I don't know," I replied rubbing my arm. "But I've been accused of some pretty unpleasant things today—not to mention being called a name or two I don't care to repeat—and I've taken about as much as I can for one twenty-four-hour period."

"You were right," he said staring out the windshield. His faint smile suggested a sort of black humor. "What you said a couple of months ago when I told you that Rowan had taken it upon herself to tell Lizzy about us. I said I wouldn't let them direct my life, and you said they already were. You were right."

He turned to me and, with a warmer smile, touched the back of his hand to my cheek. I started to recoil, but stopped myself.

"I'm sorry about what I said before."

"What? Accusing me of abandoning my husband and children?"

He pulled his hand away and rubbed it across his face. "What do you say we find a more comfortable place to continue this conversation?"

"Fine," I replied, crossing my arms and staring straight ahead. "As long as you aren't also going to blame me for world hunger, climate change, or the general demise of civilized society."

The best place to talk, Will seemed to believe, was my hotel room. I wasn't sure I agreed, but I didn't argue. We stopped at a grocery store and picked up some bread and cheese and fruit to make up for the lunch we didn't have at the Hallorans' and brought it into the room with us. He took the chair next to the writing desk, and I sat cross-legged at the foot of the bed.

"So, you want to talk?" I asked with just a touch of sarcasm. I kept my eyes on the orange I was peeling. The tension in the room was thick.

Will swiped a napkin across his mouth and took a slug of water from the bottle on the table.

"Callie, I didn't mean it when I said you walked out on your family," he said. "Or, maybe I did, but not the way it came out."

"Okay," I replied. "So how did you mean it to come out?"

He responded slowly, almost hesitantly. "Joanna and I—we had a lot of problems—I've told you that. But, we were never able to work them out, or to reconcile anything. She was gone before we could really try. And after she died, it didn't seem to matter because I was so focused on my kids and on work. There wasn't space for much else." He took another long sip. "But now everything's different."

"How do you mean?" I asked.

"I mean my life isn't static anymore. It's moving in the direction where you are. And it's hard as hell because I have all this baggage that's moving with me."

He read the confusion on my face.

"And I don't mean my kids," he continued. "I mean all the unresolved stuff between us—between Joanna and me." He sat back in the chair. "You and Joe had problems, and splitting up was the right thing to do." He gave me a sheepish glance. "You know I didn't mean to imply otherwise. Hell, if you hadn't, you never would have come back to Westin, and ... well ..."

"Okay," I replied cautiously. I reached out and gave him part of the orange as a peace offering, which he accepted. He pulled off a section and took a bite.

"But you were able to reconcile things," Will continued. "You were able to close some doors because both of you were here to do it. I think I sort of envy that."

I was beginning to understand the enormity of the burden he'd been carrying. Guiding two young children through their own grief and helping them begin the slow and painful process of learning how to survive without their mother; staying one step ahead of the Hallorans so he could protect his children while at the same time giving them the family connections they needed; and continuing to run the hospital's trauma center, where he faced varying degrees of pain and anguish on a daily basis. Even if he were so inclined, he'd never had the time or opportunity to address his own feelings.

"Toward the end, I couldn't say that Joanna and I were happily married," he said, "but we had Lizzy and Wiley. And, there was Joanna's illness to contend with. Doing anything else but take care of them—and be some kind of husband to Joanna—wasn't an option. It wasn't anything I ever considered."

"And when she died, she released you from all that."

"In a way, yes. But in some ways I'm still as stuck as I ever was. And Joanna's family and their need to keep her as much alive as a dead person can be, has made it next to impossible to find any kind of closure." He glanced up at me and leaned forward, his elbows on his knees and his head in his hands. "God, I hate that word," he muttered.

I reached out and touched his shoulder. The muscle was hard as a rock.

"Will," I asked. "Have you actually said goodbye to her?"

He lifted his head. "What do you mean?"

"You're right that Joe and I were able to come to some kind of reconciliation. We couldn't stay together, but, after a time, we forgave one another for everything and stopped trying to assign blame. In the end, it didn't matter who did what to whom. And that has made it possible for each of us to move forward, I think. Maybe you need to do the same thing with Joanna."

# 37

Will had no particular destination in mind when he left Callie's hotel room. After wandering the quiet streets for a time, stopping here and there at places he and Joanna used to frequent, he found himself at the park. He sat down on the bench where they often met on summer afternoons when he'd take a break from the hospital.

The night sky was clear, and he could make out a few constellations. Maybe Callie was right, he thought. Maybe a simple goodbye would help him lay Joanna to rest—finally.

He kept his eyes peeled on the heavens, hoping in some strange way to catch a glimpse of her, although he wasn't sure what form she would take, and whether he'd recognize her even if she miraculously appeared.

He heaved a sigh, keeping his eyes fixed on the stars. "Joanna," he said out loud. He was not calling out to her as much as simply acknowledging her existence in the universe. "Joanna, I'm sorry. I'm sorry for not being able to give you everything you needed. I loved you the best I could—I still do—but I know it wasn't enough."

He stared down at his hands, at the finger of his left hand where he'd once worn the wedding ring that bound him to her. "I know the road was rocky a lot of the time, and I didn't always do everything I could to smooth it out," he said, just above a whisper. "I can only ask you to forgive me and know that I will never forget you."

It was after midnight when I heard a faint knocking on the door of my hotel room. I knew it was Will. Scrambling out of bed, I threw on my robe. I turned the deadbolt and opened the door. He stepped inside and pulled me into an embrace. He smelled of night air and what I thought might be whiskey.

He didn't say anything, but raised his hand and touched my cheek. I didn't move, only looked into his face, trying to read his expression. It was a blank page.

He kissed me then, slowly and intensely, pressing his body against mine. It was whiskey—I could taste it. "I need you, Callie." His breath was warm on my neck. "God, I need you."

He looked completely spent, emotionally and physically, and ready to collapse at any second. His face was pale, with dark smudges under his eyes. I took his hand and pulled him toward the bed. He stood on one side of it, so still I could barely see him breathing. I pushed his jacket off his shoulders and down his arms, and tossed it onto the chair. I did the same with his shirt. He kicked off his shoes himself and undid his jeans and stepped out of them.

Lifting the covers, I urged him to get into bed. "Come on," I said gently, "before you catch cold." He slid between the sheets and watched me as I untied my robe and let it slip off my shoulders. He wore an odd expression, as though I were a stranger. I crawled in next to him, but kept a slight distance between us.

"Are you okay?" I asked. He was lying on his back, staring up at the ceiling. He didn't respond, and I repeated the question.

He turned to look at me. "I left her at the park." His voice was barely audible.

"What?"

"I said goodbye at the park, and I left her there."

I brought my hand up to his face and caressed his cheek. His eyes brimmed with tears. "Oh, Will," I murmured.

I fell asleep next to him, with his hand resting softly on my thigh. Aside from that limited connection, our bodies were entirely separate from one another. It didn't seem right for me to touch him. And as I slipped into unconsciousness, I wondered whether it was, in fact, me he meant to hold— or her.

# 38

Will was gone when I awoke the next morning. I opened my eyes to sunlight streaming in through the window and expected to find him sound asleep next to me. He was clearly exhausted when I helped him to bed the night before. Slightly alarmed, I sat up and looked around. I listened for the shower or the sound of water running in the sink, but everything was quiet.

I leaned back against the pillows, wondering where he went, and why he didn't tell me he was leaving. A few minutes later I heard the key in the lock and he walked in with a newspaper and two cups of steaming coffee.

"Hey, you're awake. Good morning. I brought you some coffee." He handed me a cup and sat down next to me.

"Uh, thanks," I said taking a sip. I was puzzled—and more than a bit disquieted by the change in his demeanor. This was not the same man who'd come to my room last night. I set the cup on the nightstand, pulled on my robe, and padded to the bathroom. "I'll be right back."

When I returned, he had taken off his shoes and was lying back against a couple of pillows he had propped against the headboard. He had the TV remote in one hand and was flipping through the channels.

With my robe still wrapped around me, I crawled back into bed and brought the covers up to my chest. I was feeling oddly shy.

As usual, Will read my mind.

He turned off the TV, set the remote on the nightstand, and reached over and pushed back the sheets just enough so he could loosen the sash on my robe. He brushed aside the cloth, leaned forward, and dropped a line of kisses along my newly exposed chest. "Don't worry," he whispered. "It's me."

He rose abruptly, removed his clothing, and slid back into bed next to me. Wrapping his arms around my waist, he pulled me over him so my body was stretched across the length of his. He buried his face in my hair and inhaled. "You smell so good."

I sat up so I was straddling him, my knees on either side of his hips. I was still wearing the robe, but a quick shrug of my shoulders and the silky dressing gown fell away. Will gazed up at me and his hands circled and caressed my breasts. I let my upper body fall forward slightly so I hovered over him like a butterfly. My hair fell in a veil around us as I inched downward, and my mouth met his, open and warm and moist.

"Be kind," he said only half-jokingly. "It was one hell of a party."

"So, where did you go last night?" I asked later. My head was cradled in the crook of his shoulder, and his arm was around my waist. His fingertips just brushed my naked hips.

He took a deep breath and exhaled heavily. "Well, among other places, I went to a bar. The King's Head. Joanna and I used to go there. Actually, it's more like an old English pub."

"Ah, so that's why you came back smelling like whiskey."

"Yeah, Joanna and I sort of had a drink or two together." He brushed my hair away from his face. "And then I went to the park." He hesitated. "I told her about … everything." I hoped he'd leave the explanation at that. I didn't want to hear more, didn't want to be privy to what passed between him and his memory of her. Either possessing that same sensibility or reading it in my demeanor, he fell silent. He focused his gaze on the floral border that ran along the top of the far wall. My hand rested on his chest, and I watched it rise and fall with each slow, quiet breath. "I went to the cemetery, too," he said finally. "Someone had left flowers at her grave." He glanced down at me. "Probably Eleanor."

I kissed him lightly on the chest and moved my thumb gently over his abdomen. "Eleanor didn't leave them," I said. "I did."

He sat up abruptly and studied my face for a long minute. "You?" he exclaimed. "Why?"

"I'm not exactly sure," I said.

He lay back down and pulled me close to him again. "I guess I felt I owed her some kind of acknowledgment, too," I said.

When Will left my hotel room the day before, he drove off in search of absolution. It had to come from Joanna herself, but only he knew where he would find it and what form it would take.

Alone in the room, I had begun to feel a little anxious. The walls were getting close and I needed some fresh air, so I walked out into the hallway and through a side door that opened to the hotel garden. The light, transitioning from afternoon to early evening, was soft and slightly unfocused.

I found myself surrounded by dozens of roses in varying colors and styles. A gravel path meandered around and between the individual bushes. Plaques next to each bush gave their common names—pink damask, red floribunda, Persian yellow, purple passion, white polar star. The summer air was thick and sweet. The scent of roses—and carnations—always reminded me of my junior prom and the first time a boy ever brought me flowers. I smiled at the thought.

I followed the path a short distance and came to a wooden bench nestled in the shade of a large, old oak tree. The shadows were cool on my face. I sat down and began to think.

I tried to imagine how Joanna might be feeling, if she still existed somewhere and was watching her children. I imagined how I would feel if I were her and another woman stepped into my children's lives while I looked on from afar. Would I take comfort in the fact that they were being cared for in my absence, or would I simply resent the woman who was taking my place? I wondered for a moment whether my own mother, from some heavenly post, had watched as Lila appropriated her home and her family, and I wondered whether she was saddened or relieved.

It suddenly seemed very important that I show my own respect for Joanna, a woman I'd never even met, but whose children were, in some way, being entrusted to me. And the best place to accomplish that was the cemetery where she was buried.

I remembered Will casually pointing it out to me earlier in the day when we drove past on the way to the Hallorans'. It wasn't all that far from the hotel—no more than a couple of miles—and I asked the manager at the front desk to write out directions so I could walk there. It was early enough that I could get there and back before sunset.

A small flower shop was conveniently—if not strategically—located across the street from the cemetery. I went in and bought a small bouquet of brightly colored flowers.

I wasn't a fan of cemeteries, a sensibility no doubt rooted in my earliest encounter with one. The first burial I'd ever attended was my mother's, and I could still picture the white brocade casket being lowered into the freshly dug grave, the displaced dirt waiting in a pile to be shoveled back into the hole to fill whatever space remained.

When my father brought Lucas and me back to the cemetery a few weeks after the funeral, it struck me that the ground over her grave was nearly flat, and the grass showed no signs of ever having been disturbed.

Using the directory at the entrance to the cemetery, I located Joanna's grave. It was situated on a small hill, in the company of other Halloran family ancestors who had, as one epitaph read, "slipped the surly bonds of earth."

I found the headstone easily. It was a white marble square, uneven and rounded at one corner. It rested on a solid base, with the figure of an angel draped lithely over the rounded side.

I read the words engraved on the front—*Joanna Halloran Tremaine, Beloved wife of William*. My chest tightened involuntarily and my throat closed. For a moment I thought I might be sick. Beloved wife of William. Will. My Will.

Hers, too.

I closed my eyes and took a deep breath.

*Beloved mother of Lizzy and Wiley*, the inscription continued, *Beloved Daughter, Sister, Friend*.

I searched the ground in front of the headstone for the metal canister that was set there to hold flowers. I found it easily, and removed the cylinder from its base. Looking around, I caught sight of a water spigot several yards away. I filled the canister, put it back in place, and carefully set the flowers inside. Still on my knees, I reached out and lightly touched two of the names carved on the headstone. *Lizzy. Wiley*. My fingertips traced the grooves in the marble. The letters were smooth and cool, and dark against the white background. I'm not sure how long I sat there, but by the time I became aware of myself again, shadows were starting to fall and the evening air had turned chilly. I got to my feet and wiped my hands on my jeans. I took a step back and gazed at the headstone.

"They'll always be yours," I promised, and walked away.

## 39

Now that I'd met Will's children—and he'd met mine—the only introductions yet to be made among the six of us involved the children
themselves. We decided to bring everyone together in San Sebastian, around
the annual Harvest Festival, which took place during the last weekend of
August. A twist on the old-fashioned county fair, the four-day event ran
from Thursday through Sunday and featured all the traditional activities,
plus a carnival with rides, games, and fortune-tellers.

Wiley didn't require much convincing, especially when he learned that
something called The Hammer was part of the carnival ride lineup.

Lizzy was not so keen, but Will told me he'd made it very clear that on
this occasion she had no choice in the matter. Her presence was required,
and that was that.

They arrived in San Sebastian the day the fair opened, and settled into the
cottage. It didn't seem proper for me to share quarters with them under the
circumstances, so Bailey and I moved over to Alice's place for the duration
of their visit.

According to the plan, Will, Lizzy, Wiley, and I would spend Friday at the
fair, and Ben and Justine would drive down to San Sebastian on Saturday morning, arriving in time for breakfast. Then we'd all spend the rest of the weekend
together and see how everything went. There was no set schedule or itinerary.
We might go to the fair again, or perhaps on a hike, or maybe to the beach.

The idea was simply to spend time together.

❦

"I don't want to be here," Lizzy complained shortly after her arrival. "I don't
like this place. We don't belong here."

Wiley, more or less comfortable in any unfamiliar environment as long as his father was with him, had turned on the television and become engrossed in a Discovery Channel program about sharks.

Will took a seat on the couch and motioned for Lizzy to join him. She plopped down beside him, arms across her chest, chin pushed out in its usual display of defiance. He put an arm around her shoulder and pulled her enough so she fell against him. She smiled despite herself, and kept her head against his chest.

"How about you give it a chance, huh, LZ?" Will rested his cheek on the top of Lizzy's head. "It could turn out better than you think."

"Doubt it," she grumbled. "Where is she, anyway?"

"She—Callie—is staying with her friend at the other house," Will replied, "the one we passed when we were coming up the long driveway."

"How come she's not staying here?" A commercial had diverted Wiley's attention from the sharks. "She lives here, doesn't she?"

"Well, she does," Will explained, "but she thought—and I agreed—that you and Lizzy and I would be more comfortable if we were here by ourselves. We'll see her tomorrow."

"*I'd* be more comfortable at home," Lizzy declared.

"You know, Liz, someone once said that people are about as happy as they make up their minds to be. You could learn something from that." Will's patience was wearing thin. He'd been listening to Lizzy grouse and complain since they left Westin.

Before he could continue—or she could respond—they all heard the sound of a door creaking and then of bags rustling in the vicinity of the laundry room. They glanced at one another. Will rose and crept toward the back of the house to investigate, with Wiley tiptoeing close behind. Lizzy chose to stay in the living room.

"Hey, what are you doing here?" Will laughed when he saw Bailey peer at him from around the corner. The dog was biting down on an old piece of rawhide, his brown eyes shining with delight.

He trotted over to Will, tail wagging enthusiastically.

"How did you get in?" Will stood at the open back door and looked from one side to the other. He was sure that if Bailey was here, Callie must be nearby. The dog stuck to her like Velcro. He heard the loud chirp-chirp of a cricket, but he didn't see any sign of Callie. He frowned in disappointment. They'd not had even a minute together since he and the kids arrived that afternoon. He hadn't seen her in a month, and he ached to touch her, even if it meant just holding her hand.

"Is this Callie's dog?" Wiley asked, scratching the soft fur behind Bailey's ear. Bailey continued to wag his tail, but refused to drop his treasure. He sat down next to Wiley and pressed his body against the boy's leg. His tail swished across the floor.

"Hey, Dad, I think he likes me!" Wiley beamed.

Will turned to his son and saw two pairs of eyes staring back at him. "I'm sure he does," he agreed.

He took another look outside just in time to see a narrow beam of light pointed in his direction. A few seconds later, he made out Callie's form in the darkness. His heart lightened and he walked out to meet her.

## ৪১

"I don't suppose you've seen an errant pooch anywhere," I said raising my eyebrows. "He escaped from Alice's yard."

"As a matter of fact, I have," Will replied. He pointed behind him with his thumb. "He's introducing himself to Wiley." Then glancing in the same direction to make sure his son was still occupied, he pulled me into the shadows of the house. He pressed me against the fence and kissed me urgently, his mouth devouring mine.

"Hey, Dad!" Wiley's voice rang out in the dark.

Will let go of me, dropped his forehead onto my shoulder, and exhaled heavily. He lifted it again, and I shrugged. I gave him a half smile as I started to turn toward the door. Taking my arm to stop me, he kissed me again, only briefly this time.

"Dad! Where are you?" Wiley called out one more time, a little louder and with a hint of alarm.

"I'm right here," Will hollered back. "I'm with Callie. She's looking for Bailey." He cupped my cheek lightly with his hand. "You and I aren't finished," he whispered. I heard the smile in his voice.

"So, I see you two have met," I said to Wiley, who sat cross-legged on the kitchen floor with Bailey at his side.

"He likes me." Wiley said brightly, his arm around the big dog's neck. "He keeps licking me." With perfect timing, Bailey's tongue swabbed Wiley's round face. He, in turn, let out a chortle and fell over backward, lying in a sprawl while the dog, with much fervor, continued his demonstration of affection. Will and I stood back and laughed.

Lizzy wandered in to see what the commotion was. She caught me in close proximity to her father and her face went blank. Preferring to fade into the background, I didn't say anything. I hadn't meant to join them at all this evening—I thought they should have Will to themselves while they got accustomed to the place. They had arrived in San Sebastian sometime in the afternoon, and Will, who knew the way, had picked up a rental car and driven from the airport to the cottage. All the contact they'd had from me thus far was a note in the kitchen welcoming them and inviting them to make themselves at home.

"Hey, LZ, want to say hello to Callie?" Will asked with a nod of his head that signaled an order rather than a suggestion.

"Not really," she said coldly.

"Liz," Will warned.

She glared at me through narrowed eyes. "Hello."

"Well, welcome, Lizzy," I said as warmly as I could. "I hope that while you're here, you'll make yourself as comfortable as you can."

"Mmph," she grumbled, rolling her eyes. Will scowled, and I turned the subject to Bailey.

"Well, I guess I'll take the happy wanderer back to the house with me," I said. I picked up the flashlight and was about to call for Bailey to follow me when he, as usual, had another idea. He padded over to Lizzy and sat down, leaning against her leg this time. He gave me a look that told me he wasn't going anywhere. She reached down to pat the scruff of his neck, and he gazed up at her with doleful eyes. A hint of a smile touched her lips, but it quickly faded and her mouth assumed its usual straight line.

"C'mon, Wiley," she addressed her brother. "Let's go watch TV. Dad probably wants to be alone with her." She jerked her chin toward me.

Will opened his mouth to respond as she turned and walked into the other room, but I touched his arm and shook my head. "It's okay. Let her say what she wants to. She'll figure out when she's crossed the line. And she won't stop pushing until she does. Believe me, I know the drill."

"But I won't let her be rude. She was brought up to be respectful, and that's what I expect."

My hand was still resting on his arm. "Look at all of this from her perspective," I said quietly. "She has no control over what's going on in her life right now, particularly the things she doesn't like. She had no control over what her mother did, and she has no control over what you do. What she can control, though, is how she reacts to those things. And you have to give her that. You cannot demand warmth or even respect." As an afterthought, I added, "A little civility, maybe, but not much more."

"Then I will demand that," he said. He looked over at Lizzy and Wiley sitting on the floor in front of the television. Bailey lay curled up between them. "Quite the peacemaker, isn't he?" Will nodded in the dog's direction.

"He does have a way of bringing people together." I made a move to say goodnight to Lizzy and Wiley and to call Bailey to come with me. I thought better of it, though, when Wiley laid himself down on the rug and used Bailey as a pillow. Bailey groaned happily and rolled onto his side.

"Why don't you keep him here with you tonight?" I said. "He'll be fine without me as long as he's at home."

"Well, he might be, but I sure as hell won't," Will groused.

I smiled up at him teasingly and caressed his cheek. "Oh, poor boy. How you do suffer."

Out of the children's line of sight, he rested his hands on my waist. "Why don't you sneak into your own room tonight?" he asked wryly. "It's your place, after all. I'll leave the door unlocked for you."

I stood on my tiptoes and brought my mouth close to his ear. "Don't worry about the lock," I whispered. "It's my place. I have a key."

And so it was that a few hours later, when Lizzy and Wiley were sound asleep in the guest room—she in the bed, he on the cot, and both in the presence of one snoring canine companion—I crept into my own room, undressed quietly, and curled up next to Will. He had dozed off himself, but as soon as he realized I was there he reached for me and pulled me to him.

Shortly thereafter, he lay next to me again, his breathing heavy and body damp from exertion, and a smile spreading across his face.

# 40

Callie was gone when Will awoke in the morning. Still on the edge of sleep but ready for her again, he moved toward the spot where he'd last held her. He opened his eyes and sighed when he encountered only bed-clothes. He didn't have time, however, to give much thought to his current predicament—or to the previous evening, which was closely related to his current predicament. It was only moments before Wiley bounded into the room with Bailey at his heels, and they both jumped onto the bed.

"Hey, there! Watch out, you two," Will cried, extending his arms in an attempt to protect himself.

"Come on, Dad, get up. We have to get ready to go." Wiley pulled at his arm.

Will lifted himself into a sitting position, tucked a pillow behind him, and smiled playfully. "What are you talking about?" he teased. "Go where?"

"To the fair! You promised to ride The Hammer with me!"

"Ah, yes. Now I remember. The fair. The Hammer. So you're still up for it, huh?"

"Da-ad! Come *on*, let's go!"

Wiley hopped off the bed and ran back to the guest room to find his clothes, slamming the door on his way out. Will flinched and then sighed in exasperation, wondering if his son would ever be capable of closing a door quietly. He arose quickly and pulled on the pajama bottoms and worn T-shirt he'd tossed haphazardly onto the floor the night before.

Meanwhile, Lizzy had gotten out of bed and knocked quietly at his door.

"C'mon in," Will called. Lizzy opened the door but stood just outside the room. She was clad in dark blue sweatpants and a sweatshirt with the words Westin Girls Softball emblazoned on the front in stark white letters. She'd pulled her long brown hair into a ponytail before going to sleep. It had loosened during the night, and silky strands fell in wisps across her face.

"Good morning, LZ," Will said. "Ready for the fair?"

Lizzy glanced around the room. "Where is she?" she asked with a sneer. "I figured she'd be in here."

Will took a breath and sat down on the bed. "Liz, come here for a minute."

Lizzy hesitated. Her eyes darted from the perfume bottles on the dresser to the photographs of Callie and her children, to the books on the night-stands, and to the overstuffed chair next to the window. All these things were Callie's—the books, the trinkets, the clothes. They belonged to her. And now her father did, too. Lizzy felt a sharp pain in her abdomen, as though she had eaten glass shards. She tightened her muscles and put her hand over the area of pain.

Will eyed her with concern. "Are you okay, LZ? It looks like something hurts."

She wanted to tell him that everything hurt, from the inside out. Nothing was the way it was supposed to be, and there wasn't anything she could do about it.

"I'm fine," she replied sharply.

"Well, come here for a minute anyway," Will said again.

She obliged—grudgingly—and, following her doctor-father's orders, stretched out on her back so he could give her a cursory exam.

"Does this hurt?" he asked as he pressed in around her appendix.

"No."

"How about here?" He moved his hands across her abdomen, feeling for evidence of anything equally serious.

"No."

"And here?"

"No, Dad. I said I'm fine. Stop being a doctor."

She sat up.

"Sorry," he said. "Can't help it. Can't help being a dad, can't help being a doctor."

They were both leaning back against the headboard. Will put his arm around Lizzy's shoulder and drew her close to him.

"I want to tell you something," he said thoughtfully. "Lizzy, I knew your mom for a long time—a lot longer than you did." He tweaked her ponytail and she responded with a glimmer of a smile. "And I know how much she loved us. And I also know that she would want us—all of us—to be as happy as we can be, even if she isn't here. Lizzy, she was one of the kindest, most understanding people I've ever known, and the thing she would most want for you is that you live as full and happy a life as you possibly can."

"Gran says Callie will make us forget her," Lizzy said. She was playing with the sheet, making little pleats between her fingers.

"Could you?" Will asked.

"No."

"I'm glad. Because I wouldn't want you to." He tilted his head so it touched hers. "And I don't want Wiley to forget her, and I don't want to forget her. That's one reason I'm so glad I have you. Because when I look at you, sometimes I see her."

Lizzy looked up and gave Will a brief smile. Turning her attention back to the sheet, she continued. "Gran said Callie wouldn't want us to remember Mom. She said Callie wouldn't let us have any of her pictures or any of her things."

Will closed his eyes and sighed heavily. "LZ, your grandmother says a lot of things—and so does your Aunt Rowan—and not all of them are accurate. I promise you that Callie doesn't want any of us to forget. She knows herself how important it is. She was your age when her own mother died. She knows how it feels."

Lizzy stiffened. "Well, she doesn't know how *I* feel."

She pulled away from Will, got off the bed, and left the room.

# 41

Much to Wiley's delight, we reached the fairgrounds just in time to catch the pig race quarterfinals. While pig racing was a regular event at the San Sebastian County Fair and Exposition, it was not something he'd had the good fortune to witness elsewhere. From our vantage point in the bleachers we could see the pigs—eight in all—milling around at their respective starting gates, waiting to be called to their marks.

They ran in pairs, and the four who completed three full laps with the best time would move on to the semifinals; the top two from that race would compete in the finals at the end of the day, and the champion would take home the coveted Winged Pig trophy.

"The smart money's on Porky," I whispered to Will. "At least that's what the couple next to me seem to think." I tilted my head in their direction. "And from what I can tell, they seem to be experts on the sport."

"Which one's Porky?" he asked.

"I don't know. But if I were a betting woman, I'd put my wager on that one over there." I pointed to a female rooting around in the dirt and grunting rather loudly. "Petunia. She looks ready to race like the wind."

"Mm, I'd be inclined to go with Arnold Ziffel over there," Will replied. "Or maybe Wilbur—you know, Zuckerman's famous pig."

"Well," I said, surprised by his demonstrated familiarity with *Charlotte's Web*. "I am impressed."

"Hey, listen," he replied with a wink, "you aren't the only one who knows great literature."

After the pig races, which were dominated by Arnold Ziffel, Petunia, and a pair of long shots named Hamhock and This Lil' Piggy, we strolled over to the carnival area to check out the games, the rides, and, more specifically, the infamous Hammer.

Apparently, a number of Wiley's friends had become fans of this particular apparatus at a carnival or fair near Westin a month or so earlier, but Wiley had missed it because he'd gone on a fishing trip with Edward and Chase. The ride boasted two hammer-shaped contrivances, each of which moved in the opposite direction of the other but appeared to be on a collision course at the bottom and top of the rotation. The whole idea made me shudder, but Will, who apparently had a stronger constitution—and stomach—than I, had promised his son initiation into that carnival ride club.

"Hey, Dad, think I can win a goldfish?" Lizzy asked as we passed a booth where fifty or so tiny round fishbowls were arranged in rows on a section of brightly painted plywood. Each contained a small goldfish, and players paid two dollars for four chances to toss a ping-pong ball into a fishbowl. If one hit the mark, the resident goldfish became the prize.

"I hope not," Will replied. "If we managed to get it home, your cat would probably eat it."

"Or leave it on your pillow," Wiley added. "With one fish eye staring up at you."

"You're disgusting," Lizzy said, giving him a shove.

Turning a corner, we came upon The Hammer, and Wiley let out an audible gasp.

We stopped and watched the long arms of The Hammer move back and forth, back and forth, reaching greater altitude with each swing. "Awesome!" Wiley cried. He reached for Will's arm. "C'mon, Dad, let's get in line!"

"Go ahead, I'm coming." Will smiled at the exuberance on his son's face.

"You're really going to do it, huh?" I asked quietly. I was not a fan of carnival rides, except maybe the merry-go-round and, on rare occasions, the Ferris wheel. The idea of being flung into the air and then tossed and turned in all directions was not the least bit appealing. "You've gotta be nuts—both of you." I looked at the ride again and shook my head in disbelief.

We'd stood in line for a half hour or so, waiting for Wiley and Will to take their turn when Lizzy announced she had to go to the bathroom—now!—and wanted Will to walk with her to the restroom. It was a few buildings away, in the main exhibition hall. I think she was hoping to keep him occupied long enough that I'd be forced either to pull Wiley out of line and make him wait for his father to return—in which case Wiley would be angry with me—or accompany him myself on this amusement park monstrosity and then spend the rest of the afternoon trying to get my psyche—and my stomach—back under control. Little did she know that was not going to happen, no matter how she tried to manipulate the situation.

"Dad can't go with you, Liz," Wiley whined. "He has to stay here with me. We're in the next group."

Will looked at me and raised his eyebrows. I caught his meaning immediately.

"How about if you and I walk over," I said to Lizzy. "We can look at the jewelry on the way back. By that time maybe Wiley and your dad will have been thrown around enough by that miserable contraption."

Lizzy responded as if I hadn't spoken. "Dad, I need you to come with me. You said I can't go over there by myself."

"That's right—you can't," Will replied. "And you won't. Callie said she'd go with you. Wiley's been waiting in line for over half an hour. It's not fair to make him wait longer when he doesn't have to."

Lizzy pursed her lips, narrowed her eyes, and looked straight ahead. "All right!" she muttered and started walking away.

I glanced over at Will, let out a sigh, and followed her. What had proved to be an almost enjoyable morning now looked like it might be on a downward slide into an unpleasant afternoon. I watched Lizzy as she walked, and noticed she held her hand over her abdomen as though she were in some kind of discomfort. Probably an upset stomach from the stress, I thought. It wasn't likely due to anything she'd eaten, considering that she'd barely consumed a bite since they arrived. She refused to touch any food I had a hand in preparing or providing.

Ignoring me, she stayed at least five paces ahead as we walked to the restrooms. A line had formed outside the stalls, and she waited in silence. As soon as one opened up, she ducked inside. When she reemerged a minute or two later, she was white as a ghost.

"Lizzy, what's wrong?" I asked.

I could tell at once from her expression that something serious had happened. I could also tell she was deciding how much of it she wanted to share with me.

She approached me, her hand still hovering over her abdomen.

"Lizzy," I asked again, "what's the matter? Are you all right?"

She looked at me wide-eyed. "Blood," she whispered. Where, I demanded. Her underwear, she replied. A few more details, and it wasn't hard to figure out that she had gotten her period, and had no idea what to do about it.

"Have you had it before, or is this the first time?" I asked quietly.

"First time," she answered tersely.

I took a breath and thought for a moment. This was a situation that required careful negotiation.

"Well, tell you what—" I tried to sound nonchalant. "Why don't we get the car keys from your dad and you and I will find a pharmacy and get whatever you need."

A wave of panic washed over her. "Don't tell him. Promise me you won't tell him."

"Honey, he's your father—and he's a doctor. This won't be a surprise. And he'll want to know about it."

"I don't care," she cried. "He'll ask me questions and I don't want to talk about it. Promise me you won't tell him."

I didn't want to keep any secrets from Will, particularly one that involved his daughter. On the other hand, neither did I want to violate Lizzy's confidence. She was none too pleased with me already, and revealing something she wanted kept just between the two of us would only alienate her further.

"What if I tell him quietly, so no one else can hear, but also tell him that you don't want him to ask or say anything about it, and you'll bring it up with him when you're ready?" I suggested. "That way he won't keep asking if you're feeling all right."

She considered the idea and then sighed with obvious resignation. "Okay."

I touched her shoulder very lightly. "Lizzy, this isn't a bad thing. The timing may not be great, but it's something we can take care of."

We found Will and Wiley sitting on a fence just outside the area of The Hammer. They were laughing as Wiley relived their carnival ride. Clearly the adrenaline rush still had him in its grip. Will brightened when he saw us.

"There you are," he said. "We were starting to wonder what happened to you."

"Yeah, Lizzy," Wiley teased, "I told Dad I thought maybe you fell into a port-a-potty."

"Be quiet, jerk," Lizzy replied coldly. She looked at me then, almost pleadingly, and I turned to Will.

"I need your car key," I said, putting out my hand. "Lizzy and I have something we need to do." I looked over at Wiley, who was about to make a comment. "And it doesn't involve either of you."

Will eyed me suspiciously. If Lizzy was getting in the car with me of her own volition, the situation had to be somewhat serious. At the same time, though, Lizzy's willingness to go anywhere with me, no matter what the circumstances, was a step in the right direction. Realizing he had no choice but to trust me, he reached into his pocket, pulled out his keys, and dropped them in my hand.

"We won't be long," I promised. "Lizzy'll call you when we get back, and we'll figure out where to meet up again."

Will searched Lizzy's face for signs of illness or injury, and saw the anxiousness in her eyes.

"Is everything okay?" he asked. Lizzy, in turn, looked at me.

"It's fine. Everything's fine. We'll be back soon," I said. I put my hand on Lizzy's shoulder and we walked away.

Addressing this particular issue with Lizzy was tricky. It required a degree of sensitivity and support, but I also had to keep a certain emotional distance. I was not her mother, nor was I any other female relative, friend, or even well-regarded acquaintance. Right now I just happened to be the person who could provide the assistance she required.

We drove to a pharmacy near the fairgrounds to pick up whatever Lizzy thought she might need. I knew she understood what was happening to her physically, but I wasn't sure how much she'd talked with anyone about the particulars. Will had never mentioned it, but that wasn't a surprise. He still thought of her as his little girl. This momentous event would undo him a little.

Lizzy and I stood in the middle of the aisle, side by side, while she examined the various products. She didn't touch any of them, just studied the packaging.

"Do you know what you want?" I asked cautiously. I wanted her to know I was available, but I also wanted her to decide my level of involvement. "Have you talked about it with anyone?"

She shook her head. Her face was pale, but her ears were bright pink.

"Well," I said, picking up a box. "When my daughter was your age, she used these. Do you want to give them a try, or would you rather have something else?"

She nodded toward the package in my hand. "Those, I guess."

"Okay. Let's get a couple of boxes so you won't have to worry about running out for a while." She shrugged nervously.

I grabbed a small basket from a stack at the end of the aisle and dropped the boxes inside.

"Anything else? Do you have any discomfort? Do you need some Tylenol or ibuprofen?"

Again, she shook her head. We started walking to the front of the store, and as we approached the checkout line she suddenly stopped in her tracks. "I don't have any money," she said, almost in a panic.

"That's okay. I'll take care of it," I reassured her. She was clearly still uncomfortable, and I suspected it had something to do with the young man working the cash register. "And, here—" I dug in my purse for the car key. "Why don't you wait for me in the car? I'll pay for this and be right out."

With great relief, she took the key and went outside.

We made a quick stop at home and then headed back to the fairgrounds. Lizzy was silent as we drove, but I could tell she had something on her mind. She watched the scenery pass, and every so often took a breath as though she were going to speak. Each time, though, she stopped herself.

Finally, as we pulled into a parking space back at the fairgrounds, she asked her question.

"Did your mom help you? The first time, I mean."

I switched off the engine and took the key out of the ignition. "No," I replied quietly. "She was gone long before that."

"Who did then?"

I turned to face her. "You know, I honestly don't remember."

She looked down at her lap. "Well, thanks for helping me," she said, her voice barely a whisper.

"You're welcome," I replied.

We found Will and Wiley in the arcade playing pinball. Wiley was up to 78,420 points, and Will had reached an even 80,000.

"Hey, you're back!" Will said when he saw us. "And just in the nick of time." He put his hands on Wiley's shoulders. "This boy here is poised to take the lead away from his old man."

He gave Lizzy a quick visual once-over. "You all right, LZ?"

"Yeah, Dad, I'm fine. Can we get something to eat? I'm hungry."

"Sure. You and Wiley can go on ahead and decide what you want," Will said.

When Lizzy and Wiley were out of earshot, Will asked about Lizzy's and my impromptu excursion. I told him where she and I had gone.

"Jeez," he said looking a little overcome. I was right about his being undone by the news.

"You can't talk to her about it, though," I warned him. "She's feeling awkward and a little embarrassed, and she doesn't want you to ask any questions."

"There's nothing to be embarrassed about," he argued. "And, anyway, I'm her father. We talk about everything."

"Not this," I said firmly. "Wait until she brings it up."

He stopped and looked at me for a moment. "All right." He rubbed his hand over his face. "Wow. I guess she's not a little girl anymore."

"Uh, yeah, she is," I replied. "She's only thirteen. And she needs her dad as much as ever. In some ways, even more."

He took my hand as we continued walking, worming our way through the throng of people. Ahead of us, I could see Wiley's blond head and Lizzy's purple tank top. "Thanks for stepping in," Will said. "I'm sure she appreciates it—I know I do. God, I don't know what I would have done. Probably handled it all wrong."

"Oh, I doubt that very much," I replied. "You love her, and she knows it, and that's all that matters."

By the time we got home it was close to evening and everyone was worn out. Bailey, who had been left to his own devices all day, was beside himself at our arrival and immediately demanded that someone join him outside for a game of fetch. Fortunately, he found a willing partner in Wiley, so I was able to sit down for a few minutes and relax. Lizzy, meanwhile, had gone upstairs to take a short nap before dinner. I think she was feeling a bit undone herself.

Will joined me on the couch in the living room. I sank into the cushions, my legs stretched in front of me. He extended his arm across the back of the couch, and I leaned against his chest. His shirt smelled of hay and woodsmoke and something sweet—funnel cake, maybe. I reached up and pulled him toward me. My lips brushed his. He returned the favor—but more fervently.

"I've wanted to do that all day," he whispered.

"So have I."

Dinner that evening consisted simply of scrambled eggs and raisin bread toast. Between the cotton candy, hot dogs, and other Harvest Festival delicacies consumed over the course of the day, no one was particularly hungry.

I was doing cleanup in the kitchen, ably assisted by Wiley, and Will and Lizzy were in the living room. They had found a deck of cards and were engaged in a game of gin rummy. I put away the last pan and was about to join them when I heard Lizzy's voice.

"Did Callie tell you?"

I turned toward the living room. Lizzy sat across from Will, her eyes focused on her cards.

"Yeah," he replied, rearranging his own hand. "How do you feel?"

"Okay."

He paused briefly and looked at her. "Do you want to ask me anything?"

Lizzy stared at him with an expression that suggested both disbelief and utter disgust. He may as well have asked if she wanted him to go along on her first date. "No!" she replied. "Jeez, Dad!"

"Okay," he said, raising his hand to his chest. "I just want to make sure."

Lizzy was pensive for a moment as she studied her cards again. "Did you know Callie's mom wasn't there when—" She paused, apparently deciding not to continue. "Never mind," she muttered, tossing the cards on the table and getting up to leave. "I'm going outside." She glanced over in Wiley's direction. "Hey, jerk, want to come?"

# 42

I was in the kitchen flipping slices of French toast the next morning when Ben and Justine arrived. Justine had called me the evening before to tell me she'd gotten to Ben's place and they'd drive over from Kentfield together. They were going to spend two nights, which I hoped would be enough time for them to become acquainted with Lizzy and Wiley—and vice versa—but not so much that anyone would be overwhelmed.

I wasn't really worried about my two because I knew Ben would be wearing his big brother hat, and would do his best to make everyone comfortable. He had a talent for that. And Justine would be, well, Justine.

Will had told Lizzy and Wiley that Ben and Justine were coming, and Wiley's eagerness to meet them was matched only by Lizzy's indifference. I hoped that a few minutes with Justine would spark a little enthusiasm. Both she and Ben were well aware of Lizzy's opposition to the prospective family unit.

"Hi, Mama," Justine said cheerfully as she and Ben walked in through the back door. She gave me a hug from behind and showed me the small bouquet of flowers she had brought. She held them up to my nose so I could smell them. "Look—I brought these for the table," she said, and began rummaging around for a vase.

"They're beautiful, honey, and they smell wonderful," I said.

"Hi, Mom." Ben peered over my shoulder. "Smells good." He glanced around the kitchen and living room. "Where is everyone?"

"Um, I think Wiley is outside somewhere with Bailey—they've gotten to be great friends—and Lizzy is upstairs." I stacked the slices of French toast on the griddle and then slid them onto a serving plate.

Will walked in from the garage.

"Will!" Justine held her arms out to him. "It's so great to see you again."

As I watched them, I noticed Ben turn toward the stairs and smile. "Hey, you must be Lizzy," he said warmly.

Lizzy took a few steps forward and stood very close to her father. She was obviously uncomfortable in the presence of my children.

Justine extended her arm to shake hands. "That's Ben, and I'm Justine. And I'm really happy to meet you, finally."

Lizzy glanced quickly at Will and then back to Justine, taking her hand. "Thanks," she said huskily.

"Okay, Mom," Justine said turning her attention to me. "What do you need me to do?"

"Well, the table still needs to be set. Maybe Lizzy can help."

Justine rotated on the balls of her feet so she faced Lizzy again. "Well?" she said. "Table or flowers?"

As it turned out, Lizzy and Justine worked together on both the table and the flower arrangement. Justine chattered on about nothing important, and Lizzy, who moved along beside her, listened attentively but had no comment.

Just as we were getting ready to sit down, Will went outside to find Wiley.

I heard him call Wiley's name two or three times, and when neither came back inside after a minute or two, I went out to check on them. Will was standing on the driveway, hands on his hips, looking concerned.

"I don't see him," he said. "I've looked around and I've called him, but he hasn't answered me."

"How about Bailey?" I asked, surveying the area. "Have you seen him? They were out here together. If he went off anywhere, Bailey would have followed him, I'm sure."

We were joined by Ben, Justine, and Lizzy, all wondering what was going on. Wiley had been outside playing with the dog, and now both seemed to have disappeared.

Will ran his hand through his hair. I could see the panic starting to rise.

Ben suggested we split up and look around. There were a lot of nooks and crannies around the property—and near the house in particular—that might have caught Wiley's interest.

"Could he have followed Bailey?" Justine asked. "I mean, could Bailey have run after a rabbit or something and Wiley just went with him?"

"Not likely," I replied. "When Bailey goes after something he doesn't stay with it for long, and he always comes back. If he's not here, I'm sure he's followed Wiley somewhere."

We fanned out to conduct a search, with Justine and Lizzy taking the area between the cottage and Alice's house, Ben heading off toward the orchards, and Will and me making our way to the bluffs.

It was late morning, and the temperature was already high enough to be uncomfortably warm in the direct sun, although it remained fairly tolerable in the shade. I realized about a half mile into our trek that we should have grabbed a couple of water bottles. I hoped that Wiley had simply wandered off to investigate something, with Bailey in tow, and then lost track of time. If that were the case, then depending on where they'd gotten to, the worst they'd be is hot and thirsty. If something more serious had happened, though, or if Wiley were hurt, thirst might be the least of our worries.

Will cupped his hands around his mouth and shouted Wiley's name. No reply. The only sounds, besides our own footsteps on the gravely dirt, were the birds calling to each other.

"Wiley!" Will called again. And again, no reply.

I hollered for Bailey. If he were anywhere in the vicinity, he'd bark for me.

We followed the trail for another quarter mile or so as it wound through groves of sycamore and eucalyptus trees.

"God, Callie, where could he be?" Will scanned the immediate vicinity. I could hear the fear in his voice.

"He's got to be here somewhere. It would be impossible for him to go very far. He'd run out of space. And there aren't—" I stopped.

"There aren't what?"

I closed my eyes, chastising myself for bringing the idea to the forefront. But it's the first thought I would have had if one of my children was missing. "I was just going to say that there aren't many people—I mean strangers—wandering around here. It's not likely he'd encounter anyone."

Will rubbed his hand across his face. He'd gone completely pale, and looked as though he might be physically ill.

"So he has to be here," I said forcefully. "And Bailey with him. We just have to keep looking."

We followed the trails that ran along the bluffs above the ocean, as well as those that cut through the meadow to the east. There was no sign of boy or dog. And now I was really starting to worry. They hadn't been gone long enough to get much farther than this. I checked in with Ben and Justine to see if they'd found anything. They hadn't.

The mugwort, white sage, and golden eardrops had grown tall across the bluffs and meadow, and along with the native grasses, they created a very effective screen that made it nearly impossible to see anything at any distance. If Wiley were out here, we'd have to practically stumble across him.

Will continued to shout Wiley's name, and I continued to call for Bailey. I prayed one of us would get a response. After another half hour or so, as we turned a corner that brought us close to the edge of the bluff, I heard what I thought was a soft cry. I stopped and grabbed Will's hand.

"Shh," I said, putting my forefinger up to my mouth. I cocked my head and listened. From somewhere below me I picked up the sound again. I called Bailey's name and waited for a response. This time I was rewarded with a high-pitched whine. I peered over the edge of the bluff, scanning the grass and shrubs for anything that resembled either boy or dog. The terrain was fairly rugged and in some places nearly perpendicular to the ocean below. The tide was out, and huge rocks jutted out from the sand.

"Bailey," I called, "where are you?" A sharp "rrrf-rrrf" came from several yards away.

From the trail, some sections of the bluff appeared to drop straight to the ocean. In reality, however, many of them fell only ten or twelve feet to outcroppings, some of which were the size of, maybe, a queen-size bed. It was on one of these that we found Wiley and Bailey.

Will spotted them first, and immediately scrambled down the steep but manageable ocean side of the bluff to the grassy plane where Wiley lay stretched out with Bailey curled around him. I remained on the trail that edged the bluff. At one point Will's foot slid on some loose dirt and he grabbed onto a handful of scrub brush to keep himself from falling. I stifled a scream and then begged him to be careful, but he wasn't listening. His focus was entirely on Wiley.

I pulled out my phone and quickly called Ben to tell him where we were. From his location near the orchard, it wouldn't take more than ten minutes for him to get here. He was closer to Alice's house than he was to the cottage, so I told him to look in her garage for some rope. I also told him to get a few bottles of water from her and bring them with him. And finally, he should call Justine and let her know what was going on so she and Lizzy could meet us.

As I spoke to Ben, I watched Will descend farther down the side of the bluff. It crossed my mind that, depending on the situation, we might have trouble getting both of them back up to the top. I stood with my hand over my mouth, contemplating the various possibilities, as Will reached Wiley. Bailey refused to move, but the end of his tail wagged slightly as Will got closer. I called to him, but he only looked at me.

Wiley was lying on his side with one leg curled and the other outstretched. His head was resting on his arm. His eyes were closed, and I prayed that he was not unconscious. Will put one hand on Wiley's forehead and the other on his shoulder. I saw that he was speaking to him, but I couldn't hear his words.

Wiley opened his eyes and smiled slightly at his father. He started to get up, but Will stopped him. He must have asked questions then as he examined the boy for broken bones and other damage, because Wiley nodded occasionally or shook his head. Finally, Will focused on Wiley's left ankle. The boy howled in pain.

I heard footsteps behind me and turned to see Ben approaching with the rope and water. I heaved a tremendous sigh of relief.

"His ankle is sprained, but I'm pretty sure it's not broken," Will called up to me. "He has pretty significant abrasions on his elbow, but the ankle's the only major thing. I'll need help getting him up to the top."

Ben tossed one end of the rope down to Will. He caught it and wrapped it around Wiley's hips, securing it with a bowline knot. Will and Ben decided that Ben and I would pull on the rope from above, while Will hoisted Wiley upward as far as he could. Wiley would assist on his own behalf by climbing up the side as best he could, using his arms and his uninjured leg. Will told him what he needed to do, and Wiley nodded. The rescue effort would be successful, as long as neither Will nor Wiley slipped. If that happened, one or both of them could easily fall over backward and plummet to the rocks below. My heart pounded in my ears.

Justine and Lizzy arrived just as Ben had his arms around Wiley's chest and was hauling him up over the ledge and onto the trail. I knelt down beside him and handed him a bottle of water, which he accepted gratefully. His face and neck were grimy, and damp with sweat, but I didn't see any significant contusions or abrasions other than the skinned elbow. He wanted to take off his shoe, but I told him to keep it on to help control the swelling.

When Lizzy caught sight of Ben and me peering over the side of the cliff and calling down to Will, she screamed and started to run toward us. Justine grabbed her by the arm and held her close. Lizzy clung to Justine's shirt, whimpering, with tears streaming down her face. Justine hugged her tightly, and Lizzy buried her head in Justine's arms. She had already lost one parent to a steep, rocky dive; the idea of the other meeting a similar fate must have terrified her.

Getting Wiley up onto high ground had been a fairly easy proposition because Ben and I were at the top, pulling, and Will was underneath, pushing. Wiley hadn't had far to go on his own strength. And, of course, he wasn't particularly heavy. For Will, it would be more difficult. Tying the rope to a tree and having him rappel up the cliff would have been one possible solution, except that no trees were within reach of the rope. My inclination was to call in professionals—as in a rescue team—but Ben and Will refused. Nor would they take my suggestion that Ben find Alice's foreman and his pickup and bring both of them here so they could attach the rope to the bumper and haul Will up that way. Will didn't want to waste the time, and he and Ben had no doubt they could manage.

The best option, they decided, was for Ben and Justine and me to hold the rope while Will climbed up. I uttered another brief yet heartfelt prayer, took my place behind Ben, and held on for all I was worth. The dirt on the trail was dry and loose, but deep ruts carved into the ground by the winter rains made getting a good foothold at least possible. Still, at one point, when Will was halfway up the cliff, Ben lost his footing and Will slid back down to the outcropping. It happened again when Will stepped on a branch that collapsed under his weight. But, finally, on the third try, he heaved himself over the ledge and collapsed on his back in the scrub grass. I wanted to take hold of him and never let go, but Lizzy, who had been standing next to Wiley, rushed to him. She fell on her knees beside him, sobbing. He sat up and took her in his arms.

"Shh, it's okay," he murmured, stroking her hair. "Everyone's safe. We're all safe."

I dropped to the ground several yards away from them. I pulled my knees up to my chin, wrapped my arms around my legs, and hid my face.

Meanwhile, Ben and Justine sat down next to Wiley, who, aside from the ankle and elbow, seemed not much the worse for wear now that he'd had some water. The one among us who managed the best was Bailey. The bluffs were his playground, and once he'd seen Wiley and Will to safety, he scrambled like a mountain goat up the cliff side and onto the trail. He parked himself at my feet. I lifted my head, and he gave me a quick sniff and licked my face.

"Good boy!" I praised, scratching his ears. "What a good boy!"

With her arm around his waist, and his arm around her shoulder, Will and Lizzy walked over to Wiley. Will squatted beside him and examined his ankle again, poking and prodding as gently as possible. Nope, he said with certainty, not broken.

"You're lucky. But you do have a decent sprain. Let's get you home so we can elevate it and put some ice on it." Bailey moved from my side to Wiley's, and Will stopped to give him a pat. "Good work, pal," he said. "There's a soup bone or a steak with your name on it." Bailey merely swished his tail back and forth in the dirt.

It was nearly a mile back to the cottage, and this time Will and Ben gave in to my suggestion regarding Alice's foreman and his truck. Fifteen minutes later, Will and Ben lifted Wiley into the bed of the pickup, and climbed in, along with Lizzy—who wouldn't leave her father's side. Justine and I squeezed into the cab alongside the generously proportioned driver.

Once home, we settled Wiley on the couch in the living room, his ankle propped on two pillows, and a bag of ice draped across the swollen joint. I brought over a basin of warm soapy water and a washcloth and towel and Will cleaned out the abrasion on Wiley's elbow. The patient grimaced and made hissing sounds as he inhaled through his teeth, but otherwise handled the pain stoically. Afterward, I applied layers of lavender and calendula oil and covered the whole thing with a large bandage. Then I took another cloth and a fresh bowl of water and wiped his face, neck, and arms. He smiled at me appreciatively.

"Can I bring you anything?" I asked when I'd gotten him as clean as he was going to be under the circumstances. "Something else to drink? Are you hungry?" He shook his head. I got up and carried the basin, washcloths, and towel back to the kitchen.

Will sat down on the couch, just next to Wiley's feet, and Lizzy curled up on the chair by the window. Ben and Justine joined me in the kitchen. It didn't seem appropriate for any of us to be present for the exchange between Will and Wiley.

"So, how about telling us what happened?" Will prodded.

"Are you mad?" Wiley asked.

"Well, that depends. Start talking."

Wiley had been playing ball in the yard with Bailey, but got bored after a while and decided to investigate the surrounding area.

With Bailey as his trusty and enthusiastic guide, Wiley roamed farther and farther until he found himself along the bluffs. At one point, Wiley said, he saw a snake slither across the trail and decided to follow it. He didn't mean to go down so far, but his foot slipped and he tumbled. I saw Will cringe; Wiley could quite easily have continued tumbling—all the way down to the rocks.

"I mostly slid down on my butt," he explained. "But my foot got caught on a branch and it sort of twisted. And when I tried to get up, I couldn't walk because my ankle hurt." Bailey parked himself next to Wiley, placing his own body between Wiley and the drop to the ocean. "I wasn't scared, though, 'cause Bailey was with me. And I figured you would come and find us. I was just hot and kind of thirsty. And after a while I guess I sort of stopped thinking about where I was."

Will gazed at his son, shaking his head.

"So, are you mad?" Wiley asked, lowering his head so he could avoid looking his father in the eye.

Will snorted. "Well, I can't say I'm not angry about you wandering off without telling anyone. You know better than that. You had everyone really worried. And what's more, you could have gotten seriously hurt."

"I'm really sorry, Dad," Wiley murmured. "I didn't mean to."

"The most important thing right now is that you're okay. But we aren't finished talking about this, and there will be some kind of punishment to help you remember what you did wrong." Will reached over and chucked Wiley under the chin. His expression softened. "Mostly, though, I'm just glad you're okay." He picked up the bag of melting ice to refill it with fresh cubes.

"Hey, Dad?" Wiley turned his face upward.

"Yeah?"

"Thanks for getting me."

"You're welcome."

# 43

It was well past noon by the time we got Wiley settled, and Justine suggested that she and Ben—and Lizzy, if she wanted to join them—make a run to a nearby burger place and pick up lunch for everyone.

Lizzy, who was still plastered to Will's side, passed on the invitation.

After Ben and Justine left, however, she went up to the guest room and closed the door. Wiley dozed on the couch, and Will found me in the kitchen, cleaning up what was left of breakfast.

He came up behind me and pulled me into an embrace. "That was scary as hell," he said holding me tightly. "He came way too close to falling off that outcropping."

"No kidding. So did you." I caressed the muscles of his back, taking great comfort in his solidness. "Do me a favor and don't try that again — either one of you — okay? I don't think my heart could stand it."

"Mine, either," he said.

With Wiley laid up, we abandoned the rest of the day's plans. We'd intended to pack a picnic lunch and take a short hike up around Rock Creek, but that was clearly out of the question. We'd had enough excitement for one day anyway. Ben happened to have his DVD set of *The Lord of the Rings* in his car, and after lunch, he and Wiley and Will became engrossed in part one of the trilogy. Lizzy wandered into the living room a few minutes after it started, and she settled in to watch it, too. Justine sat down with her computer on her lap, and I went up to my room for a few minutes of quiet. I was surprised at how tired I felt from the morning's adventure.

Bailey was sacked out on his cushion, but woke up when he heard me. He jumped up onto the bed and we stretched out next to each other.

I reached over to take a book off the nightstand, but caught sight of a photograph album Justine had tucked away on the bottom shelf. She'd found it in a closet in the house where we—the Winwoods—had lived as a family. Joe owned the house now and lived there with the new Mrs. Winwood. And the new Mrs. Winwood was only too happy to see the photo album—and everything else associated with her husband's first marriage—removed from her home. I picked up the album and began looking through the pages. There were Ben and Justine at four and six in their Halloween costumes. Ben was an astronaut and Justine a butterfly. She adored that costume—the brightly painted wings and the splashes of color I'd applied to her face. So enamored was she, in fact, that she continued to wear the wings well into November, and for three days after Halloween she refused to let me wash the makeup off her face. I smiled at the memory.

Turning the page, I glimpsed images of Ben and Justine again, still children, and of me and Joe, still married. I studied my face—and his—and saw for the first time the expressions of general unhappiness that we must have presented to Ben and Justine every day for years. Terrible models of how to live one's life, I thought.

There were photos from family vacations, school plays, birthday parties, and a host of special events—Ben's high school graduation, Justine decked out for a Homecoming dance. And always, Joe and me in the background. And always, some kind of strain between us.

I'd gotten through about a quarter of the album when Will knocked softly on the door. It was partway open, and he peeked in. He was carrying two glasses of iced tea.

"What are you doing up here all by yourself?" He sat down next to me, and set the glasses on the nightstand.

"Oh, just enjoying a little solitude," I said. "I happened upon this photo album Justine brought, and started looking through it. I haven't seen it for years." I glanced up at him. "Taking a short stroll down memory lane, I guess."

He looked over my shoulder. "Pleasant journey?"

"Yes and no, I suppose." I turned my attention back to the page in front of me for a moment. Justine's third-grade face smiled up at me. I glanced back at Will. "But I'm glad this is where I live now."

He sat down next to me.

"What are you thinking about?" he asked after a short time. "You've been staring at the same picture for five minutes now." The photograph was one of Ben and Justine, taken the day Joe and I brought Justine home from the hospital. Ben was so proud of his new baby sister.

"Actually, I was thinking about lasts," I replied.

"As opposed to firsts, you mean?"

A shiver ran through me and I reached for the throw at the foot of the bed. Will took it from me and draped it over my legs. "A funny thing about lasts," I remarked. "You never know when they happen."

Will eyed me quizzically—and clearly a little worried. "How do you mean?"

"Well, you always know when something has happened for the first time, because it's brand new. But as milestones, lasts are tricky because you don't know they've happened."

"I'm not sure I follow."

"There is a last time, for example, that you hold your child on your lap or rock her to sleep. Or nurse him. Or fix a bottle. Or change a diaper. Or read a bedtime story. Or pack a lunch for school. Things you do over and over again, sometimes for years. And then at some point, each one happens for the last time. You never do that thing again."

"I think I know what you mean," Will said. "When Lizzy was just a toddler, she'd climb up on my lap when she was tired, stuff her thumb in her mouth, and go to sleep with her head on my chest. She was warm and soft, and I loved that she felt so safe with me." He looked out the window as though he were seeing her somewhere in the distance. "And then she stopped doing it. Probably got too old, or too big. I don't remember when, or why, but I missed it."

"That's exactly what I mean. You never know that the last time has occurred. So you don't savor it the way you might if you knew it was never going to happen again. It's sad, in a way." I paused briefly. "And maybe that makes lasts even more significant than firsts."

Will reached over and picked up his glass. He took a long sip. "You could be right. We've certainly had our share of lasts without realizing it."

"Mmm," I agreed. "Remember the night before you left for Boston? God, we were so young. We had no idea it would be the last time we'd sleep together. And the following morning—I never would have dreamed the last kiss you gave me before you drove away would, indeed, be the last kiss."

"Well, not exactly the last on either count," he whispered and lightly brushed his lips against mine. "It just took twenty-five years to get to the next one." He touched my cheek with the back of his hand. "So much has happened for both of us between then and now," he continued, "some of it pretty incredible, and some of it not so great." We exchanged glances. "But I feel so lucky to have another chance with you."

"I wonder what would have happened if we hadn't gone our separate ways all those years ago," I thought out loud. I toyed with the pearl ring on my right hand. It was an anniversary gift from my father to my mother, and had been passed on to me after she died. "Would we have gotten married, do you think? Had children of our own?"

Will lifted one shoulder and let it drop. "I don't know," he replied. "But I do sort of regret that we won't."

"Won't what?" I asked tilting my head to look up at him.

"Have children—well, one, anyway—yours and mine."

"Just short of impossible now," I quipped. "But I know what you mean. And I sort of regret it, too. Except if I hadn't married Joe, I wouldn't have Ben and Justine. And, you know, I really think they are my greatest contribution to the world—well, his and mine, I suppose. I truly believe they will do spectacular things."

"Yeah, I feel the same way about Wiley and Lizzy. Wiley has a tremendous ability to make people laugh, and Lizzy has an extraordinary kindness and sensitivity about her." He glanced at me and shrugged. "Even if she does hide it from you."

His expression turned pensive then. "They are what's left of Joanna. I guess they're sort of her gift to the world."

I shivered again and sat upright. It was beginning to hit me that whatever family Will and I built together, Joanna would always be a part of it. Her ghost would follow Lizzy, Wiley, and, to some extent, Will, for the rest of their lives. Like it or not, I would have to find a way to live with her, too. It was a daunting prospect, and once again I found myself feeling oddly sympathetic toward Lila, who never figured out a way to coexist peacefully with my mother's memory.

Will put an arm around me. "I'm sorry, Cal. I shouldn't have said that."

"Don't be silly," I said, trying to sound unfazed. "Of course you should. You have children with her. It's not like you can erase her from your life—or that you'd want to."

"And you can't do that with Joe, either."

"Well, I can't erase him from my past, but I can remove every trace of him from my present and my future. That's the beauty of divorce papers—and grown children who don't require joint custody." I closed the photo album and set it aside, as though temporarily closing a door on some part of my personal history. "Unfortunately, your situation is not so clear cut. Joe and I wouldn't be together right now, no matter what. But you and Joanna …"

Will sighed heavily and held my hand against the muscle of his thigh.

"Cal, when I married Joanna, I did love her. And I expected that, aside from a few bumps in the road, we'd live happily ever after. Obviously, I was wrong about that. And I don't know what would have happened if she hadn't died—maybe she would have wanted something else, and everything would be different. But I *do* know that I have never in my life loved anyone the way I love you."

I leaned against him, eyes closed, breathing in his musky scent. "Well, I guess things happen the way they're supposed to," I said. "If you and I had gotten married way back when, there's a good chance we wouldn't have stayed together. We were pretty young, after all. Maybe we needed the long separation—and all the experiences that came with it."

He took my hand and began playing with the ring himself, rotating it around and around on my finger.

"Maybe," he said, "but I still consider myself very lucky to have another chance with you."

He picked up the photo album, held it between us, and opened it to a page in the middle. He pointed to an older woman standing hand in hand with four-year-old Justine in front of Cinderella's castle at Disneyland. "So, who's this?"

℘ℨ

In search of her father, Lizzy climbed the stairs and followed the sound of his voice. She had a good idea where she'd find him. Callie's laugh floated into the hall, and Lizzy's stomach tightened. She was right.

Standing just beyond the door, she saw them. They were sitting on Callie's bed, looking through what appeared to be a photo album. Callie's shoulder was pressed against Will's chest as she pointed out pictures and identified subjects and places that had nothing to do with him. Lizzy watched her father. His eyes sparkled, and he smiled easily. He took Callie's hand and lightly kissed her palm. Lizzy's eyes burned. She didn't remember him looking at her mother that way or taking her hand with the same ease and tenderness.

Lizzy stood quietly, close enough to watch Will and Callie together, but too far away to hear the words that passed between them. They interacted in a calm, light-hearted manner, entirely unaware of her presence.

Callie reached up and touched Will's cheek. Lizzy's hands curled into fists and she clenched her teeth, swallowing the rage that grew from somewhere deep in her belly. She was losing him, she thought. She was losing her father, and the idea of it petrified her. He was all she had, and she couldn't survive without him. It was hard enough trying to get through every day without her mother.

She brought her hand up and quickly wiped away the tears that spilled onto her cheeks. She wanted her mother. If her mother were alive, none of this would be happening. They'd all be back in Westin together, in their own house, as the family they were meant to be. No intrusions, no intruders, no step-anything. Just Will, Joanna, Lizzy, and Wiley.

She closed her eyes and imagined the feel of her mother's hands stroking her back or pulling her hair into a braid. If she quieted her mind, she could hear Joanna singing a lullaby to her, and she could smell the floral fragrance of Joanna's perfume. If she closed her eyes and remembered hard enough, she could conjure not just a fleeting image of her mother but an almost complete resurrection.

Inevitably, however, reality hit her head-on. When she opened her eyes again, she crashed into the truth of what her life had become—was becoming. Her mother was gone. Had left her. And in his way, her father was getting ready to do the same.

"Hey, LZ, is that you?" Will's voice broke into her thoughts. Startled, she took a few steps backward. "Are you looking for me?"

She moved forward again, into a shaft of light that filtered in through the bedroom window and struck the carpet in the hall. It reflected off the warm brown streaks in her hair. "I was just wondering where you were," she said. With unmistakable bitterness, she added, "I guess I should have known."

He held his arm out to her, but she remained just outside the doorway. "Come here," he said softly.

❧

Figuring that my exit would be welcomed by at least one of them, I closed the photo album and stood up. "I think I'll go downstairs and check on Bailey. And maybe I'll see if Wiley needs anything."

"He doesn't," Lizzy responded sharply, fixing a glare in my direction. I felt a distinct sense of relief that I wasn't anywhere near the edge of the bluff when she had come on the scene earlier in the day. "I'm taking care of him. He's fine."

"Watch the tone, Liz," Will scolded.

"No, it's okay," I said to Will, but kept my eyes on Lizzy. "I will check on Bailey, though. He hasn't been out in a while."

Downstairs, I opened the back door and shooed Bailey outside. He immediately took off after a butterfly, jumping and cavorting like the carefree spirit he was. If I wasn't tempted to join him, I was certainly envious of him.

Wiley was still on the couch, and I did look in on him. The movie had ended, and Ben and Justine had gone over to Alice's house to help her move a dresser and rearrange some bookshelves.

"How's the ankle?" I asked. Wiley glanced up from the TV.

"It hurts a little, but not bad," he replied. I took a seat next to him on the edge of the couch.

"What are you watching?"

"A cartoon." He turned his face to the screen. "It's *The Jetsons*. Ben said he used to watch it when he was little. But I've never seen it."

I chuckled. "He did. And you know what's really funny? So did I when I was your age. It's a pretty old show. I always liked Rosie, the robot maid. And Astro, of course, but then, I'm partial to dogs."

Wiley had pressed the mute button on the remote control, so we sat together in silence and watched the animated action on the screen. The only sound was the quiet tick-tock of the clock on the shelf as it marked the passing seconds.

"I have a question," Wiley said suddenly.

"What is it? Maybe I have an answer," I replied.

He looked down at the remote and then at me. "If you have your own children, how can you care about me and Lizzy?"

I took a deep breath. This was not what I'd expected. I wasn't prepared for any serious life discussions—my mind was still on cartoon characters. Wiley gazed at me with round blue eyes and an expression that was frighteningly serious. My immediate inclination was to pull him close to me and hold him tightly. Instead, I paused for a moment, chewing on the inside of my bottom lip as I thought about how to respond.

"Well," I began tentatively, "my feelings for Ben and Justine are very special because they are my own children—just like your dad's feelings for you and Lizzy are very special. But that doesn't mean I don't care about you, too. And I do, very, very much. And even though your dad loves you and Lizzy more than anything, that doesn't mean he can't care about Ben and Justine."

"But could you love me and Lizzy?" It was clear he'd put a lot of thought into this particular topic.

"Yes, I'm sure I could."

"But we aren't your children." Every answer I gave him seemed to elicit a new concern, or take his current concerns in a new direction.

"Well," I answered thoughtfully, "there are also different kinds of love. You love your dad and you love your grandmother, but not in the same way, right? And you love your sister, but that's different, too."

"Do you love my dad?" Wiley asked.

"Yes, I do. Very much."

"Does he love you?"

"Yes, I think he does."

Wiley drew his eyebrows together into a scowl. He was thinking hard about something. "But what about my mom?" he asked finally. "Does that mean he doesn't love her anymore?"

I heard a creak and looked over at the stairs. Will was standing on the bottom step with Lizzy at his side. She was watching Wiley and me, taking in the words I addressed to her brother. I turned back to Wiley, who didn't seem to notice his father and sister were nearby.

"Of course not," I replied. "He loves your mom, and he always will."

Wiley cocked his head and gave me a look of total bewilderment. "But how can he if he loves you?"

I took another deep breath. "Well, you love Winslow, right?"

Wiley nodded. "Uh-huh."

"But you also love Hank, even though he's not here anymore."

He nodded again.

"Winslow didn't make you forget Hank, did he? Or feel any differently about him?"

Wiley shook his head.

"It's like that with people, too," I said. I reached out and brushed a few strands of hair away from his eyes. "I've learned an interesting thing about love. It never runs out. Our hearts just keep making more and more and more, so we always have enough."

"Do you love Ben's dad?"

That question caught me by complete surprise.

"Ah, er," I hesitated. "Well, yes, I suppose I do."

"But why don't you live with him?"

Now the conversation was taking a decidedly uncomfortable turn. I glanced over my shoulder at Will, hoping he'd step in. He merely raised his eyebrows. Apparently, he was as puzzled about Wiley's line of questioning as I was—and about how to respond.

"Well, I don't live with him because we aren't married anymore," I explained.

"If you aren't married anymore, how come you still love him? And if you still love him, how come you aren't married anymore?" Wiley's questions drew me deeper and deeper into a very complicated—and thorny—topic, and I tried to keep my answers simple.

"I think that love doesn't go away, but sometimes it changes. Not between parents and children," I assured him, "but sometimes between grown-ups. Not always, but sometimes." I hoped that would satisfy him.

"Maybe it's like pizza," he said seriously.

I looked at him quizzically.

"I used to only want plain cheese pizza," he explained. "But now I only get pepperoni. I still like cheese, though."

I heard Will chuckle behind me.

"Yeah," I replied. "It's a lot like that."

Clearly troubled by the exchange between Wiley and me, Lizzy pushed her way past Will and ran out the front door. From my position on the couch, I peered out the window and saw her pacing across the front walkway. Her arms were folded across her chest, and she was breathing heavily. She stopped for a moment, sat down on the worn wooden bench near the garden, and wiped her eyes with the heels of her hands. My heart went out to her. I understood—perhaps better than anyone—how she was feeling, and I wished I could say something to make her feel better. If she'd allowed me to speak to her, I would have told her what I think I needed to hear when I was her age and my father married Lila. I would have reassured Lizzy that her mother's memory was safe. I would have promised her that whatever she needed to keep her mother close would be there for her always. And I would have made it clear that her father was hers forever.

None of that mattered, though. As far as Lizzy was concerned, I was the enemy—the source of all her current unhappiness. And in that capacity, I could provide no comfort whatsoever.

Will, who also had been watching her through the window, made a move toward the front door. He stopped, however, when he saw Ben approach her in the yard. He was concentrating on his cell phone—checking for messages from his girlfriend, most likely—but when he caught sight of Lizzy perched on the bench, he turned it off and tucked it in his pocket. I could see him asking her a question. She responded with barely a nod. He took a seat next to her, and continued talking.

Will apparently changed his mind about going to her, and, instead, sat down in one of the chairs across from Wiley and me. He laughed softly and pointed with his chin toward his son, who, as I sat next to him, had nodded off to sleep. I patted Wiley's arm.

"Poor guy. He must be exhausted. I'm sure he had quite a fright this morning, no matter how much he argues otherwise." I turned back toward Will, who was monitoring the scene as it unfolded outside the window.

"Ben's good," I commented. "He'll make her feel better. He has a knack for that—and Justine's given him plenty of practice."

Will smiled and raised an eyebrow. "And Lizzy certainly could use a perspective other than mine," he said. "Or Eleanor's."

I rose and moved closer to the window. Ben's head was tilted close to Lizzy's, and he was saying something that, given how intently she was listening to him, must have been serious.

"Look," I said to Will, motioning toward them. He stood next to me and wrapped his arm around my shoulder.

"That's a beautiful sight," he murmured.

# 44

After a casual dinner of—not coincidentally—pepperoni pizza and salad, with ice cream sundaes for dessert, we all gathered in the living room for a game of Pictionary. The Tremaines battled the Winwoods, with the losing team promising to bake a batch of the winning team's favorite cookies. Confident to a fault, Will and Wiley were already discussing what kind they wanted. Will preferred chocolate chip, while Wiley favored oatmeal raisin. Lizzy remained silent.

Given that I had no drawing ability whatsoever, I was not a huge fan of Pictionary, and in my mind was already scanning the cupboards to make sure I had all the ingredients for both kinds of cookies. Fortunately, Ben had a decent hand, and Justine seemed to pull the correct responses out of thin air. Still, we were no match for Wiley, who appeared to be channeling Rembrandt or Norman Rockwell. When it became clear that the Winwoods would come up on the short end of the cookie deal, we nixed the formal game, and, as one big team, guessed the clues as Wiley drew them. Even at that, spontaneous teams formed, with Lizzy aligning herself with either Ben or Justine, depending on the clue. She even laughed when Ben pretended to mistake Wiley's llama for a camel. Will and I sat back and watched, both of us aware of the significance of the moment. Maybe, I thought to myself, just maybe, we actually can make this work.

It was getting late when the game finally wound down, and I announced to Ben and Justine that it was time to walk the short distance to Alice's house. I knew she'd be waiting up for a report on how the day had gone post-sprained ankle.

Before we left, though, Will and I cleaned up the kitchen. And while we did that, our respective children tuned in to a television sitcom. I don't know what show it was, but I heard laughter as I was stacking plates in the dining area.

243

"You were really great with Wiley earlier today," Will commented as he wiped out the wooden salad bowl. "Those were some tough questions."

I rinsed the sponge and began wiping down the counters. "He's such a sweet kid," I said. "So serious, though. I had no idea he had all that on his mind."

Will folded the dishcloth and hung it on the hook next to the sink. "I think he's really starting to like you," he said. "Lizzy on the other hand ..." He nodded toward his daughter, who sat next to Wiley on the couch. She pressed herself up against him, trying to keep as much space as possible between her and Justine. I knew that drill, too. As much as she'd extended herself earlier, she had to retreat to an equal degree right now. Her emotional equilibrium had been upset and she had to regain control. Next time maybe it would shift, and she'd extend herself a little more and retreat a little less.

"I don't know what to do," Will continued. "Part of me wants to hug her, and part of me wants to throttle her—she can be so miserable. But most of all, I just want to take the pain away."

I pulled the bag of trash out from the cupboard under the sink. "How about taking a walk with me to dispose of this?"

After the heat of the day, the evening air was pleasantly cool. Will took the bag and put his arm around my waist as we walked to the garbage can by the back gate.

"Pretty pathetic way to get a moment alone," he joked as he dropped the bag into the can.

"Well, we take what we can get." I put my arms around his neck and kissed him soundly. "That will just have to do for now."

"You are coming back tonight, aren't you?" he asked with some urgency.

"I hadn't really thought about it," I replied with a teasing half smile, "but I suppose I could." In reality, nothing would have kept me away from him.

He held me close. "How about, you suppose you *will* ..." he murmured, and kissed me again.

After a few minutes, we turned back to the cottage. "You know, Will," I said thoughtfully, "as much as you may want to, and as much as you may try, you'll never be able to take Lizzy's pain away. No one can." We walked slowly, arm in arm. "I mean, think about it—she lost the most important person in her life. The grief will be with her forever. The intensity will vary, and she'll learn to live with it, but it will never go away."

We stopped, and I took Will's hand. "You are a great father. And I truly mean that. You are as loving and present for her as anyone can possibly be.

And that's the best thing you can do for her. But it still won't take away the pain."

"So, how did you manage?" he asked.

I took a deep breath and gazed beyond the yard, to the point where the familiar landscape melded with the darkness. "You know, I often wonder about that. Sometimes I think my mother must have been with me somehow, in spirit, maybe, protecting me, guiding me. Because God knows no one else did, and yet I somehow managed to get to adulthood relatively unscathed." I glanced up at him, shaking my head. "And when I think of some of the situations I got myself into along the way, and some of the things that could have happened, well ..."

We reached the steps leading to the back door and sat down. Will held my hand.

"But I'll tell you this," I added, "not a day has gone by since I was eleven years old that I haven't thought of her and felt her absence to one degree or another. It's the kind of loss that informs who you are. It defines you in many ways. And it never goes away."

Will took a deep breath and exhaled heavily. "She has a huge burden, doesn't she? So does Wiley."

"Yeah, but they also have you. And, believe me, that makes up for a lot."

The next day passed uneventfully, much to everyone's relief—no injuries or incidents—and by Monday afternoon I had the cottage to myself again. Ben and Justine left for Kentfield in the morning, and Will headed off to the airport with Lizzy and Wiley a little later.

"Why am I always saying I wish I didn't have to leave you?" Will grumbled shortly before he and the kids piled into the car. We were curled up on the couch in the living room. Lizzy was upstairs, avoiding me, and Wiley was outside with Bailey—and staying in the yard this time. His ankle had already healed enough that he could walk on it fairly easily, as long as it was well wrapped and he moved slowly.

"Because we live in different places and because you always do have to leave," I said. "Or, I do."

I leaned against him and rested my head on his shoulder. His cotton shirt was soft beneath my cheek. "Soon," he murmured stroking my neck. "We'll have it figured out soon. Now that everyone's met, we can start putting it all together."

He turned his head and softly kissed my brow. "I love you, Cal, and I just don't want to leave you anymore," he murmured. "I want you with me. Always."

I nestled in closer and breathed in the scent of soap and aftershave. "I know," I whispered. "I want that, too."

He took my hand and brought it to his mouth. He kissed my fingers and held them to his lips. He was pensive for a moment. "How long has it been since we met up again in the ER? Eight months?" he asked.

"About that," I replied. "Why?"

"I just ... I want us to be ... I mean, what's between us is ..." He paused, and looked down at me, scowling as he tried to find the right words for whatever it was he wanted to say.

"Why, William Tremaine," I said. "If I didn't know better, I'd think you're asking me to go steady."

"No," he said contemplatively. "Well, sort of. What I'm asking is if you'll marry me."

I stared up at him, certain he was making a joke. "You're kidding, right?"

"No." He held my hand to his chest. "I'm not kidding at all. I love you, and I want to spend the rest of my life with you."

"But we've only known each other for eight months."

"We've known each other a lot longer than that. And besides, we're not kids. It's not like we don't know what we're doing or what we're getting ourselves into."

"Getting ourselves into, huh?"

"You know what I mean." He frowned. "This isn't going the way I wanted it to."

I tucked myself into the crook of his shoulder. "I think it's going just fine."

"So," he murmured, "will you marry me?" His fingertips stroked the length of my back.

"Really?"

"Really."

I leaned forward and kissed his chest, just near his heart. "Yes."

# 45

Rowan watched from the window as Paulette greeted Lizzy at the top of the front steps, and both waved goodbye to Will. He swung the car around the circular driveway and headed down to the street. A minute later, Lizzy burst into the living room, dropping a pink and white backpack on the floor near one of the wingback chairs.

"Didn't your dad want to come in?" Rowan asked, and gave her a hug.

Lizzy shook her head and leaned backward, her arms still around her aunt's waist. "Nah, there was an emergency or something he had to take care of at the hospital. He said he wouldn't be very long, though. He's gonna pick up Wiley and they're both coming back here."

"Oh, okay." Rowan smiled and smoothed Lizzy's hair. "Well, Gran will be down shortly. We can't wait to hear about your trip."

She took a seat in the chair closest to the couch. Lizzy parked herself in the other, and pulled the backpack onto her lap. "I have something for you," she announced. "I got it in San Sebastian. Dad won it for me at a fair. I told him I was going to give it to you." She reached inside and pulled out a stuffed elephant. It had been Will's prize for knocking down all ten wooden bottles in one of the carnival games. It had taken only three tries with a baseball.

Lizzy handed the stuffed animal to Rowan, who accepted it thoughtfully, fingering one of its large gray ears. "I remembered what you said once about you and my mom riding the elephant at the African safari park when you were little," Lizzy explained. "I thought this one might make you think of that and remind you of her."

"Oh, Lizzy, that's so sweet of you." Rowan's voice cracked slightly and she held the stuffed animal close to her chest. "You're right. It does make me think of that. Boy, that elephant was huge. Your mom was in front, and I was behind her. I had my arms wrapped around her waist so tight she could barely breathe. She kept trying to make me let go. She was so brave and I was so scared."

"I remember that, too," Eleanor said as she walked into the living room. Lizzy sprung forward and wrapped her arms around her grandmother's waist. Eleanor returned the embrace and kissed the top of Lizzy's head. "Joanna never let you live it down, either," she said to Rowan.

"You were the older sister, and your father had instructed you to look after her," Eleanor continued, laughing softly. "As it turned out, she had to look after you."

Rowan gazed at the elephant, holding it out at arm's length. She shook her head and sighed. "What did your dad say when you told him you wanted to give it to me?"

"He said he thought it was a good idea," Lizzy replied. "He said maybe we could share it."

Rowan didn't respond; she simply returned her attention to the elephant.

Eleanor sat down on the couch and patted the cushion next to her. "Now, Lizzy, tell us all about your trip to San Sebastian. So, we know you went to a fair, but what else did you do?"

Lizzy shared highlights of the weekend. She described the cottage, and its proximity to the ocean; and she told them about Bailey, and about Ben and Justine. Eleanor and Rowan expressed both concern and relief when Lizzy recounted details of the fair, particularly of the trip she and Callie made to the drugstore.

"My goodness!" Eleanor exclaimed, affectionately tucking strands of hair behind Lizzy's ear. "That's certainly a momentous event. How did you feel about it?"

"Mmm, okay, I guess." Lizzy concentrated on the straps of her backpack. Her ears turned a warm shade of pink. "I wished you or Aunt Rowan or Aunt Sarah had been there instead, but Callie helped me. And she didn't make me tell my dad."

Eleanor and Rowan looked at one another.

"Well, that was very thoughtful of her," Eleanor acknowledged. "But why not tell your father?"

Lizzy scowled. "I just didn't want to talk to him about it for a while. But Callie told him, and said he shouldn't ask me about it until I brought it up."

Eleanor stiffened, hands folded in her lap, and lips pursed. "That was very perceptive of her."

Lizzy continued her rundown of the weekend. They watched wide-eyed as she described The Hammer, Wiley's adventure the morning after the fair, and his subsequent sprained ankle. She avoided any discussions related to her father and Callie, or to the longing for her mother that arose from watching them together. She chose not to mention how effortlessly Will and Callie interacted, or how his face lit up when she came into the room.

"And what about her children?" Rowan asked. "Tell us more about them."

Lizzy hesitated. "They were nice. Justine's pretty, and she laughs a lot. And Ben's funny. He told me and Wiley a lot of stupid jokes." She paused briefly, twisting a lock of hair around her finger.

Eleanor watched her granddaughter. "Anything else?" she asked.

Lizzy shrugged and slumped down into the cushion of the couch.

Rowan, who had been quietly listening to Lizzy's report, leaned forward and placed her hand on Lizzy's knee. "You can tell us, you know," she pressed. "Whatever you want to say. It's okay."

Frowning, Lizzy chewed her lip. She opened her mouth to speak, but was interrupted by Paulette bringing in a pitcher of lemonade and a plate of cookies. She set the tray on the coffee table in front of Eleanor.

"I thought you might be hungry or thirsty," she said to Lizzy.

Eleanor nodded to Paulette. "Thank you."

"What were we saying?" Eleanor asked both Lizzy and Rowan after Paulette left the room.

"Lizzy was going to tell us something about her visit," Rowan replied. Then, addressing her niece, "Go ahead, honey."

Lizzy rubbed her eye with the heel of her hand. "On one of the days, I was feeling sort of sad, and angry, and I was missing my mom," she began. "And I went outside to sit on the bench in the front yard. I didn't want to be where Callie was. But Ben came over and talked to me. I think he wanted to make me feel better."

"Well, that was kind of him," Eleanor said casually as she poured lemonade into the tall glasses. She handed one to Lizzy, who sat back against the sofa cushion. "And did he?"

"He was nice. He just put his arm around my shoulder and said he could understand why I was feeling that way." She took a sip of lemonade and reached for a cookie. "He was really nice," she continued. "So was Justine. I liked them. But I still don't want my dad to marry Callie."

"Well, it sounds very much like he's headed in that direction," Eleanor concluded. "Does your father know how you feel?"

Lizzy frowned again. "Yeah. But he says I should trust him. And he says I should give Callie a chance." She paused, glancing from her aunt to her grandmother. "But I don't want to. I want things to be the way they were—when it was just us."

"When you were all a family, right?" Rowan asked pointedly.

Lizzy set her glass on the table. "I just want my dad back," she sighed.

Eleanor raised her glass to her lips. She glanced at Rowan, and then faced Lizzy. She spoke cautiously and deliberately, choosing her words with care. "Lizzy, when Ben put his arm around you, did he do anything else?"

"What do you mean?"

"She means, honey, did he just put his arm around you, or did he get close to you in any other way?" Rowan responded softly.

"No," Lizzy replied nervously, her eyes flitting from her aunt to her grandmother. "Why?"

"We just want to make sure he didn't make you feel uncomfortable," Eleanor added.

"It seemed kind of weird that he'd do that since we didn't really know each other," Lizzy replied. "But I thought he was just being nice."

Once again, Eleanor and Rowan exchanged glances, each manifesting a controlled sense of alarm.

"Why are you asking all these questions?" Lizzy glanced from her grandmother to her aunt. "Did someone do something wrong?"

Eleanor set her cup on the table. "Come here, honey." She held her arms out to Lizzy, who nestled in closer to her. "I'm just not sure it's appropriate for someone who hardly knows you to … to … be that close to you. Especially a young man."

"Lizzy, baby, if it bothered you at all, you need to tell us." Rowan leaned forward in her chair and spoke kindly but firmly. "We can make sure it doesn't happen again."

Lizzy played with the hem of her shirt, running the edge of the fabric between her fingers. "He was really nice to me. We talked, and he made me feel better."

"What did he say?" Eleanor asked.

"He said he understood how I felt, and that he'd probably feel the same way if it were him. He said he knew I was mad, and he knew I didn't like his mom. And he said it was okay. He said that maybe after a while we'd all be more comfortable with each other, but right now everything was too strange."

Lizzy tilted her head upward to look at Eleanor. "Gran, do you think he was only pretending to be nice?"

"I don't know, honey," Eleanor replied. "But I do know that if you have problems you should talk to your father, or to me or Aunt Rowan. We can help you. Ben doesn't know you; he doesn't know what's best for you." She hesitated for a moment. "And if your father doesn't seem to understand, then Aunt Rowan and I—or your grandfather or Uncle Chase—can help you. We love you very much, and all we want is for you to be safe and happy."

Lizzy scowled. "Everything was okay until Callie came along. Now my dad just wants to be with her. It's like Wiley and I don't matter anymore."

Eleanor stared at Lizzy for a moment and then rang the small silver bell she kept on the table next her. A few minutes later, Paulette walked in.

When Eleanor spoke, she addressed Lizzy, but her words were meant for Paulette. "Lizzy, Paulette was planning to bake some cookies this afternoon, and was waiting for you because she thought you might like to help."

She turned toward the housekeeper and raised one eyebrow. "Isn't that right, Paulette?"

"Yes," Paulette said. "As a matter of fact I was just about to get started. The sugar cookie dough is all ready. Perhaps Lizzy would like to decide on the shapes. I have a brand-new set of cookie cutters. Different kinds of leaves— for fall."

Eleanor nodded. "I think that's a splendid idea. And you can make some extras to take home with you. I know how much Wiley enjoys them—and your father, too."

"Okay, huh. More comfortable later, huh. I'll bet," Rowan exclaimed when Lizzy was out of earshot. "How *dare* he touch her? How dare he lay one finger on her! And where was Will when all this happened? Did he just leave his daughter to fend for herself while he was off ... doing God knows what?" Her eyes shone like dark beads.

Eleanor sat back and brought her hand up to her chin. She shook her head. "It could have been perfectly innocent."

Rowan leaned forward. "But what if it wasn't? What if it's just the beginning of something horrible? Mother, we can't let anything happen to her."

Eleanor studied her daughter's face. "I've always worried about something like this. Will's done his best, I'm sure, but—"

Edward appeared in the doorway.

"Well, from the looks of you two, I'd say Chicken Little was right, and the sky really is falling." He bent down and dropped a kiss on his wife's cheek.

"It very well may be, Edward," Eleanor replied. "It just may be."

"Elly, we have to be reasonable here," Edward admonished when Eleanor finished recounting their conversation with Lizzy. "You can't even be sure anything happened. Or that there's even any danger."

Rowan responded first. "And you can't be sure it didn't—or that there isn't. Are you willing to take chances with your own granddaughter?"

Edward addressed his daughter firmly. "You know damn well I'm not. But I am also not willing to act precipitously—or, worse, overreact."

Eleanor glared at him. "All I know is that my granddaughter—your granddaughter—Joanna's child—may not be safe with that young man." The muscles around her neck and jaw tightened. "And I am not going to risk something more serious—and perhaps irreparable—happening to her. If Will won't protect Lizzy, then I'll have to!"

Edward loosened his tie. Tiny beads of sweat glistened high on his forehead. "All right. And what do you propose to do?"

"I think we should consult with the district attorney," Eleanor said. "Tell him what we know, and ask his advice. He should be of some help. After all, we contributed enough to his reelection campaign last year."

Edward sighed. "I suppose that's a place to start. But we have to be careful." He pointed a finger at Eleanor. "If Will catches wind of this, he'll be furious—and I wouldn't blame him. These are serious accusations, and if they're unfounded—"

"My concerns are not unfounded," Eleanor retorted. "This young man has already made some kind of advance toward Lizzy. And if we don't stop him, who knows how far it will go."

Added Rowan, "Lizzy as much as told us she was uncomfortable being alone with this guy. And if Will marries this woman, it'll be like throwing Lizzy to a shark."

Eleanor stiffened.

"And he did put his hands on her, don't forget," Rowan continued. "Whatever his intention, it was entirely inappropriate. He's ten years older than she is."

Eleanor nodded in agreement. "If you'd heard Lizzy this afternoon, you'd understand. She's a child, Edward. She doesn't see the potential for danger. And apparently her father doesn't either. It's up to us to keep her safe."

Edward studied his wife's face. "All right, Elly. I'll call the district attorney and see where we go from here."

# 46

"The first thing to decide is where to live," Will said during one of our regular telephone conversations. "I was thinking we could rent a house until we find a place we all like. You know, someplace that'll be ours from the very beginning."

I was in the kitchen making a batch of brownies to bring to school the next day for the teachers' fall bake sale. It took place every year, during the last week of October.

I had combined the ingredients in a large mixing bowl and was just beginning to stir it all together when Will called.

"That sounds like a plan," I said.

"But not one that garners much enthusiasm, it seems," Will commented. "What's going on?"

I took a deep breath and exhaled. "I don't know."

"Yes, you do. What?"

I rested the spoon handle against the inside of the mixing bowl. "I hate when you do that."

"Do what?"

"Read my mind. Know when I'm trying to ignore something."

"So, what are you trying to ignore?"

"It's just …" I paused, unsure how to continue. We'd both waited so long and worked so hard for this second chance, and now that it was here—and beginning to take full form—I found myself becoming more and more reticent, nervous, and afraid. Much like I was when Will and I first reconnected.

"Cal, you have to be honest with me," Will said. "I promised I would always tell you the truth, even if it hurt, remember? You have to do the same."

I thought for a moment. "I love you, Will. I love you with all my heart." My voice trembled and I was sure he could hear it.

"But ..."

"I guess I'm just realizing what a huge thing this is," I answered. "All the changes, all the adjustments."

"Are you having second thoughts?" he asked. I could hear the tension in his voice.

"Not about my feelings for you."

"But about something else. Do you want to wait?"

"I don't know. Maybe."

Will was silent.

"Here's the thing," I said, beginning to speak quickly—a sure sign of my own nervousness. "It hasn't been all that long since I struck out on my own—I mean without Joe. And I finally have a place that's just mine—and a life that's just mine. I'm finally able to arrange things according to how I want them to be, without having to take anyone into account."

"Anyone, meaning me," he broke in.

"Anyone, meaning anyone," I replied. "And now it'll be you and Lizzy and Wiley. I'm beginning to see how great an undertaking this is. And I suppose it's a little daunting."

I heard Will draw a breath, but he didn't say anything.

"I love you, Will. But what if it doesn't work? What if everyone's miserable? I mean, we seem to be doing fine at a distance. What will happen when we're together every day? What if we drive each other nuts? What if it turns out we made a huge mistake?"

My fears poured out like water from a spigot. I knew how ridiculous I sounded, but I couldn't stop myself. "And how are we going to deal with Lizzy? She's your daughter—not mine—and she clearly wants to have you to herself. What if—"

He interrupted me mid-sentence. "Stop, Cal. Just stop." He paused briefly. "Tell me what this is really about."

I switched the phone to my other hand and rubbed my forehead. Tell him what this was really about. It was really about my inability to jump in with both feet, and my inability to fully commit myself to him—or anyone else. It was about that constant need to protect myself from the pain of inevitable loss.

Because as far as I was concerned, it was inevitable. It lurked around every corner, waiting to catch me unaware. Somehow, under some set of circumstances, and when I was least prepared for it, Will would be taken away from me. Or he'd take himself away from me. I knew it. And I couldn't bear it.

I needed to reestablish a safe distance from him—the distance between San Sebastian and Westin.

"You know, it could happen the other way around," he said. He knew where I was heading.

"What do you mean?"

"You worry about losing me, but it could happen the other way around. I could lose you just as easily." He paused. "But that's a chance I'm willing to take."

Tears stung my eyes. We were both silent for a long moment.

"Jesus, Callie, it's like you have this brick wall around you, and every time I tear one section down, you build another right back up!" I heard the frustration in his voice, and I couldn't blame him. "What do you want me to do? Write out a guarantee? Sign a contract?"

"No," I answered, barely above a whisper.

"Cal, for any of this to work, you have to be willing to take a chance." He spoke evenly but forcefully. "At some point you just have to trust me, and have faith in how much I love you—how much we love each other."

I closed my eyes and exhaled. I hadn't realized I was holding my breath. There was no way I could make him understand. Things like trust and faith came more easily to him. He grew up with a mother and a father who loved one other and loved him. Lucas and I grew up alone. Will didn't know what it was like to live where Lucas and I did—on the periphery, watching other people love and be loved, while we contented ourselves with whatever morsels were tossed our way. Will was part of a storybook family that spent holidays and vacations together—he spent a month of every summer with his grandparents, for crying out loud. They took pleasure and pride in one another's successes. They quarreled and disagreed, but ended every argument with a handshake, or a hug, or a kiss.

Will never knew how it felt to be on the outside looking in, to crave a sense of belonging somewhere—anywhere—but never finding that place, because it didn't really exist.

He grew up practically swaddled in faith and trust, and that's why he was willing—and able—to take a chance. While I stood on the precipice wondering whether and how I'd survive the unavoidable hard landing, he took a running leap and soared over the edge. It wasn't that he had some misguided notion that everything would always work out—God knows he'd suffered his share of hardship—but he was taught early on that, in general, giving one's heart—taking the risk—was a good thing to do. He had loved and been loved, and knew how to manage both.

I, on the other hand, held tightly to my own heart, parsing out little pieces as I saw fit, and never giving anyone too large a portion—except to Will the first time, when I was too young to know better. And when he handed it back to me, I placed it in a box, sealed it all around with strapping tape, and tucked it away on a dark shelf so I wouldn't have to look at it.

No wonder my marriage failed.

"I'm trying Will, I really am," I said more defensively than was necessary. "And I mean it to the core when I tell you I love you—that's not something I say lightly. It's just …" I paused, exhaling heavily.

"What it comes down to," he said, "is you're either willing to take a risk or you aren't."

"I know," I said. "I know."

Will was silent for a moment. "Well, can you still commit to Thanksgiving at least?" he asked, and only half-jokingly.

Relieved, I smiled and began stirring the batter again. "Of course. Whatever else, you think I'd pass up a chance to play pilgrims and Indians?" We both laughed.

"Good," he said. "Because I had the buckles on my shoes polished just for the occasion. And, I already told Eleanor and Edward that the kids and I wouldn't be spending the holiday with them."

Upon hearing that piece of news, I froze mid-stir. "Wow. That can't have gone over well. What did they say?"

"Not a lot, really," Will acknowledged. "I was actually kind of surprised."

With the phone cradled between my head and shoulder, I poured the batter into the baking dish and then collected up the wooden spoon, mixing bowl, and measuring cups, and put everything in the sink. "I can't imagine they'll take it lying down, though."

Will stretched and yawned. "Well, there's not a lot they can do about it."

I heard muffled voices in the background. Lizzy and Wiley must have come home. Will hollered something I couldn't make out.

"Sorry about that," Will said. "Wiley just got home from soccer practice."

"Okay, well …"

"I wish you were here," he murmured. "I miss holding you. I miss touching you. I miss … well, you know what I miss."

"Thanksgiving's not so far away," I reminded him. "Remember, pilgrims and Indians."

# 47

Will set the oilcan on the ground and ran a cloth across the bicycle chain. "Okay, pal, try that and see how it feels." It was Sunday morning, and they were giving Wiley's bike a tune-up.

Wiley swung his leg over the seat and straddled the crossbar. With one foot on the pedal, he rotated the crank in reverse a few times. "I think it's good now," he said.

"Why don't you take it for a spin just to make sure," Will suggested. "But put on your helmet."

Squinting into the sun, which shone brightly for late October, Will smiled as he watched Wiley ride down the street. He was strong, but also possessed a certain grace, like an athlete.

And he was growing like a weed. Joanna was right when she predicted he would be tall.

Will was putting a wrench back in the toolbox when he heard the phone. Wiping his hands on a clean rag, he hurried into the kitchen, thinking it might be Lizzy. He reached for the phone, and frowned when he saw the Hallorans' number on the screen. He was tempted to ignore the ringing, but it was probably Eleanor, and he knew from experience that the more politic—and, hence, easier—course was simply to find out what she wanted, and respond accordingly.

"Good afternoon, Will," Eleanor said in her usual formal manner. "Edward and I were hoping you could come by the house this afternoon. We have something important we'd like to discuss with you."

Will's shoulders dropped. Her request felt more like a summons than an invitation. He could put her off, but he knew it would be only a postponement. When Eleanor demanded an audience, the operative word was demand.

"Important, huh, can you at least give me a hint?" he asked with a touch of sarcasm.

"I think it's something better discussed in person," she said, ignoring his tone. "Is three o'clock convenient?"

Will pressed his hand to his forehead and thought for a minute. Three o'clock. Wiley would be at the movies with Tanner, and Lizzy would most likely be at the mall with Amy and her mother. "Sure," he said, "three is fine."

The large grandfather clock in the foyer chimed the hour when Paulette showed Will into the living room. Edward and Eleanor were waiting for him, seated next to one another on the couch. He glanced around the room, expecting to meet Rowan's cold stare, but was pleasantly surprised to discover she was not there. He took a chair on the other side of the coffee table, across from Edward and Eleanor. The configuration, he noted with a touch of foreboding, was decidedly adversarial.

Paulette poured coffee into a china cup and handed it to him. He accepted it graciously.

"So, Eleanor, what do you want to talk about?" Will asked.

"I won't beat around the bush," she said after Paulette had left the room. "I'll just come right out with it." Her voice wavered. "Will, you know that Edward and I have always considered you an exemplary father to Lizzy and Wiley." She glanced at her husband. "But some things have come to our attention that make us quite concerned about their physical and emotional well-being. These ... incidents ... give us pause to wonder whether they continue to be truly safe in your care."

Will eyed his mother-in-law. "Excuse me?"

"We're convinced that with this new ... person ... in your life, the children are not receiving adequate attention, particularly when she is present." Eleanor paused as she set down her cup, and then folded her hands in her lap. "Therefore, Edward and I have consulted an attorney, and intend to seek legal custody of Lizzy and Wiley. We regret that it has come to this, but we can't think of any other way."

Will glanced from one in-law to the other. He wasn't sure he'd heard correctly. "You've done what?" he demanded. She couldn't seriously mean to take his children away from him. Not even Eleanor Halloran was that vindictive.

"We have met with an attorney," she repeated. "We want custody of the children. Quite simply, we don't feel you can be trusted to look out for their welfare. And since Joanna—their mother—is our daughter, we believe they belong with us. Our attorney assures us we have a very strong case."

Will looked at Edward, who nodded in agreement.

"What the hell are you talking about?" Will slammed his cup down with such force that it turned on its side. Hot liquid spilled into the saucer and overflowed onto the polished wood of the table.

Eleanor grabbed a napkin and dropped it over the puddle.

Will didn't move.

"I'm talking about the fact that the children aren't safe in your care when you are with that woman." She waved her hand in a gesture of contempt. "Your attention is, quite obviously, focused in another direction."

Will glared at Eleanor, and she returned his gaze. Her face was nearly expressionless, but with one cocked eyebrow she practically dared him to challenge her.

His eyes narrowed. "You can't be serious," he said. "And even if you are, you have no grounds. No judge in his right mind would even entertain the idea that Lizzy and Wiley should be anywhere but with me—their father."

"That would certainly be true, if, indeed, you were acting as a father. As it is, they're allowed to roam unsupervised, and are left to fend for themselves while you focus all of your attention … elsewhere."

"Roam unsupervised, fend for themselves—what the hell are you talking about?" Will's face had gone white with anger. Eleanor opened her mouth to speak, but Edward put his hand out. She yielded to her husband and leaned into the cushion behind her.

"We know about Wiley's sprained ankle and how it happened," he said to Will. "Thank God it was only a sprain. From the way he and Lizzy described it, he could easily have been seriously injured—or worse. He told us about falling from a bluff above the ocean and lying there, overheated and in pain, while he waited for someone to find him." He pointed a finger at Will. "If you'd been doing your job as a father, he wouldn't have been free to wander off in the first place."

Will leaned back and rubbed a hand across his face. They were serious. Jesus Christ, they were serious. They really intended to take him to court and fight for custody of his son and daughter. The idea seemed wholly preposterous on its face, but at the same time, he wouldn't put anything past Joanna's family—and Eleanor in particular. Joanna told him once that if anything ever happened to her, Eleanor would try to take the children. She said it in passing, almost like a joke, but now he wondered if she had been issuing a warning.

"What happened to Wiley could have happened anywhere, and you know it," Will said, his teeth clenched and the muscles of his jaw contracting. "It could have happened when he went fishing with you." He gave a nod in

Edward's direction. "Or when he and Lizzy went snowboarding with Chase and Sarah."

"But it didn't," Eleanor snapped. "Neither Wiley nor Lizzy has suffered so much as a skinned knee when they've been with any of us. Clearly, we take the responsibility for their care very seriously."

Will wanted to punch the smug, self-righteous expression off her face, but he resisted the temptation.

"And you dare to suggest I don't?" he asked.

"The evidence speaks for itself," Eleanor continued. "We're suggesting that you are too involved with that woman to pay proper attention to your children. And if she's more important to you than they are, well then …"

"This is insane," Will declared. He rose and took a few steps toward the door. "Go ahead and try if you want to, but you won't get anywhere. You'll never be able to convince a judge that I am an unfit parent. The most you'll accomplish is losing your grandchildren entirely."

"You might think otherwise if you knew what Lizzy had to say about that woman's son," Eleanor said coolly as she picked up the silver coffee server and refilled her cup.

Will started. "What? What did she say about him?"

Eleanor added cream to her coffee, stirring slowly. She tapped the spoon lightly on the rim and set it in the saucer.

"Not surprisingly, she was very uncomfortable discussing it," Eleanor continued. "She clearly has a certain loyalty where you are concerned. But it was evident from what she did say that he got closer to her—physically—than was appropriate."

Will's breathing quickened. "*What* did she tell you, Eleanor?"

"I won't violate her confidence. You'll have to ask her yourself—and hope she feels safe enough to tell you the truth." Eleanor lifted her cup to her lips and took a sip. Although she appeared calm and composed, her hands trembled.

Will raised his voice. "*What did she say?*"

Edward responded. "Will, I think Eleanor's right that Lizzy should be the one to tell you."

Will closed his eyes, taking a few seconds to rein in his temper. He spoke softly then. "I will talk to her, of course. But I would like to know what you heard."

The grandparents looked at one another. "All right," Eleanor said. She set her cup back in the saucer. "Apparently, he treated her with more familiarity than seemed appropriate given the nature of their relationship—they'd only just met." She eyed Will cautiously.

"What else?" he demanded.

Eleanor took a deep breath before continuing. "She said he put his arm around her and held her close to him. You—and she—may prefer to think it was innocent, but anyone with half a brain knows someone his age should never lay a finger on a thirteen-year-old, no matter what the circumstances."

A heavy wooden credenza stood next to the door, and Will grasped the edge to steady himself. For the first time since Joanna died, he felt a burst of white-hot anger toward her. Goddamn it, he thought to himself. They had created these children together, and they were supposed to raise them together. That was the deal. She was not supposed to take the car and drive herself off a cliff. She was not supposed to leave him to protect their children from this pack of wolves that was her family. Maybe Callie was right, that Joanna *had* committed the unforgivable offense of abandoning her children.

Will rubbed his eyes. He couldn't believe what he was hearing. He wanted to talk to Lizzy and find out exactly what she'd said so he could know how Eleanor—and Rowan, he was sure—were misinterpreting her words.

"Lizzy is an innocent young girl, Will." Eleanor's voice cut into his thoughts. "Her grandfather and I will to do whatever it takes to make sure she stays that way. We will protect both of Joanna's children at any cost."

He was about to say, "Over my dead body," but thought better of it. As far as the Hallorans were concerned, that would present the best of all possible circumstances. Instead, he turned toward the door. He placed his hand on the jamb and, as he was about to walk out, made an about-face in the direction of his mother- and father-in-law.

"Why now?" he asked. "It's been two months since we went to San Sebastian. Did Lizzy only just now tell you about it?"

Edward and Eleanor glanced at one another again. Eleanor took another sip so she wouldn't have to speak.

It was Edward who answered. "We only now realized the necessity. When you told us you plan to take the children back there for Thanksgiving—and place Lizzy within that young man's reach—it became imperative that we take action."

Will shook his head. "Well, Edward, you do what you think you have to." His eyes blazed as he struggled to keep his anger under control. "I'll continue to take care of my children. But know that from this point on, they'll have no contact with you. Your visit with Lizzy and Wiley yesterday is the last you'll have with them. If you want to communicate with them, you'll do it through me."

He didn't wait for a reaction, but spun around and walked out the door.

Paulette called to him in the foyer. He didn't immediately see her, but turned toward the sound of her voice. She was approaching him from the direction of the kitchen.

"Dr. Tremaine, I'm glad I caught you before you left." She extended her arm and held out a brown paper bag. "Cookies," she said, "the kind Lizzy likes so much."

Will nodded. "Thanks, Paulette. That's very thoughtful of you. I know she'll appreciate them. Wiley, too."

"Well." Paulette dropped her gaze. "I don't guess we'll be seeing them anytime soon." It was clear she had overheard his conversation with Edward and Eleanor.

"No," Will replied, taking the bag. "Probably not."

"Will you tell them I'm thinking about them?"

"Of course." Will reached out and squeezed her hand. "Of course I will."

# 48

I was struggling to hold two overflowing bags of groceries while fumbling for my house key when I heard the telephone ring. I set one of the bags on the porch next to the door and managed to get the key in the lock and the door open just as the answering machine was taking a message.

I heard only a few words—"on our way right now"—but the voice that spoke them was forceful and urgent.

I plopped one grocery bag on the chair, brought in the other, and listened to the message in its entirety. Ben's girlfriend, Gina, had left it. Some crisis had arisen, and they needed to see me. They were on their way up from Kentfield and would be here in an hour or so.

I called Ben's apartment, but didn't get an answer. Likewise his cell phone. I left the simple message that I'd gotten Gina's call and that I'd be here when they arrived. I didn't have Gina's number, so all I could do was wait for them.

I started to put away the groceries, sidestepping Bailey, who was stretched out in the middle of the kitchen floor. I tried to guess what would cause Ben to make a special trip up here in the middle of the week, but nothing came to mind. It wasn't work-related, I was sure, and I knew he and Gina weren't coming to tell me they were getting married or doing something equally crazy. It couldn't have to do with Joe or Justine, because if it did, I would have heard from Justine. The best course was simply to wait.

They pulled up just as I was setting a pot of tea to brew. The minute I saw Ben I knew the situation was serious. He was ashen, but his eyes were round and dark. His mouth was nothing more than a thin, pale line.

I rushed to him and took his arm. "Ben, what's going on? What's happened?"

He looked at me and opened his mouth as if to speak, but no words came out. He stood there shaking his head.

I turned to Gina and raised my eyebrows.

She glanced at Ben. "You're not going to believe it," she said. "I don't believe it."

"Believe what?" My heart was beginning to race as I prepared for a contingent of possibilities that included both serious illness and death.

Ben sat down at the table and Gina pulled a chair around to be right next to him. Ben leaned forward, with elbows on the table and his head in his hands.

"The grandparents of those kids," Gina said, "the Hallorans—they're claiming Ben did something to Lizzy when she was here with her dad and her brother."

"What do you mean, 'did something'?"

"They're saying he touched her," Gina replied. "Inappropriately."

I fell backward against the counter.

Ben lifted his head. "They say I touched her, Mom. They're claiming she told them I did, when they were here in August." His voice trembled. "But I didn't. You know I didn't." His voice cracked and he was shaking.

I stared at both of them in disbelief. My heart was pounding, but I tried to remain calm. "Okay," I said, my breath quivering as I inhaled. "Tell me what happened."

Ben looked once again to Gina, and once again hid his face in his hands. She caressed his arm and then rested her hand on his leg. He seemed to relax slightly in response to her touch. I noted—appreciatively—the effect she had on him. In a calm, even tone, she gave me the details.

She had stayed over at Ben's apartment the previous night, and they were just finishing breakfast when someone knocked on the door. Gina answered it, and a man, casually dressed, stood facing her.

"He asked if Ben Winwood lived there, and if he was home. I told him he was, and closed the door partway while I went to get Ben. So Ben came to the door, and the guy introduced himself. He said his name was John Wyatt, and he was an investigator with a law firm in Westin. He told Ben he needed to ask him some questions."

I broke out in a cold sweat. John Wyatt. The Hallorans were digging up dirt again, only this time pitching their shovels at Ben. I nodded for Gina to go on.

Ben invited Wyatt inside, and they all sat down in Ben's small living room.

"He asked if Ben knew a girl named Lizzy Tremaine," Gina continued. "Ben said he did, and the investigator asked how he knew her. Ben told him they'd met here, a couple of months ago, when she and her brother and father came to visit. Then he asked if Ben had been alone with Lizzy at all during the few days everyone was here. Ben said he couldn't remember, and then asked what the questions were all about."

At that point, Ben took over the telling of the story. He got to his feet and began pacing back and forth. "He said Lizzy told her grandmother and aunt that I'd made advances toward her." He put special emphasis on the word "advances." "He said she told them I'd gotten too close to her, and that I—" He stopped mid-step and ran his hand through his light brown hair. "Mom, you know I didn't do anything. You know I didn't."

My stomach turned. So this was the full-on assault. This was the Hallorans' battle plan. This was how they would divide and conquer—or, rather, conquer and divide.

"Mom, you know I didn't do anything," Ben repeated anxiously.

I reached out and grasped his hand. "Of course I do, honey," I replied.

He turned toward the window for a moment and then faced me again. His shoulders dropped. "It was the day Wiley fell and sprained his ankle," he said with a tone that was equal parts realization and despair. "Lizzy was outside. I saw her sitting on the bench when I came back from Alice's house. She looked so sad." Ben was pacing again, trying to recall every detail of that encounter.

I remembered, too. Will and I had watched the exchange from the window—and it had lightened our hearts to see her interacting so freely with Ben.

"I sat down next to her and we just started talking," Ben continued. "She said she hated it here, and she hated—" he stopped himself.

"Hated what?" I asked.

He hesitated, but I had a good idea of what he was going to say. "Hated you." I was right. "She was kind of sweet about it, though. She said she was sorry to say that about my mom. And she said it wasn't you, exactly, but what you were doing to her family. She said you were taking her dad away from her."

A lump formed in my throat. As far as Lizzy knew, I was taking him away. Or, at the very least, coming between them. My throat ached so that I couldn't say anything. I simply nodded again.

"I told her I was sorry, and that I understood how she felt. I told her I'd probably feel the same way."

She had started to cry, then, and he put a big brotherly arm around her and drew her close to him. She cried on his shoulder.

"But, Mom," he exclaimed almost in desperation, "Aside from that, I didn't touch her. I didn't. She was crying, and I just wanted to comfort her a little."

I took a deep breath and recovered my voice.

"Could there maybe have been something accidental? Something that you don't immediately remember?" I asked.

"Oh, God, you don't believe me, do you?" The color drained from his face again, except for the darkness in his eyes. Even his lips had gone white. He looked stricken.

Seeing the anguish on Ben's face, my empathy toward Lizzy turned all at once into rage against the Hallorans. I walked over and stood directly in front of him. I grasped his arms tightly and stared directly into his eyes. His muscles were rigid under the cotton of his shirtsleeves.

"Ben, listen to me. I do believe you. I don't doubt for a second that you're telling the truth and that you did nothing wrong. But Eleanor and Rowan—and even Edward—somehow got a different idea, and they had to get it from Lizzy. I just need to know if there's something she could have misinterpreted."

"That's all it was. I promise. I don't know how she could have misinterpreted that." He dropped down onto the couch and grabbed one of the throw pillows, hugging it to his chest.

Gina sat down next to him and took his arm. "You haven't heard all that happened this morning, though," she said ominously.

I took another shaky breath. "Okay, what else is there?"

She glanced at Ben, who now had one hand over his eyes, and with the other had taken hold of hers. "Do you want to tell her, or should I?"

He gestured for her to continue.

"When Ben realized what the investigator was talking about—was accusing him of—he got really angry." Even without hearing another word, I could guess what followed. Ben was easygoing by nature, and rarely worked up a temper. Even when he did, it was fairly mild. Still, I could count a few occasions when the flames roared out of control—facing Joe alone for the first time after he learned about the divorce, for example. All Joe would say about it was that after Ben stormed out of the house, Joe made arrangements to have the glass in the living room window replaced, and took one of the chairs to the dump.

A shiver ran down my back, and the hairs on my arms stood erect. "What happened then?" I asked Gina.

"Ben pushed him—hard. He fell against the wall. And when he took a step forward, Ben pushed him again."

"Oh, Ben," I whispered, my hand covering my mouth.

"Ben pulled his fist back, like he was going to hit Wyatt," Gina continued, "but I got between them. I knew that no matter what, Ben wouldn't let anything happen to me. Wyatt told Ben he'd be lucky if all he faced was assault charges after that. And then he said Ben would be hearing from the DA's office."

I closed my eyes and took a deep breath, absorbing Gina's words and what they meant for all of us—Ben, Lizzy, me, Will, Will and me together.

Every so often, something happens that causes one's private world to shift slightly on its axis. Sometimes it's wondrous and joyful. Other times, however, it's nothing but devastating.

I sat quietly, looking at Ben and adjusting to the certainty that all of our lives had changed and would never be the same.

# 49

Will walked in the front door, dropped his keys on the table, and called to Lizzy and Wiley. Silence. Neither one was home. He closed his eyes and took a breath. He remembered they were out with friends, and felt both disappointment and relief. Disappointment because after Eleanor and Edward's announcement this afternoon, he felt an overwhelming need to see his children—to have them close to him. At the same time, he felt a sense of relief because he had a little while to pull himself together before he had to face them.

He wasn't sure how he'd handle the situation. Joanna's family had been a big part of the children's lives, and the separation from them would be difficult for everyone. The Hallorans provided a haven for Lizzy and Wiley, a place they could go anytime and know they were loved and wanted. And it gave them a connection to the mother they sorely needed. Even more, Will had come to rely on the Hallorans' assistance in looking after Lizzy and Wiley when he wasn't able to do it himself. His hours at the hospital were often unpredictable, and knowing he could call on Eleanor—or Rowan, or Chase—to pick one of them up from somewhere, or drop the other off somewhere, or simply fill in at a moment's notice gave him a tremendous sense of security.

For now, however, all of that was gone. For now, it was as though the Hallorans didn't exist—certainly not in any way that would be of help to him.

Will pulled a container of leftover pot roast out of the refrigerator and opened the lid. He took a whiff and set it on the counter. He had no appetite, but Lizzy would not have had dinner yet. Wiley, he assumed, would make a meal of popcorn and Milk Duds at the movie theater with Tanner. Popcorn and Milk Duds. He pressed his fingertips to his eyes. What kind of a dinner was that? Maybe they were right. Maybe he wasn't taking proper care of them.

He yanked a pot from the cupboard and slammed it onto a burner. No, he argued with himself, no. They were not going to make him doubt himself. Wiley would have a proper dinner when he got home, and that would be fine.

Will glanced at the clock. It was four thirty. He expected Lizzy home in another half hour. Wiley wouldn't be back until seven or so, which would give Will some time alone with Lizzy.

He moved to the living room and stood at the window, looking out onto the street. The view extended from one end of the short block to the other. One of the reasons he and Joanna had chosen this particular house was because of the big picture window in the living room. She loved basking in the afternoon sun that poured in at an angle, particularly on those days when her mood was dark and cold.

"Jesus," Will muttered out loud, "how did this happen?" He rubbed his hands across his face as though the action would wipe away the confusion and reveal at least a hint of clarity.

He wasn't sure how he'd broach the subject of Ben's interaction with Lizzy. How would he raise the question as to whether or not he had done anything inappropriate? What words would he use? What would she consider inappropriate? And if Ben had done anything, why didn't she tell him about it? He'd always taken great pride and pleasure in the openness of his relationship with Lizzy, and their ability to communicate with one another freely and easily. It gratified him to know his daughter felt comfortable talking with him about the important—and, often, sensitive—issues in her life.

Yet, she'd kept this to herself, until she chose to reveal it not to him, but to her grandmother and aunt. That could mean Ben hadn't done anything truly improper, and Eleanor and Rowan were trying to turn some minor contact into a major criminal offense. Or, Ben really did make an inappropriate advance, and Lizzy didn't want to tell him because of his feelings for Callie. Worse, maybe Lizzy felt she *couldn't* tell him because of his feelings for Callie. If that were the case, Lizzy was living with the belief that Callie meant more to him than she did. That possibility turned him cold. Lizzy had already lost so much.

He sat down on the couch. Lizzy's cat jumped up and brushed against him, turning back and forth and pressing her face into Will's hand. Will gave her a pat, and she curled up in a half circle beside him. He stroked the top of her head, and she responded with a meow and a loud purr.

But how could Ben be guilty of anything like this, Will wondered? He hadn't known Ben very long, but he knew Callie. He couldn't imagine her son to be capable of something like this. At the same time, though, he knew his daughter wouldn't lie.

The possibilities played over and over in his head.

He didn't want to believe any of it could be true.

The sharp ring of the telephone startled him back into the present moment. He saw Callie's number on the screen, and with feelings of both relief and dread he reached for the handset.

# 50

Although none of us was particularly hungry, I sent Ben and Gina out to pick up something for dinner. As soon as they drove away, I picked up the telephone to call Will. He answered almost immediately.

"What the hell is going on?" I asked, trying to keep my emotions under control. "Have you *heard* what Eleanor and Edward are saying about Ben?"

"Yes," he replied quietly. "They told me just today. In fact, I got back from their place only a little while ago."

"And did they also tell you they sent the investigator from their attorney's office to question Ben? The same one they had asking questions about me. He paid Ben a visit this morning."

"What?" he exclaimed. "No, I had no idea."

"The investigator as good as told him he'd be facing some kind of charges." My son facing charges—if the whole thing weren't so frightening it would be laughable.

"It gets worse," Will said.

Once again, my stomach turned over. "What do you mean?"

"Eleanor and Edward are suing for custody of Lizzy and Wiley," he said plainly. "They're claiming I'm an unfit parent because of Wiley's sprained ankle a couple of months ago, and because of Lizzy and—well, you know."

I sank down onto the couch, my anger collapsing all at once under the weight of Will's announcement. My fingers tingled, but my lips went numb. I tried to speak, but nothing worked. I swallowed hard. Custody of Lizzy and Wiley. He was right—it did get worse.

"H-how can they do that?" I stammered finally. "How can they th-think that?"

Will must have rubbed his hand across his face, and he must not have

271

shaved this morning, because even through the telephone I could hear the rasp of his stubble.

"Jesus, Cal, I can't believe this is happening. I can't believe they'd actually do this." The anguish in his voice traveled through the phone line and into my heart.

"How in God's name can they claim you're an ... unfit parent?" I argued. Just saying the words "unfit parent" made me feel sick. Lizzy and Wiley couldn't have a more devoted father.

"They're claiming it's because of—" He stopped abruptly, holding his breath.

Bailey jumped up beside me and laid his head in my lap. I clutched the fur around his shoulder. "Because of what?" I asked nervously. He didn't have to say, though. As with Ben, I already knew the answer.

He exhaled heavily. "Because of you. Because they think that when I'm with you, I don't pay enough attention to the kids. According to them, Wiley's fall and Lizzy's—whatever it was—are proof I can't be trusted."

"Oh, God, Will." I didn't know what else to say.

"They can't possibly have a case," Will said with sudden determination. "I told them that what happened to Wiley could have happened anywhere, with anyone, even with them. And Lizzy—" He stopped again. Lizzy posed the greater issue.

Bailey adjusted himself and groaned softly. I stroked his ear. "What did Lizzy say?" I asked tentatively. "About Ben, I mean."

"Nothing yet," he replied. "I haven't asked her. She won't be home until later."

I hesitated for a moment, toying with Bailey's collar. "Will, you do believe Ben when he says that nothing happened, don't you?"

He didn't respond.

"Lizzy's mistaken," I continued. "She has to be. I'm not saying she's lying, but at the very worst, she misinterpreted something. You know Ben isn't capable of doing anything like that, right?"

"I don't think so," he replied, and then added, "I have to talk to Lizzy."

"You don't think so?" I cried. "What the hell do you mean, you don't think so?" I sat upright, my face suddenly hot with fury. "Are you seriously suggesting that Ben has to explain himself and declare his innocence? Are you telling me you don't know him well enough by now to know that he would never—and I mean never!—do anything to hurt Lizzy or Wiley in any way, let alone like that?"

I couldn't believe I was having this conversation, and with Will of all people. Did he actually believe my son was not only capable of mistreating his daughter, but guilty as well?

Tears burned in my eyes. The room began to spin, and I suddenly felt very sick. I hung up the telephone and ran upstairs to the bathroom and slammed the door. I stood there, bent forward, my elbows resting on the cool marble counter, and my head in my hands.

My heart pounded and I broke out in a cold sweat as I fought waves of nausea. I was absolutely certain of Ben's innocence, but for Will to question it—even in the slightest—cast doubt on everything I thought I knew about him.

After a few minutes, I heard the murmur of voices in the living room. Ben and Gina had returned. The telephone rang a couple of times before someone picked it up. Probably Will calling back.

I turned on the faucet and splashed cold water on my face. A quiet knock sounded on the bathroom door.

"Callie?" It was Gina. "Are you all right?"

I dried my face on a towel and pulled my hair up off my neck, securing it with a clip. I glanced at myself in the mirror, took a deep breath, and opened the door.

"Ben's on the phone with Will," Gina said. "Are you okay?"

I smiled and patted her shoulder. "I'm all right," I replied. "It's just a lot to take in."

"No kidding," she snorted.

We headed downstairs and into the living room, where Ben was still talking with Will. He was recounting his morning visit from the private investigator.

Ben glanced at me. "I know, I know! I shouldn't have pushed him. But what would you have done if someone made disgusting suggestions like that about you?"

He was silent, apparently listening to Will's response.

"No!" he bellowed suddenly, his face going white again. "No! Goddamn it! I didn't touch her! Aside from the conversation we had the afternoon Wiley hurt his ankle, when she was crying and I put my arm around her shoulder—and just her shoulder!—I never had any contact with her!" Ben was practically screaming at Will. "And you know what? If you don't believe that, then you can just fucking go to hell!"

Ben threw the phone against the wall and stormed outside. Gina and I stared at one another. She followed Ben, and I picked up the receiver.

"Are you there?" I asked hesitantly.

"Yeah, I'm here," he replied. "But I'm surprised the phone still works. Is he all right?"

"Of course he's not all right," I snapped. "He's been accused of molesting a thirteen-year-old girl. How can he possibly be all right? None of us is all right!"

Will sighed heavily. "Callie, for what it's worth, I do find it very hard to believe anything … inappropriate … happened between Ben and Lizzy. But she's my daughter. What kind of father would I be if I didn't protect her?"

In some ways the current situation was hardest for him. The ugliness of the accusation aside, I knew Ben would quickly be exonerated—he was innocent, after all—but, in the meantime, Will was facing the threat of losing his children altogether. It was within the realm of possibility that he'd be forced to turn them over to Eleanor and Edward Halloran. They had power and resources, and they weren't afraid to use them.

Silently, I cursed Joanna for bringing all of this about by deserting her family in the first place. At this particular moment, it didn't matter that if she were alive Will and I wouldn't have found each other again, and the last eleven months wouldn't have happened. If she were alive, my son would not be facing this sickening accusation.

"I can't just dismiss it like it's nothing," Will continued. "*Something* happened with Lizzy. She wouldn't just make it up."

I shook my head in disbelief. The lump in my throat was the size of a grapefruit. I could barely draw in a breath. I closed my eyes and swallowed hard. So this was it. He'd defend his child as vehemently as I would mine. It was a brilliant strategy on Eleanor's part. No other circumstances would have pitted Will and me against one another.

"You do what you have to do," I replied, "and so will I."

"Funny," Will responded dryly. "That's what I said to Edward."

# 51

An hour later, Will heard the slam of a car door and watched as Lizzy hurried up the front walkway. She hugged her arms tightly across her chest, holding her jacket closed, and she clutched a small paper bag in one hand. He met her at the door, opening it for her before she pulled out her key.

"Hey, LZ, how was the shopping trip?"

Lizzy stepped across the threshold. Will waved to Amy's mother, who waited at the curb to make sure Lizzy got safely inside. She waved back as she and Amy drove away, and Will closed the door.

"It was good. Amy's mom is really fun. She let us stop at the makeup counter and get makeovers." Lizzy turned her face, still flushed from the cold, as though posing for a camera. "What do you think?"

Will smiled. "I think you're beautiful—with or without makeup. Although," he added, "I also think you're still a bit young for it."

"Yeah, Amy's mom said the same thing. But everyone at school wears at least a little. So she got each of us some mascara and an eye pencil." Lizzy held up the bag. "She said she hoped you wouldn't mind."

Will sighed. "No, I suppose not," he said. "But don't go crazy with that stuff. I want to be able to look at you and see *you*, okay?"

"Yes, Dad." Lizzy turned and moved toward the stairs. "I'm gonna take a shower. Someone in the food court dropped a milkshake, and it splattered all over everything—including me."

"Well, don't take too long," Will called after her. "Dinner's almost ready and you need to set the table." He paused. "And there's something I want to talk to you about."

"Okay, I'll be quick," she hollered.

Will turned down the heat but left the pot roast on the stove to keep warm. He reached into the refrigerator, pulled out a bag of mixed greens, and poured some into a bowl. He chopped up a cucumber and some carrots, tossed them in with the greens, and set the bowl aside.

When he went back into the living room, Lizzy was waiting for him. She sat on the couch with her knees drawn up to her chin, and her cat at her feet. She was dressed in a pair of dark leggings, a light-blue pullover sweater that had belonged to Joanna, and purple polka-dot socks. Her damp hair fell across her shoulders and down her back.

"So, what do you want to talk about?" she asked. He sat down across from her. He wanted to be able to look at her face-to-face, to watch her expressions, and see the truth in her eyes.

"LZ, what did you think about the trip we took to San Sebastian last August?"

She raised one shoulder and let it drop. "I don't know," she replied unemotionally. "I didn't want to go, if that's what you mean, and I didn't like being there. I told you—I wanted to be home."

Will brought the fingertips of both hands together and looked down at them. He kept his eyes focused on his hands when he spoke.

"Lizzy, I need to know if anything happened between you and Ben."

He lifted his eyes and gazed at her then, straight on.

"Did Gran tell you?" she asked warily.

"She didn't say much. She thought what you told her was in confidence, and she wanted to respect that," Will explained. Respect, he thought to himself, right.

Lizzy fidgeted with the cuff of her sweatshirt. Will couldn't mistake the nervousness. "Lizzy," he said gently, "if there was anything that made you … uncomfortable in any way, I really want you to tell me."

"What are you going to do?"

"That depends on what you tell me."

Lizzy chewed her bottom lip. "Will Ben get in trouble?"

"That also depends on what you tell me," Will replied. "He might, but that doesn't matter. The only thing that matters is that you tell me the truth." He looked at her intently. "I want to hear it, LZ, whatever it is."

Lizzy turned her attention to a thread that had come loose in the seam of her leggings. She was silent for a minute or so. "Gran said what Ben did was wrong," she said finally. "I heard her telling Grandpa."

Will rubbed his hand over his face. What if Edward was right? What if he'd been so consumed by his feelings for Callie—by his own need to be close to her—that he hadn't looked out for his daughter's welfare? He had left Lizzy and Ben alone together, but it never occurred to him that she'd be anything but safe. He's Callie's son, for God's sake.

Will stroked Lizzy's hair. "Maybe it was wrong, and maybe your grandmother is overreacting. But I won't know if you don't tell me."

"What about Callie?"

"What about her?"

Lizzy pulled the thread loose and began playing with it, wrapping it around her finger. "If you and Callie get married, I'll see Ben a lot. And if Gran's right ..."

"Liz, please, just tell me what happened. We can figure all the rest out later." Will's heart hammered in his chest. His palms were sweaty, and his stomach was pitching and rolling like a dinghy on a stormy sea, but he kept his voice calm and even. If Eleanor was right—he could barely bring himself to contemplate the possibility. If Eleanor was right, he and Callie would be finished.

"He put his arm across my shoulder," Lizzy whispered.

Will swallowed hard and nodded. "Okay, what else?"

"That's all."

Will sat back and looked at his daughter. "That's all?"

She nodded, wide-eyed.

"Tell me how it happened," Will pressed.

Lizzy rolled the thread into a tiny ball and dropped it onto the coffee table. She hugged her legs and rested her forehead on her knees. When she looked at her father again, her eyes glistened with tears. "I was outside, on the bench. It was after Callie was talking to Wiley—about how he could love Winslow and still love Hank. Like you could love Callie and still love Mom."

Will nodded again, encouraging her to continue.

She closed her eyes and two tears trickled down her cheeks. Then, as though something inside her suddenly broke, she dropped her forehead onto her knees and began to sob. "But you can't, Daddy, you can't. You can't love Callie. You just can't!" Lizzy's body shook with the full force of her emotions. Will reached out to her, but she pushed him away and wrapped her arms more tightly around her knees, forming herself into a ball.

"Lizzy," he murmured, lightly touching her hair. "Lizzy, please. Come here." Relenting, she moved toward him and pressed her head against his chest, allowing his arms to enfold her. He stroked the back of her head. She held on to him, clutching his shirt in her fists as she wept.

"Oh, Lizzy," he said, "I'm so sorry." At that moment, he was sorry for everything—for Joanna, for Eleanor, for Callie, and for all the hurts he might have caused, and all those he knew he couldn't prevent. Perhaps this was his penance for not loving Joanna properly—he could have his daughter, or Callie, but not both.

After a few minutes, Lizzy began to calm down. Her sobs relaxed to little hiccups, and her breathing became more regular. She sniffled, and Will reached behind him, grabbing whatever was close at hand that could serve as a handkerchief. It happened to be one of Wiley's T-shirts.

"Here," he said with a half smile. "Wiley won't know the difference."

Lizzy chuckled and blew her nose.

"Liz," Will asked tentatively, "did anything else happen with Ben? I mean, what did he do—or you do—when he put his arm around you?"

"I didn't know what I was supposed to do," she replied. "I just sat on the bench."

"He saw you were crying, didn't he? Do you think he could just have been trying to make you feel better?" Will wanted to get a complete picture. He needed the truth—Lizzy's version of it anyway.

Lizzy stared at him. "You think I'm wrong, don't you?" she cried. "You think Gran's wrong! You just want to make everything okay so you can be with Callie!" She broke away from him, ran upstairs to her bedroom, and slammed the door. Will flinched at the sound. He fell back against the cushion and closed his eyes.

He had to understand what went on between Lizzy and Ben. Eleanor and Edward were building their custody case around it. If Eleanor was, indeed, imagining the worst about Ben—and wrongly accusing him—he had to do everything in his power to uncover the truth. It was the only way he could keep his children. At this point, it was within the realm of possibility that the Hallorans could convince a sympathetic judge that Lizzy was safer with them than with her own father.

And if Eleanor was not imagining the worst—a possibility Will could hardly bear even to contemplate—well, he had to know that, too, so he could protect his daughter.

Will trudged up the stairs and stopped at Lizzy's room. He knocked softly on the door. "Hey, LZ? Can I come in?"

He found Lizzy curled up on her bed, hugging an old, worn teddy bear. She was facing the wall, and thick sections of her long brown hair had fallen over her face, hiding her eyes. She didn't bother to move them. Will sat down next to her. He reached out and tucked the locks behind her ear.

"Lizzy, I want you to know that I believe whatever you tell me. And I will always—always—take care of you. No matter what." He caressed her cheek. "I love you, LZ."

"I know," she whispered and closed her eyes.

A blanket was folded across the foot of the bed, and Will pulled it up over Lizzy's shoulders.

She turned to face him. "Dad?"

"Yeah?"

"What about Callie?"

Will's breath caught in his throat. He paused before responding. What about Callie? That was a question to which he didn't have an answer. He loved her as much as ever—that wasn't in doubt. But whether they still had a future together was another issue entirely.

"I don't know, LZ, I don't know." He leaned toward her and kissed her forehead. "But that's not anything you have to worry about."

Will slept in his bed that night instead of throwing a pillow and blanket on the family room couch, as was his usual habit. He wasn't sure why, but it seemed appropriate somehow.

He didn't fall asleep easily, though. The conversation he had with Callie earlier in the evening kept replaying in his mind. He'd never heard her so angry. He could hardly blame her. He'd react the same way if it were his son whose character was being impugned in such a revolting way.

He rolled over and stared at the ceiling. It was only a few days ago that they were planning their first Thanksgiving together. He and the kids would fly out to San Sebastian and, like they did in August, they'd have the cottage and Callie would stay at Alice's. They'd gather there for Thanksgiving dinner, with Alice and Callie in charge of the meal. Ben and Justine would be present, as would Alice's daughter, Sally.

And after Thanksgiving, Christmas would follow. For the first time in years, he was actually looking forward to the holidays. He imagined everyone together on Christmas morning, and his heart warmed. Callie would be his Christmas gift, the only thing he wanted.

Within seconds, however, the feelings of joy and anticipation gave way to a sense of loss and loneliness. It would be a long time before he saw her again, and God only knew what would transpire between now and then.

# 52

None of us had much of an appetite. The hamburgers Ben and Gina brought back for dinner went largely uneaten as each of us played with the food on our plates, pushing it from one side to the other. I had been lost in my own thoughts, trying to figure out how we were going to manage this mess.

I shoved my plate aside and addressed Ben. "Well, I think the most important thing to do is talk to Miranda. She's my best friend, she has complete faith in you, and, best of all, she's an assistant DA in Westin."

Ben brightened. "I completely forgot about that." A smile crossed his lips. "Can you call her tonight?"

"I already did. She wasn't home, so I left a message for her to get back to me right away. I told her we're in crisis mode. Even if she's out of town, she'll check her messages, and when she hears that, she'll know what it means."

As close as we were, Miranda and I didn't speak all that often—she had her life, and I had mine. Sometimes a month would pass before one of us called the other to check in. But it had somehow been established years ago that if either of us heard the words "crisis mode," the other would spring into action, no matter where we were or what we were doing. I'd used them most recently following the revelation of Joe's second affair, and Miranda landed on my doorstep ready to start overseeing the distribution of property.

Later, sitting in the living room, Ben turned to me. Gina was curled up against the arm of the sofa with her legs drawn up, and he sat with his back pressed against her knees. Her forearms were draped over his shoulders, her hands locked and resting on his chest. As I looked at them together, I realized that from the moment she and Ben walked into the house this morning, she had not voiced one word of uncertainty about Ben. I issued a silent thank-you.

"Do you really think it will all be okay?" Ben asked.

I was in one of the chairs across from them, Bailey on the floor beside me. He lifted his head at the sound of Ben's voice. I gave him a pat and he settled back down. "I do think it will all be okay. It's going to be hard, and probably pretty ugly—the Hallorans are nothing if not tenacious, and they're used to getting what they want—but it will all be okay." I leaned forward and touched his knee. "I am not going to let anything happen to you," I promised. "I don't care what I have to do."

I was right about Miranda. It was nearly midnight when the telephone rang. Ben and Gina had settled into the guest room, and I was lying in my own bed. Bailey snored quietly, while I tossed and turned, replaying my conversation with Will earlier in the day. His words rolled over and over in my head: "*Something happened with Lizzy. She wouldn't just make it up.*"

Ben knocked on the door just as I picked up the phone. "Come on in," I called.

I sat up, pulled a pillow behind my back and pressed the talk button. "I just got your message," Miranda said anxiously. "What's going on? Are you all right?"

I heaved a sigh of relief. Miranda would bring a sense of reason to this whole crazy, sordid mess, and together we'd figure out how to deal with it.

I glanced at Ben and my expression softened. "You are not going to believe it."

I related the whole story—from the allegation, to the supposed assault, to the brewing custody battle.

"Son of a bitch," Miranda said.

"Yeah, my sentiments, too," I replied. "But what are we going to do about it?"

Miranda took a deep breath as she made the transition from friend to legal adviser. "Well, first, Ben isn't going to talk to anyone unless he has a lawyer in the room with him—I'll take care of that. And second, *you* aren't going to discuss this with anyone outside the immediate family—not even Will."

"Jesus, Miranda, how am I supposed to manage that?" I exclaimed. "He *is* my immediate family—or will be."

"Right now, he's the father of the girl Ben is accused of ... er ... mistreating, shall we say? The situation is complicated enough without it appearing that either of you is influencing the other in any way."

Miranda's words cut through me like a knife. Over the last year, Will and I had carefully arranged the individual pieces of our lives into a fragile mosaic that represented what we hoped our family would become. The glue hadn't even set, when along came Eleanor Halloran. She delivered one blow and it shattered into a thousand tiny fragments.

Gina tapped on the bedroom door and opened it enough to peek in. She beckoned to Ben, who got to his feet and followed her. He stopped at the door and glanced back at me. I put my hand over the phone and told him I'd come in shortly and fill him in. He nodded and slipped out into the hall.

"The truth of the matter is that Will stands to lose the most by any communication the two of you have," Miranda continued.

"How do you mean?" I asked.

"Think about it," she replied. "Your son is accused of doing something horrible to his daughter. How is it going to look if he continues his relationship with you?" She paused for a few seconds then answered her own question. "It's going to look like he's more interested in you than in the welfare of his own kid. And in a custody fight, that won't go over well with a judge."

A wave of nausea passed over me again. It didn't matter whether Will believed Ben or not. The accusation had been made. The proverbial bell had been rung, and the echo would reverberate in whatever direction the wind took it. The fact that there was not one scintilla of truth to the allegation involving Ben and Lizzy didn't matter. At this point, the accusation was enough. Will could lose his children because of me.

And my relationship with him could cause untold damage to my son.

With complete clarity—and overwhelming heartbreak—I knew what I had to do. First, however, I was going to be sick.

# 53

Ben and Gina headed back to Kentfield after breakfast the following morning. My conversation with Miranda left Ben feeling more optimistic. He had an ally now, a professional with expertise who could actually do him some good. She had promised to check in with the Westin district attorney to find out what he knew, and also find out how Eleanor and Edward had managed to have an investigator question Ben here.

She also suggested that a visit to Eleanor on Ben's behalf might be in order.

"Well, be careful," I warned during our telephone conversation the previous night. "I don't want you to find yourself up to your neck in quicksand—personally or professionally—because of your friendship with me."

Miranda laughed and assured me she could take care of herself.

After Ben and Gina left, I sat on the couch wondering what to do next. I didn't know whether I should call Will and tell him all that Miranda had said, or wait for him to call me. I assumed I'd hear from him after he talked to Lizzy and learned firsthand what had transpired between her and Ben.

I spent the rest of the morning trying to occupy myself with small, mindless tasks. Every so often I glanced at the phone, wondering what Will was doing. I felt entirely disconnected from him. The situation was almost too surreal to contemplate. I kept thinking—hoping—I would wake up to find Will lying next to me and realize this had all been a bad dream.

And when I focused on the reality of the situation, I prayed for some miracle that would set things right again. At the same time, I tried to ignore the voice in my head that said, simply, "I told you so."

As the day wore on and I didn't hear from Will, I became more and more uneasy. I picked up the phone and put it down again several times before finally giving in and dialing his number. He picked up after a few rings.

"Hi, Cal," he said wearily. "I was just about to call you. Lizzy went out with a couple of friends, and I was waiting until she left. How are you?"

"I've been better," I said. "And you?"

"The same."

The conversation immediately turned serious. He related his discussion with Lizzy, and confirmed that her version of the incident matched Ben's. I heaved a huge sigh of relief. The Hallorans would have a hard time pressing any accusation that Lizzy couldn't affirm.

"My guess," he continued, "is that Lizzy told Eleanor and Rowan—probably very innocently—about Ben, and they either read more into it or took it as the first step of something worse."

"And you?" I asked, holding my breath. "Do you think it's the first step of something worse? Do you think Lizzy isn't safe with Ben?"

Will didn't respond immediately. I licked my lips and swallowed hard.

"No, I don't," he answered finally. "But the truth is, it doesn't matter what I think."

I motioned for Bailey to jump up on the couch with me. "Yes, it does matter," I argued. "It matters enormously to me. I couldn't bear it if you believed my son capable of such a thing."

"Well, the question now is, where do we go from here?"

I told him about my conversation with Miranda, including her legal advice, and what it meant for the two of us.

"So, here we are," I concluded. "You on one side with your kids, and me on the other with mine." My eyes brimmed with tears and my voice wavered. "The answer to your question about where we go from here is, we go nowhere—not together, anyway. We have no choice."

We argued back and forth, Will vowing to fight Eleanor and Edward, and me refusing to join him. "If we go up against them, it will be my son they drag through the mud and muck. I can't do that to him. I won't do that to him. And, I won't put Lizzy in the middle of it."

Will was silent.

"Miranda's right," I continued. My throat ached. "If we go on as we have been, the Hallorans will keep fighting for Lizzy and Wiley. And they could win. If we don't, they'll have no reason to go after Ben, and no ammunition to use in a custody fight."

In the end, Will conceded. "You know, I've always known I had to protect Lizzy from the Hallorans, but I never imagined it would come out of something like this."

I thought back to the conversation we had a week or so earlier, when he told me he'd announced that he and the children would not spend Thanksgiving with them. Now I understood their seemingly calm reaction. This had been their plan all along. They were simply waiting for the right moment to put it into action.

"I promised I'd never say goodbye to you again." Will's voice cracked. "Remember? In San Sebastian. After the first time."

Tears spilled down my cheeks. I did remember. "We both made a lot of promises," I whispered. "And meant every one of them."

"I love you, Cal, no matter what. And I refuse to believe, no matter what, that this is how it ends."

I could barely speak. "I love you, too."

After I hung up the telephone, I sat on the couch feeling completely empty. The finality of our conversation hadn't sunk in yet, but at the same time, I knew something was different.

No more than ten minutes had passed when the phone rang again, and Joe was on the other end demanding to know how his son could be accused of mistreating Will's daughter. And he wanted to know what I was doing about it.

I couldn't blame him for being furious.

"Well, I'd say it's a misunderstanding," I replied, "but that's kind of an understatement."

I told him the whole story, beginning with Eleanor and Edward Halloran's unwillingness to accept the death of their daughter, and ending with the allegation against Ben, the sole purpose of which was to separate me and Will so the Halloran family—immediate and extended—would remain intact.

"And they succeeded," I concluded. "Will and I are no longer ... together. So they have no reason to pursue this craziness with Ben. And even if they wanted to, they couldn't make any kind of case. The threat was enough."

"Then it's all been dropped?" Joe asked.

I sat back and rubbed my eyes. I was exhausted. Getting through the last day and a half had required all the strength I could muster, and I was beginning to wear pretty thin.

"I think so," I sighed. "I can't imagine they'd want to take it any further and risk alienating Will any more than they already have—if that's possible."

"Callie, I just don't know how you could let this happen in the first place," Joe snapped.

"Let's not go there, all right?" I replied coldly. "It's not like I saw this coming and sat back and let Ben take a hit. For Christ's sake, I just said goodbye to the one man who means more to me than anyone ever has or ever will just so all this would go away and Ben would be safe." I didn't bother trying to protect Joe's feelings. He responded with an awkward silence, and I made no effort to fill the empty space between us.

"Well, I am sorry about that," he mumbled finally. "From what I've heard, he sounds like a decent guy."

"He is a decent guy," I said. "That's why all this happened in the first place."

# 55

Following Miranda's advice, I avoided all further contact with Will. I went to school, taught my classes, took Bailey out with Alice and Bingo, and did little else. I felt an overwhelming sadness so deep that I couldn't even cry anymore. Unless I was actively occupied with something else, I simply sat and stared out the window.

Finally, however, *against* Miranda's advice, I decided I had to see Will one last time. I had to speak with him in person. The telephone call wasn't enough. I had to look in his eyes. We both deserved at least that. The good-byes we'd spoken twenty-five years earlier had taken place over the phone, and while we wished each other well in the end, that exchange seemed incomplete. Will and I were parting again—for good this time—and we needed to say goodbye properly.

So with Miranda trying to convince me otherwise even up to the final boarding call, I took a couple of days off and caught a plane to Westin.

"Remember," I said to Ben as we were about to leave for the airport, "dry food in the morning, wet food at night." He had agreed to look after Bailey. "I left the cans on the counter."

He tossed my suitcase on the backseat and slammed the car door. "I know, Mom, I know. I've taken care of him often enough. He'll be fine."

I patted Bailey on the head and got in the car.

Ben glanced at me as we headed down the driveway to the main road. "Are you okay?"

I put my hand up. "We're not going to talk about this now, all right?" It was taking every ounce of strength I had to keep myself from falling completely to pieces.

Ben turned silent, but his guilt and remorse were as loud as artillery.

I sighed, feeling a bit of my own guilt and remorse. I reminded myself that none of this was his fault. "But you don't have to worry," I assured him. "I am okay. Everything's going to be okay."

Heading to Westin in July to meet Will's children, the flight seemed to take hours. This trip, however, the time passed more quickly than I might have preferred, and before I knew it we had landed and I was walking out of the terminal, with my suitcase in tow.

I hopped on a shuttle bus to the rental car area, and then it was on to Miranda's house. I was planning to stay only a couple of days, just long enough to settle things with Will. I also wanted to formulate a game plan with Miranda in the eventuality one might be necessary, although neither of us really believed the Hallorans would take the issue any further now that Will and I had separated.

I'd arranged to meet Will at her place in the morning. She made clear her opposition to a face-to-face talk, but agreed that if one was going to take place, it should be somewhere private. She'd make herself scarce so Will and I could talk alone.

"What are you going to say to him?" Miranda asked over dinner. I toyed with the food on my plate.

"The same things I said before—that whatever plans we made aren't going to work. I can't risk Ben's well-being, and Will can't risk Lizzy's and Wiley's. The Hallorans have won."

Miranda reached out and rested her hand on my wrist. "You can fight, you know. It'll be hard, but not impossible. I had a talk with the boss and he believes the Hallorans are taking the custody route only because he made the professional decision that, as far as Ben is concerned, there isn't any action to prosecute right now."

I set my fork down and patted her fingers. "I know it's not impossible, but it would get pretty damn ugly. And I just can't do that to Ben. If the Hallorans pursue this and manage to make something stick, my God, it could follow him for the rest of his life."

"They couldn't, though," Miranda replied. "You know that."

"Yeah," I sighed. "But even so, what will happen to Ben if this drags out? People will make assumptions. They'll consider him guilty, no matter what. If we end it here, we can minimize the damage."

I sipped my water. "And what about Will? He could actually lose his kids because of this." I pressed the glass to my temple. My head was beginning to ache. "If he and I go our separate ways, the Hallorans won't have this relationship—or Ben—to use against him."

I looked hard at Miranda. "I will not be part of Will being separated from Lizzy and Wiley. And you can't guarantee that isn't going to happen."

"I'm so sorry, Callie." Miranda squeezed my hand. "I know how really hard this is."

I closed my eyes and tears dampened my lashes. My throat closed for a moment and I swallowed hard. "Thanks," I whispered. "I just can't believe it's come to this. And yet I don't see how it can be any different."

"Well, speaking as your attorney, you're doing the right thing—at least for now. Even if you and Will decide to put up a fight later on."

"I know," I sighed. "But being right doesn't make it any easier."

I set the alarm on my phone to wake me early the next morning, but it was unnecessary. Aside from dozing off for a few minutes here and there, I spent the night tossing and turning; by the time my phone jingled, I'd already been awake for a good two hours.

Showered and dressed, I met Miranda in the kitchen. She was heading off to work, and as she walked to her car she turned to me and expressed three words of warning: "Just be careful."

I was cleaning up the few dishes in the sink when the doorbell rang a half hour or so later. I wiped my hands on a towel and walked slowly to the foyer. My heart felt like a jackhammer in my chest. I wanted desperately to see Will, but, at the same time, I was terrified.

I opened the door, and there he stood in front of me. He looked haggard and worn. His face was lined, and his eyes were tired. He was dressed plainly in jeans, a button-down shirt, and a brown corduroy jacket.

"Hi, Cal." He said softly.

I opened the door a little wider and gestured for him to come inside. "Will," I whispered. He pulled me into his arms and held me tightly for a minute or so. I caressed his back through the thick fabric of his jacket. He felt solid and strong, and I didn't want to let him go.

With his hands cupping my face, he kissed me, long and deeply.

"Will," I whispered again when he stopped for breath.

"Not yet," he implored. "Don't say it yet." He kissed me again.

I opened my mouth to him, overcome by the familiar desire that flooded through me whenever he was near. "Will," I breathed.

At once remembering the situation, however, I took a step backward, and pressed my hands against his chest to establish some distance between us. "Come sit down. We have to talk about this."

He closed his eyes and exhaled. I took a seat on the couch and he dropped down next to me.

"We don't have any choice," I said simply. He knew what I meant. Eleanor and her forces had triumphed. They'd achieved an all-out victory. I was waving the white flag of surrender—the war was over.

"There's no way we can fight this," I continued. "Not without risk to my son—or your children. Jesus, Will, they could get custody of Lizzy and Wiley. We can't let that happen."

"I know." With his head down, shoulders hunched, and forearms resting on his thighs, he displayed total defeat. Lifting his head, he snorted quietly. One corner of his mouth turned up slightly. "You're still using 'we,' as though we are in this together."

"I wish we could be," I replied, "but it just isn't possible. We're on opposite sides—my son, your daughter. The fact that nothing happened between Ben and Lizzy doesn't even matter."

"I know," he said again.

I reached out and touched his hair. "I love you, Will. And all I want right now is to spend the rest of my life with you." My voice broke. I brushed a tear off my cheek and cleared my throat. "But more important than anything else, you're Lizzy's and Wiley's father—I can't be part of anything that could take you away from them."

Will grasped my hand and pressed my fingers to his mouth. "I know," he acknowledged a third time, adding, "And you know what the hell of all of this is?"

"What?" I sniffled.

"After that first visit to San Sebastian, in February, I thought—" He stopped himself but still held on to my hand.

"Thought what?" I pressed.

"I thought everything would finally be okay. From the minute I saw you standing by the gate at the airport, I knew I wanted you. And by the time I left on Monday, if there had been any doubt, there wasn't anymore. After that weekend, I knew I could handle anything, as long as you were with me. And here I am facing one of the biggest fights of my life—needing you more than ever—and you're the one person I can't have."

We sat in silence, the truth of the situation like a deep chasm between us. The only sounds came from the birds in the maple tree in Miranda's front yard.

"Cal," Will said suddenly, his eyes narrowed and brows pulled together. "Why did you come here?"

"What do you mean?" I asked.

"You haven't said anything different from what you told me over the phone a week ago. So why are you here?"

I kept my eyes on him.

"Don't get me wrong, it's not that I don't want to see you," he continued. "I just don't entirely understand."

Miranda had wondered the same thing as she tried to convince me to stay in San Sebastian. I gave Will the same answer I gave her.

"I had to. I couldn't just hang up the phone and never see you again. I guess I needed some kind of goodbye, no matter how hard it is."

Will rose and walked to the window. He didn't say anything, but stared outside.

"If I shouldn't have, I'm sorry," I said. "I just—oh, hell, I don't know." I dropped my head into my hands. "I don't know."

I didn't hear him approach, but I felt his weight on the cushion next to me when he sat down. I gazed up at him and he wrapped his arm around me. He leaned forward, and kissed me softly. I let my body fall backward so he was above me. Miranda's words of caution echoed in my mind.

"We shouldn't," I cautioned as he leaned in to kiss me again.

He looked at me then, his expression somber. The shine in his eyes was gone, and for the first time, I saw how worn he was. And how worn *down* he was. Fighting the Hallorans while continuing to care for his children and do his work at the hospital was taking all his strength.

"Cal, remember what you said to me about lasts? About how they're more significant than firsts because you don't know when they've happened?"

I nodded.

"I want—I need—a last time with you, and to know that's what it is." His face was no more than a few inches from mine. "I love you, Callie," he whispered. "Nothing has changed that. Whether we're together or on the other side of the world from each other, I love you."

Tears ran down my cheeks. Unable to speak, I turned my gaze to the front window, concentrating for a moment on the gray clouds. I looked back at Will and brushed my fingers through his hair. I stood up, took his hand, and led him upstairs.

Settling into the unmade bed, Will pulled the rumpled sheet over us. Wasting no time, he leaned forward and kissed me hard. There was a roughness in his touch, a sense of desperation. I recognized it—I felt it, too. I turned slightly and he rolled onto his back. With my hand tracing the curve of his shoulder, I brought my face close to his chest, caressing the warm skin with my lips. I ran my hand down the length of his body as I moved lower, across the muscles of his abdomen, and beyond the thicket of coarse, dark hair. He gasped when I took him in my mouth, and then let out a quiet moan. His fingers gripped the bedclothes, and he arched his back slightly.

"Come here," he whispered after a minute or so. When I didn't immediately comply, he tugged at my shoulder. "Come here!" I released him and sat up, my knees straddling his hips. With his hands tangled in the waves of my hair, he drew me toward him and kissed me again. He rolled over so his body hovered above mine. He gazed at me for a moment, and I saw in his eyes a look of tremendous joy mingled with deep sadness.

He stroked my cheek with his finger. "I mean it, Callie. Wherever you are, and whatever comes between us, I love you."

"And I love you. Always."

I kissed him again, and, for what we both knew would be the last time, he pressed himself into me.

# 56

Miranda turned her car up the long circular driveway that led to the house. Keeping her eyes focused forward, she glanced to the side occasionally to take in both the structure and the landscape.

"Holy shit," she said out loud as she pulled to a stop twenty feet away from the house. "Callie was right. These people do have more money than God." And with that, access to some of the best attorneys in the country. This was not going to be an easy fight.

Her objective in visiting the Hallorans, however, was to help avoid a fight. Miranda walked toward the front door, the heels of her shoes clicking on the brick pathway. The Hallorans' housekeeper answered the bell and led her into the living room, where Eleanor and Rowan were awaiting her arrival.

"Good afternoon, Mrs. Halloran," Miranda said, extending her hand in greeting. "Thank you for taking the time to see me."

"I'm happy to meet you, Ms. Wilkes." Eleanor took Miranda's hand. "And may I introduce my daughter, Rowan." Seated on the sofa, Rowan gave Miranda a slight nod. "Miss Halloran," Miranda acknowledged.

"Please, Ms. Wilkes," Eleanor said cordially, "make yourself comfortable."

Miranda sat down on one of the wingback chairs in front of the coffee table and across from the sofa. Eleanor took her place next to Rowan, who eyed Miranda suspiciously as she toyed with the diamond pendant that hung from a thin gold chain around her neck.

"Now, Ms. Wilkes, what can we do for you?" Eleanor asked, interlacing her fingers and laying her hands in her lap.

"Well, as you know, I'm here on behalf of Ben Winwood. I'd like to discuss the accusation you have leveled against him," Miranda replied.

Eleanor and Rowan looked at one another.

"I'm not sure such a conversation should take place without our own attorney present," said Rowan.

"Miss Halloran, this is not a legal proceeding of any kind, and whatever is said in this room, this afternoon, will remain in confidence among the three of us—unless, of course, either of you chooses to share it with anyone."

"Very well, Ms. Wilkes, what would you like to say?" Eleanor's voice had a slight edge, which Miranda chose to ignore.

"Quite simply, I want to let you know what will happen if you pursue this baseless accusation and try to use it as evidence to support your equally baseless claim that their father is an unfit parent," Miranda said quietly but firmly.

"If you do choose to continue, you can be certain that the moment Ben is exonerated—and he will be—I'll have a suit brought against you."

She leaned forward, bringing her face nearer to Eleanor's. "And I will bury you."

Their eyes locked, neither woman looked away or even blinked.

"And to make that happen, the attorney—a former colleague—will put Lizzy on the stand—you won't be able to prevent it—and he'll question her," Miranda continued. "And I'm telling you, he'll break her. He was a prosecutor for a lot of years. He knows how to do it." She paused for a moment. It was a bluff—she had no intention of involving Lizzy, no matter what the legal circumstances—and she wondered if Eleanor was perceptive enough to call her on it.

Eleanor kept her eyes fixed on Miranda's.

"And when he finishes with Lizzy," Miranda continued, "when she's sitting in the witness chair sobbing, you'll have only yourselves to blame."

Eleanor sat back against the cushion and took a deep breath. "Do you think you can frighten me away from fighting on behalf of my granddaughter?"

"I don't mean to frighten you, Mrs. Halloran. Nor am I issuing a threat. I am simply stating what will happen if you continue along this path. When all is said and done, Ben will be completely absolved of any wrongdoing, and your actions—and motives—will be exposed. Lizzy and Wiley will remain with their father, and, in all likelihood, you will never see your grandchildren again."

Miranda picked up the china teacup that Paulette had set in front of her a few minutes earlier. She took a sip, allowing Eleanor to absorb everything she had said.

In response, Eleanor took another deep breath and raised her own cup. Rowan, who until now had been sitting quietly at her mother's side, opened her mouth to speak. "Mother, you aren't really going to let this two-bit hack decide the future for Lizzy and Wiley, are you? They are Joanna's children. They belong with Joanna's family."

"As far as that goes, Miss Halloran," Miranda responded calmly, "their father contributed half of their DNA. He is more their family than you are, both legally and biologically." She paused for effect. "And regarding your description of me as a two-bit hack—a term, by the way, that applies to journalists, not attorneys—I suggest you consult the Westin Law Review and study my conviction rate. I am very good at what I do, and I credit a good deal of my success to the colleague I mentioned earlier."

Rowan crossed one leg over the other and glared at Miranda. She drummed her fingers against her thigh. "So you may think," she said with a sneer. "I guess we'll just see, won't we."

Miranda turned her attention back to Eleanor. "It might also be worth noting that I haven't even touched on the issue of damages. When the lawsuit is filed and you lose—and I guarantee you will, just ask your attorney—you and Mr. Halloran could find yourselves handing over quite a hefty sum to Mr. Winwood as compensation for the pain and anguish you've caused, as well as for the damage to his reputation.

"And, of course," she added as an afterthought, "we'll be more than happy to keep the two-bit hacks at the local press apprised as the case moves along."

Miranda set her cup down and rose to leave. "And now, Mrs. Halloran, I'll entrust the situation to you." She picked up her purse and slung the strap over her shoulder. She gave Rowan a brief nod and walked toward the foyer.

Eleanor followed. "Ms. Wilkes," she said as she opened the front door, "please know that my husband and I will do whatever we believe to be in the best interests of our grandchildren."

Miranda stepped outside and turned to face Eleanor.

"Well, Mrs. Halloran, given your concern for them, I have every confidence that you will. Good afternoon."

# 57

The high-pitched hum of the motor and the whir of three huge rotating brushes created a four-part harmony as the soft bristles spun along the sides of the car, over the windshield, and across the roof.

Will and Wiley stood next to each other at the Plexiglas wall, watching the car move slowly down the track. Both stood with their legs slightly apart and their arms folded across their chests. One looked like a miniature version of the other. The water jets switched on for the final rinse and a fine mist floated over the wall, dampening their faces.

The car rolled off the track, and Will took a seat on one of the wooden benches, watching the attendants work on his car. With spray bottles and rags—and nearly the same degree of efficiency he saw from the doctors and nurses in his emergency department—they wiped down the interior, dried the exterior, and polished the windows.

Wiley chattered away beside him, but Will paid no attention to what he actually said. His mind was focused on something—or, rather, someone—that had nothing to do with cars or the ER.

One of the attendants raised an arm to indicate the car was ready.

"C'mon, let's go," Will said. "We still have a lot to do."

He handed the attendant the receipt and a tip.

In exchange, the attendant handed him an earring. "Found it under one of the seats," he said. "Hope you still have the other one."

Will held the earring in the palm of his hand and studied it for a moment. It was Callie's. A smooth violet-colored teardrop attached to sterling silver filigree and wire. She'd lost it during her trip to Westin, when she came out to meet Lizzy and Wiley. She and Will were in her hotel room when she noticed it was missing. She was slipping off her jewelry, and when she reached up to take out her earrings, one of them was gone. They joked that it must have come dislodged in the heat of passion earlier that evening. They looked for it the next day, but never found it.

Will sighed and wrapped his fingers around the lone earring. He rested his hand against his chest and closed his eyes, remembering the feel of her.

Will and Wiley had several errands to run. Pharmacy, hardware store, car wash—check, check, and check. Their next stop was the sporting goods store to pick up a new set of wheels for Wiley's skateboard. After that, it would be the market for a gallon of milk, a loaf of bread, and a jar of peanut butter. He couldn't handle any more than that today. He'd leave a list for Isabel, and she could pick up the rest of the things when she shopped for ingredients for next week's dinners.

"Hey, Dad," Wiley asked as they turned into the grocery store parking lot, "can we go see Gran and Grandpa today? We haven't been over there in a long time."

Will took a deep breath. The question wasn't a surprise—he'd been expecting it. In fact, what did surprise him was that it had taken two weeks for Wiley to comment on not having visited his grandparents.

"Not today, pal," Will replied, trying to steer away from the topic. "We have to go home and put those wheels on your skateboard so you can go the skate park with Tanner tomorrow."

"Oh, yeah," Wiley replied. "I forgot about that."

Will still hadn't figured out how he would explain the estrangement from Joanna's family. For the last two years Lizzy and Wiley spent at least one night a week with them. Since Eleanor's declaration, however, the children hadn't set one foot in the Halloran house. And they wouldn't as long as the custody issue continued. He couldn't tell them the truth, but he didn't want to tell an outright lie either. They were too smart for that—particularly Lizzy. Will was fairly certain she knew the situation had something to do with her and Ben.

Still, the last thing they needed to hear was that their grandparents wanted to take them away from him because they believed he was a lousy father.

"But when *can* we see them?" Wiley asked, pressing the point.

Will sighed loudly. "I don't know, Wiley, okay? I don't know!"

Wiley stared out the window, straight-faced and quiet.

Will glanced out his own window and frowned. He couldn't blame Wiley. His grandparents had been a big part of his life for almost as long as he could remember.

ANDREA WEIR

"I'm sorry, pal," Will apologized. "I didn't mean to snap at you. It's just that we have so much to do today."

"It's okay," Wiley murmured, his face still turned toward the window.

When they finally arrived back home, Will checked on Lizzy, who was in her bedroom finishing a book report. He went into his own room, closed the door, and sat down on the bed. He'd tucked Callie's earring into his pocket, and he withdrew it now, gazing at the silver and amethyst resting lightly in his palm. It was warm from his body.

It crossed his mind that he should return it to her so she'd have the pair, but he couldn't bring himself to do it. He needed to keep it—to possess it—as a part of her that he could still see and touch. At this moment, it was as close to her as he could get.

# 58

It was a cold November evening, with an early winter storm pummeling the area. The cottage was cozy and warm, but the wind rattling the windows and huge raindrops pounding against the glass made me a little uneasy. I was glad to have Ben with me.

He had stopped by shortly before dinner, and when the rain started coming down sooner—and harder—than expected, I convinced him to stay overnight.

I was just turning down the quilt when Ben knocked lightly at my bedroom door. "Mom," he called softly, "can I come in?"

I sat down on the bed and faced the door. "Of course, honey, come on in."

He took one step into the room, stopped, and stood with his hands at his sides. His face was drawn and tired. The events of the past month were, not surprisingly, taking their toll.

I extended my hand to him, inviting him to come closer. He accepted it and sat down next to me.

"What is it, Ben?" I asked. "What do you need?"

He leaned forward with his elbows on his knees and his head in his hands. His shoulders vibrated slightly, and I knew he was crying. *Damn the Hallorans*, I thought bitterly to myself. *Damn all of them, including Joanna.*

I wrapped my arm around his shoulder and drew him to me. He rested his head on my chest just like he used to do when he was little and needed comforting after a skinned knee or bad dream. Bad dream, indeed; this was a waking nightmare. There was little I could do for him, except be here with him.

Tears stung my eyes as I considered all he had endured because of Eleanor and Rowan Halloran—and me. And when I brushed those away, a fresh round took their place when I thought of my own situation. The Hallorans' strategy couldn't have played to their advantage any better—Will and I were separated for good, and the precious memory of their dead daughter was safe. No one would come between any of them now.

"I'm so sorry about all of this," Ben whispered. He sniffled and wiped his eyes on his sleeve. I reached across him to the nightstand and picked up a box of Kleenex. He plucked a couple of tissues and gave his nose a solid blow.

"Ben, you have nothing to be sorry for. The situation is what it is, and there's very little anyone can do about it now."

"But you and Will ..."

"There is no me and Will anymore." A lump caught in my throat. I swallowed hard, but it didn't go away.

"That's what I mean," Ben reiterated. "I'm so sorry it turned out this way."

I sat up and swiveled Ben's body so he faced me. I had to make him understand that what happened between Will and me was not his fault. It was not what I wanted, but it was the result of a choice that *I* made in response to a situation that someone else had created. "Listen to me," I said, my voice suddenly clear and strong. "I will be honest with you—except for you and Justine, I have never loved anyone in this world the way I love Will—not even your father, who I have always believed is, in many ways, an extraordinary man. But Will is my heart and soul. I would sacrifice almost everything I have and everything I am for him."

Ben dropped his gaze to the hands in his lap. My words must have cut like daggers. But I had to tell him the absolute truth about my feelings for Will so he'd believe I was telling the truth when I explained why I made the decision to leave him. I lifted Ben's chin with my thumb and forefinger so he had to look at me.

"What I won't sacrifice, though, are my children," I continued. "I don't care what Eleanor or Edward or Rowan Halloran do to me, but I will not allow them to hurt you or Justine. It's that simple. And if their actions come between Will and me, well, that's for the two of us to deal with—not you."

I brought my face close to Ben's so I could look into his eyes. "Ben, you are involved in this situation because of the Hallorans. But you are in no way the cause. You have done nothing wrong. Saying goodbye to Will was my choice. I hate that I had to make a choice at all, or that it has turned out this way, but I'd do it again and again and again if I had to, no matter what it cost. You are that important to me."

He rose and walked to the dresser. He stood with his shoulders hunched and his head bowed. His hands rested on the front edge. He looked up, glanced at my reflection in the mirror, and then slammed his fist on the dresser top with such force that the perfume bottles rattled and one fell onto its side. The outline of his back muscles, tightly contracted, showed through his cotton T-shirt. "You don't know how much I hate them—all of them," he snarled.

"I can guess," I replied quietly, "and you wouldn't be out of line."

"God, Mom, it shouldn't be this way," he said more softly. His eyes shimmered in the lamplight and his cheeks were damp. "I've never seen you as happy as you've been since you and Will got together. It kills me to have that taken away."

"You're right, it shouldn't be this way. But like I said, this is how it is. And unless things with the Hallorans change—and that doesn't seem very likely—this is how they're going to stay."

I'd left a basket of clean laundry by the bed, and I grabbed a towel from the pile and started folding. It felt good to have a simple task to occupy my mind. I shook it out and something fell to the floor. I picked it up, and my heart sank. It was one of Will's T-shirts. It was gray, the words Westin Track Club in faded lettering on the front.

I had been resolute with Ben—he was in desperate need of it—but one look at Will's shirt, and my resolve melted. A tidal wave of pain and sadness was about to break over me. And I had to be alone to meet it.

Ben must have read something in my face or manner, because he moved to the door without saying a word. I looked at him and we smiled faintly at one another. He walked out, closing the door quietly behind him.

I sat on the bed again, and ran my hand across the quilt. We had lain here together, Will and I. We had made love here, made plans here. It was here that we gave ourselves to each other, and here that I felt most complete. Now it was the place where I felt the most achingly alone.

I pressed his shirt to my face, hoping to breathe in his scent, but getting only the fragrance of detergent and fabric softener. "Will," I whispered. The wave broke. My chest was heavy, and my heart literally hurt, as though someone had taken a broadsword to it. Bailey jumped up on the bed and arranged himself next to me. He looked at me for a long moment, then sat up and licked my cheek.

"Thanks, buddy," I murmured. My voice cracked. I tried to hold back the tears, but the effort was fruitless. They pressed like raging water against a dam constructed of nothing but stones and twigs. I couldn't contain them. With my face buried in Will's shirt, I collapsed alongside Bailey and wept. I wept for myself and for Will, for the past we didn't share and for the promises we wouldn't keep. I wept for Ben, for the pain and humiliation he was being forced to bear. I wept out of desperation for my mother, and I wept for Lizzy and Wiley, feeling their loss as keenly as I felt my own.

# 59

"Hey, Dad, tell me again why we're going to Alex and Julie's house for Thanksgiving, and not to Gran's like we always do."

It was Thanksgiving morning and Lizzy sat at the small round table in the kitchen eating a bowl of Cheerios while Will scrambled eggs for Wiley, who was sprawled out on the family room floor watching television.

"Well, Alex and Julie have been wanting us to spend the holiday with them for a long time now, and I thought it would be good to do something different this year."

Will had been enormously relieved when Alex told him he and Julie were staying in town for Thanksgiving, rather than traveling back to Connecticut to visit Julie's family. When Julie heard about the battle brewing with the Hallorans—and the abrupt change in Will's travel plans—she insisted on preparing dinner for him and the children.

"Oh," Lizzy replied, taking a spoonful of cereal. She chewed and swallowed. "What about Christmas then? We're spending Christmas Eve at Gran's, aren't we?"

"I don't know." Will tried to sound noncommittal. Christmas with the Hallorans this year was out of the question, but he didn't want to take the tradition away from Lizzy—or Wiley—until he'd replaced it with something else. He wasn't sure what that would be, though—Alex and Julie were certain they *would* be in Connecticut for Christmas.

"I was thinking maybe we'd go away somewhere. Just the three of us. How does that sound?"

"Dad, what's going on?" Lizzy asked. "I know there's something with Gran and Grandpa, and that's why we haven't seen them since before Halloween. Every time Wiley or I ask to visit them, you always have some reason why we can't."

Pretending to concentrate on the eggs, Will didn't answer immediately. He'd hoped to stall her indefinitely, even though he knew she was far too perceptive for that.

When he turned to face her, her eyes met his. She didn't adjust her gaze. She wanted an answer. He'd always been honest with her, he thought, and maybe that was the best way of dealing with this situation now.

He turned off the stove, moved the frying pan to a cool burner, and sat down across from her.

"It's kind of complicated, LZ," he said quietly. He took a breath as though to continue speaking, but stopped himself.

"What, Dad? Tell me."

"LZ, you know your grandmother loves you a lot, right?"

"Yeah."

"Well, she thinks—and your grandfather seems to agree—that it would be better for you and Wiley if you lived with them instead of with me." Will studied Lizzy's face for her reaction.

She dropped her spoon. It landed in the near-empty cereal bowl with a loud clank, sending droplets of milk onto the table. She fell back in her chair and stared at him. "But I don't want to do that," she cried. "I don't want to live with them. I want to stay here—with you."

Will reached out and laid his hand over hers. "I know. I want that, too. I don't want you or Wiley to be anywhere else. And I won't let it happen."

"So that's why we haven't been able to visit them? Because Gran would make us stay there, and wouldn't let us come back home?"

Will rubbed his chin as he contemplated his response. "Well, sort of. But it's more complicated than that," he said finally.

"But I don't understand," she argued. "Why can't Wiley and I just tell her we don't want to live there? And why does she think that would be better anyway? It's stupid. She's just—"

Lizzy stopped abruptly and swallowed hard. "It's because of me, isn't it? Because of what I said about Ben?" Her face went ashen.

Will sat back, unsure how to respond. The entire situation *was* because of Lizzy—because of what she had told Eleanor and Rowan, even though, at the time, she had no concept of the implications. And while Lizzy was at the center of this whole mess, he wouldn't allow her to assume any of the blame or take any of the responsibility.

In the most basic terms possible, and sparing her feelings for her grandparents as best he could, Will explained that Eleanor and Edward were, indeed, concerned about the interaction between Lizzy and Ben.

"Like I said before, they love you and care about you, and they want to protect you," he said. "And sometimes when people have strong feelings like that, they overreact. And that's what your Gran and Grandpa are doing." He looked closely for clues to what she might be thinking. "Do you get what I'm saying?"

"I think so," she replied. She sat quietly, and Will waited for her to speak. "That's why we didn't go to Callie's for Thanksgiving like you said we would, isn't it?"

Hearing Callie's name was akin to having salt poured on a gaping wound. Now Will sat quietly, figuring out what kind of spin to put on this aspect of the issue. "Yes," he said, adding quickly, "but it's also true that Alex and Julie have been asking us for a long time to spend Thanksgiving with them."

Lizzy scowled and chewed the inside of her lip. "Can Gran really do that? Can she make us live with her and Grandpa?"

Will pressed his hand to his daughter's cheek, stroking it lightly with his thumb. "No one's taking you or Wiley anywhere, LZ, I promise."

As Will transferred Wiley's eggs onto a plate, Lizzy dumped her bowl in the sink and ran up to her room. She pushed the door shut behind her, plopped down on her bed, and reached for her old teddy bear. This turn of events was not what she had intended.

She was aware that telling Eleanor and Rowan about Ben's familiarity with her had somehow affected her father's relationship with Callie. She didn't know what transpired between the various parties, but she noticed that his frequent telephone conversations with Callie had ceased completely. Even more telling, though, was the abrupt change in their Thanksgiving plans. She knew how excited he was about going to San Sebastian and seeing her.

But that part of it was just fine with Lizzy. She wanted her father back, and she got her wish. If what she said about Ben had something to do with it, well, that was fine, too. After all, what she told her grandmother was the truth. Ben did put his arm around her, and while her thirteen-year-old sensibilities never perceived anything improper, the action did strike her as a bit odd. If that statement resulted in her father and Callie going their separate ways, she'd not explain it any further. Let Eleanor read into it whatever she wanted.

But the situation with her father was something else entirely. She had no idea her grandparents would react this way. It never crossed her mind that they might use her words as an excuse to wrench her—and Wiley—away from him.

She sat on the bed, cross-legged, and looked out the window at the gray sky juxtaposed against the pink and lavender floral-print curtains that framed the image. She shivered and reached for a sweatshirt.

She knew her father would put up a fight—and she knew how tough he could be when circumstances required it—but her grandparents were equally formidable. She knew that, too. While she took her father at his word, she had a keen sense of her grandmother's determination—when Eleanor wanted something, she generally got it.

Lizzy gazed down at the teddy bear's black button eyes, as though expecting it to speak and offer words of either encouragement or wisdom. She had landed herself between a rock and a hard place, and didn't see an immediate way out. If she made clear to Eleanor what she believed from the outset—that Ben had been showing kindness to her, and nothing more—Eleanor might abandon this crazy notion that Lizzy and Wiley would be better off with her rather than with their dad.

On the other hand, if everyone knew that Ben posed no danger to her, the one obstacle that kept her father and Callie apart would be removed. They would get married, and Lizzy would have to stand by and watch another woman take her mother's place.

A quiet knock sounded on her bedroom door.

"Yeah?" she answered.

The door opened partway, and Will poked his head around so he could see her.

"Are you okay?" he asked.

"Um, yeah," she replied, tossing the stuffed bear onto the pillow next to her. "I was just thinking."

"About anything in particular? Or anything I can help with?"

She paused for a moment, began to say something, and then thought better of it. "No, it's fine."

Will nodded once, unconvinced. Everything wasn't fine, but he wasn't going to push her to talk about it. Whatever she wanted to say, she'd bring it up with him when she was ready.

"Well, we're supposed to be at Alex and Julie's house at two o'clock. Can you be ready in time?"

"Sure," Lizzy replied.

Will winked at her and started to close the door.

"Dad!"

"Yeah?"

"Never mind."

# 60

Contrary to the nature of the holiday, I wasn't feeling a lot of gratitude this Thanksgiving, even with Ben, Justine, and Miranda around the table sharing in the bounty. We all gathered at Alice's house, joined by Alice's daughter, Sally, and my friend Mr. Lowell. He'd expected to spend the holiday with his niece in Chicago, but their plans fell through at the last minute. That malady seemed to be contagious.

"How are you doing?" Miranda asked as we sat on the couch. Alice, Sally, and Justine were in charge of dinner, and Miranda and I had the luxury of doing nothing more than enjoying the aromas wafting from the kitchen.

Ben and Gina were out walking on the bluffs with Bailey. Gina had abandoned her plans to visit her own family in favor of spending the holiday with Ben—a circumstance for which I was grateful.

"I'm fine," I said, toying with the zipper on one of Alice's throw pillows. "Really."

Miranda drew her eyebrows together and gave me a stern look. "This is me you're talking to, not one of your kids. You don't have to pretend, and I can see right through it anyway. So you might as well be honest."

I hugged the pillow and sighed. "I miss him. I miss him, and I want him, and I feel like some part of me is dead. Is that honest enough for you?"

"I'm sorry, sweetie. I really am. I know how hard this is." She shrugged a shoulder in a way that was meant to be comforting. "But who knows—maybe it won't always have to be this way."

"Maybe, but I'm not counting on it." I glanced toward the front door, through which Ben and Gina had left with Bailey a half hour or so earlier. "At least things are okay for Ben now. As long as Will and I are apart, the Hallorans can't use him to advance their cause. They've no need to."

Miranda picked up her tea, blew away the steam, and took a sip. "Well, the thing I find most amusing right now is the fact that while they've succeeded in separating the two of you, they've also alienated Will to the point that they aren't seeing the grandkids anyway."

"How do you know that?" I asked, startled.

Miranda hesitated before answering. "I've, uh, spoken to Will a couple of times since this whole thing erupted. Legal matters," she added.

My heart fluttered and I felt the familiar lump in my throat. I coughed, hoping to dislodge it.

"Why didn't you tell me?"

"What good would it have done?" she asked.

I shrugged lightly. "None, I suppose." I stared into my cup, watching the steam swirl upward. "How is he?"

"About as well as you are," Miranda replied. "He's hurting, too. And scared. He's worried about what all this is doing to the kids."

I closed my eyes, fighting back the latest round of tears.

"The funny thing is, though, Eleanor is further away from Lizzy and Wiley than she was when you and Will were together. And there isn't a damn thing she can do about it right now."

"What do you mean?"

"Everyone knows the one incident between Ben and Lizzy doesn't represent anything on its face. I mean, he didn't actually do anything but put his arm around her shoulder. She acknowledged that herself."

"I know," I replied sharply. "That's the whole point."

"So, on its own, it doesn't give Eleanor much to pursue—especially because you and Will aren't seeing each other anymore. That would look to a judge like Will became aware of a potential danger and took steps to protect his daughter—as any good parent would."

I was beginning to see the Hallorans' predicament.

"It has sort of backfired for Eleanor, though. I think she believed that if she got you out of the picture, everything would go back to the way it was. But all she's really managed to do at this point is estrange Will—and her grandchildren—even more. She can't force him to let her see them. Not legally, anyway. And right now she has no leverage."

"Do you know what they're doing for Thanksgiving?"

"Spending it with his friends Alex and Julie, is what he told me."

I smiled, heartened by the fact that he and Lizzy and Wiley would be with the two people who were most like family.

"While we're on the subject, he also said one other thing the last time I spoke with him," Miranda noted. "Asked me to pass it along to you. I had second thoughts about whether to do it, though. You're already hurting enough. But now that you know I've been in touch with him, you may as well hear it."

"What?" I asked anxiously.

"It doesn't mean anything to me, but he said you'd get it. It's one word … a name—Etta."

Tears filled my eyes, but I smiled anyway. "Here we are in heaven," I whispered.

# 61

Will stepped out of the shower and wrapped a towel around his waist. Leaning over the sink, he studied his face in the mirror, deciding whether Thanksgiving protocol required that he shave.

He walked into the bedroom, and the glint of Callie's earring on the dresser caught his eye. He picked it up, examining the smooth, cool stone and the intricate pattern on the silver. He remembered the last time she wore it. He remembered the look of it falling delicately against her hair, the feel of it against his hand when he caressed her neck.

His heart quickened with the memory. She had been so free with him that night in Westin. She had taken him so fully into herself—not just his body but his entire being. She had wrapped her arms around his very soul.

All at once, he felt the familiar rousing, and became aware of his own hardness. He touched himself lightly through the towel, not out of any kind of self-gratification, but simply as an acknowledgment of the physical response the thought of her evoked.

He closed his eyes. He could satisfy himself, picturing her in his mind, but he would not. He was drawn to her physically, like steel to a magnet, and his imagination could easily conjure up every aspect of her, but at this moment it seemed to him almost profane to use her that way.

He opened his eyes, set the earring down on the dresser, and went into the bathroom to shave.

Seated at the table later in the afternoon, Will glanced around and felt a rush of gratitude for Alex and Julie. He had no idea how he and his kids would have spent the holiday if his friends hadn't decided to have a gathering at their house.

He still had to figure out what they would do for Christmas, but he decided not to worry about that now.

Alex sat at one end of the oblong table, with Wiley to his immediate right. Julie was seated at the other end, and Lizzy had the chair next to her. Will occupied a space near the middle, with Wiley on one side, and Julie's administrative assistant on the other. Across from him—and next to Lizzy—were Alex and Julie's neighbors, an older couple whose children lived out of state and were trading Thanksgiving with their spouses' relatives for a big family Christmas in Westin.

Will kept a careful eye on Lizzy, who seemed especially quiet. No surprise, given their conversation earlier in the day. She glanced over at him and their eyes met. He raised his eyebrows and she smiled shyly.

The Hallorans would *not* take her away from him, and he vowed to do whatever it took to make her believe it.

As usual, thinking of Edward and Eleanor and the custody issue brought Callie to mind. She was never far from his thoughts. He felt a sharp stab in his chest, wondering what she was doing and who was with her. Ben and Justine, certainly. And Alice. Probably Miranda, and maybe even Alistair Lowell.

Will closed his eyes, waiting for the pain to recede.

When the holiday meal was over and everyone had eaten their fill, Lizzy helped Julie clear away the dessert dishes while Alex pulled out a deck of cards. He invited everyone sitting around the table to join him in a few hands of poker.

"Draw or stud?" the administrative assistant asked enthusiastically.

"Poker? Really?" Will asked. He gestured toward Wiley. "He's twelve years old!"

"He's gotta learn sometime," Alex said, giving Wiley a wink. "Who better to teach him than the old men? Think of it as a rite of passage."

"What old men?" the neighbor retorted as he began shuffling the cards. "Speak for yourself. So what are we betting? Pennies? Matchsticks?"

Julie excused herself and suggested she and Lizzy withdraw to the living room to work on their latest knitting project—a pink cardigan.

"Okay, let's see what we have here," she said as she pulled a front section out of her knitting basket. It was the color of ripe watermelon, with a set of thin white stripes running along the bottom. "I think this is the piece you've been doing." She studied the rows of stockinette. "This looks great, sweetie. You've really got the hang of it. See how even those stitches are? You're already a pro."

Lizzy sat down next to Julie and picked up the needles and ball of yarn.

She completed two rows, and then stopped. She looked to see that her father was occupied with the card game and then turned to Julie.

"I think I did something wrong," she said.

Julie reached over to take the knitting from her. "Let's have a look. If you did, I'm sure we can fix it."

"No, I don't mean with the sweater."

Julie stopped her own work and looked at Lizzy. "What *do* you mean?"

"My dad told me that Gran and Grandpa want to make me and Wiley live with them," Lizzy began. "He said it's because they love us and they're worried about us and they think it would be better for us if we were at their house instead of at home with him." Julie listened carefully as Lizzy recounted the conversation she'd had with Will that morning. Lizzy also acknowledged that it might have been what she'd told Eleanor and Rowan about Ben that set her grandparents on their present course.

When Lizzy got to the end, she sniffled and wiped her eyes with her fists.

"Your dad told us about that," Julie responded. She reached over and patted Lizzy's arm. "All of this is really hard for you, isn't it?"

Lizzy nodded.

"You know, none of it's your fault. Even considering what you said—or didn't say—to your grandmother." Julie picked up one of the knitting needles and pretended to be counting stitches. "Lizzy, when you were in San Sebastian, at Callie's house, what did you think about Ben putting his arm around you?"

Lizzy shrugged. "I don't know anymore. Like I told Gran, I didn't think it was bad; I thought he was just being nice. But then she and Aunt Rowan made it seem like what he did was wrong."

Letting the needles and yarn fall to her lap, Julie held Lizzy's chin with her thumb and forefinger and looked at her straight on. "Well, you know that if anything like that does make you uncomfortable, it *is* wrong, plain and simple. And you should tell your dad so he can take care of it." She picked up the knitting needles again. "But, in this case," she added, "maybe you were right that Ben really was only trying to be nice."

Lizzy shrugged again.

"Sweetie, I'm not trying to tell you how it was, or how you felt," Julie continued. "Only you know that. And whatever you felt is completely okay. But it's important that when people take action—like your grandparents are—they do it for the right reason, and they make their decisions based on facts, not on what they think *might* be true."

"I don't want Gran and Grandpa to do this," Lizzy whispered. Her eyes shimmered, and she brushed away a tear just as it fell onto her cheek. "I don't want to live with them. I only want to be with my dad."

"Would you like to tell them that?" Julie asked. "Your grandparents, I mean?"

Lizzy hesitated. She picked up a separate ball of yarn and began unwinding and winding it. "I don't know … maybe …" She looked up at Julie. "But I can't. My dad won't let me. He won't let me see them—Wiley can't, either. He's afraid they won't let us go home."

"But if you could see them," Julie pressed, "would you want to tell them how you feel?"

Lizzy nodded.

"How about if I talk to your dad?"

Lizzy chewed her bottom lip anxiously.

"Honey, your dad doesn't *want* to keep you from your grandparents," Julie continued. "Believe me, he knows how much you love them, and they love you."

The two sat wordless for a moment, their eyes fixed on one another. When Will's voice suddenly broke the silence, they both jumped.

"So, what's going on in here?" he asked. He approached Lizzy and squeezed her shoulder. "Are you okay, LZ?"

Lizzy didn't reply.

"We're just talking," Julie replied. "How are things in there?" Her conversation with Lizzy had been punctuated and interrupted by the occasional whoop and holler as one or another of the poker hounds played a particularly good hand.

"They're turning Wiley into a card shark," Will replied. "He's beating all of them—with Alex's assistance, of course."

"Of course," Julie smiled.

Will sat down next to Lizzy. "So, what *is* going on in here? You two look so serious. Did you forget today is a holiday?" He gave Lizzy a nudge with his elbow.

"Lizzy and I have been talking about some important things," Julie explained. She glanced over at Lizzy. "Shall I?"

Almost imperceptibly, Lizzy moved her head up and down.

"Well," Julie began, "Lizzy has some things she'd like to say to her grandparents, and they have to do with you, and with Ben Winwood."

The rest of Thanksgiving weekend passed quickly. Ben and Gina stayed in San Sebastian until Saturday morning, Justine headed back to Middlebrook by midafternoon, and Miranda had an evening flight to Westin. I hated to see her go, but I looked forward to having the cottage to myself again.

"What do you have planned for tomorrow?" she asked as she packed her things. "Something pleasant, I hope. And away from this house." She had earlier expressed her concern that I was spending too much time either at home or by myself—or both. "You have to be out in the world," she argued.

I told her I intended to spend most of the day preparing for the following week's classes. My honors students were about to tackle *Hamlet*.

"'There is nothing either good or bad,'" she quoted in response, "'but thinking makes it so.'"

"My point exactly," I said.

# 62

It was well after New Year's by the time arrangements were made for Lizzy to visit her grandparents. It had taken some doing for Julie to convince Will that calling on the Hallorans could actually be good for Lizzy; and even then, he refused to let the meeting take place over the holidays.

"She has the right to speak her piece," Julie argued during the last of several conversations on the topic. They were sitting in a small café near the hospital—the same place he'd met Callie just over a year ago. "Lizzy is part of this, and she has something to say about it."

Will shook his head. "You know damn well they'll discount anything she says on my behalf or in my defense. They'll think I put her up to it just so I can get back to Callie. It will only make things worse."

He wadded his napkin into a ball and tossed it onto the table. "They're looking for any reason to believe what they want to believe. Nothing Lizzy says will make a difference."

Julie set her cup down. "There you're wrong," she argued. "What Lizzy says *will* make a difference—to her. Like I said, she has the right to speak her piece. However they want to take it is up to them. All that matters is that she knows—and you know—what she says is the truth."

Will sat back in his chair and scowled. "This whole thing has been so hard on her. I just don't want her to have to deal with any more than she has to."

"You can't shield her from it, Will. She's too smart for that." Julie paused while the waitress refilled their coffee cups. "Besides, letting her speak up for herself will give her some power. And she needs that."

Will rubbed his hands across his face. "All right," he sighed, finally surrendering. "But when they bare their claws," he added, in an icy tone she had never heard from him before, "just make sure they don't get anywhere near her."

And now here they were—Lizzy and Julie—on their way to the Halloran family compound. Lizzy still hadn't figured out exactly what she wanted to say to her grandparents. It had been so long since she'd seen them that they had become almost like strangers to her. After Thanksgiving with Julie and Alex, Will brought the children to Wyoming to spend Christmas with an aunt, uncle, and cousins he hadn't seen since he graduated from medical school. It was a bit awkward at first, but what the hell, he thought. Lizzy and Wiley may as well get to know the few relatives that remained on the Tremaine side of the family.

Julie took the long way from Will's house to the Hallorans'. As she drove, she reminded Lizzy that the sole purpose of the visit was to give her a chance to say whatever was on her mind.

"What if I hurt their feelings?" Lizzy worried.

Julie glanced over at her and smiled reassuringly. "Sweetie, it's not your job to protect anyone—not Ben, not your father, and certainly not your grandparents. Your job is simply to be honest."

Lizzy stared out the passenger window. "Maybe my dad was right," she muttered.

With her coat still zipped, Lizzy walked tentatively into her grandparents' living room, where the four Hallorans, plus Sarah, waited to greet her.

"Hi, Gran."

Eleanor rushed toward her, arms extended. "Oh, Lizzy, darling, I'm so glad to see you. We've all missed you terribly."

Lizzy made no move to return her grandmother's attention.

Realizing very quickly this would not be the happy reunion she had anticipated, Eleanor stopped a few feet from her granddaughter.

"Will you come sit down?" she asked, gesturing toward the couch.

Lizzy turned toward Julie, who stood behind her. Julie nodded once or twice, and Lizzy sat down in one of the wingback chairs.

The Hallorans, including Sarah, looked at one another nervously and found their own seats—Eleanor and Edward on the couch, Rowan in the second wingback chair, and Chase and Sarah on the love seat. Julie remained standing, positioning herself slightly behind Lizzy. She rested her forearm on Lizzy's chair.

"Well, tell us how you are, sweetheart," Rowan began. "It's been so long since we've seen you or your brother, and we've missed you so much. It was very unkind of your father not to let us spend any of the holidays together."

Lizzy fixed her aunt a cold stare. Startled, Rowan pressed herself into the back of her chair. An awkward tension filled the room.

"Ahem." Edward gave his daughter a look of reproach, then glanced at Eleanor before addressing Lizzy. "And how is Wiley," he asked. "And your father?"

Lizzy carried the burden of everyone's attention. They waited anxiously for her to speak, but she responded with silence.

Julie rested her hand lightly on Lizzy's shoulder and addressed the group on her behalf. "From the way all of you look, I'd say Wiley—and Will—are doing about as well as you are," she said.

Cutting to the chase, Lizzy addressed her grandmother. "Gran, I want to know why you're trying to take me and Wiley away from our dad."

Eleanor faltered for a moment, taken aback by her granddaughter's straightforwardness. She moved from the sofa to the ottoman in front of Lizzy's chair. "Honey, your grandfather and I love you and Wiley very much, and we only care about what's best for you." She reached out and gently tucked a few strands of Lizzy's hair behind her ear. "Can you understand that?"

Lizzy pulled away from Eleanor's hand and leaned closer to Julie. "That's what my dad said," she replied. "That it's because you love us. But he's wrong. I don't think you care about us at all. And I don't want to live here with you. And neither does Wiley. We only want to live with our dad."

"Lizzy, if this is a better place for you and Wiley, then this is where you should be," Eleanor argued.

"This isn't a better place," Lizzy replied coldly. "We're supposed to be with our dad. No matter what."

Eleanor folded her hands in her lap, sighed, and gave Lizzy a sympathetic smile. "Sweetheart, I know that you—"

"You don't know anything," Lizzy interrupted.

Eleanor drew a quick breath. She paused for a moment then continued. "Lizzy, your grandfather and I—and your Aunt Rowan and Uncle Chase— only want to make sure you and Wiley are safe. And we're not sure your father is doing the best job of that."

Lizzy scowled as she listened to her grandmother.

"When you told Aunt Rowan and me about your trip to San Sebastian last summer and the interaction you had with Ben Winwood, it worried us very much. You were smart enough to know he did something inappropriate. You said it made you uncomfortable."

Julie snorted quietly and shook her head.

She opened her mouth to speak, but Lizzy responded first. "You said that, not me."

"And didn't you say you just wanted to be the family you were—you, Wiley, and your father?" Eleanor pressed.

Lizzy's eyes moved from her grandmother to her aunt and back to her grandmother. "I want my dad," she said flatly. "He loves me and Wiley, and he always takes care of us, no matter what you think."

"I'm sure you believe that, Lizzy, but you're a child. That's why you need your family to look after you." It was Rowan who spoke, but Lizzy ignored her.

She stared at the crystal vase on the coffee table. No one in the room made a sound. Slowly, she raised her eyes to meet her grandmother's. "My dad said my mom was the kindest, most understanding person he ever knew." Her voice was barely audible. "He said she loved me and Wiley more than anything. And she loved him, too." She watched her grandmother for a few seconds. Gently shaking her head, she added, "And I don't think she'd like this."

Without waiting for a response, Lizzy turned to Julie. "Can we go now?"

"Whenever you're ready," Julie said.

Chase stood at the window, his arms folded across his chest, and watched Julie and Lizzy drive away. "Out of the mouths of babes, eh, Mother?"

He swung around to face Eleanor, who, following Lizzy's abrupt departure, now sat rigid on the couch. "Are you satisfied?" he asked brusquely. "Will wants nothing to do with you, and now Lizzy has said all but the same thing. What's more, she seems to know her mother better than you do."

Chase's words struck their target with stunning accuracy, although Eleanor demonstrated no visible response.

"I've had enough of this whole thing, Mother," he continued. "Joanna was my sister, and I loved her. And if the last three months have taught me anything, it's that I don't want to be estranged from her children. You can do whatever you want, but I'm calling Will." Sarah touched his arm lightly in a show of support, and he took her hand.

"I never thought there was any truth to your claims about him being an unfit father," Chase went on. He spoke quietly, but decisively. "And, to be honest, right now I'm pretty damned ashamed that I didn't speak up."

Again, Eleanor showed no response. She simply stared straight ahead. A muted ray of sunlight stretched across her shoulder, casting one side of her face in shadow. Chase released Sarah's hand and moved closer to his mother.

The loathing in his voice, thick and bitter, was undeniable. "Joanna was sick, Mother. She was sick. And she spent years calling out for help that none of us provided because we didn't want to admit—*you* didn't want to admit—that anything was wrong. But something *was* wrong—and now she's dead because of it."

Eleanor closed her eyes and her entire body contracted in a spasm of realization and pain.

"Will was the one who looked after her," Chase went on. "God knows we sure as hell didn't." Reaching behind him, he grasped Sarah's hand again. "I've always said Will was nothing but good to Joanna—and to Lizzy and Wiley, too. So I'm going to call him and try to make amends. I lost Joanna, but I'm not going to lose her kids, too. Not when I don't have to."

He glanced quickly at his father as he and Sarah left the room.

Edward put an arm around his wife's shoulder and laid one hand softly over hers. "Elly," he murmured. "Do you really want to continue this fight?"

Eleanor remained silent.

"Your greatest fear when Will told us he had met someone was that we'd lose Joanna's children," Edward said. "And we have. But not because of Will's actions—because of our own."

Rowan responded sharply. "But what about that someone's son? What about what he did to Lizzy? Would you ignore that?"

Edward let out a weary sigh. "Rowan, there is nothing to suggest the young man intended anything more than a simple show of kindness. The district attorney concluded that himself." He eyed his daughter coldly. "I made the mistake of allowing myself to be caught up in your false panic and letting all of this get completely out of hand."

Rowan opened her mouth to speak, but decided otherwise. She returned her father's icy stare and, without another word, rose quietly and walked out of the room.

Edward turned his attention back to his wife. "Elly, please, look at what's happening. Joanna's children need us. They need you. *And* they need their father."

Eleanor shook her head, tears welling in her eyes. "Chase is right," she said, her voice little more than a whisper. "Chase is right—about all of it." She turned toward her husband, slowly, her body shaking. "Dear God, Edward, what have I done?"

# 63

Paulette directed Miranda to the living room and offered her a chair. "Mr. and Mrs. Halloran will be down momentarily," she said. Paulette made no mention of Rowan, which Miranda took as an indication she would not be joining them.

Miranda still had no idea why she was here. Edward had arranged the meeting, but hadn't given a clue as to its purpose.

She gazed around the room, noting the baby grand piano in one corner, the game table in another—with hand-carved marble chess pieces properly arranged on the board waiting for someone to make the first move—and the family portrait hanging over the mantel. Eleanor did look the matriarch, Miranda thought to herself as she studied the older woman's features. "As flexible and accommodating as a steel rod," she muttered under her breath.

"Good afternoon, Ms. Wilkes, thank you for coming on such short notice."

Miranda turned when she heard Edward's deep voice. He extended his hand to her, and she accepted graciously.

"I was happy to," she replied, making note of Eleanor's conspicuous absence. "Your call yesterday sounded quite urgent."

Edward motioned toward one of the chairs. "Please, have a seat. My wife will not be joining us this afternoon. I'm afraid she is unwell."

"I'm sorry to hear that," Miranda replied. She sat down and paused for a moment. "So, Mr. Halloran, what can I do for you?"

Edward took a seat across from her. "You're right, Ms. Wilkes, my call was urgent. So I'll get right to the point. I'm hoping you can deliver a message to my son-in-law."

"I think I can do that," Miranda said.

Edward nodded. "I'd like you to tell him that we've considered the

319

situation carefully, and have decided it is in our grandchildren's best interests that they remain with their father. We are no longer pursuing legal custody."

"Well," she replied, masking her elation behind a calm exterior. "I am pleasantly surprised. May I ask what brought you to this decision?"

Now Edward paused. "Ms. Wilkes, my wife and I love our grandchildren very much, and their physical and emotional well-being is of paramount importance. However, we realize now that in our zeal to protect them, we may have acted precipitously with regard to custody."

"I see," Miranda said. "And how about with regard to Ben Winwood?"

Edward took a deep breath. "Yes, Ms. Wilkes. With regard to him, too." He got up, walked to the sideboard, and poured a drink from the crystal decanter. He turned toward Miranda and raised the bottle, questioning.

"No, thank you."

"When my wife and daughter spoke with Lizzy, she left them with the impression that the young man had made certain ... advances when they were all together in San Sebastian. Of course, our immediate response was to do whatever was necessary to protect her from what we believed was a dangerous situation."

He returned to his place and set his glass on the table next to him. "After further discussion with Lizzy, we realize we may have perceived a greater threat than actually exists."

"Are you sure you don't mean that you perceived a threat where none exists, Mr. Halloran? Your statement would indicate you still have some reservation." Miranda said.

"We were mistaken in our belief that Ben Winwood is a threat to our granddaughter," Edward conceded.

Miranda asked what the Hallorans expected her to do for them, and how they intended to compensate Ben for the pain and suffering he had endured over the last four months, as well as any damage to his character—potential or otherwise.

"We leave that to our attorney—and to the Winwoods," he replied.

# 64

Miranda sat in the front seat of her car and dialed Will's number. She wanted to give him the good news first. Then she'd call Callie. She wasn't sure what either would do with the information, but she hoped Will would catch the first plane to San Sebastian and put everything right with Callie. Now that the issues between the Hallorans and the Tremaines—and the Winwoods—had been resolved, maybe he could convince her to put everything aside and accept that entangling alliance with him she'd craved for so many years.

"Hello, this is Dr. Tremaine." Will's voice sounded tired. It was late afternoon, close to the end of what had turned into a long and complicated day in the ER. Between the day's work and the thoughts of Callie that were never far away, his mood was somber.

"Prince Charming," Miranda chirped. "I have good news."

Will recognized Miranda's voice and salutation. "Oh, yeah? Well, I could use some," he replied heavily.

"I've just met with the Hallorans," she said. Will detected a particular bounce in her voice. "They've seen the light and decided to drop the custody case."

"What?" he cried. Realizing his response attracted the interest of several bystanders, he turned his body so he faced the wall.

"And that's not all." Miranda couldn't help smiling as she spoke. "They're withdrawing their complaint against Ben and issuing him a written apology."

"My God, Miranda, this is … this is … Jesus … I can't believe it!" He ran his hand through his hair. The weight in his voice evaporated, and he spoke quickly and excitedly. "How did you do it? And do Callie and Ben know? God, they'll both be so relieved."

"No, I haven't talked to Callie yet. I'm going to call her next," Miranda said.

"And as far as how I did it, well, the fact is, the credit goes to your daughter." Then, more seriously, she added, "You know, Will, Rowan Halloran may be angry and vindictive, but I think Eleanor truly loves Lizzy and Wiley, and really believed she needed to protect them."

Will snorted.

"Well," Miranda corrected herself, "she wanted to believe it was necessary to protect them—just like she wanted to believe her daughter's death was an accident and that if she kept you and Callie apart, the family could continue on just as it was when Joanna was alive."

"Yeah, well …"

"Simply stated, I think Lizzy proved the main point I made to Eleanor back when this whole thing began," Miranda continued, "and I think they finally realized that all they were gaining from this endeavor is a lot of animosity—from you and from Lizzy and Wiley, the very people she's trying to keep so close."

Miranda didn't go into the specific details of the earlier conversation she had with Eleanor, back when the whole sordid mess began.

"Jesus, Miranda, I don't know what to say," Will exclaimed, pressing his hand against the back of his neck. "I don't know how to thank you."

"I'll tell you how you can thank me," Miranda said. "Make Callie happy."

Will was silent.

"Hello? Are you still there?"

"Yeah, I'm here." The heaviness had returned. "Miranda, I'd like nothing more than to do exactly that. But after what the Hallorans did to Ben, it's pretty clear she wants nothing to do with anyone associated with them—including me."

Miranda sighed. If there was one personality characteristic she knew best about Callie—and disliked the most—it was her obstinacy. "Will, if you know Callie at all, you know two things about her: First, she's as stubborn as a mule."

"That's true," Will acknowledged. He transferred his phone from one hand to the other.

"And second, while she'll fight like a rabid dog when it comes to her children—or anyone else who needs protecting—she won't do the same for herself."

"I suppose that's true too."

"There's no supposing about it," Miranda said firmly. "Will, you have to know how much she loves you. But if she thinks her actions are detrimental to her own children, or that her presence makes life difficult for you or your children in any way that she can't help resolve, she's going to step away. That's just how she is."

"I agree with all that, and God knows I love her just as much, but the fact remains that she doesn't want to see me."

Miranda took a deep breath and exhaled loudly. "How is it that I—the one person in this group with no romantic inclinations beyond a date for dinner next week—have the best insight into male-female relationships?" she asked. "Tell me something. Do you really think that if you showed up at her door, she wouldn't invite you in?"

Will paused.

"Well," he concluded after a minute or so. "I guess there's only one way to find out."

# 65

Despite the January chill, Justine was sitting out on the front porch step with Bailey when I turned into the driveway. Were it not for the big grin on her face, I would have assumed something terrible had happened.

I pulled my book bag and purse out of the car and walked over to her. "So what's got you looking like the Cheshire cat?" I asked. I wasn't surprised to see her—her school semester wouldn't begin for another week, and she was spending the last few days of her winter vacation with me—but her glad expression was a little suspicious.

She stood up and bit her upper lip to try to keep from smiling.

"Justine, what's going on? Did you win the lottery, or something?"

"Better," she declared. "Miranda called. She left a message."

We walked up the front steps and into the house. She handed me a piece of paper on which she'd written two words—"It's over."

I looked up at her. "What does she mean? What's over?"

"Mom, the Hallorans have given up. They've acknowledged they were wrong about Ben, and they're not trying to get custody of Lizzy and Wiley." She grasped my arm. "Do you know what this means?"

My heart quickened and I had a little trouble catching my breath. I dropped my purse and book bag and sat down on the couch. Bailey jumped up next to me and pressed his head against my hand.

"Does Ben know?" I asked. "We have to tell him. He'll be ecstatic."

"Relax, Mom, I called him right after I got off the phone with Miranda. He and Gina are on their way up here now. We're going to celebrate."

She sat down next to me and touched my arm again. "Mom, do you know what this means?"

"It means Ben's going to be okay," I answered with a heavy sigh of relief. "We don't have to worry about this anymore."

I fell back against the couch. All my fears and concerns seemed to flow out of me, and I went completely limp. I brushed away a tear that trickled down my cheek.

"Right. But do you know what else it means?" She stared at me with her eyes wide.

"Yes," I breathed. "It means Will isn't going to lose his kids."

"Right," she said again. "And what else?"

I raised my shoulders questioningly. "What?"

With a look of utter exasperation, she rolled her eyes and shook her head. "It means you and Will can pick up where you left off."

That was one thought that hadn't even crossed my mind.

"No, Justine," I corrected her. "We can't pick up where we left off. It's not that simple. I am relieved for everyone, but I don't believe for a minute that the Hallorans are giving up. They're only changing tactics."

# 66

The light shining though the cottage window was a welcoming sight. Will brought his rental car to a stop several yards short of the white picket fence that outlined the perimeter of the front yard. He switched off the ignition, and looked at the house. He wondered why Callie hadn't closed the curtains yet. It wasn't like her to wait until after dark. When he glimpsed her moving from the kitchen to the living room, his fight-or-flight response kicked in and a burst of adrenaline flooded his body. His heart raced, his breathing quickened, and his hands and feet tingled. He pressed his damp palms against the denim fabric of his jeans. If fight or flight were his only options, he intended to fight—for her and for whatever future they might have.

He wanted to jump out of the car, burst through the front door, and take her in his arms. He wanted to hold her, to feel her warm softness. He longed to make love to her. Not for the physical satisfaction—although he couldn't deny the power of his desire—but for the closeness it brought them. He never felt as safe anywhere as he did lying next to her, particularly in the moments after they'd completely dissolved into one another, when nothing existed in the world save the two of them.

But he didn't jump out of the car or burst through the front door. He moved slowly and deliberately. He had no idea how he'd be received. All the way from Westin, he clung to Miranda's assertion that Callie wanted him as much as he wanted her, but now he was beginning to worry that it had been wishful thinking.

At best, she'd welcome him with open arms. At worst, it would be a repeat of the last time he saw her, when she told him their only future was in the past and bade him goodbye.

He got out of the car and walked up to the porch. The night air was cold, but when he shivered, it had nothing to do with the temperature. The rest of his life would be determined by the next few minutes. If she welcomed him, they might find a way to retie the threads that had bound them to one another. If she turned him away—well, he didn't know what he'd do. He hadn't allowed himself to contemplate that possibility.

Will lifted his hand tentatively, but before he had a chance to knock, Callie opened the door.

§∂

Bailey heard the car pull up and lifted his head at the crunching sound of feet walking along the gravel path up to the front porch. He responded with a low growl.

I wasn't expecting anyone at this time of the evening, but assumed it was Ben dropping in to make sure I was all right. He'd done that quite often over the last couple of months, sometimes bringing Gina along, but usually coming alone. When Bailey heard footsteps on the porch, he sat up and barked. I shushed him and went to open the door in anticipation of Ben.

Someone else stood on the threshold, and my heart leapt.

Will smiled tentatively. "Hi, Cal." The porch light shining on him gave him an almost angelic glow.

I wasn't sure what to say—or do. I wanted to throw myself at him, but given the circumstances, that didn't seem entirely appropriate. "Will—I'm surprised to see—I mean, I didn't expect—I—oh, I don't know what I mean."

He spoke softly, almost hesitantly. "Can I come in?"

"Of course." I moved to the side, and he stepped into the living room. Bailey, a one-canine welcoming committee, was as happy to see Will as I was. He wagged his tail ferociously while running in circles around Will and yipping excitedly. Will squatted down and returned the welcome, and when Bailey finally calmed down, I ordered him to his bed near the fireplace.

"I was kind of afraid you'd close the door on me," Will said. He made no move to take off his jacket or present any other show of familiarity. He didn't even sit down. "I wasn't sure you'd want to see me."

I bowed my head. "Will, it was never the case that I didn't *want* to see you," I said. "Saying goodbye to you was one of the hardest things I've ever done."

We stood across from one another, awkward and tentative, neither of us knowing quite what to say or do. He shifted from one foot to the other.

"How are Lizzy and Wiley?" I asked.

ANDREA WEIR

"They're fine." He pulled a piece of paper out of his jacket pocket and held it out to me. "Wiley asked me to give you this."

I unfolded it and saw that he'd drawn a picture of Bailey—and quite a good likeness—sitting on the front porch.

I was touched by Wiley's thoughtfulness, and warmed by the affirmation that he and I had formed some semblance of a relationship. I hadn't imagined it after all. "Wow," I exclaimed as I studied the drawing. "He really does have such an amazing talent!" I gave another quick glance at the paper in my hand. "Please thank him for me and tell him I'll frame it and hang it on the wall in the living room."

Will gazed down at me. "I'd rather you told him yourself." His lips curved into the smallest hint of a smile. "I think he'd prefer that, too."

"Well," I replied a little uncomfortably. I turned away from him and set the drawing on the table.

Will coughed lightly. "And Lizzy wanted me to give you this." I turned back and saw an envelope in his hand. It was sealed. I looked up at him, questioning.

He shrugged one shoulder slightly. "I don't know what's in it. She didn't tell me, just asked me to give it to you."

I reached out cautiously and took the envelope from him. She'd written my name on the front in small, bold letters. I took a deep breath and ran my thumb under the flap to open it. It contained one thin sheet of plain white paper.

*Dear Callie,*

*I just want to say I'm sorry about everything with Ben. I didn't think any of it would happen. I didn't know Gran and Aunt Rowan would be so mean. And I didn't know Gran wanted to take Wiley and me away from my dad. I just wanted us to be a family, like we were. But I guess we can't be anymore.*

The letters blurred as my eyes filled.

*You were nice to me, especially at the fair, and I appreciated it. I don't know if we can be friends, but if you're mad at me, I hope you won't take it out on my dad. I think he really misses you.*

She signed it, simply, *Lizzy.*

So, I wondered, was this her way of giving her blessing—or, at least, acquiescing—to a relationship between Will and me?

I licked my lips and took another deep breath. I handed the letter to Will so he could read what his daughter had written.

"She's right, you know." He refolded the paper and slid it back into the envelope. He dropped the letter onto the table next to Wiley's drawing. "About all of it."

I sat down on the couch. "It's a very sweet note. And I'm sure she means every word." I picked up the envelope and held it lightly. I glanced up at Will. "She's just a little girl. She had no idea what was going on. I certainly hope she doesn't think I'd hold anything against her. Or that Ben would. I'm sure he doesn't."

Will didn't move. "How is Ben?"

I looked up at him again. A good three feet separated us. It may have been three hundred—or three thousand.

"He's well, for the most part," I said. "He's been moving forward as best he can. He's still affected, but he has a wonderful girlfriend who stood by him throughout the whole ordeal, and she's helping him figure out how to put everything behind him. So is Justine," I added. "And Joe has been extremely supportive—angry, but supportive."

"I'm glad." Will took a step forward, reached out his hand, and lightly brushed my cheek. "I wish we could do that—put all of this behind us, I mean." His eyes searched my face. "You know, it's finished, Cal. Everything with Eleanor and Edward is finished. They won't cause any more trouble." We continued to study each other. "That means something for us, doesn't it?" he asked after a moment.

He sat down in the chair across from me. He still wore his jacket, as though he didn't intend to stay. Perhaps he didn't want to get too comfortable.

I rested my head in my hands. "It'll never be finished," I muttered. I looked over at Will. "You have no idea the pain Ben has gone through because of Eleanor and Edward. And even though their plan for *him* didn't work, how can I be sure they don't—or won't—have something else brewing? That they aren't planning to sabotage Justine in some way?"

"I think I might know something about the pain they've caused," Will noted sharply. "It was my daughter they used for their scheme. Do you think she hasn't suffered as well?"

"Of course I don't think that," I replied just as sharply. "She's as much a victim in all of this as Ben is."

Bailey scratched at the front door. I took a deep breath and got up to let him out. I felt Will's eyes on me as I walked across the room.

"Cal, the bottom line is they realize what a huge mistake they made."

I stood at the open door and kept an eye on Bailey. The almost-full moon swathed the ground in silvery light, and I could smell the dampness in the cold winter air. I watched Bailey perhaps more intently than was necessary. I welcomed the temporary distraction as an opportunity to process Will's words and sort quickly through my own thoughts.

When Bailey came back inside, he sneezed a few times and curled up on his bed again.

"Cal, they can't hurt us," Will said. This time it was his head that bowed. "That is, assuming there is an 'us.'" He paused, and then rose suddenly and walked toward where I stood by the door. He was in front of me in no more than three strides. "Callie—"

His fingers closed firmly around my arms. "Callie, I love you." Dark and fierce beneath tightly knitted brows, his eyes captured mine. "I love you," he repeated, almost pleading, and shaking me just slightly. "Tell me that means something."

"It means everything to me—everything," I replied. He loosened his hold on me and I reached up to touch his cheek. We stood silent and motionless for a moment. "But you're wrong when you say they can't hurt us anymore," I continued. "They can. If one way doesn't work, they'll find another."

Will dropped his hands to his sides and I stepped away from him. I picked up a pillow, sat down on the couch, and hugged it to my chest. Flimsy though it was, I meant it to serve as a barrier between us.

"They won't let you have a life that doesn't include Joanna, no matter who they have to destroy. It's that simple."

"No," Will argued. His hands, still at his sides, curled into fists and then relaxed again. "I've said over and over again that what's simple is the fact that I love you and you love me. That's simple, and that's all that counts."

I wanted to believe him, to share his confidence. But I was afraid of the Hallorans. Will and I could fight them, were we willing, but did I want to?

When I didn't respond, Will brought his hand to his forehead, hiding his eyes. I couldn't make out his expression.

"All right, then." He took his hand away and gazed down at me, his eyes narrowed and hard as steel. "I guess this is how it's going to be." He took a breath. "Callie, I'll fight for you any way I can, but I can't fight possibilities. I don't have contingency plans for everything that might happen, or could happen. I can't make any guarantees, except that I will always love you, and will always do my best to protect you—and Ben and Justine—from whatever Eleanor or Rowan or anyone else might dream up."

He paused, and I saw his eyes soften for a moment before turning cold again. "But if that's not enough for you …"

I rose and watched him as he walked to the door. With his hand on the knob, he turned to face me. "Bye, Cal. Take care of yourself." He opened the door and walked out to his car. Without looking back, he got in and started the ignition.

I continued to watch him out the window. He was leaving again, only this time it was at my bidding. And this time it would be for good. When he had driven off to Boston all those years ago, I fully expected to see him again. And even during the years that I was married to Joe, I had the strange idea—the everlasting hope—that I'd find him again. And I did. But I wouldn't have another chance. That kind of lightning wouldn't strike twice. And even if I changed my mind and flew to Westin tomorrow, it would be too late. If I let him drive away now, it would be forever.

And that, I realized, was more frightening to me than anything the Hallorans could do. I couldn't go back to being half alive.

I rushed out to the porch just as he had turned the car around and begun heading slowly down the driveway into the darkness. He didn't see me. I called to him, but he didn't hear. I cut across the yard and then thoughtlessly dashed between the hedges and in front of the car.

He slammed on the brakes, jumped out, and ran toward me. "Jesus, Callie, I could have killed you," he cried.

I threw myself against him and wrapped my arms around his neck.

"And if I let you go, I may as well kill myself," I whispered, with my cheek pressed against his chest. His heart pounded in my ear.

He held me close, his hands warm on my back and his face buried in my hair.

I looked up at him, tears streaming down my cheeks. "I love you, Will. I love you and I don't want to live without you. It *is* that simple."

He tilted his face toward mine, his head eclipsing the moon, and kissed me very gently. He pulled away, and with one arm around my shoulders, and the other arm behind my knees, he scooped me up and carried me to the porch. He stopped abruptly just as we reached the door, and set me down on the worn wooden planks.

"Wait here," he directed and walked back to the car. He turned off the engine and smiled broadly as he approached me. The keys jingled in his hand. "I guess I'm not going anywhere after all."

331

"No," I said as we walked inside. "I guess you aren't."

Will and I had made love many times since his first visit to San Sebastian, but on this night it was as though we'd only just found each other. And, in a way, maybe we had.

When we got upstairs, each of us dropping shoes, shirts, and other articles of clothing along the way, he held me to him and kissed me feverishly.

"I want you, Cal. More, I think, than I ever have."

"Me, too," I replied breathlessly.

With his hands on my shoulders and our eyes locked, he directed me toward the bed. The backs of my knees hit the mattress, and I dropped down. With one hand, Will pulled me to my feet again, and with the other he tore back the quilt and sheets. He eased my body onto the bed, and then lay down next to me.

The need in him was strong. I felt it when he touched me. His hands trembled as they moved up and down my body, reacquainting themselves with the curves and lines they already knew so well. I reached down and took hold of him. He was hard and solid, and he moaned softly at my touch. He rolled onto his back, and I kissed his chest, breathing in the smell of him. He pulled me down so my body lay atop his. With lips parted, I pressed my mouth to his, caressing his bottom lip with my tongue. He wrapped his arms around me and rolled over so I was on my back as he hovered above me. I stroked his hair, and he gazed down at me. "I will never lose you again," he murmured. "If I have to move heaven and earth, I won't be separated from you."

My eyes filled. "No, you won't be. I'll be moving heaven and earth right with you." He touched my cheek, and kissed me again. His hips pressed against mine, questioning, and I ran my fingertips along his shoulders and back. I ached to feel him deep inside me.

"Now," I whispered. And with a breath of utter satisfaction he drove himself into me.

Afterward, Will and I lay wrapped in each other. The room was silent, except for Bailey's quiet snore. Will reached up and pushed my hair away from his nose. He tucked his arm around me again and let out a sigh. I thought he was drifting off to sleep, but instead he spoke. His voice was barely audible.

I tilted my head up. My eyes had grown accustomed to the dark, and I noticed the lock of dark hair that fell over his forehead, and two vertical lines set deep between his furrowed eyebrows. The corners of his mouth turned up slightly, but not in amusement. His expression was altogether serious.

"I need you, Cal," he said urgently. "I need to know that every day is going to end this way—with you, here, in my arms."

"That's a pretty tall order seeing as how we live in different states," I replied, caressing the solid muscles of his shoulder and upper arm.

He turned onto his side so he could face me. His breathing was slow and steady. His fingertips stroked my face while mine played with the curls at the back of his neck. He lifted his head and looked at me with an almost startling intensity; the blue of his eyes was so dark as to appear black.

"Marry me," he whispered, his gaze intent on mine. "Marry me, finally."

He took my hand and held it to his chest. "I love you, Callie, with every particle of my being."

A single tear trickled down my cheek. I took his hand in both of mine. "And I love you," I murmured.

He studied my face, waiting for my response. I nodded, almost imperceptibly, and he smiled, his own eyes shining in the dull light. He cupped my cheek and wiped the tear away with his thumb.

"Till death do us part."

"And then some."

# Acknowledgements

Many people helped make this book a reality and I am indebted to all of them.

Judi Stauffer, my friend and soul sister, who taught me to trust myself and to be present in my own life. Your wisdom knows no bounds, and I am a grateful beneficiary.

Rebecca and Catherine, my wildly brilliant, talented, and beautiful daughters. You are the best role models I could ask for.

Rose Crowther, my best friend since sophomore year in high school and keeper of all the secrets.

Stanley Weinstein, who encouraged me to follow my dreams and believed in me even when I didn't believe in myself.

Marcia Meier, editor extraordinaire, gifted writer, and literary cheerleader. The words "thank you" seem wholly inadequate. Without you, I'd still be blushing and this book wouldn't exist. It's that simple.

My sister, Susan Hamlin, who knows the history and in more ways than I can name helped me become the person I am today.

My aunts, Adele and Libby, who for the last year have started every telephone conversation with, "So, what's happening with the book?" Here it is, and I hope you decide it was worth waiting for.

ANDREA WEIR

My mother, Faye, whose absence has been the strongest presence in my life and without whom I wouldn't have a story.

And, of course, Duane, who gave me the creative space I needed—literally and figuratively—to tell the story. Thanks for the morning coffee (it's a wonderful way to wake up), for walking the dogs, and for the countless other things you do that make life possible.